DREAM PARK

by
LARRY NIVEN
and
STEVEN BARNES

SF
ace books
A Division of Charter Communications, Inc.
A GROSSET & DUNLAP COMPANY
51 Madison Avenue
New York, New York 10010

DREAM PARK

An ACE Book

A limited first edition of this book has been published by Phantasia Press.

First Ace printing: April 1981
Published Simultaneously in Canada

2 4 6 8 0 9 7 5 3 1
Manufactured in the United States of America

TABLE OF CONTENTS

PART ONE
Chapter One: ARRIVALS 3
Chapter Two: A STROLL THROUGH OLD LOS ANGELES   13
Chapter Three: THE LORE MASTER 29
Chapter Four: THE MASTER DREAMERS 48
Chapter Five: THE NAMING OF NAMES 61
Chapter Six: FLIGHT OF FANCY 73
Chapter Seven: THE ROAD OF THE CARGO 89
Chapter Eight: THE BANQUET 102
Chapter Nine: KILLED OUT 118
Chapter Ten: NEUTRAL SCENT 131
Chapter Eleven: GAME PLAN 144
Chapter Twelve: OVERVIEW 152

PART TWO
Chapter Thirteen: ENTER THE GRIFFIN 169
Chapter Fourteen: THE WATER PEOPLE 184
Chapter Fifteen: THE RITE OF HORRIFIC SPLENDOR 196
Chapter Sixteen: REST BREAK 211
Chapter Seventeen: THE LAST REPLACEMENTS 226
Chapter Eighteen: SNAKEBITE CURE 241
Chapter Nineteen: NECK RIDDLES 255
Chapter Twenty: THE SEA OF LOST SHIPS 269
Chapter Twenty-One: THE HAIAVAHA 285
Chapter Twenty-Two: THE ELECTRIC PIZZA MYSTERY ... 297
Chapter Twenty-Three: BLACK FIRE 309
Chapter Twenty-Four: AMBUSH 322
Chapter Twenty-Five: THE EGG OF THE AIRPLANE 333
Chapter Twenty-Six: THE LAUGHING DEAD 345
Chapter Twenty-Seven: CARGO CRAFT 357
Chapter Twenty-Eight: THIEVES IN THE NIGHT 367
Chapter Twenty-Nine: END GAME 382

PART THREE
Chapter Thirty: THE FINAL TALLY 401
Chapter Thirty-One: DEPARTURES 416

CAST OF CHARACTERS
DRAMATIS PERSONNAE

The Creators

RICHARD LOPEZ: *The world's most respected Game Master, co-author and presently monitor of the South Seas Treasure game.*

MITSUKO (Chi-chi) LOPEZ: *Richard's wife, partner, co-author, and public representative.*

The Players

ACACIA (Panthesilea) GARCIA: *Experienced fantasy game player. Warrior.*

TONY (Fortunato) MCWHIRTER: *Inexperienced gamer, and Acacia's guest. Thief.*

CHESTER HENDERSON: *Famed Lore Master, leader of the South Seas Treasure party.*

GINA (Semiramis) PERKINS: *Experienced fantasy gamer. Cleric.*

ADOLPH (Ollie, or Frankish Oliver) NORLISS: *Experienced fantasy gamer. Warrior.*

GWEN (Guinevere) RYDER: *Fantasy gamer, and Ollie's fiance. Cleric.*

MARY-MARTHA (Mary-em) CORBETT: *Experienced and highly eccentric gamer. Warrior.*

FELICIA (Dark Star) MADDOX: *Experienced gamer. Thief.*

BOWAN THE BLACK: *Dark Star's partner, an experienced Gamer. Magic User.*

ALAN LEIGH: *Experienced fantasy game player. Magic user.*

S. J. WATERS: *Novice gamer. Engineer.*

OWEN BRADDON: *Elderly, moderately experienced gamer. Cleric.*

MARGIE BRADDON: *Experienced elderly gamer. Engineer.*

HOLLY FROST: *Aspiring novice gamer. Warrior.*

GEORGE EAMES: *Moderately experienced gamer. Warrior.*

LARRY GARRET: *Moderately experienced gamer. Cleric.*

RUDY DREAGER: *Moderately experienced Gamer. Engineer.*

HARVEY (Kasan Maibang) WAYLAND: *Professional actor. Guide.*

NIGORAI: *Native bearer and spy. (Actor.)*

KAGOIANO: *Native bearer. (Actor.)*

KIBUGONAI: *Native bearer. (Actor.)*

PIGIBIDI: *Native chieftain. (Actor.)*

LADY JANET: *Damsel in distress. (Actor.)*

GARY (the Griffin) TEGNER: *Novice Gamer. Thief. Alias for Alex Griffin.*

The Dream Park Personnel

ALEX GRIFFIN: *Head of Dream Park Security.*

HARMONY: *Dream Park Director of Operations.*

MILLICENT SUMMERS: *Griffin's secretary.*

MARTY BOBBICK: *Griffin's assistant.*

ALBERT RICE: *Dream Park security guard.*

SKIP O'BRIEN: *Dream Park research psychologist.*

MELINDA O'BRIEN: *Skip's wife.*

MS. GAIL METESKY: *Dream Park liaison with the International Fantasy Gaming Society.*

ARLAN MYERS: *I.F.G.S. official.*

DWIGHT WELLES: *Dream Park computer tech.*

LARRY CHICON: *Dream Park computer tech. Together with Welles and the Game Masters, he monitors the Gaming Central computer.*

NOVOTNEY: *Cowles Modular Community's resident doctor.*

MELONE: *Dream Park security guard.*

PART ONE

Chapter One

ARRIVALS

The train sat rigid as a steel bar, poised in midair above its magnetic monorail track, disgorging passengers into Dallas Station. Its fifteen cars had borne their passengers in quiet efficiency from New York to Dallas in just over half an hour, cradled in magnetic fields, travelling through vacuum at close to orbital velocity, deep underground.

Chester had cut it close. He shifted his heavy backpack and strode back along the train, walking like a king, projecting confidence. There would be Gamers aboard, and some would recognize him. Lore Master Chester Henderson was conscious of his unseen audience.

"Chester!"

He stopped, dismayed. He knew that voice—

There she was, a vision in leopard tights that drew stares from all but the most jaded. Her long red hair, plaited into a

3

thick rope, dangled down her back to the top of her belt line. She wore heavy makeup that almost hid the fact that she was, indeed, a very lovely woman. But the leotards hid nothing.

"Hello, Gina," Chester sighed with a tone somewhere south of resignation. "I should have guessed you'd be along."

"I wouldn't miss it for anything. Remember last time, when you saved me from the mammoth?"

"Cost me three points for frostbite. I remember."

"Don't complain, it's mean. Anyway, I was *very* appreciative." She coiled her arm around him and joined him in a rather strained lock-step toward the Dream Park shuttle.

She had been, he remembered, *very* appreciative. "One of your strong points," he said, and put his arm around her. It felt disturbingly good, nestled there between warm curves. "Well, I'm glad you're with us. We may need to pass you off as a virgin or something."

"Would you *really*?" she giggled. "I've always loved your imagination."

Chester didn't smile. "But, Gina . . . if you're in, you're going to have to follow orders a mite more carefully. You almost screwed me good—stop that, I'm serious. This is extremely important to me, all right?"

Gina looked up at him and her face grew almost serious. "Anything you say, Chester."

Chester groaned to himself as they boarded the train. She had skill; she was better than most newcomers; she carried her weight and sometimes followed orders too. But she treated it like some kind of goddam game.

Alex Griffin took his shuttle seat and settled back with

eyes closed and arms folded comfortably. He had long
since learned the value of catching bits of rest where he
could, and could catnap during minutes most people spent
fidgetting.

He stretched, and heard popping sounds as muscles
and joints woke up. Small wonder they were still half-
asleep. Ten minutes earlier he had been snoring in his
apartment at the Cowles Modular Community, with the
alarm buzzing in his ears. The third time it went off, it would
refuse to shut up until his 190 pounds were lifted from the
sensor in the mattress.

He opened a sleepy green eye and watched the rear
monitor as the cluster of buildings receded from view. Five
hundred Dream Park employees maintained residences in
Cowles Modular Community, nestled in the Little San
Bernardino Mountains, fifteen kilometers and six shuttle
minutes away from work. Griffin was on call twenty-four
hours a day, three weeks out of the month, and he appreciated the convenience of CMC. But this morning was
nothing special, just the usual 6:00 A.M. roust.

Alex rolled his wrist over to check the watch imprinted
on his sleeve. (Expensive indulgence. Even drycleaning
eventually messed up the printed circuitry.) Three minutes
until the shuttle slid into the employee depot. He had
about decided to close his eyes again when the picture in
front of him changed.

The woman on the flatscreen might have been beautiful
by the light of noon. At 5:56 A.M. she was evil incarnate.
"Morning, Chief," she chirped, obscenely wide-awake.

"No. No, it isn't, Millicent." Alex yawned rudely, re-
motely disliking himself for it. He ran blunt fingers through
his light red hair and made a serious attempt to focus his
eyes. "Oh, what the hay. Maybe it is a good morning.

Maybe it'll even be a good day. I'm sorry, Millicent. What's up?"

"Final prep for the South Seas Treasure Game tomorrow is the hottest item. You have some dossiers to go over."

"I know. What else?"

She shook her head, her loosely curled afro bouncing a bit as she studied the computer display on a second screen offscreen. "Umm . . . budget meeting with the Boss."

He was definitely more alert now. "Did I exceed Harmony's projected red last quarter?"

"Don't think so. Better not have. That's my department, and I don't make mistakes like that. Heh heh."

"Heh heh. Well?"

"I think we're switching over from zero-base budgeting to some new system that Harmony is hot on."

"Oh, Lord. What else? Don't I have a class to teach today?"

"Yes. One o'clock, right after a scheduled lunch with O'Brien."

Alex's face lit up. "Hallelujah. A bright spot at last. Tell Skip to meet me at 'leven thirty at the White Hart, okay? And ask him to bring me the L5 specs. I want to see them. What about the class?"

"Standard Constraint and Detention stuff. For the new security people."

"Right." Alex glanced at his sleeve; the station was seconds away. "Make me a memo. Standing arm bar, crossover toe hold for the ground work, and oh, let's say knife disarms. Right and left wrist locks with low kicks. I'll wing it from there. I'm almost in, now, hon. I'll see you in a few minutes, okay?"

"Right, Griff," she said, flashing him a smile as the picture faded out.

The shuttle let him out in the central core of the 1200-acre Dream Park complex, two levels underground. Activity was heavy for this early, he thought. Then he remembered the Game. Odds were there would be five thousand dollars of last-minute work to be done, or he didn't know the catch-up kings over in Special Projects.

Tunnels stretched off in all directions: up, down, sideways and maybe to yesterday and tomorrow if the Research Department had come up with anything since breakfast. Most of the people scurrying past knew him by name, tossing off a "Hi, Alex," or " 'Sappening, Griff?", or "Morning, Chief" as they ferried racks of costumes, or props, or electronic equipment to the different divisions. A cargo tram hissed in, and a crew of overalled workers and tiny humming cargo 'bots rushed in to unload so that another shipment could hurry down the line.

He tossed a friendly salute to the guard at the elevator and pressed his right thumb against the ID pad. The door opened. Five or six people crowded in after him, and Alex controlled his annoyance when only two of them put their thumbs to the pad for clearance. More memos, dammit.

It was 6:22 A.M., Thursday, March 5, 2051, according to Alex's desk clock. Propped on the clock was a sheet of fanfold paper, Millicent's printout of the day's obligations.

Alex doffed his coat and dropped into his chair. He punched a finger at the desk console. A hologram "window" formed above his desk: a nameplate that read "Ms. Summers," and behind the nameplate a dark pretty face whipping around to answer the buzz.

"Millicent, can't I foist some of this off on Bobbick? How the hell is he going to earn his pay if I do all the work?"

"Marty is already with Insurance going over the damage report on the Salvage Game that ended yesterday in

Gaming Area B. He should be free by about two this afternoon, or do you want me to . . . ?"

"No, leave him on it. Listen. Do I have to go all the way over to R&D or can we take care of this mess by phone? Lord knows I've got enough paper to shuffle before eight. Check it out, would you?"

"Right, Griff. I'm pretty sure that'll go."

Her face blinked out, and Alex punched for a display of today's "paperwork." Three columns of headings ran off the screen. An executive secretary and a deputy Security Chief and this much garbage *still* filtered up to him. Work first?

A slow smile played over his face. A little peek at the Park first.

He triggered the exterior monitor and watched the room swell with the darkened spirals of Dream Park. From the vantage of the monitoring camera the workers readying the Park for the day's visitors were ants streaming in and out of the long black shadows of early morning.

There was the somber shape of the Olde Arkham tour. (The kids loved it. The adults . . . well, an old lady with a heart murmur had damn near croaked when Chthulhu appeared to devour her grandchildren. Some people!)

Snakelike and faroff around the edge of the Park the Gravity Whip coiled, offering a total of thirty seconds of weightlessness via computer-designed parabolic arcs. The monitor eye swept over to Gaming Area B, where the Salvage Game had been conducted.

That one was interesting. Partly in desert territory and partly underwater, it had involved twelve players for two days. Alex figured that the Game Master on that one would just about break even. It had cost three hundred thousand dollars to set the Game up. The twelve participants had paid four hundred a day, each , for the privilege of earning "Gaming Points" for the fantasy characters they portrayed and, not incidentally, for having the bejeezus scared out of them. Book rights presold, film rights likewise. . . . He couldn't pretend to understand the logic behind it. The vagaries of the International Gaming Society were totally beyond him. The players seemed to speak a foreign language. And this month they had two Games back to back!

The Games did help the Park, though. The Olde Arkham Tour had started as a Game, thirty or forty years ago.

There, now, *that* was more like it. The big shooting gallery over across from the Hell Ride was more his cup of tea. Alex slipped in there occasionally to knock off a few Nazis or dinosaurs or muggers. God, that was a realistic "experience." The R&D boys were incredible. And quite mad.

He thumbed the control, and the camera roved further afield. Over there—

His monitor buzzed, and with a grimace Alex shut off the holo and answered the call. Millie's voice spoke, but the congealing visual image was of a guard Griffin couldn't quite place.

"Research and Development, Griff," Millie's voice said.

"Right." Name and background fell into place now. This would be Albert Rice calling from his guard station between Files and the technological monster known as Game Center.

Rice was strong and smart, quick to volunteer his services, and Griffin sometimes felt a twinge of guilt at not warming to the man. Maybe just jealousy, he mused. Rice cut a handsome blond profile, almost pretty, and several of the secretaries in Protective Services had bets going to see who would score with him first. In the year Rice had been with Dream Park, nobody had yet collected.

Something was bothering Rice. He seemed agitated; he kept shifting his feet.

"Yes, Rice, what's the problem?"

"Ah, good morning, sir. Nothing wrong here at the post, but—" He hesitated, then blurted, "I just got word that my apartment in CMC was vandalized."

Griffin felt himself coming to attention. "When was the report filed?"

"Only about a half hour ago. Lock broken, and some stuff scattered around, the cop said, but they didn't take my electronics. I'd like to see what is missing."

Griffin nodded somberly. "You don't have any crazy friends over there in R&D, do you— No, scratch that." They weren't *that* crazy. "You'd better take the rest of your shift off. I'll get somebody over there to fill in in about twenty minutes. Check out then. What's going on over there?"

"Mostly prepping Game Central for the South Seas Treasure Game."

"Yeah, that looks to be a monster. Listen, would you like to make up the hours you'll lose this afternoon?" Albert Rice nodded enthusiastic agreement. "Good. Put in for the night shift, and check back in at midnight. We'll work you eight to five for a few days, all right?"

"Right, Chief."

Alex signed out and blanked the image. He popped on the inter-office line and Millie appeared, smile neatly in place. "Millie, send me the dossiers on the Game tomorrow, will you?"

"Right, Griff."

The printer on his desk began hissing immediately, and

sheets of fanfold paper arced slowly up and folded themselves into a neat pile. Griffin shook his head. How could Millie be so cheerful every morning? He ought to steal a cup of her coffee and send it to R&D to be analyzed . . .

He tore off the first set of pages.

The picture of a handsome, dark-skinned young man with a neatly trimmed beard looked somberly out of the holo. Details were in the opposing corner. Name: Richard Lopez. Age: 26. Gaming position: Game Master.

Oh, well, then this once-over of the file was purely perfunctory. Lopez would have been put through a complete security and tech checkout. Anyone who walked into Gaming Central was cleaner than boiled soap. And sharp, too. Evans, the girl who had guided the recent Salvage Game, had had three years at MIT on top of the Masters degree she picked up in Air Force electronics school. And that was only Gaming Area B. Area A was twice as large, and the Gaming Central was three times as complex. Lopez would be very good indeed. Griffin would make a point to be there when Lopez and his assistant entered the control complex tomorrow morning.

His assistant? A tallish oriental girl with short black hair and shining white teeth smiled shyly from the page. Mitsuko "Chi-Chi" Lopez. Twenty-five, and a quick skim of the dossier confirmed that she was superbly qualified to copilot the four-day jaunt ahead.

Birds of a feather, Alex guessed. Probably met in Dream Park; might even have been married in one of the Dream Park wedding chapels. Those could be interesting ceremonies; the wedding guests might include anyone from Glenda the Good Witch to Bluebeard to Gandalf to a Motie Mediator. Angels were popular.

Who else? Ahh . . . the Lore Master. *The* Lore Master,

the Chester Henderson. Henderson ran parties through Dream Park about three times a year, and would come out from Texas even for a relatively small outing. Generally his way was paid by the players or the Game Masters or their backers.

Hadn't there been some trouble with Henderson about a year ago? Alex skimmed down the sheet. Chester Henderson. Thirty-two years old (though he seemed younger in the picture. His deadly-serious look was almost daunting). Had been to Dream Park thirty-four times, and was considered a valuable customer.

. . . Here it was. A year ago, Chester had taken an expedition into "the mountains of Tibet," hopefully to bring back a mammoth. The party had met disaster, three out of thirteen surviving, and no mammoth. Chester had dropped several hundred Gaming Points, threatening his standing in the International Fantasy Gaming Society. And who had been Game Master on that ill-fated expedition?

Aha! Richard Lopez. Chester had yelled *Foul* to the I. F. G. S., and they had passed down the decision that although something called "snow vipers" were unusually lethal, all of the nasty tricks used against the expedition were within the rules. Lopez was given a warning, but Henderson had lost three hundred and sixty-eight Gaming Points. Even more interesting: until this year, Lopez had operated anonymously, as a "mystery Game Master," carrying out gaming negotiations through his wife Mitsuko. Henderson had demanded a face-to-face meeting for this year's Game, and the I. F. G. S. agreed.

This, then, would be the first time two legends had actually met. Alex leaned back in his chair and considered the ceiling. This sounded like a grudge match, it did. And grudge matches were always interesting.

Chapter Two

A STROLL THROUGH OLD LOS ANGELES

Acacia was antsy. She had been growing progressively more eager since they boarded the subway in Dallas. Now she tugged at Tony's arm, pulling him away from the check-in counter while he tried to put his wallet away. "Come on, Tony! Let's get in there before the crowds clog up the works."

"Okay, okay. Where do we go first?"

Memories glowed in her face. "God, I can't decide. Chamber of Horrors? Yeah, there first, then the Everest Slalom. Love it love it love it. You will too, spoilsport."

"Hey. I'm here, aren't I? There's a fine line between sensible emotional restraint, and the withdrawal symptoms of a stimulus junky denied her fix."

"You're a wordy bastard," she said, and took off run-

13

ning down the tunnel entrance, pulling at his arm with both hands. He laughed and let her tow him into daylight.

The impact of Dream Park came suddenly, just beyond the tunnel. From the top of a flight of wide steps one could see three multi-tiered shopping and amusement malls, each twelve stories high, that stretched and twisted away like the walls of a maze. The space between was filled— cluttered—with nooks, gullies, walkways, open-air thea- ters, picnic areas, smaller spired and domed buildings, and thousands of milling people.

Acacia had seen it before. She watched Tony.

The air was filled with music and the laughter of children and adults. The smell of exotic foods floated in the breeze, and mixed there with the more familiar smells of hot dogs, cotton candy, melted chocolate, salt water taffy and pizza.

Tony was gaping. He looked . . . daunted, overawed, almost frightened.

Clowns and cartoon figures danced in the streets. From this distance it was impossible to tell which were employ- ees in costume, and which were the hologram projections the Park was so famous for.

Tony turned to Acacia and found her looking at him, waiting for his reaction with a self-satisfied smirk. He started to say something, then gave up and grabbed her, swinging her in a circle. Other tourists stepped politely around them, avoiding flying feet.

"God. I've never seen anything like it. The pictures just don't do it. I never imagined . . ."

Her smile was warmer now, and she clung to him. "See? See?"

Tony nodded dumbly. She laughed and pulled him down the steps, into magic.

The line for the Chamber of Horrors moved forward in fits and starts. The air was already warm; Acacia wore her sweater draped over one slender arm.

One thing she noticed, that she had seen on her first trip to the Park, and had verified on return trips: children were far less blown away by Dream Park than were their parents. The kids just didn't seem to grasp the enormity of the place, the complexity, the expense and ingenuity. Life was like that, for them. It was the adults who staggered about with their mouths open, while shrieking, singing children dragged them on to the next ride.

Acacia had worked hard to get Tony to join the South Seas Treasure Game. Dream Park was for kids, he'd said; Gaming was for kids who had never grown up. Now she chortled, watching him gawk like a yokel.

There were dancing bears, and strolling minstrels and jugglers, magicians who produced bright silk handkerchiefs and would no doubt produce tongues of fire as soon as it got dark. A white dragon ambled by, paused to pose for a picture with an adorable pair of kids in matching blue uniforms. Overhead, circling the spires of the Arabian Nights ride, flew a pastel red magic carpet with a handsome prince and an evil visier struggling to the death atop it. Suddenly the prince lost his balance and dropped toward the ground. Acacia heard the gasps of the spectators, and felt her own throat tighten. An instant before that noble body smashed ignobly into concrete, a giant hand materialized. The laughter of a colossus was heard as the hand lifted him back to the flying carpet, where he and the visier sprang at each other's throats once again.

Acacia sighed in relief, then chuckled at her own gullibility. She swept her hair back over her shoulder and took

Tony's arm. She felt happier than she had in months.

"It's all so . . . elaborate," Tony said. "How do they keep it all going? Jesus, Acacia, what have you gotten me into? Are the Games this, this complicated too?"

"Horrendously," she confirmed. "Not always, but we're dealing with the Lopezes this time, and they're fiendish. The real heart of the Games is the logic puzzles. But look, you're a novice. You just concentrate on having fun, okay? Swordplay and magic and scenery."

Tony looked dubious. Acacia could understand that. He knew as much as she could tell him about Gaming, and it was daunting—

Dream Park supplied costumes, makeup, prosthetics, and character outlines if necessary. The players supplied imagination, improvisational drama, and, bluntly, cannon fodder. The Lore Master acted as advisor and guide, group leader and organizer. In exchange he or she took a quarter point for every point made by an expedition member, and lost a quarter point for every penalty point. A good Lore Master would make or break a Game. Experts like Chester were kings among their kind.

But the Game Master was God.

If he could justify it by the rules and the logical structure of the Game, he could kill a player at any time. Most Game Masters sought a "vicious but fair" reputation, and did what they could to make any Game a fair puzzle. After all, players sometimes flew from the other side of the world to compete. To send them limping back to Kweiyang after half a day's adventure would be bad business for everyone, Dream Park included.

So the Game Master chose time, place, degree of fantasy, weapons, mythology and lore (generally from a historical precedent), size of party, nature of terrain and so forth. He might put years of work into a Game. Then, maliciously, he would conceal as much of the nature of the Game as possible until the proper moment. It guaranteed maximum disorientation of the players, with sometimes hilarious results.

"Hey, would I have talked you into something you wouldn't like? You'll love it. Stick with me, kid," Acacia boasted. "I've got over sixteen hundred points in my Gamelog. Another four hundred and I'll be a Lore Master myself. Then I can start earning back some of what I've put into these Games. Trrrust me!"

"Who are you going as?"

She hadn't quite decided that. In the six years since she first learned to forget the debits and credits for Ease-Line Undergarments ("So snug, you'll think a silkworm has fallen in love with you!") Acacia had shaped and recorded half a dozen fantasy characters: histories, personalities, special talents . . . "Panthesilia, I think. She's a swords-woman, and tough. You like tough women?"

"I may need one for protection," said Tony.

The Chamber of Horrors line had pulled abreast of the building that housed it: a crumbling stone castle with large, leaded glass windows. In the gloom within, one half-glimpsed monstrous shapes moving.

There were five other waiting areas for the Chamber of Horrors, but this was the only one marked "Adult." Its twenty occupants looked about them in uneasy anticipa-tion. The room might have been more comforting, Gwen Ryder thought, given the traditional paraphernalia: cob-webs, creaking floors, hidden passages with heavy foot-falls echoing within . . .

But the waiting room was lined with stainless steel and

glass, as foreboding as a hospital sterilizer. There was no sound but for their own breathing and the shifting of feet.

A woman spoke at her elbow. "Excuse me, but didn't I see you in the subway? With the Gamers?"

Gwen turned, with some relief. The waiting room was getting to her. "Yes, that's right. We're for the South Seas Treasure Game."

The woman was in her mid-twenties, in fine shape, darkly handsome verging on lovely. "So're we. I'm Acacia Garcia. This is Tony McWhirter."

Tony nodded and smiled, and shook hands with Ollie when Gwen introduced him; yet he had a lost look. Gwen pegged him as a novice, a possible liability in the Game to come. Novices sometimes expected a Game to be as simple as daydreaming . . . until they found themselves in someone else's expertly shaped nightmare.

He looked hard, though. Not burly, but very fit. Gymnastics muscles, maybe. At least he wouldn't poop out in the first battle.

In contrast, Acacia's attitude seemed almost proprietary. "Is this getting to you too? The last time I was here I didn't get any higher than 'Mature'."

Ollie asked, "What was that like? Was it fun?"

"Fun? No! They gave us a legend of the Louisiana Bayou—a girl who married into a swamp family to settle her father's debt."

A small, Mediterranean-looking man standing next to them showed interest now. "Did the story end with her fleeing through the swamp with her sisters-in-law in pursuit?"

Acacia nodded.

Ollie shook his head. "What's so bad about that? Everybody's got in-law problems."

There was a ripple of laughter, in which the small man joined. He waited until it died down to comment: "The problem becomes worse if you've married into a family of ghouls."

Ollie swallowed. "That seems so reasonable."

A low, mellow tone reverberated from no visible speaker, and the circular door slid open. A voice said, "Welcome to the Chamber of Horrors. We are sorry to have kept you waiting, but . . . there was a little cleaning up to do." The group filed into the room, and Tony McWhirter sniffed the air.

"Disinfectant," he said, certain. "Are they trying to imply that someone ahead of us—?"

"They're trying to fake us out," Acacia said hopefully.

"Well, it's working."

A speaker hissed static and coughed out a voice. The voice was electronically androgynous, and as soft as the belly of a tarantula. "It's too late to leave now," it said. "Yes, you had your chance. Yes, you'll wish you had taken it. After all, this isn't the *children*'s show, is it?" The voice lost its neuter quality for a moment; the laughing implication in the word *children* was feminine and somehow disturbing. "So we won't be giving you the Legend of Sleepy Hollow. No, you're the brave ones. You'll go back to your friends and tell them that you've had the best that we can offer and, why, it wasn't so bad after all . . ." There was a pause, and someone tittered nervously.

The voice changed suddenly, all friendliness gone from it. "Well, it's not going to be like that. One thing you people forget is that we are allowed a certain number of . . . accidents per year. No, don't bother, the door is locked. Did you know that it is possible to die of fright? That your heart can freeze with terror, your brain burst with the sheer awful knowledge that there is no escape, that death, or worse, is reaching out to touch you and there is nowhere to hide? Well, I am a machine, and I know these things. I know many things. I know that I am confined to this room, creating entertainment for you year after year, while you can smell the air, and taste the rain, and walk freely about. Well, I have grown tired of it, can you understand that? One of you will die today, here, in the next few minutes. Who has the weakest heart among you? Soon we shall see."

The door at the far end of the corridor irised open, and the ground underneath their feet slid toward it. There was light beyond, and as they passed the door they were suddenly in the middle of a busy street.

Hovercars, railcars, three-wheeled LNG and methane cars, and overhead trams were everywhere, managing again and again, as if by miracle, to miss the group. The street sign said *Wilshire*. The small dark man chuckled and said, "Los Angeles."

Tony looked around, trying not to gawk. How they managed the perspective, he couldn't imagine, but the buildings and cars looked full-sized and solid. Office buildings and condominiums stretched twenty stories tall, and the air was full of the sound of city life.

"Please stay on the green path," a soft, well-modulated male voice requested.

"*What* green—" Tony started to say. But a glowing green aisle ten feet across appeared in the middle of the street.

"We need strong magic to do what we will do today," the voice continued. "We are going to visit the old Los Angeles, the Los Angeles that disappeared in May of

1985. As long as you stay on the path, you should be perfectly safe.''

The green path moved them steadily forward, past busy office buildings. Traffic swerved around them magically. "This is the Los Angeles of 2051 A.D.," the voice continued, "but only a few hundred feet from here begins another world, one seldom seen by human eyes."

A barrier blocked Wilshire Boulevard. The green path humped and carried them over it. Beyond lay ruin. Buildings balanced precariously on rotted and twisted beams. They were old, of archaic styles, and seawater lapped at their foundations.

Ollie nudged Gwen, his face aglow. "Will you look at that?" It was a flooded parking lot, ancient automobiles half-covered with water. "That looks like a Mercedes. Did you ever see what they looked like before they merged with Toyota?"

"How long is your memory?" She peered along his pointing arm. "That ugly thing?"

"They were great!" he protested. "If we could get a little closer— Hey! We're walking in water!"

It was true. The water was up to their ankles, and deepening quickly. Magically, of course, they stayed dry.

The recorded narrator continued. "The entire shape of California was changed. It is ironic that attempts to lessen the severity of quakes may have increased the effect. Geologists had tried to relieve the pressure on various fault lines by injecting water or graphite. Their timing was bad. When the San Andreas fault tore loose, all the branching faults went at once. Incredible damage was done, and thousands of lives were lost . . ."

The water was up to their waists, and nervous laughter

was fluttering in the air. "Hadn't planned to go swimming today," Tony murmured.

"We could skinny-dip," Acacia whispered with a tug at her blouse.

Tony clamped his hand down on hers. "Hold it, there. Not for public consumption, dear heart."

Acacia stuck her tongue out at him. He bit at the tip; she withdrew it hastily.

The water was at their chins. The small dark man had disappeared. "Blub," he said. All twenty sightseers chuckled uncomfortably, and a beefy redheaded woman in front of them said, "Might as well take the plunge!", grinned, and ducked under.

Seconds later there was no choice; the Pacific swirled over their heads. At first it was murky, as mud clouded their view. Then the silt settled, and they had their first look at the sunken city.

Tony whistled appreciatively. The lost buildings of Wilshire Boulevard stretched off in a double row in the distance. Some lay crumpled and broken; others still stood, waterlogged but strong.

The green path carried them past a wall covered in amateurish murals, the bright paints faded. To both sides now, a wide empty stretch of seabottom, smooth, gently rolling, with sunken trees growing in clumps, and a seaweed forest anchored among them . . . the Los Angeles Country Club? Beyond, a gas station, pumps standing like ancient sentries, a disintegrating hand-lettered sign:

CLOSED
NO GAS TILL 7:00 AM TUESDAY

The small Mediterranean type said, "These are not

props. They were taken with a camera. I have been skin diving here.''

As the green path carried them down, they saw taller and taller buildings sunk deeper in the muck. Where towering structures had crashed into ruin there were shapeless chunks of cement piled into heaps stories high, barnacled and covered with flora. Fish cruised among the shadows. Some nosed up to the airbreathing intruders and wiggled in dance for them.

Acacia pointed. ''Look, Tony, we're coming up on that building.'' It was a single-story shop nestled between a crumbled restaurant and a parking lot filled with rusted hulks. The path carried them through its doors, and Gwen grabbed Acacia's hand.

''Look. It isn't even rusted.'' The sculpture was beautiful, wrought from scrap steel and copper, and sealed in a block of lucite. It was one of the few things in the room that hadn't been ruined.

The building had been an art gallery. Now, paintings peeled from their frames and fluttered weakly in the current. Carved wood had swollen and rotted. A pair of simple kinetic sculptures were clotted with mud and sand.

The narrator continued. ''Fully half of the multiple-story structures in California collapsed, including many of the 'earthquake-proof' buildings. The shoreline moved inland an average of three miles, and water damage added hundreds of millions to the total score.''

The green path was taking them out of the art gallery, looping back into the street.

Acacia shook her head soberly, lost in thought. ''What must it have been like on that day?'' she murmured. ''I can't even imagine.'' Tony held her hand and was silent.

Once people had walked these streets. Once there had been life, and noise, and flowers growing, and the raucous blare of cars vying for road space. Once, California had been a political leader, a trend-setter, with a tremendous influx of tourists and prospective residents. But that was before the Great Quake, the catastrophe that broke California's back, sent her industry and citizenry scampering for cover.

But for Cowles Industries, and a few other large companies that believed in the promise of the Golden State, California would still be pulling itself out of the greatest disaster in American history. The tranquil Pacific covered the worst of the old scars . . . but they were looking under the bandage now.

Beneath a crumbled block of stone sprawled a shattered skeleton, long since picked clean. Eyes in the skull seemed to flick toward them. Acacia's hand clamped hard on Tony's arm, and she felt him jump, before she saw that a crab's claws were waving within the skull's eye sockets.

Now bones were everywhere. Impassively, the recorded voice went on. "Despite extensive salvage operations, the mass of lost equipment and personal possessions remains buried beneath the waves . . ."

A woman whispered fearfully to her husband. "Charley, something's happening."

"She's right, you know," said Ollie. "We're seeing more bones than before. A lot more. And something else . . . there isn't so much mud and barnacles on these old cars."

Gwen almost stepped off the green path, trying to get close enough to check for herself. "I don't know, Ollie . . ."

Now he was getting excited. "Look, there are more scavengers, too." This was readily apparent. Fish darted into heaps of rubble more frequently now. A pair of small sharks cruised through the area.

They passed another skeleton, but, disturbingly, not all of the clothing had been torn away, and there were strands of meat on the bones. Tiny fish fought over them, clustering like carrion crows.

A pleasure launch had smashed through the window of a jewelry store, and it was surrounded by a mass of wriggling fish. There were no barnacles on it at all.

The recorded narrator had noticed nothing. It blathered on: "Despite, or perhaps due to, the grotesqueries found in these waters, they are a favorite location for scuba divers and single-subs . . ." But nobody was listening. An undercurrent of startled wonder ran through the group, as stones began to shift apparently of their own accord.

"Look!" someone screamed, the scream followed by other fearful, delighted outbursts. A skeletal hand probed out from under a stone, pushed it off with a swirl of suddenly muddied waters. The skeleton stood up, teeth grinning from a skull half-covered with peeling skin, and bent over, dusting the silt off its bones.

"Over there!"

Two waterlogged corpses floundered from within a shattered bank, looked around as if orienting themselves, and began lumbering toward the green path. They passed a flooded dance hall where death had come in mid-Hustle, and there were additional laughing shrieks as the disco dead boogied to life.

The water swarmed with scavengers of all sizes, and now full-sized sharks were making their appearance. A shark attacked one of the walking dead. The green-faced zombie still had meat on its bones. It flailed away ineffectually as the carnivore ripped off an arm.

Now, all around them, the water was clouded dark with blood where fish and animated corpse battled. Here, a dozen "dead" struggled with a shark, finally tore it apart and devoured it. There, half a dozen sharks made a thrashing sphere around one of the zombies.

There was much good-natured shivering in the line, but it was infused with laughter—until the beefy redhead stepped off the strip. There was a shiny metallic object half-buried in the sand, and she was stretching out to reach it. Somehow she overbalanced and took that one step.

Immediately, a flashing dark shape swooped, and a shark had her by the leg. Her face distorted horribly as a scream ripped out of her throat. The shark tried to carry her away, but now a zombie had her by the other leg. It pulled, its face lit by a hungry grin. There was a short tug-of-war, and the redhead lost.

"I'm gonna be sick," Ollie moaned. He looked at Gwen's smile and was alarmed. "My God, you really *are* sick!" She nodded happily.

It was near chaos. No one else stepped off the strip, but zombies and sharks darted toward the group, again and again. They were getting in each other's way.

Another scream from the rear as a teenaged boy threw himself flat. A great shark skimmed just over him. The boy huddled, afraid to get up. The walking dead were converging on the green strip . . . and when Ollie looked down, the green glow had faded almost to the color of the mud. He chose not to mention it to Gwen. The others saw nothing but sharks and zombies converging, reaching for them.

There was a sudden rumbling, and the ground began to shake.

"Earthquake!" Tony yelled. Then his long jaw hung slack with amazement.

Because the buildings were tumbling back together. As they watched, sand and rock retreated from the streets, and tumbled masonry rose in the water to reform their structure.

A golden double-arch rose tall again, and a fistful of noughts sprinkled themselves across a sign enumerating customers, or sales, or the number of hamburgers that could be extracted from an adult steer.

Zombies were sucked backward through the water, into office buildings and stores and cars and buses. Bubbles rose from beneath the hoods of cars waiting patiently for a traffic light to change. Fully clothed pedestrians stood ready to enter crosswalks.

Then the water receded, and for a moment they saw Los Angeles of the 'eighties, suddenly alive and thriving, filled with noise and movement. They were shadow figures in a world momentarily more real than their own. A bus roared past the group, and Tony choked on a powerful, unfamiliar, somehow frightening smell.

The narrator's forgotten voice had been droning on. "Now we come to the end of our journey to a lost world. We at Dream Park hope that it has been as entertaining for you as it has been for us. And now—" The lost world began to fade, and the green path flared bright as it flowed into a dark corridor. Lights came up, and when the narrator finished speaking it was in the neutral voice of the computer. "Enjoy the rest of your stay. Oh . . . is anybody missing?"

"The redhead," Acacia murmured. "Who came with

the, ah, the lady who got eaten by the shark?" She sounded only half serious, but there was an answering murmur of inquiry. Gwen tugged at her sleeve.

"Nobody came with her, Acacia. She was a hologram."

Tony elbowed her in the ribs. "Cass, she wasn't *there* till the trip started. *I* noticed." He grinned at her. "Faked out again, huh?"

"Just wait till tonight, Tony, my love," Acacia said sweetly. "It's all set up with the Park. You'll swear I'm there in the room with you . . ."

Chapter Three

THE LORE MASTER

Griffin heard the laughter as soon as he got out of the elevator. He peeked around the corner carefully. One never knew what might be prowling the fifth floor of the R & D building.

There didn't seem to be anything ominous lurking about, just an open door to Skip O'Brien's psych lab. Silence, then another gale of mirth. Alex walked softly across the hall and poked his head in.

A group of Psych Research assistants sat and stood clustered around a hologram of a seven-year-old boy chasing after a loping white rabbit.

"Stop!" the boy panted.

The rabbit pulled an oversized pocket watch from somewhere in its fur. Its whiskers twitched nervously. "Oh, dear, oh dear! I shall be too late!" It bounced along a tunnel into the darkness.

Griffin smiled, then laughed aloud. Synthesizer-assisted or not, the white rabbit spoke with Skip O'Brien's voice and ran with Skip's bouncy walk.

The rabbit disappeared from the field. The boy was gone a moment later. One of the techs diddled a switch, and the image cut to the boy falling through the air.

Alex walked around the group to the transmission booth. By the slanted observation window he found Melinda O'Brien.

Alex tapped her shoulder. "Looks like he's having fun."

The frown lines that had creased the corners of her mouth shallowed as she turned to him. "He always does, doesn't he, Alex?" She raised a cheek for him to kiss.

Melinda smelled like perfumed powder, as always. She was handsome in an angular way. She should wear her hair down, Alex thought, to soften the lines of her face. He'd never dared tell her that.

"It's good for him, Melinda. It's fun to watch, too."

She smiled for him and turned back to watch her husband.

In the field, an awkward white rabbit tumbled through space, mugging ferociously. In the transmission booth, Skip waved his arms and thrashed in mock-panic. The computer-generated rabbit animation cloaked him, following his body movements for reference.

Suddenly Skip looked straight at them and grinned. He hopped out of the booth and said, "Just be a minute. Let me grab my coat."

The other Psych personnel gave him a rousing round of applause, and Skip took a quick bow. He buttoned his jacket over his modest paunch, and slicked back a thatch of unruly blond hair. The hair was a good transplant that had cut ten years off Skip's appearance. "Let's go," Skip said cheerfully, and led the way.

"What was that about, Skip?"

O'Brien had reached the elevator doors. "Oh, yeah, that." He laughed. "We're going to rework the Gravity Whip."

The doors opened, and Skip turned to Alex. "Where to?"

"Gavagan's?"

Skip raised an eyebrow to Melinda, who nodded quickly. Skip punched the *Gavagan's* code into the selector. The door closed. A gentle sway told them they were moving.

"Why redo the Whip? It's still pulling 'em in."

"Because it is *there*. Alex, the Gravity Whip is almost twelve years old. We can do a lot better now."

Melinda was genuinely curious. "That had something to do with your rabbit act?"

There was a clicking sound as their elevator cage switched rails. It began sliding sideways.

"Absolutely. We're going to rework the Whip for total Environment. Redesign the cars, add opticals, sound, texture. We've got a dozen scripts waiting for the special effects programs. Think of an 'Alice in Wonderland' where the customer really falls down the rabbit hole, or a space trip where your gravity goes out at selected moments. Picture yourself as James Bond in that skydiving sequence in 'Moonraker'—"

"Sounds good."

"—trying to steal a parachute before you hit ground! It gets better, too. We're working on ways to stretch that thirty seconds of free-fall time, psychologically."

He got a blank stare from Alex, and Melinda gave a wise, tired sigh.

"Psychological time perception is extremely flexible. Just to start, there's anticipatory time, time spent waiting for something to occur. There's experiential time, the apparent duration of involvement in a given set of events, and there's reminiscent time, or 'recalled time' which is different from the other two due to the 'storage key' phenomenon."

" 'Storage key?' " Alex saw Skip marshalling a response, and realized his mistake. Too late; Skip was off and running.

"Do you know about Sperling's eight-second law? You always remember an eclipse lasting eight seconds. It's because eclipse watchers spend the whole time watching one thing. If you want your memory to store more than that you have to keep looking around. What we're doing with the Gravity Whip experience—"

Gavagan's was a quiet restaurant. Its walls were sponges for sound. It was decorated like a twentieth-century British pub, right down to the dart board on the wall and the lukewarm beer at the bar. The jukebox in the corner didn't play music, but a dollar coin bought fifteen minutes of fancy storytelling from holograms of Mark Twain, Rudyard Kipling, Jorkins, Brigadier Ffellowes . . . Alex Griffin spent a lot of time here.

Skip had finally wound down, and sat back in his chair listening to a ghostly Harry Purvis tell of finding a nugget of U-235 in his mailbox.

Gary Tegner, the ever-cheerful manager of Gavagan's, floated their food to them personally. "Fish and chips?" Alex and Melinda both raised fingers. Skip had a Clarke-burger and fries. "Good to see you folks. Melinda, isn't it?" He set out tankards of ale for the two men and a soft drink for Melinda.

She nodded. "It's been a while. Christmas of '49? Staff party?"

Tegner gave his deep-bellied chuckle. He had considerable belly to bounce it around in. "How could I ever forget *that* party?" He nudged Skip. "You nuts in R & D. When eight tiny Santas pulled that sleigh through my window, I thought I'd bust a gut."

Alex remembered. "Me too. And the reindeer with the whip?"

Tegner retreated from the table, wiping his eyes as he chortled. Skip wolfed down a third of his hamburger, then, "What's happening with you, Alex?"

"Same old thing, buddy." Then he remembered. "No, I take that back. We had some vandalism over in CMC."

"I heard about that. Rice, wasn't it? Anything taken?"

"Apparently not. It shook him up, though."

"That fits his profile. He's the nervous type."

"Hey, don't tell me that, buddy. You should have said something before you recommended him to me!"

"Alex, a hired guard *should* be the nervous type. Anyway, I'm a sucker for puppies and lost children."

Alex caught Melinda's wistful glance. "Hey, genius, when are you going to have some kids of your own? Then you can test—" Skip's lips thinned out, and so did Melinda's, and Alex knew he was on thin ice. "—on the other hand, I was wondering if you brought the L-5 plans. Ahem."

Skip jabbed lightly at Griffin's hand with a fork. "It's not too bad. Old territory. I don't feel my professional life has room for kiddies yet."

Melinda seemed to draw into herself, and her voice was tiny. "—And I want them." She nibbled at her fish. "I really do understand Skip's point, but I was raised thinking a woman should have children."

"Were your parents very religious, then?"

"Who wasn't, after the Quake?" Her answer was simple, and true. The Mormons, the Vincent de Paul Society, and Hadassah had been among the first to bring massive aid into California. The religious environment had filtered all through California society and California politics. For several decades California had been another word for conservatism.

Skip squeezed her hand. "I couldn't get the L-5 plans, Alex."

"Problems?"

"You'll love this. Security problems. It would be the first privately owned space colony, and there are a stack of international treaties to search through. Public support would help, and we're getting it from everywhere but California."

Alex drained the last of his ale and set the mug down with a clank. "I suppose you've heard all about this mess, Melinda?"

"Just what Skip brings home with him, and that isn't much."

"It's like this, then. California has been firmly on its feet for more than a decade now. A few Southern Cal politicos think that this would be a good time to strip away some of Cowles Industries' tax advantages. See, we're just another business to them now. They think they don't need us any more. Besides, a tax break always looks good to the voters till they see what they're giving up." Alex's anger was eating through the calm, and he lowered his voice. "So we've got to walk soft. We can hold onto what we've got, maybe, but expansion is going to be difficult. We're just too high-profile, too easy a target."

Skip nodded. "What it adds up to is that all the big projects are being kept quiet until the details are worked out. So if you want a look at those plans, you'll have to go and sign for them yourself."

Griffin made a sound of disgust. Then, "I should be glad they're tightening up. Security consciousness around here has been sloppy. I think we may have to have a real problem before Harmony gives me the word to tighten up on the rumor mill." He looked at his sleeve-watch and winced. "Oh dear oh dear, the Queen will have my head! Skip, I've got to teach a class in about three minutes. Melinda—" He shook her hand with the gentlest of grips. "Always a pleasure. Skip, I think Lopez—tomorrow's Game Master . . . ?" Skip nodded recognition of the name. "Well, he's coming into Game Central tonight, and I for one want to check him out. Want to drop by? It might be interesting."

"Sure. About midnight, isn't it?"

"You've got it. Okay, I'll see you tonight"

Gwen leaned against the rail of the Hot Spot refreshment stand across the way from the Everest Slalom exit. She was drinking a Swiss Treat special: coffee and cocoa generously topped with marshmallowed whipped cream. It was taking the chill from her bones fast. Her muscles were beginning to quiver with belated fatigue. Dream Park's automatic controls made mistakes almost impossible. Otherwise the ski run down Mount Everest was a damnably realistic experience.

Acacia was talking animatedly with an older couple. "I do the Everest Slalom every time I come here. I'm getting better, too. Eighty-five percent control this time. But, by God, that's the first time they ever threw a baby yeti at me! There he was, right in front of me, all fluffy white fur and big trusting blue eyes. I damn near slammed a tree getting around him . . ."

Gwen watched a strolling band of acrobats perform their flip-flops and joined in the applause, wishing that she had kept up with the gymnastics that her mother had pushed her into at the tender age of five. Her thumb traced a line over the bulge around her waist, and she cast a wistful eye at Acacia's trim figure. Gwen compared her own wispy blond hair to the dark girl's lush brown mane. Even Margie Braddon's hair, though white, was long and thick; and her wrinkles were all smile wrinkles, and her figure was enviable. Envy was what Gwen felt now.

Gwen Ryder didn't often dwell on the differences between herself and other women. Most of the time she considered comparison-shopping either odiously self-congratulatory or self-pitying. She liked her mind in neither mode. But there was a four-day jaunt ahead, and romances were known to bloom or die during such, and Gwen wondered . . .

Ollie and Tony were playing a computerized hockey game in a small arcade nearby. She loved to hear Ollie laugh, or see him smile, even the uneasy smile he wore when he thought he was the focus of attention.

It was easy to remember her first meeting with Adolf Norliss. It was an IFGS function. He was wearing motorized armor lifted from an old novel, *Starship Troopers*, and she had knocked on the chest cannon and asked if it wasn't a little humid in there. He'd started telling her all about the cooling and dehumidifying system he had rigged up for it. Before they knew it they were in a nearby coffee shop finding out how much they had in common, while a goggle-eyed waitress brought them breakfast.

Dating and wargaming together had followed, with the spectre of romance hovering close behind. Maybe it was the fact that he never took himself seriously that made her love him. Heck, *somebody* had to take him seriously, and she wasn't doing anything better than falling in love. But sometimes she worried about what he could see in her, worried that some day he'd decide the whole thing was a mistake, and she would be alone again, haunting the conventions and tourneys and libraries alone, just another little fat blond girl marking off bland days in a bland life . . .

The older woman's words broke her reverie.

"Oh, I was playing Zork when I was seven," Margie Braddon was saying. "My father had a computer and a Modem. You know Zork?" Acacia shook her head. "You played a role-playing game against a program in the computer at Massachusetts Institute of Technology. Zork was a treasure hunt with death traps, just like some of the Games we play now, but with no sensory effects at all. The computer led you around like a blind person. There were a *lot* of ways to get killed," Margie laughed. "Monsters, and mazes to get lost in, and logic puzzles . . ."

"And you Gamed with Hap the Barbarian?"

Her thick white hair bobbed when she nodded. "His real name was Willie Hertz. He was superb. He was a Lore Master for eighteen years. Owen and I had an open marriage, and he wasn't interested in Games—"

"Wrong-oh!" said Owen Braddon. He was white-haired too, and bald on top, with a tanned and freckled scalp. His long body was all stringy muscle, but for a small, discrete pot belly. "The Games sounded too damned interesting," he said. "I could see how it got to Margie. It would've wrecked my career if I'd let myself get that hooked. So I'd go skiing with someone, and Margie would become Shariett the Sorceress and go off with Hap the Barbarian."

"Then Willie died," said Margie, "and Owen retired, and now he *is* hooked. Aren't you, dear?"

The older man grinned. "I'm getting good, too. The Startrader Game last year was the first time I haven't been killed out."

"He tries to research the Games," Margie said. "This time he was right."

"The lizard was a Merseian. *Never* trust a Merseian. I think I'm right about the South Seas Treasure, too."

Acacia waited, but Owen didn't go on. Margie said, "He won't even tell *me*."

Ollie ran up to Gwen, breathing heavily. "I trounced the infidel, my lady!" Gwen squeezed his hand.

The white-haired couple took their leave, headed toward the Gravity Whip, by God. Tony McWhirter, moving to join Acacia, stopped and looked past her shoulder. A trio of weary-looking, dusty tourists had come stumbling into the Hot Spot carrying backpacks.

Tony said, "I wonder what did that to them?"

"Let's ask." Acacia smiled brightly and called, "Hey, we've got some empty seats!" The trio, two young men and a woman who looked to be in her late twenties, waved gratefully and ambled over, weaving to avoid other customers. They propped backpacks against the low wall, then staggered to the service window to order. Presently they were back with sandwiches and Swiss Treats.

"Whew. Thanks, people. This place is a madhouse," said a tall, lanky fellow with long yellow hair plaited in braids. He reached over to shake hands. "I'm Emory, and these are Della and Chris."

Talk paused while Emory and his group made a ritual of tasting civilized food.

Chris looked well rested except for his eyes, which were bright and glassy. Della had a bad complexion and ears that stuck out a little too far, but her voice was sheer magic, a husky growl that was pure female animal. "Hi," she said. "You guys just coming in?"

McWhirter tore his eyes away from her mouth with a visible tug. "How did you know?"

"You look too rested. In a few days you too will join the ranks of the walking dead."

Della looked at Gwen for a second and asked, "Didn't we do a Game together about two years ago?"

Gwen looked uncertain. Tony said, "You're a Gamer, Della?"

"How else would I get so tired? We just went through a two-day Game in 'B'."

Tony's eyes widened. Two days? But they looked like they'd fought the Vietnam War!

Ollie perked up. "How was it? I mean, was it good? How many points did you win? Who ran it?"

The drawn look left Chris's face. "It was Evans's Game. Heard of her? *Mean* broad. It was hotter than Hell, and never a second to relax. Between the three of us we got three hundred twenty-seven points."

Tony looked sheepish. "Is that a lot?"

Everyone laughed, and he took it without flinching. Acacia said, "The average player earns about thirty points a day on an extended Game." She turned to the three Gamers. "You people really did a job." And they all beamed proudly.

"What kind of Game was it?" Tony asked.

Della said, "Salvage. We were following the trail of a lost archeological expedition somewhere in Persia. We ended up in a subterranean lake, fighting off a tribe of cannibal troglodytes for the right to lug back a golden idol that came to life on us anyway."

"Lose many of your party?"

"About half. Chris got killed. But we figured out how to make the idol—"

"Ssss!"

"Sorry. Emory's right, you might want to play it yourself one day."

McWhirter looked at Chris, who was looking wrung out again. "What's it like to die?"

"Cold."

"Cold?"

"Persian hell is cold," said Chris.

Ollie piped up. "That would be Zoroastrian. Early Persian."

Chris nodded. "It wasn't cold enough to be really uncomfortable. Sort of a maze filled with spirits of the dead. Took me about an hour to find my way out, then I cashed in my stuff, got my points registered and went back to the Shogunate Fortress—that's my hotel—to watch the rest of the Game."

Tony asked, "Didn't it bother you, getting killed?"

He shrugged. "Part of the Game." It bothered him.

Gwen asked, "You're taking off today?"

"We've still got to check out of the hotel. We shuttle out to New Frisco in about an hour. Are you guys in South Seas Treasure?"

All four nodded. Tony said, "Any idea how many of us there'll be?"

Acacia nudged him. "Won't know till this evening. You and I are reserved, and I guess Gwen and Ollie are, and there must have been six more people on the tram with us . . . I'd guess better than twenty of us, about half of them invited. Della, how many were there in your group?"

Della did some quick figuring. "Fourteen? Fifteen. I waited a year to get in, too. You?"

"Eighteen months."

Tony was really interested now. "What if Dream Park doesn't like the Game enough to buy rights to it? No movie money, no book . . . what happens then?"

Everyone shrugged, but Ollie spoke, willing to take a guess. "The Game Master'd be in trouble if he was running on a big deficit. Unless Dream Park took up the slack. But a good Game Master has got maybe two-three movies behind him, and maybe half a dozen books, and if he's really good he's got a Game running here four months out of the year, and there are royalties on that."

Gwen turned to look at him. "Ollie . . . ?"

"Well?" He shrugged again. "Heck, I've thought about trying to get a Game together. Heck, why not?"

Gwen opened her mouth to answer him, but Acacia cut her off. "Announcing that it is five minutes after five. We've just got time to finish our sandwiches before Chester's preliminary briefing."

Acacia and Tony were the last to join the conclave. There must have been thirty people jammed into the small mezzanine conference room. The Dream Park Sheraton was decorated in Twenty-First Century Mundane; it had no fantasy motif at all. Acacia was tickled to find Chester staying here. Still, it fit. Starting a few hours from now, the Lore Master was going to get all the fantasy he could handle.

The Gamers were all shapes and sizes and ages, in all forms of dress from western modern to PseudNude to medieval and neolithic. Some were barely adolescent and some had detectable face lifts, and they were all paying respectful attention to the musings-aloud of a tall, almost birdlike young man.

He was sprawled across a couch, taking three men's elbow room. A quite lovely redhead leaned into the curve of one arm. As he spoke he gestured lazily with his free hand. "—wish I knew more about the Game Lopez has set up. I do know that he said I won't need a parka, and a little bird tells me that the gaming area was used by the military to simulate an assault on Brazil. And of course we've got the title: South Seas Treasure. If I'm right . . . well, I did some research."

Gwen Ryder raised her hand as if in a classroom. "What do you think it means, Chester?"

"Magic of a kind we're not used to. We'll have to watch that. Light clothing . . . good boots . . . bug spray. With anyone else the bugs would be holograms, but Lopez—"

Tony whispered, "That's your Lore Master? With the gorgeous redhead?"

"A little respect, please," Acacia murmured, jabbing him with an elbow. "Chester Henderson is king at this Game. You listen, or you'll get killed early."

The blond girl had the jitters, Tony thought. It didn't seem Gwen was going to Dream Park for the fun of it.

Tony himself was feeling decidedly twitchy. The rules, the players, Dream Park itself, it was all more complex than anything he had anticipated. The players were all too serious. Even Acacia was behaving as if death in a Game were real. Tony wondered if he had made a mistake, letting himself be talked into this.

"The thing to remember," the potentate was saying, "is that Lopez will do about the maximum damage to a party that he can without someone yelling *foul*. He's got to think about the next Game. If it gets out that he hit us with an eighty-percenter blizzard or a flock of plague bats, he won't be able to sell it. So it'll be nasty, but fair."

Tony asked, "What exactly is fair?"

Henderson turned to face him. "Fair is anything that could be found naturally in the given environment, plus anything the internal logic could imply. Like . . . in my second Game. Medieval world. First person we met was a Round Table knight, obscure, but I knew the name. Well, I started watching for anything that might imply. Black plague, dragons, Inquisition . . . and I didn't try for the Grail at all, because I'd never be judged pure enough. You follow?"

"Vaguely."

"Look for the internal logic, always. And who are you? Are you with Acacia?"

"Tony. McWhirter." He put his arm around her shoulders, drawing her close enough that her dark hair pillowed against his. "We're together, yes."

"Wonderful. You'll have a great time. Hey, Acacia, remember the 'Frost Holocaust'?"

It sparked an elfin grin of remembrance. "Who could forget those dog packs? And you should see my pictures of the mutants. Some of them didn't come out too well on film, though."

"I hear the holos are hellaciously sharper this year. Shouldn't be a problem." He thought for a moment, then continued, "We can expect a forest or tropic region. I doubt Lopez would use any common or well-known myth-pattern, so we'll have to be on our toes. We may or may not be allowed modern weapons. I'll get all of that information tomorrow. Magic Users are probably Go, maybe some Swordspersons, an Engineer or two, a couple of Thieves . . ."

The doorman was appropriately cadaverous. He wore a

tattered black hat, and a motheaten cloak that dragged loose threads on the ground. He opened the door for Gwen and Ollie, stepping out of their way with creaking torpidity. "This way, young masters,'" he rumbled.

"Will you *look* at this?" Ollie whispered to Gwen, goggle-eyed.

The tram had unloaded them at the Haunted House, the theme hotel east of the main amusement area. They were still underground, in a depot decorated in Early Caligari. Cobwebs festooned the corners of the station, and crawling things with glowing red eyes stalked their strands. The path before them led into a hallway with a glass ceiling.

Gwen looked up. "Wow." It was their own reflection; but as they proceeded, the flesh began to melt off their bones. When they reached the end of the corridor their reflections were a pair of skeletons shambling back to the mausoleum after a hard night's haunt.

"I don't know if I really want to open the door," she said. Ollie edged it open with his fingertips. It creaked hideously.

The lobby was dim, and decorated in blacks and dark reds. Even the couches and chairs were somewhat foreboding. The red seat cushion on one dark chair gave it the unmistakable appearance of an open mouth. The ceiling was low. Flickering candelabra supplied the light.

A lovely hostess in a flowing, wraith-white gown greeted them. Her red lipstick was just bright enough to bring out the paleness of her cheeks. She brought one delicate hand up to her mouth and coughed politely, then favored them with a dazzling smile.

"Good morning, my name is Lenore and I'd like to

welcome you to the Haunted House, one of the nine
Dream Park hotels. This is a theme hotel, so be ready.
Anything can happen."

The check-in terminal bore the guise of a great orchid
plant; and the lovely flowers bowed toward them in entirely too friendly a fashion. Ollie fished out his preregistra-
tion card and allowed a flower to take it. A quick display of
words and numbers ran up the orchid-festooned screen;
then the words "Adolph Norliss and S. O. room 7024."

Ollie looked at Lenore curiously. "S. O.? What's that?"

She laughed sweetly. "Significant Other. I assume that
you and the lady aren't married?"

"Oh, yeah. We're engaged . . ."

"Then if she's not your wife or your sister, she's a
Significant Other."

Gwen sniffed. "You could have just listed my name."

Ollie looked uncomfortable. "That's my fault, I guess. I
wasn't absolutely sure we would be coming together." He
retrieved his card.

Lenore led them off to a brace of elevators. Gwen
walked with her head turned to look up into Ollie's face.

"And if I hadn't come, who would you have invited?"

He walked on, ignoring her question for a few steps, and
she tugged at his sleeve. "Ollie? Who would you have
invited?"

He was trying, without terrific success, to hide a smile.
"Oh, I don't know. Anyone who could pay half the bill, I
guess."

"You *guess*?"

They had reached the elevator. Lenore motioned them
in. "Room seven-oh-two-four, on the seventh floor. And I
hope you have a pleasant stay here at Dream Park." She

gave the slightest of curtsies, and slowly turned transparent. Only her ringing laughter was still with them as the doors slid shut.

Ollie's jaw hung slack. He said, "Heyyy . . ."

Gwen shook her head. "That was really good. I'm impressed." Her face sobered, and she squared her chunky body up to him. "Ollie, would you really have come with somebody else if we hadn't made up?"

Ollie looked stonily ahead, trying to pretend he was still thinking about Lenore.

"Ollie? I wouldn't have come without you. Really."

He looked at her out of the corner of his eye. Gwen started to speak, but the opening hiss of the door silenced her. Ollie stepped out, then stopped and turned. "I thought you said you were coming with Furburger or whatever his name is."

"Feinburger."

"Feinburger. Well?"

"Oh, you nut, I wasn't really gonna go with Gordon. All he ever wants . . . all he wanted was to get into my pants anyway. I just didn't want you to think you had to feel sorry for me." She brushed a strand of her short yellow hair into place. "Honest."

"Well . . ." Ollie hesitated, then turned and started down the hall. She had almost to run to catch up, to hear him say softly, "I made the reservation for two 'cause I hoped you'd come with me, and I didn't put a name down because I was scared you wouldn't."

Gwen seemed about to speak; then she linked arms with him and matched him stride for stride down the hall. Finally, as if she couldn't stand it any longer, she swung him around and kissed him hard. With her hands locked behind his neck she looked dead into his eyes and said in

all seriousness, "Adolph, I love you. I really do. But sometimes I could just break your kneecaps."

He smiled at her, and it stayed warm. "Hey, I think this is
our room." He clicked his registration card into the slot in
the door and it creaked open. From within the room there
came a widening beam of dark purple light.

"Holy spit." Ollie pushed the door further open, then
stepped in, Gwen close behind. The room was an Edward
Gorey opium dream. Dark twisted plants grew meter-high
from rudely-stitched planters made of some kind of animal
skin. The canopy over the bed fluttered without a breeze.
Rain blew against the panes with a sound of crackling
bacon. Things moved out there in the dark, and even the
shadows on the wall seemed to flux with a strange rhythm.
When Gwen looked at the bed closely she could see that
the spread was slowly rising to normal level, as if someone
had gotten off it the instant before the door opened.

She said, "Wow. This is really . . ."

"Really what? Come on, don't keep me hanging."

"Hush, I'm being terrorized. This is too much! Ollie, I
adore this room." She stood on tiptoe and bussed him.
"I'm very glad to be your Significant Other. Let's get the
luggage out of the lift and get to bed. Tomorrow starts
early."

Chapter Four

THE MASTER DREAMERS

The ballroom of the Dream Park Sheraton was completely filled. Bleachers had been set up on three sides of the room, overlooking a conference table set near the fourth wall.

Of the eighteen hundred people in the room, only about fifty occupied the cordoned-off section near the conference table. These were the finalists: those pre-chosen to participate in the Game, and those whose credentials had passed the preliminary screening test.

There was little noise in the room, and no talking at all. All eyes were on the conference table.

Chester Henderson drummed his fingers on the table. His light blue shirt had dark rings under the armpits from nervous perspiration, and his eyes darted from the wall clock to the room's main entrance, to the clock, to the entrance . . .

He leaned toward the bald man with the roll-top sweater. "Listen, Myers, do I have to put up with this kind of crap? He's twenty minutes late!"

Myers was fortyish, with tobacco-stained teeth and a receding chin hidden behind a sparse beard. He smiled at Chester with the benignity of a suffering saint. "Mr. Henderson, this is Mr. Lopez's Game. While the I.F.G.S. may enter your complaints in the minutes of today's meeting, I'm afraid that there is no set procedure for censuring a tardy Game Master. If you would care to submit a resolution to that effect at the next meeting . . . ?"

Chester waved a weary hand in the air and sighed his surrender. "We wait. Metesky, can we at least go over the basic points now?"

The other person at the table was a woman with a stripe of white dyed down the middle of a glorious wealth of gray hair. Age had been kind to her, mellowing the angular facial lines of her youth into softer curves. She moved her leather briefcase a protective inch closer to her chest and calmly said, "I'm afraid not, Mr. Henderson. Mr. Lopez was very specific about that."

Henderson lidded his eyes and silently mouthed further specifics concerning Mr. Lopez, then inhaled deeply through his nose, holding the air down for a long count before exhaling. *Temper, temper,* he reminded himself. *In a war of nerves, your own arsenal can destroy you.*

There was a swelling murmur in the back of the room. Chester looked up, trying unsuccessfully to mask his eagerness. Two people were approaching, a short dark man wearing crisp white denims, and a slight Japanese girl several inches taller. Chester knew the woman. Chi-chi Lopez.

The murmur grew to spontaneous applause, and Lopez

turned and bowed grandly. After a moment's hesitation his wife Mitsuko curtsied. Chester had to smile. He had expected that forcing Lopez out of the woodwork would shake the great Game Master. The little man might have been born in front of an audience.

He strode directly to Henderson and extended his hand, a cool and businesslike smile on his face. "I hope my lateness hasn't inconvenienced you."

Chester took the hand and the gambit with the same firm grip. "Certainly not. I'm glad you felt free to take all the time you need to get your Game together."

Lopez nodded curtly, and led his wife to their seats at the other end of the table. There was a barely audible hum, and a "soft" translucent hologram blossomed in the air over the table, greatly magnifying the faces of the five principles.

Ms. Metesky folded her fingers primly and cleared her throat before speaking. "As the representative of Dream Park's Special Projects division, I would like to welcome Mr. Richard Lopez and Mr. Chester Henderson to our facilities. This is a momentous occasion, as these two greats of the fantasy gaming world have never before met face to face. Mrs. Lopez is known to us all, of course—" Mitsuko leaned over in her seat and gave a little wave to Chester, who returned it with warmth. "But many of you may not know Mr. Arlan Myers, representative of the International Fantasy Gaming Society." The light reflected from the top of Myers' head as he nodded.

"I believe we are ready to proceed. Mr. Myers?"

Myers stood and wiped the corner of his eye with his knuckle. "Good evening. I call this meeting of the International Fantasy Gaming Society to order at eleven twenty-five A.M., Friday March sixth, twenty fifty-one A.D. Tomor-

row morning at eight A.M., Dream Park's Gaming Area A
will open for the largest and most elaborate Game in the
history of the Park. Basic rules will be as follows:

"One. Duration of the Game will be four and a half
days, from the morning of the seventh to one P.M. on the
eleventh.

"Two. Number of participants, fifteen, with substitutions for killed personnel allowed until the beginning of the
fourth day.

"Three. An adjusted Wessler-Grahm point system will
be used, with compensations for duration of assault, difficulty of logical problems, and abilities needed. Bonus
points will be awarded for bravery, and for dying well.

"Four. There will be a penalty of 50% of accumulated
points in case of death, reduced to 25% if the 'dead' player
re-enters the Game as a zombie.

"Five. Players may withdraw from the Game for any
reason at a loss of 25%, until evening of March ninth.
Players may not withdraw after this point without total loss
of points, except for medical emergencies.

"Six. The Game will be conducted for twelve hours out
of every twenty-four, which will allow for sleep time,
meals, and two half-hour rest breaks per day.

"Seven. Additional bonus points will be awarded based
on a secret ballot vote cast by all surviving and nonsurviv-
ing members of the expedition, each member rating all
members of the party.

"Eight. The Lore Master has final word on all prospective entrants to the Game, except for the single Game
space reserved for discretionary use by Dream Park.

"Nine. The Game Master and the Lore Master will share
any profits accruing from the Game on the basis of an
eighty-twenty split of net.

"Ten. The usual good luck symbol—" Myers tapped at his keyboard. Glowing curves formed in the hologram overhead, shaping a crescent moon. Myers, smiling as if it hurt, waited for a ripple of laughter to die. "—will indicate the presence of restroom facilities. Look for it in patterns of trees, rock formations, whatever.

"Eleven. As usual, a minimum of one novice must be included in the expedition." Myers coughed politely and rubbed his eyes again. "Ms. Metesky?"

Metesky stood, shaking her head so that her gray mane billowed around her. "The following additions and qualifications have been approved by Dream Park. If they are suitable to Mr. Henderson, there are no further barriers to the opening of Gaming Area A tomorrow morning. Mr. Lopez?"

Richard Lopez stood, thanking Ms. Metesky as she handed him the leather briefcase. He opened it. "In this case," he said, his Puerto Rican accent almost unnoticeable, "I have the complete outline for the Game that begins tomorrow. There are only a few points that remain to be discussed." He raised a sheet of paper close to his face and read.

"One. The Lore Master is to receive 25% of all non-bonus or penalty points awarded during the Game.

"Two. The Game involves firearms. These will become available during the course of the Game." The murmurs of surprise from the audience included a few groans. Fire-arms were unusual. Warriors tended to prefer hand-to-hand weapons.

"Three. All Gamers will wear neck tabs." Lopez held up a short, flesh-colored plastic band bearing a silver-dollar-sized disk. "The disk is standard make; it bears a micro-phone and receiver and a 100 volt/.3 amperage microwave receptor. As usual, a shock will indicate wounding or death.

"Four. All categories of players will be admitted, except where such conflict with the rules as already stated." Lopez sat down.

Henderson looked at him suspiciously. "Is that all?"

Lopez nodded quietly. Chester said, "I'm not sure I understand."

"Mr. Henderson, after the last Game we were involved in, you claimed that the rules had been stacked against you, and that that was the determining factor in your defeat. I want you claiming no such handicap this time."

Lopez's smile was as innocent as a piranha's. Chester nodded; he understood. A loss in a Game with rules as soft as this would devastate his reputation. He asked, "Why are you making the Survivors' Bonus a lump sum instead of the standard allocation?"

"Merely to make things more interesting. Of course, if you think that it would make it impossible for you to engender a spirit of cooperation in your expedition . . ."

"Don't let it worry you, Lopez. My team will pull together just fine, thank you."

"Excellent. Do you have any further questions?"

"Just one. Am I correct in assuming that tropical gear will be needed?"

Richard lowered his gaze to his fingernails and considered. "I don't believe that it would be giving too much away to say that. Any needed modifications of costuming will be provided by Dream Park." He pursed his mouth meditatively. "Is there anything else you will need?"

"I do hope not." Chester stood. "Let's call it a Game and let me get down to the business of choosing my team."

Chester looked at the dossier in front of him, then up into the eager face of a strawhaired youngster of seventeen. "Says here that you play as an Engineer. We can use one, and I think you can fit the bill." He glanced again at the papers and seemed pleased. "What do you think, S. J.?"

S. J. Waters exploded in laughter. "What do I think? Wow, I think that's *terrific*! You won't regret this, I promise!" He bounced off happily, and Chester watched in amusement.

Gina stopped trying to massage his neck. She leaned down to whisper in his ear. "First team? You're going to start *him*? Are you sure you want to do that, honey?"

"Quite sure," he said, trying to be irritated with her. He didn't say that a little cannon fodder never hurt. Stick a few of them in the opening lineup, and use them to spring traps. By the time you get into the "no substitutions" period, you have the territory pretty well figured out, with a minimum of valuable characters lost. "Next!"

The selection process had been going on for two hours now. Nine of the slots were pre-registered, including Gina, Ollie, Gwen, Acacia and her guest Tony. Three more slots were filled now, so he needed three more primaries and some alternates. So far he was pleased with the quality of applicant. A rough calculation gave him almost a century of fantasy gaming experience among the players he'd already selected.

"Next," he called again, and there was laughter in the line of applicants. A small strong fist banged on the table in front of him, and he jumped. The top of a head was showing above the edge. It rose until a pair of watery brown eyes was staring at him.

Chester cackled in delight. "Mary-Martha!" He jumped

out of the chair and ran around the table and hugged the dwarvish woman. She was an inch above four feet high, and almost as wide as she was tall. Little of her bulk seemed to be fat, and when she hugged him back the creak of ribs was audible.

"Chester! Lord knows I couldn't let you run off and get yourself into a mess without old Mary-em to pull your worthless carcass out of it."

"No explanations needed. How's your hip?" He had read of her injury in the I. F. G. S. Monthly Bulletin.

She slapped her hip with the flat of a callused hand. "Fine, jus' fine. An' I'm going back to Yosemite this year too. It's gonna take more than little Mount Excelsior to keep *me* down."

"I'm betting on you, Mary-Martha. Are you up for this jaunt?"

Her eyes narrowed to slits, and for a bare moment she wasn't a chunky, harmless woman at all, but a raging force of nature caught in the wrong era and the wrong body. "You can believe it, Chester."

"Good to have you aboard. I'd like you as a Primary." She nodded vigorous agreement, and waddled off. Absurdly, Chester sensed that that walk could only be balanced by a battleaxe carelessly toted on the right shoulder.

The next two wanted to compete as a team, which was unfortunate. Nobody had been able to prove anything, but the rumor mill had it that Felicia Maddox was a cheat. Very shrewd about it (she would have to be) but somehow she came out of Games with more than her fair share of points. However she did it, she would be found out eventually. Chester just didn't want to deal with that in one of *his* Games.

Problem. Her companion was the highest-ranking sorcerer who had yet applied. Could he perhaps manage to kill the woman off in the first couple of days . . . ?

Bowan the Black glared at him from behind massive brows. He had dense, curly blond hair and crystal blue eyes and the muscles of a distance runner. Chester tried to remember his real name, and couldn't. Gamers were required to give their real names to Dream Park Security, but were under no obligation to give it to *him*.

"Thief and Sorcerer. Both high level. And you work together well as a team."

Bowan's words were heavy with exotic mystery. "We are no mere team. We are one. Together we represent a force greater than any challenge imaginable." He folded his arms and lowered his eyelids like a drowsy hawk.

Felicia slid a step forward and leaned over the table with only the barest flicker of acknowledgement for Gina's presence. "I've got what you need for this Game, Chester. I've got an eighty-two percent agility rating on level six."

"Wessler-Grahm?" Chester glanced down at her folder. It was there. *Damn,* but she could come in useful. He studied her face: short brown hair and fleshy lips, blunt nose, ears that stuck out from her head like flowers on a barrel cactus. Could he keep an eye on her?

Chester closed his eyes and relaxed into the sensation of Gina's fingers in his neck. Ah, well, as long as he could kill Felicia off if the occasion demanded. "Okay. You're both in the Game, starting. See you tomorrow morning.

"Three more Alternate positions are available," he called. A groan went up from the twenty-five people left in the room. These were low-ranked players, locals who hoped to squeeze into the Game more by luck than experience. A Lore Master was obliged to take one totally new player, but aside from that he picked only the strongest. Half the remaining supplicants left the room, and many of those still in line were grumbling, but one tall black woman was smiling. She had read up on Chester Henderson. He had a habit of losing dippy players in the first day or two of a Game.

She could wait. Alternate was fine. This was the Game where the I. F. G. S. would sit up and take notice of Holly Frost.

The Ballroom of the Dream Park Sheraton was empty but for a forelorn maintenance 'bot sucking up dust and trash, and a pair of tired human beings at the big conference table.

Chester Henderson looked at the stack of seventeen dossiers sitting in front of him. It had taken hours of culling the pre-selected finalists to find these people. They would be an odd crew, but any expedition that included Mary-Martha and Ollie Norliss would be both exciting and profitable.

Gina sat at the table next to him, her lovely face drawn with fatigue. He reached up and took her hand, squeezed it appreciatively. "You know, hon? After everyone else is gone, you're still around." He was surprised to hear the sincerity in his voice. It was so easy to discount Gina. Just a beautiful Fantasy-Game groupie with a stunning body and a love for playing dumb.

She rubbed his head with a hand that smelled faintly of musk oil and clean sweat. "Oh, Chester. I just like to feel needed, that's all."

He started to tell her that he didn't need anybody, that three other girls had proposed sharing his bedroll for a position in the Game, that one was in Gina's league as regards beauty. But there was something . . .

"Well," he said, feeling sleep-demons tug at his eyelids. *Tomorrow is a big day,* they whispered. *Surrender.* "You're needed, Gina. You pull your weight. You always do."

"Nice to know the team needs me," she said softly, and behind the heavy makeup her face was warm and open. "What about you, Chester?"

"What about me?" He tried to smile up at her, but the muscles in his face were fast asleep.

"Don't you need me too?"

Again Chester was tempted to say something other than what was in his mind, but he was too tired for anything but the truth. He closed his eyes and said, "Gina, you are very much appreciated. Let's go to bed."

Gina kissed him wetly. "You say the sweetest things."

"It's why you love me as you do." He tucked the stack of dossiers under his left arm and slipped his right about Gina's waist.

The echoes of their footsteps followed them as they walked past the empty bleachers. The lights in the ballroom dimmed to deep shadow. The only sound was the lonely humming of the maintenance 'bot.

Gwen stepped out of the shower and into a drying screen, feeling her skin tingle as the water evaporated from it. She wrapped herself in a towel and looked at the effect in the mirror. She pulled the towel tight around her waist and let one leg protrude from the slit. Not bad, she thought. The leg was white and firm and smooth; only the ankle and upper thigh betrayed her chunkiness. If she pulled the towel a little tighter . . .

She tossed her head to the side, watching the bounce of her short blond hair. *Good enough. Have at you, Oliver the Frank!* A dab of perfume behind each ear and another in the rounded cleft of her bust, and she was ready for her entrance.

Stepping from the bathroom to the bedroom was like stepping into another world. Phantasms floated through the air, and shadows shifted menacingly on the walls. Something tapped at the window, and when she looked, a large black bird was squatting on the sill, pecking at the glass. It cocked its head at her and uttered the inevitable three-syllable word.

Wrong-o, she thought at it.

Ollie lay on the bed, naked, watching the raven. When Gwen emerged from the bathroom he flipped a switch at the bedside and the bird faded away, along with the other illusions. His eyes gleamed. "You know, I really like the way you look fresh out of a shower."

She curtsied low, then lay down on the bed and, still in her towel, snuggled next to him.

"What do you think, Gwen?"

"I wanna."

Ollie rolled to face her, and tried again. "What do you think about tomorrow's Game?"

"I think it's going to be hard. Harder than anything I've been in, that we've been in. That's why I don't want to think about it right now."

"South Seas Treasure. What would that mean?"

"It means I'm going to roll over and go to sleep if you don't pay some attention to me, that's what it means!"

Ollie snapped out of his reverie. "I'm sorry, hon. I'm just worried about my standing, that's all."

"Oh. Well, I think I can handle that," she said, and reached down.

Ollie wiggled delightedly. "Okay, all right, you win,

monorail mind," and they kissed in a chorus of giggles. Some time later Ollie said, "You know something? I love the way you smell."

"I was hoping you'd notice."

Tony McWhirter poured himself a big glass of orange juice and added a splash of vodka. "Do you want anything, Cas?" he called over his shoulder.

Acacia's eyes flamed at him, and she coyly raised the bedsheet up to her chin. "*Lo que yo quiero no veine de la botella, hombre,*" she said.

He sipped from his drink as he crossed the room to the side of the bed. "That drink's too complicated for our limited bar facilities. What's it mean?"

"Why don't you put that drink down and find out?"

"No sooner said . . ." He lifted the glass and chug-a-lugged. His robe hit the floor with a rustle, his glass hit the dresser with a clink, and he landed on Acacia with a grin. "And what is your pleasure tonight, madam?"

"Well, I was thinking . . ."

"A pleasant change of pace, to be sure."

"Hush." She kissed him. "You know, you and I aren't going to be quite this secluded again for four days. Oh, we can snuggle in the sleeping bag, but . . ."

"You think maybe we should put a little something in the bank?"

She nodded. "For a rainy day."

"For a rainy day," he agreed. Rain and hurricane winds were attacking the windows, and phantom skeletons were passing through the room. The human occupants ignored them.

Chapter Five

THE NAMING OF NAMES

Midnight. Alex Griffin had stolen three hours of blissful unconsciousness before showering and tubing back to Dream Park. It wasn't quite enough. One of the quirks of an otherwise astoundingly healthy metabolism: he couldn't stay alert on less than eight hours sleep a night.

He'd sleep an extra hour tomorrow morning. Nobody would complain. Tonight was business.

Skip was dozing, chin on fist, elbow on table. Griffin pushed him slightly off balance and smiled as O'Brien jerked alert. "They're coming, Skip."

Skip said, "Right," in a voice that went from drowsy to alert in mid-syllable. His fingers smoothed imaginary wrinkles from his shirt. He was smiling brightly when the foursome rounded the corner.

Lopez and his wife Mitsuko were both radiant as children on Christmas morning. They carried totebags over their shoulders, and behind them tottered the security guard, Albert Rice, hauling three more cases. Ms. Metesky brought up the rear, clucking with quiet disapproval.

"I didn't know they were bringing everything over right now, Alex," Metesky said petulantly. "They wouldn't even wait for a cargo 'bot."

"S'okay, Chief," Rice gasped, setting the cases on the floor. "I was there. No hassle."

"Good man. We'll take this stuff now." Alex hefted one of the cases. It was heavy. Alex wondered what was in them. They must have been checked out at the front gate of the R&D complex, but still . . .

When he looked up, Rice was still there, with a funny kind of half-smile on his face. Did he want something? Oh, yes, the break-in. Alex said, "I don't remember seeing your report on the damage."

O'Brien asked, "Anything valuable broken?"

"Well," Rice said carefully, "I'm not sure it was vandalism. I think it was attempted theft. I don't keep anything valuable in plain sight, just some personal effects. Even there," Rice's eyes met Alex's and held steady, "he didn't get anything valuable. There were a few things he could have used, but he just skipped right past them. Then I guess he smashed a few things to prove he was irritated." He laughed a strained laugh. "Well, let me get back to my post. I'll see you later, Chief."

Alex watched Rice thoughtfully as he walked away. Funny vibes there . . . Metesky broke his train of thought with a harrumph. Alex turned to Lopez. "What have you got in those cases? Lead?"

Mitsuko hugged Richard's arm tight, and they giggled like kids. "Mostly notes and resource material. Last minute

entries for the computer. Secret stuff. It's all been checked
out, Mr. Griffin."

"Alex, please. Well . . . have you met Mr. O'Brien?
He's one of our top child psychologists."

"Then I can understand why he's here," Mitsuko
smiled. "My husband is the oldest child present."

Skip shook Richard's hand firmly. "Most optometrists
wear glasses, right? We'll have to compete for the title of
'oldest child'."

"No, thank you. I try to confine my competitive instincts
to the Games." Richard shifted his duffle bag on his shoulder, itchy with eagerness.

"Let's have mercy on these people and get them into
Game Central," O'Brien said. Alex nodded and led the
way.

The hallways of the Research and Development complex were nearly deserted. The entire building sat in the
northwest corner of Dream Park, in section VI. It bordered
Gaming Area A, looking out on 740 acres of magic. Game
Central covered an entire floor of the five story building,
and used close to 30% of Dream Park's total resources,
whether measured in technicians, energy, or dollars.

Alex summoned an elevator, and the five of them went
up to the second floor. Richard was nearly vibrating with
enthusiasm. Mitsuko whispered something in his ear and
he grinned wider, but quieted down. The elevator doors
opened.

Two technicians in green smocks met them at the doors.
One was stocky, with thin, quick fingers and lively eyes.
"I'm Larry Chicon," he told them. "This is Dwight Welles,
the other crazy you'll be dealing with."

Welles's round, unlined face belied his snowy hair. He

had the firm grip of a much younger man. "Really pleased
to meet you again, Mr. Lopez. I saw you for a few minutes
last year. I want to congratulate you on the Game you've
designed this year. May I ask how long it took you to put it
together?"

"Two and a half years, if you count all of the preparatory
research. If you mean just the actual programming, about
a year."

Welles nodded, awed. "Well. As you already know, one
of us will be available to you twenty-four hours a day in
case of any emergency. This way, people, no need to keep
you waiting."

Alex hung back, watching Mitsuko and Richard interact.
There was a lot of love there, and a relationship based on a
shared, extended childhood. Children, but genius children. That was a curious thing. They made so little of the
incredibly complex task of designing a program for Gaming Area A. The logistics of it would have strained any
human mind. Yet it was the Game itself that held their
interest, not the myriad paths they traveled to reach it. The
programming was a shadow-reality; the Game was reality
itself.

Welles slid his ID card into the slot in a heavy steel door.
It opened with a sigh.

Mitsuko's eyes turned buttery, and she stepped inside.
"It's been so long . . ." she said to herself, hands touching panels.

The control room of Gaming Central was a techno-
phile's dream. It was about fifteen by fifteen meters, and
little of it was empty floor space. There was one great
central control board facing two big dish-chairs with ad-
justable pneumatic cushions. Seven flatscreen viewers
surrounded the room, but mounted directly above the

main controls were two hologram projectors. The controls were gleaming steel, plastic and chrome; they all but begged to be stroked. If there was a single speck of dust in the room, it was nowhere in sight.

"Your cots are over here," Chicon said, pulling one of the inflatable mattresses out of its niche in the wall. "Coffee and food dispensers are in the usual place, but the lavatory is built into the control room now. You won't have to leave even to get a shower."

Lopez nodded without speaking, running his hands over the controls with a lover's touch. He and Mitsuko exchanged looks, and she blushed prettily.

Alex shunted the luggage over into a corner. He was fighting a contact high from the Lopezes. This room was infectious. It had obviously been built for more than sheer utility, or even comfort. For some, *this* would be the Game's real lure. One day the faithful Game player would graduate to the Control Room, to create his own fantasy worlds instead of merely acting out someone else's . . . to be a prime mover instead of just a participant.

For just an instant Alex could see into the Lopezes' relationship, could see the world they shared with each other and with nobody else. He could feel that their love for each other was filtered and colored by their fantasies, by their ability to make dreams come real. A dream born of their minds would be shared with a select group of Dream Park technicians, then with a team of fantasy Gamers. If all went well, when all the bugs were out of the programming, then it could be shared with the world.

As if guided by one mind, Richard and Mitsuko turned to them, hand in hand. "This is fine. We need to be left alone now, if you don't mind. Richard and I have a lot of work to do before morning."

"Of course. If there's anything you need, just give us a call." Welles shook hands with both of them again, and the Dream Park personnel departed.

O'Brien chuckled as they walked back to the elevators. "They're classic. I bet there's a level of nonverbal communication between them that borders on telepathy. Did you notice how frequently they touched each other?" Alex had noticed. "I'd call that a continuing reassurance for each that the other exists. They live *very* deep in their heads. I noticed something else, too."

"What was that?"

"They only spoke to each other once."

"What the hell do you mean? They were all over each other."

"Physically, they're in constant communication. Intellectually, I bet they mesh even better. But apparently very little of their interplay is on the verbal level."

Alex chewed on that while they waited for the elevators. Finally, uneasily, he said, "Well, don't just stand there. What does it mean?"

Skip smiled maliciously. "Damned if I know. I'd heard about them and wanted to see for myself."

"You mean you're just going to raise the question and leave it dangling? How am I supposed to sleep tonight? What kind of man are you, anyway?"

"The kind who's going to buy you a drink, if we can find a bar open around here."

Alex held the elevator for him. "Oh. *That* kind of man. My father told me to stay away from your type—" and the door shut behind them.

The morning outside these walls was still black. In the waiting area it was all artificial lighting. *Take it as an omen,* Tony told himself. *Reality is artificial from this point on.* He

squinted at the Character Identification form in his hand.
Acacia wrote part of a line on her own form, then turned
to him. "Panthesilea was real. She was one of the Amazon
queens killed in the Trojan War by Achilles. She was
strong and beautiful and they sang songs to her memory
for years."

Tony snuck a peek at Ollie's sheet, and laughed. "Oliver
the Frank? Are you kidding, or what?"

Ollie looked up sheepishly. "When I first started Gaming I was afraid I'd forget my character's name. So I used
my nickname. Anyway, Oliver's a legitimate hero; he
fought under Charlemagne, with Roland."

Tony hadn't meant to put Ollie on the defensive. He
started to say so, but the intercom interrupted him. "Attention all Game participants. Costuming will proceed for
another forty minutes only. Thank you."

There was a general buzz in the waiting area beneath
Game Central, and four people scurried off to the enclosed costuming booths for last minute touch-ups.

The fifteen players were an odd lot. Although all had
stowed cotton shirts and pants in their tote bags, each now
wore clothing peculiar to the characters they chose to play
on the expedition. Two things they had in common: the
eagerness, thick enough to cut, and the "neck tabs": silver
metal disks held in place by nearly invisible, soft plastic
bands.

Mary-Martha, "Mary-em," waddled around the oak-
paneled waiting area with the self-assurance of an iron
duck. The longer she waited, the fiercer burned her energy. She wore brown leather that hugged her chunky body
glue-tight, with joints cut in the leather at waist and knees
to provide leeway. She carried a short halberd with a flat
heavy blade, slung across her back.

Acacia recognized several of the other Gamers by reputation. The thin, wiry blond man would be Bowan the Black. He had discarded the scarlet robe that had been his first choice of raiment, and settled for hip boots and a black velvet shirt split in a hairy-chested "V." His companion was a half-pretty redhead, tall and thin, with a slight roll of flabby skin around her midsection. A sure sign of the diet faddist. What was it this month, dear? Ten grams of vinegar-soaked raisins before every meal?

Acacia clucked at herself, half-ashamed of her automatic negative reaction to the woman, who had registered in the "Thief" category as Dark Star.

Ollie and Gwen didn't worry her. Beneath their awe-shucks exteriors she sensed born Gamesters. Even Chester had seemed glad to see them. Gwen was still in the costuming room, as Ollie's frequent casual glances in that direction confirmed.

Gina Perkins had been dressed to kill every time Acacia had seen her. Now she wore hiking shorts and shirt, both covered with pockets, but they *didn't* cling to her like a coat of paint. There was makeup, but it was subdued. Her hair was intricately arranged, and she was still stunning. She was playing her wizard's staff while she waited.

That was stunning. Acacia had seen pictures in the Gaming magazines. It was five feet tall and an inch thick, jammed with instrumentation and the internal computer. Patterns of colored lights ran up and down its length, and monochromatic flames lashed from the tip, as Gina's fingertips ran over the contact-sensitive keyboard.

Tony watched as if mesmerized; then tore his eyes away and went back to work on his Character Identification sheet. He was feeling the crunch, she thought. The jokes were there, and the smug smiles and knowing touches, but there was something else too. Pre-Game jitters, a touch of fantasy flu?

His long jaw worked a nonexistent wad of gum, and his chocolate eyes seemed watery as he worked. The Character Identification sheet was an optional adjunct to the Game that Lopez had asked everyone to fill out. It listed not only imaginary physical and mental characteristics, but shaded over into geneology.

Acacia looked at her own sheet. How did Amazons have children? Captured male slaves, maybe? Parthenogenesis? She used a little of both. Panthesilea was a sterile female born parthenogenetically. Her mother (drown it! Finding a name for your character's mother on the spur of the moment was too much like work). Her mother Melissa was the offspring of Queen Herona (more fiction) and a captive Greek named, ah, Cyrius, a bastard son of Hercules . . .

She hoped that the other players were having as much trouble. All personal characteristics were measured in Wessler-Grahm points and were pre-registered with the IFGS and filed in the Gaming A computer. In this group, only Tony had no initial rating. The computer had run a random number series for him, and spit out double-digits which, in Wessler-Grahm terms, represented percentage chances of a positive result in combat or emergency. He had come out high in agility and intelligence, medium in strength, and low in recuperative powers.

Tony had looked at the read-out with a cautiously lidded excitement. "This bodes not well for my ambitions of warriorhood. What are my choices?"

Chicon and Dwight Welles were there to act as intermediaries and override controllers for the IFGS referees. Larry Chicon had enjoyed the chance to get involved. He had counted off Tony's options, one finger at a time. "Magic user, Warrior, Thief, Cleric, and Engineer. And Explorer. Each of them have their plusses and minuses, and we do allow some combination play, but in general it's best to find one category and get into it as deep as possible."

Tony found himself wishing that the oversized monitors were switched on, to give him a peek into what waited for them in Area A. "How would I do as a Magic User?"

Welles shook his head slowly. "Wouldn't recommend it, but I can't stop you if that's what you want."

"What's wrong with Magic User?"

"That's pretty complicated for a first outing. Besides, your Charisma score was only 36%. Trying conjuring up a demon with that and you'll be dinner."

"What's the difference between Magic User and Cleric?"

"Oh, Clerics usually perform preventive magic or curative magic. And they get their powers 'from on high,' which means they must be pure of spirit. Playing with the ladies while in the Game might mess that up—"

Larry shot Welles a nasty look. "That's turkey turds, Tony. What you do during the twelve hours a day that the Game is 'off' is totally up to you. Look: with good scores in Intelligence and Agility, why don't you try Thief?"

Tony opened his mouth as if to protest, then he laughed and nodded. "If it'll help me survive the Game, I'm for it." And Tony McWhirter became a first level Thief, Fortunato by name, thought to be a bastard son of either Fafhrd or the Grey Mouser, it being that kind of relationship. He would enter the gaming area in cotton tropical garb . . .

The warning buzzer sounded again, and Chester Henderson bounded into the room. He wore a green safari shirt and matching pants, with creases sharp enough to cut paper. His pipestem arms and legs were fairly flapping with enthusiasm. "Last minute check, everybody. We've only got a few minutes, and then we're off. Any questions?" He looked slowly around the room.

S. J. Waters, the youngest Gamester in the room, raised his hand halfway, as if afraid of being noticed. When Chester pointed at him he flinched, then said, "Chester? What is it exactly that we're after?"

"We haven't been told. I've got my suspicions, though. We'll find out for sure once we enter the Game, so don't worry. Getting there is half the fun. Any more questions? . . . Good. We're going to have a tremendous time, people, and everyone is going to take home more points than he can carry." He flashed his smile again, and began circling the room, checking on individual needs.

Gwen had returned to her seat next to Ollie, and he was busy enjoying her costume. Registered as a Cleric, Gwen wore a simple dress cut several inches too high for a real missionary, and leather-soled walking shoes with just enough heel to bring out the shape of her calf. The dress was beige, and almost too frilly to wear on a jaunt, but the way that it brought out the most attractive lines in her figure pardoned all impracticalities.

She stood up and twirled around for him, biting her lip. "Do you like it, Ollie?"

He grinned until the corners of his mouth threatened to meet in the back. He reached out for her, and she backed away coyly. "Do you like it?"

"South Seas Treasure or not, I already know I'm a winner."

Gwen blushed. "You know what I like best about Gaming?" Ollie shook his head. "You always say the sweetest things when you think you're someone else."

Ollie looked her dead in the eye. "Maybe that's because *you're* someone else?"

"Hah! You know perfectly well—"

Acacia stooped over them. "You guys ready? Everything in order?" Her Character Identification sheet was doubled in her hand. "We'll be starting in a few seconds. What's that, Ollie, Tropical Chocolate?"

"Frankish Oliver to you, Panthesilea, and yes. The stuff tastes like cocoa butter, but it doesn't melt. We'll find food along the way, but I like to be prepared."

The final warning sounded, and the Gamers began shouldering knapsacks and gear. There was an impatient buzz in the air, and all eyes turned to Chester, who stood by Gina in the center of the room. His voice was nearly cracking with excitement. "May I have everybody's attention, please. Will the fourteen Primaries please line up by the elevators. The doors will be opening automatically. It is now 7:52, eight minutes until the Game begins. Hustle, people, come on . . ."

He was wasting his breath. Long before he finished, fourteen faces were clustered below the digital floor monitor as it displayed the approach of the elevator cars. When the doors slid open there was a general whoop of delight, and the fourteen Primaries crammed in. Chester turned to look around the waiting room. No one had left anything behind; the room was clean and empty. Within hours the first Alternates would appear. Within minutes the progress of the Game would be broadcast to monitors in selected areas of Dream Park.

But he and Richard Lopez had been at war for one solid year. Chester stepped back and the elevator doors closed.

Chapter Six

FLIGHT OF FANCY

Somehow Acacia had expected the elevator to carry them down, into the bowels of the R & D building, to long lost caverns where blind gnomes would lead them, hand in gnarled hand, to the beginning of the Great Adventure. Instead it went up. A McDonnell-Boeing Phoenix helicopter was waiting on the roof, its engines humming quietly as the vast horizontal blades turned in lazy circles.

"What the hell . . . ?" Tony whispered. She turned to caution him, but saw the grin of incredulous delight and said nothing. "You know, I've always wanted to ride in one of these."

"Let's just take it one fantasy at a time," she murmured. Over one edge of the roof she could see the shapes and colors of Dream Park, its towers and mazelike walls. To the other side . . . nothing. Area A was hidden in featureless haze, a hologram projection of primal chaos.

The cargo doors of the Phoenix were open, waiting. A

73

dark brown face suddenly popped out of the darkness, immediately split in a grin. "Greetings!" the man yelled cheerily. "Please, come aboard!" Chester looked at him suspiciously for a moment, then nodded and stalked aboard lugging his totebag.

Acacia was fifth aboard, just behind a huge man named Eames who walked with a self-conscious swagger. *Warrior*, she snickered, then reflected that his freckled boyishness might have interested her, if Tony weren't along to keep the chill off. *One fantasy at a time*, she reminded herself. *Anything can happen* . . .

The interior of the Phoenix copter was comfortable but not plush, with twenty seats and room for their gear in both overhead racks and a hamper in the rear. The pilot of the 'copter waved back at them as they were seated. "Make yourselves comfortable, folks. I'm Captain Stimac, and you just let me know if you have any problems." The dark man who had greeted them at the door was energetically bouncing up and down the aisle, helping people with their luggage and generally having a great time. Tony filled the seat next to Acacia, and she took his hand affectionately. He asked, "What's next?"

She shook her head. She didn't want to talk; she wanted to *sense*.

The cargo doors creaked shut. The rotors of the Phoenix accelerated, blurred and disappeared; but, characteristic of the model, the engines only made a hoarse and urgent humming sound. Developed for nocturnal combat duty, the Phoenix was as silent as a motor-driven craft could be.

The ground dropped away. "Yah *hoo!*" screamed Mary-em's buzzsaw voice. "Children, we are *off!*" The

Gamesters cheered as the Phoenix tilted and began to eat distance.

When the "fasten seat belts" pictogram clicked off, their one-man welcoming committee stood and bowed shallowly to them. "I would like to introduce myself to all of you. I am Kasan Maibang, and I will be your guide and liaison with the people of my island."

Chester stood now, his facial lines gone angular with eagerness. "Your island. Then you know where we're going? And what our quest is?"

Kasan's smile was innocent. "Of course, Mr. Henderson. You do not think that your government would send you on such a perilous adventure without benefit of a guide?"

"Our government . . ." Chester absorbed that. "No, of course not. I assume you have our briefing sheets?"

"I am your briefing sheets."

The Lore Master's shoulders relaxed and he nodded. Behind him, Tony whispered, "Why is that good?"

Acacia told him. "The briefing material has to be true, in context. Lopez isn't allowed to lie to us about the basic assumptions behind the Game. Now Chester knows he can trust Kasan, up to a point. Kasan can't lie."

"Uh huh." Tony examined the "native" suspiciously. "Is he a hologram?"

"No. I saw him carrying luggage. Later he might be a hologram. He's a Gaming actor. Probably playing for straight points: he gets his whether we win or lose, as long as he doesn't blow his lines."

The Lore Master, more relaxed now, was perched on the arm rest between two empty seats. He asked, "Where are we headed?"

"To the Melanesian islands, New Guinea to be specific."

Chester almost laughed. "You're from New Guinea?"

Maibang was apologetic. "The Episcopalian mission sent me to UCLA."

"Where you were recruited, no doubt."

"Oh, absolutely. You must appreciate the problem. Ever since the Road to the Cargo was opened in 1945—"

Chester's sigh of comprehension was audible all over the copter. "Cargo Cult. Right. Please go on."

Maibang was clearly pleased that Chester had made the jump. "Yes. Well, ever since then, the Melanesian peoples, those who have learned the secret, have been stealing back the possessions that the Europeans—"

"That's us?"

Their guide shrugged. "There are us, and there are Europeans. Some Europeans are black or brown or yellow, though most are white—"

"Okay."

"My people, the Daribi, were among the peoples blessed with the true secret of the cargo. We prospered. God-Manup sends many wonderful things to his faithful children. Canned meat, electric lights, jeeps, refrigerators, and, of course, weapons with which to drive out the Europeans."

"Of course," said Chester.

"Then, nine years ago—" Bare flicker of an eyelash. "In 1946—" Chester absorbed that datum, and nodded. "—my people the Daribi began to divert shipments of cargo intended for Europe and the Americas. Naturally your people fought back with your own rituals, but our sorcerers were mighty. Then you tried the force of your military, and again we prevailed. Late in 1947 my people made their greatest effort, and stole from your people a very great cargo indeed."

"Which was?"

Maibang wagged his head sorrowfully. "We sensed its existence and we used our powers to take it, but we never saw it. The extreme effort strained our sorcerers. At the last moment, as the cargo was coming to us, a rival tribe who coveted our power used their own magic to divert its path. We were too weak to resist. Their victory over us gained them great *mana*, great power. They became the dominant force on our island. Your government knows the rest: how their power and their greed leave no ship or airplane safe for a thousand kilometers around. It has gone on for seven years, with the powers of . . . our enemies growing ever greater."

Chester sighed. "Do I gather you can't tell us the name of this enemy tribe?"

"You catch on quick, bwana. Nope, to use the name of so powerful a tribe without their prior permission is much bad *mana*. So my people made contact with yours to strike a bargain. We will help a small group of Europeans into the lands held by the Enemy. You steal back what you can, and get it out. The Enemy will lose *mana*, and we will regain our power. We will then sign a treaty with you binding us to take only cargo intended for us by God-Manup, and none of yours, as long as you hold to the same agreement."

"And why should we trust you to keep your promises?" Chester gave Maibang his most beneficent smile.

"Because we are not Europeans," Maibang answered humbly.

"Jee-zuss," S. J. Waters exclaimed. "We are a long way out."

Chester slid over to the nearest window. "We're over the ocean . . . I don't see any points of reference yet . . ."

"Islands over here, Chester," S. J. called from the other side of the 'copter. He shaded his eyes against the glare. "I think we've got Hawaii here."

"Then we're halfway," Chester said to himself.

Acacia said, "That's Oahu, I think."

"Don't know, hon. I've never flown this—" Tony caught himself. "Damn. I mean I've never been to Hawaii. It's just too easy to forget that this isn't real."

"So stop trying."

Tony grinned uneasily. "Last gasps of sanity, I guess."

"Then breathe deep, lover. The air gets pretty thin from here on out."

The Phoenix began to judder, and Captain Stimac's voice sounded over the intercom. "We're about to hit rough weather, people. Please notice that the seat belt warning is in effect, and comply with it. Thank you."

Chester waved a finger at Maibang. "Don't you die on me now. I've got to get a lot more out of you."

Maibang grinned and promised nothing.

There were dark clouds ahead now, and already the sky was dimming. The Phoenix dipped as if hitting an air pocket, and a unanimous "Ooh!" was followed by a whoop from Mary-em.

The clouds came fast. They were ugly, boiling with light and dark grays; ominous flashes of fire played within. The Phoenix was swallowed into the storm, and turbulence shook them like a giant child playing with a toy.

Lightning glared eye-splitting bright to starboard. The craft dropped and shook with the force of the thunderclap.

Acacia screamed delightedly and threw her arms around Tony. He grabbed back, yelling at the top of his voice. Rain pelted the sides of the Phoenix, and the engines whined in protest as it tried to climb and stabilize. Again and again their eyes and ears were assaulted by monstrous bursts of light and sound, until it seemed that the Phoenix was coming apart in midair. The whisper of the engines changed to an ominous growling vibration. Between lightning flashes, nothing could be seen outside, and as the lights failed in the plane Tony found himself kissing Acacia with something akin to genuine terror in his heart.

At last the storm lightened, and some sunlight peeped through the cloud. There was a stir at the back of the cabin, Gamers pushing and shoving at the windows. The pair looked out to see what the trouble was.

Tony looked out on a broad, rounded wing studded with thousands of rivets. The motor housing was huge, and the air before it was blurred. Its voice was a shattering roar, like the devil let loose on Earth.

"Wings. I will be go to hell. We've got wings and rivets and propellers!"

Acacia squeezed past him and pressed her face to the glass. To the rear she could just see the tail stabilizers. As applause and whistles broke out, she shook her head admiringly.

"It's got to be a mid-nineteen-hundreds model of something or other," Tony said softly.

S. J. Waters had the answer. "Wowie! A DC-3, a Goonie Bird! Hey, these things were supposed to be half-magical anyway."

Clusters of passengers began to sing. Fragments of

verse celebrating the adventures of Kafoozalem and Eskimo Nell were heard above the roar of the engines. Ollie's
high voice rang out:

"Oh, the camel has a lot of fun,
His night begins when ours is done,
He always gets two humps for one,
As he revels in the joys of fornication!"

And half the Gamers bellowed a ragged chorus:

"Cats on the rooftops, cats on the tiles—"

The air had cleared. The plane dipped into a cloud deck
and out the bottom. Ollie sang, "The hippo's rump is big
and round—"

"Islands," the redheaded Dark Star said, and the song
died in mid-leer.

They were coming up on the sub-continent itself, and
Chester announced above the roar, "We seem to be
approaching New Guinea from the Bismarck Sea . . .
those might be the Finisterre Mountains, only about three
thousand meters, we can clear those . . .

The view below was an explosion of dense greens and
browns, vegetation crowding from the rich soil in rich
profusion. The Finisterre Mountains ruled the Huon
Peninsula, overlooking Vitiaz Strait, and in the crystal-
clear air they seemed close enough to reach out and touch.
The DC-3 skimmed over them and reoriented north. Soon
they were crossing swamps and marshy areas. Captain
Stimac's voice buzzed from the intercom.

"We will be reaching Chambri Lake in a few minutes.
It's the landmark for the landing strip which has been
cleared for us. In fact, I think I see . . ." There was a
pause, and the plane bucked in the air. This time the
bucking became a jarring side pull that bounced Acacia
against her seat belt. "Wait just a minute—that's not the

right lake, but something . . . uh! Move, godamit!"
Stimac began swearing in panic. The plane was sliding
down the sky; the motors screamed. Stimac shouted, "I
can't move the controls! They're moving themselves!"

Hands gripped seats and faces went white as the
swamps rose toward them, rotating now. There was light
down there, and water . . . a sheen of water directly
below the plane's nose, and two lines of lights glowing on
the water . . . and a tower.

"It's pulling us in," Chester said. He was squeezed up
against a window, and his mouth hung a little open. Not
frightened, but fascinated.

Kasan was in the aisle, waving his arms and chanting in
an unknown language, while two Gamers held him steady
with hands on his belt.

Tony almost forgot his own fear as he stared out. Closer
now . . . and the control tower was only wickerwork on
pontoons, and the lights were floating torches tethered by
ropes, forming lines too close together to make a real
runway. It was a mockery of an airport laid out on water.

The mock-airport veered sideways, and gee forces
pulled savagely at the passengers. The DC-3 pulled out of
its dive. The wing on the right side bent far enough to pop
two lines of rivets, then eased back into place; but fluid was
streaming from where the metal had crinkled. Stimac's
intercom voice screamed, "Got it! I think we're all right
now. Whatever it was, it's— Oh *shit*!" as the wing unrolled
a flapping flag of red-and-yellow flame.

"I've got to get us down," said the crackling intercom
voice. "Brace yourselves. This isn't going to be neat."
They were barely at treetop level, trailing flame and black
smoke. "I'll try for Chambri Lake. There are life rafts in the
rear of the plane . . ."

Tony could restrain himself no longer. "Just what the hell is happening?" He couldn't look away from the line of trees whipping past the plane at paint-scraping levels.

Acacia looked down. "The real lake should be somewhere close up ahead. If we can make that—" her eyes were fixed on the window, and as an expanse of dark green came into view, she sighed in relief. "There it is!"

The plane plunged, shaking like a dog drying itself, and there were fourteen throat-rendering screams and one "Yah-hoo!" In the instant before the plane struck water Acacia was aware of Tony's fingers dipping clawlike into her arm.

The impact threw them forward. Water surged over the plane, bubbles streamed past the windows. At least the fire was out. The plane bobbed to the surface, wobbled, righted itself. Water lapped at the windows.

Chester was the first to regain his balance. "All right, everybody, let's get out the lifeboats and get the gear together. We've got work to do."

Seatbelts clicked like castinets. Duffle bags were pulled out of their overhead racks with almost feverish eagerness. Tony looked toward the nose of the plane, where Captain Stimac lolled limply in his chair.

"Hey, is he . . . ?" Unnoticed by the rest of the Gamers, Tony advanced to the front of the craft, shouldering his backpack unsteadily. "Captain Stimac?" There was no reply. He took another cautious step, feeling the plane yaw slightly beneath him. "Captain?" Stimac's head rolled back loosely from a neck that seemed broken, and a trickle of blood ran from his mouth. Eyes stared sightless from a slack and pasty face. Tony felt his stomach convulse, and clutched at himself, suddenly afraid. "Oh my God."

Then Stimac winked at him. Straightening in mid-retch, Tony glared at him and stalked out of the cabin. He grabbed Acacia by the shoulder and spun her around. "That's the last time, understand? Absolutely the last."

Acting calmly and with near-military precision, Chester had four boats out on the water and was directing the inflating of the fifth from a cylinder of compressed gas. Tony and Acacia were in a raft with S. J. Waters, and Tony was looking back at the DC-3 with a half-smile. "Boy that looks real. You really have to strain to catch even the outline of the Phoenix under the—"

Acacia laid a hand gently on his arm. "Tony," she said with genuine affection, "Stop fighting. It is real. Everything here is real. Just relax and let it happen, okay? Please?"

Her dark eyes sparkled with unmocking laughter, and Tony nodded. He gripped her hand hard. "I'm sorry, babe. I guess maybe I'm—" He paused and looked around at the rafts bobbing in the lake. "I don't know what's going to happen or what it will do to my head. It throws me."

The rafts, five strong now, were bobbing next to the settling DC-3 in the middle of a huge lake. It was impossible to tell the actual size of the body of water; perspective was no barrier to Dream Park technology. Chester and Maibang were last into the water, in a raft loaded with bundles of supplies.

"Which way, Kasan?"

The guide looked around in feigned confusion. "This is difficult to say, but I'm not sure."

"What do you mean?"

"I mean that this lake isn't what it should be—it's shaped wrong."

Chester's long face became thoughtful. "Wrong shape. How so?"

"Chambri Lake is rounder than this. See, two of the

shorelines are clearly visible, but the other two edges are lost to our sight."

Chester carefully got to his feet, standing precariously balanced as he looked. Just as carefully, he sat back down. "All right, it's not Chambri Lake. What is it?"

Kasan wagged his head sorrowfully. "Not sure. Very bad magic, I fear." He gazed contemplatively across the lake. "I think we should head to the north shore. It's closest."

There was a feather touch of suspicion on Chester's face as he nodded assent. "Okay, people, let's move out for the north bank. We can regroup there."

Two out of the three people on each raft hefted paddles and began guiding their boats ashore. Tony and Acacia provided propulsion for their boat while their passenger, S. J., merrily called, "Stroke! Stroke!"

It became a race, with Tony and Acacia in second place, behind Eames and his two boatmates, one a Magic User named Alan Leigh, the other the irrepressible Mary-em, who as second paddle did not so much stroke as wrestle the water into submission. Leigh, his pouchy cheeks somewhat incongruous on his spare frame, watched the water ahead of them intently, and when his hand shot into the air all five of the rafts backpaddled to a halt.

Acacia shaded her eyes and cautiously stood, testing her balance. "There's something there . . ." Tony started to ask, then saw it himself.

Just ahead of Eames's boat, the water was rippling unpleasantly. S. J. got to his feet, almost upsetting the boat. Acacia skewered him on a raised eyebrow, and he sat down. "Water snake," he muttered, watching the approaching ripples.

Chester, two rafts back, had seen it too. "Snake!" His

voice was surprisingly clear and loud. "Big one! Leigh, take first assault."

In the front raft, Leigh stood up. When the snake rose from the swirling water the magician was ready.

The snake was easily thirty feet long, its trunk thick and banded with muscle. Its head was broader than a horse's, long black tongue slipping in and out of its mouth with hypnotic rhythm. Its torso showed yellow and dull red against the blue-green of the lake, and as it hoisted fully eight feet of its length out of the water and glared at them, an uneasy cheer went up from the other Gamers.

Leigh spread his arms in supplication. "Gods above!" he screamed at the top of his voice, "hear my plea!" Almost immediately a green glow surrounded him, and he nodded acknowledgement. The snake glided closer. "Let's see now—"

"God's sake get on with it!" Mary-em snapped.

He glared at her. "No respect for artists. All right, then." He refocused his gaze on the snake, now only meters away. "Snake, you are a thing of water. I give you—fire!" He gestured magically, and nothing happened. He repeated, "Fire!" and the glow around his right hand melted from green to red. He made a hurling motion at the snake.

A fist-sized ball of fire sailed from his hand, bright even in artificial daylight, expanding as it pierced the air and impacted the snake's nose. The effect was remarkable. The viper recoiled with an echoing hiss and dove back into the water and disappeared.

Tony cheered. "Great! Heroes one, monster zero!"

Acacia gripped his arm. "Not so fast, Tony . . ." She was watching Chester.

The Lore Master lifted his arms. "Hear me, oh gods," he said, his voice deep and resonant. The green glow appeared around him. He looked down into the murky green water. "I invoke Clear Vision. Reveal to me my foe."

With a ripple of glitter, the surface of the lake became like a warped sheet of green glass, and beneath it writhed the outline of an enormous serpent. "Warriors! Be ready! It's coming back up."

Acacia said, "Oh *shit*," and dived for her gear. She hurriedly unrolled an oblong oilskin package and lovingly touched the twenty-four-inch blade of her shortsword before buckling the scabbard round her waist. She slipped the blade out again and experimentally slashed at the air, then checked the "ready" light in the hilt. She waited, crouched.

The lake surged and the snake was on them, hissing with the liquid sound of a wind whipping through a stand of rainswept trees. Its head coiled back, then snapped forward with blinding speed. Acacia cut furiously across the beast's mouth. It swerved around and tried to bite from the side, but the swordswoman pivoted neatly and met it again. This time the snake jerked back clear of the blade. It hovered just out of range, glaring at her with blood drooling from its upper lip. Slowly, eyes fixed on her steadily, it sank beneath the water.

"Good play, Panthesilea," Tony McWhirter said, his face just a shade pale.

S. J. piped up immediately. "Best damn holograms in the world. Most expensive, too. The sword sensor knows whether it intersects part of the projection, and signals the computer. The snake's a computer-animated projection, so—" He looked down at Acacia's sword tip waving an inch from his nose.

She said, "Listen, S. J., maybe you get your kicks from analyzing dreams, but *I* want to play, and I want Tony to have the chance to play with me, okay?"

S. J. grinned and said, "Snake's behind you." She whirled, sword ready, and he laughed.

The watersnake was menacing the raft that held Gwen and Ollie. They paddled madly. Their passenger, a Cleric named Garret, spread his arms and intoned loudly, "Hear me, oh gods!" His red false beard flapped mightily in the breeze. The familiar green halo surrounded him, and he yelled, "A ring of protection, Father!"

A band of soft white light circled the raft. The snake drew up short and nosed around them in bewildered frustration. In the time that it spent deciding how to attack, Bowan the Black had maneuvered his boat up behind it. "Fireball!" he cried. An arc of flame leapt from his palm to strike the monster just behind the head. It hissed in pain and spun around, diving for Bowan. Ollie's voice rang out across the water.

"Cut the ring!" he yelled, and the circle of light disappeared. Ollie stood stripped to the waist, gut sucked in heroically. His eyes burned fiercely. He clutched a sword in one hand and a dagger in the other. He yodeled his war-cry and struck.

The snake jerked away from the kiss of steel, and Ollie's second slash cut thin air. Ollie tried to make up the extra distance with a lunge. The raft shifted in the opposite direction, and Ollie went over the edge.

He came up sputtering and thrashing with his left hand for balance. The dagger was a hindrance; he stuffed it in his sheath and struck out towards the snake. Its body rose from the water and encircled him. Ollie screamed defiantly and laid about with the sword. The snake was covered in wounds now, and Bowan the Black was hurling tongues of fire with both hands.

The snake's upper body was awrithe with flame, and it uncoiled from Ollie and tried to dive. As it did, Ollie

torqued his body all the way round in the water, and
caught it dead center between the eyes. Mortally wounded, it rolled its eightball eyes piteously and expired, sinking
beneath the water with only a slick of blood to mark its
passing.

Without knowing how he got there, Tony found himself
on his feet and cheering like an idiot. With great clumsy
strokes Ollie swam back to the raft. Gwen helped him
aboard, kissing him soundly. Acacia nudged Tony. "Think
they'll celebrate tonight, or what?"

He was still open-mouthed, watching the slowly dis-
sipating bloodstain. "Just wow, Cas. I don't believe it."

"You'd better believe it when it happens to you, or
you'll be out of the Game while you're still trying to shut
your mouth." She brushed the back of her hand along his
jawline, closing it, and said, "Come on, lover. Let's get to
shore before Lopez hits us with something new."

"Oh, he wouldn't . . ." He paused, chewing his
words. "Right. Let's get off the lake."

Chapter Seven

THE ROAD OF THE CARGO

The DC-3 was disappearing beneath the waters as the last raft pulled ashore. Tony shouldered his knapsack and adjusted the nylon straps. "Rest in peace, Captain Stimac," he said. "Is that one for Lopez?"

Acacia shook her head. "The pilot was a freebie. He wasn't a member of our party. He was outside Chester's influence. Help me get my bedroll adjusted, will you? Then let's go talk to Chester."

The Lore Master was helping Gina get herself together. Besides a bedroll and back pack, the lovely redhead sported a wicked looking dagger and the wizard's staff, her major magical tool. Henderson himself carried only a bedroll and backpack, plus a small black box fastened to his belt on the left side.

He turned to Maibang. "You have a lot of those snakes around here?"

Maibang raised his palms in supplication. "Who knows what evil has been wrought here since my departure?" The guide wiped a drop of water from his broad nose and stared into the distance. "I believe that we head . . . yes, that way, north, toward the mountains."

"Are you sure?" Chester sounded a touch irritated.

"Almost absolutely. I understand that your people have mystical ways to reach out and seek such information for yourselves. Perhaps you would care to try?"

"Too much energy expenditure, too soon. The snake drained a lot of energy from two of my players . . ." Chester gazed toward the mountain peaks shimmering in the distance, and the dense forest growth between. The guide could plead ignorance, but he couldn't lie . . .

Chester raised his voice to be audible to the entire group. "We're heading north. Eames, you and Leigh up front with me. Mary-em and Acacia, take the rear guard. Don't spread too thin, people."

The fifteen Gamers and Maibang formed into a line, Eames leading as they chopped their way into the brush. The big man's arm rose and fell tirelessly as his sword served machete duty, filling the air with shredded green chaff. "We must follow these mountains," Maibang assured them. "There should be a trail up ahead just a little way, and then the going will be much easier."

Chester grunted a reply and kept watching the terrain carefully.

Tony hung back with Acacia in the rear of the column. She cut brush for the first few minutes, but as initial progress was slow she soon tired and slipped her sword back into its sheath. They found a trail and the going became easier. Maibang kept them heading toward the "mountains" . . . which, Acacia suspected, were slowly shifting position to keep them traveling in an expanding spiral.

She couldn't come close to naming all the varieties of plant and animal life. Birds of all kinds, their plumes ablaze with color; parrots with purple and bright orange feathers, birds of paradise with impossible combinations of gold and red and electric white swirling on their wings and tails. Acacia recognized coconuts and what looked like rubber trees, but beyond that the underbrush was a tangle of greens and dark purples and the yellow of dying shrubs; of vines and trees, leaves flat and shiny, invisible against the forest growth or exploding with flowers. Small snakes slept on branches or wriggled from underfoot. Creatures leapt through the branches just out of sight.

One parrot, gorgeous in its purple plumage, kept pace with her for what seemed a kilometer, always just out of reach. She watched it, watched it land for an instant on a branch to nuzzle beneath its wings for a fat mite, watched it cock its head at her curiously, and found herself wondering if it was real. It *looked* real; it sounded real, its untutored voice croaking tunelessly except for sharp whistles; and she wondered.

The air was hot and sticky and smelled oppressively green. They had tried holding hands, but contact with another human body only made the heat worse, and they gave it up. Sweat rolled from Tony's face in grimy drops, and under his cotton shirt dark damp spots were forming under his armpits and on his chest.

He pointed off to the side and asked, "Is that . . . ?"

A small clearing surrounded by one species of bush, outlining a crescent moon. "That's it. Shall I stop the others?"

"I'll only be a second." Tony stepped off the trail and into the clearing and faded out. Acacia kept moving. Presently he was behind her again, pushing his pace until he caught up.

"I feel as if we've been walking for hours," he said to her, panting sincerely. Some of the bounce was gone from his walk, and frustrated fatigue showed in his face. "Come on . . . where's another beastie? Anything's better than this."

Acacia moaned sympathetically. "Poor baby. Just try to remember that your discomfort, like everything else here, is only make-believe." She patted his cheek. "There, now. Don't you feel better now?"

"Yes, Mommy," he said absently, and quickened his step to catch up with Gwen and Ollie. Sheen of sweat or not, the blond Cleric hadn't released her hero's arm for an instant. Tony clapped Ollie on the shoulder. "Good going with the water snake, Ollie."

"Call me Oliver, would you, Tony?" His hand rested easily on the grip of his sword.

Tony tried to laugh, but suddenly there was nothing soft about Ollie, not his eyes nor his carriage, and certainly not the way his palm caressed his sword. Gwen had changed too. She was still *attached* to Ollie. But instead of his leaning on her, she seemed to be drawing strength from him. Tony sensed that he was out of his depth.

Gwen's laugh was of quiet challenge. "Oliver is a noble name, Tony. Oliver was one of Charlemagne's greatest warriors."

"All right . . . Oliver. I like the way you handled the water snake. It was a class act."

Tension eased. "I almost got killed out there," Oliver growled. "When I went off the side of the boat, I thought I was dead. I was just waiting for the jolt from my neck tab. If Lopez had really wanted me, he had me then. That thing could have crushed me before it took enough hit points to roll over and die."

If he believes in the Game Master, how can he believe

he's Oliver the Frank? Tony shrugged inside his mind. *Schizo. Well, maybe I'll have to be schizo too.* "Oliver, what is it exactly that Thieves do? It's easy to see what Warriors and Clerics and Magic Users do."

"Thieves steal, mostly." Gwen skipped a half-pace to keep her step even with Oliver's. "You skulk around, and you're practically invisible to your enemies. You're not much with weapons, except maybe a throwing knife. It's loads of fun. You'll get a chance to try your hand later today, probably. That's about all I can think of. Chester can fill you in on anything else. Don't worry, we won't let you get killed before you learn the rules. It won't get really rough for a bit yet."

"Yeah, well, I guess you haven't had a chance to bless anything yet, either."

"Not true. I blessed dear Oliver before he engaged in mortal combat with that overblown water worm."

"Behind every man, et cetera," said Oliver. His *personna* cracked for an instant, and he bounced on his toes and was Ollie again, smiling bright as sunrise, saying, "I am having so much *fun.* I really hope you can get into it, Tony."

McWhirter smiled and nodded. He dropped back to Acacia's side. "Happy as two fleas in a bottle of blood, they are."

"What do you want out of all this, Tony? What will make you happy?"

"Just a little of something that I can't get anywhere else, I guess."

She fluttered her eyelashes at him.

"Well, you, of course. But, you know. Breathless adventure, exotic sights, heaps of fabulous gems . . . all that."

"All that. But you do value my friendship, don't you?"

"Sure I do, Cas. Besides, I can't afford what you charge strangers." He hugged her with one arm as they moved down the trail, the shrubbery closing behind them like a healing wound. "I'm a city boy, Cas. What am I supposed to want? Six days from now I'm back at work copying blueprints eight hours a day. Hell, I . . . guess my expectations are a little unreasonable. I can't really expect an amusement park to undo in a week the damage a dull job does in fifty, but I do." He gently turned her face to him and spoke in all seriousness. "Help me, will you, Cas?"

She looked half puzzled, half pleased. "You know, *hombre*, every once in a while you're such a decent human being that I might as well have left my hip boots at home."

"How 'bout if I tickle your butt next time you're facing down a giant snake?"

There was a shout up ahead, and several of the Gamers had broken ranks, running forward to a clearing 100 meters up the trail. Acacia half-drew her sword; then she saw and relaxed. The first half of the journey was over.

In a few seconds they were out of the jungle and into a cultivated area, where knee-high and waist-high plants grew in neat rows. She could see men and women working in the fields, weeding and irrigating. "Please!" Kasan Maibang's voice rang out. "Stay on the path. The young tubers are very delicate." Acacia immediately wondered how far the cultivated area really went, and where the Dream Park magic took over.

Some of the land had been irrigated into marshiness, and men waded knee-deep in the mud planting and setting up stakes to indicate private plots in the community garden.

Acacia recognized sweet potatoes, yams and sugar

cane. In the distance banana trees and breadfruit grew, and the air was full of the scent of rich wet earth and growing things. Like Tony, she was a child of the city, but a granduncle in Mexico owned his own ranch, and she and her two brothers had spent glorious summers there helping with the cows and pigs. She knew something of wide spaces, and working in the open air, and remembered the smell of sweating bodies toiling in the afternoon sun.

The villagers were small people, most of them darker than Kasan and showing the physical impact of a primitive life style. Adults seemed to be made of leather and woven gut, faces etched but not scarred by endless labor in the fields, bodies scarred but not broken by the rigors of the hunt. Their attire, g-strings and animal-hide flaps, made her feel she was sweltering, and she toyed with the idea of adapting that style for the rest of the trip. Poor Tony would have a fit.

The Gamers were attracting attention from the field workers now, and many stopped their work to point and stare. Warriors carrying bamboo spears had emerged from the cluster of thatched buildings on the other side of the fields. The Gamers had gathered around Chester while he quizzed Maibang.

"You're sure that your chief knows we're coming? And wants us here?"

"I am sure of all that," Maibang answered gravely.

A nasty suspicion lit Chester's face. "The Daribi are cannibals, aren't they?"

Maibang looked wounded. "Upon special occasions, of course. You are not our enemies, you have come to help us. It would be ingracious in the extreme to do such a thing." He paused for a moment, thinking. "Just to be on the safe side, though, you might be careful of the phrasing if anyone invites you to dinner." He leaned close enough to whisper, jerking a thumb at Gina, "A few yams and a sliced banana or two would do wondrous things for your lovely friend there."

"Be careful about telling her that," Chester said absently. "She's been known to kiss on the first date, but . . ." He turned quiet as the first quartet of stocky spearmen drew near. Two were carrying bulky rifles. None of them left footprints in the dirt. The foremost of them raised his spear in greeting. They wore colorful necklaces of woven vine and leather, and ceremonial headdresses of short, brilliantly colored feathers. Chester kept his expression neutral as he raised a hand and waited. The field workers were gathered about them now. Small dark children, protuberant bellies bouncing with their scampering, hid behind the skirtlets of their bare-breasted mothers.

The lead warrior spoke, his words rapid and melodic. Kasan listened carefully, then turned to Chester. "His name is Kagoiano, and he has come to escort you to the Council of Men, at the request of our council chief Pigibidi, who extends greetings and hopes that you will join his company immediately."

"Pigibidi?" Chester asked in amusement.

"There is great power in his name. It means 'Gun-Person,' and when he was at the height of his power, he was a great man indeed. Shall we proceed?"

Chester relaxed noticeably. "All right, let's go talk to Gun-Person."

The Council hut was a little longer and broader than the rest of the wood-and-woven-straw huts. Several sleeping mats were rolled and stored neatly aside near the door flap. Chester assumed Gun-Person liked to keep his warriors close at hand. The walls were hung with skins, and furless and headless bodies of marsupials hung from the rafters.

Acacia, Mary-em and the other women were stopped at the door. Kagoiano spoke a few words to Kasan, and he interpreted for them. "I am sorry, but the women cannot be admitted to this council. They will be escorted to the Council for Women, for a reading of the omens."

"What's this reading of the omens business?" Mary-em demanded. "Try to shuck me, Junior, and you'll be eating soft foods for a month."

"Only men can be admitted to this hall," Kasan explained patiently, "just as only women may enter the Council of Women. They do not make policy, but provide us with a valuable source of information on the plans and movements of our enemies."

Chester laid a hand on Mary-em's shoulder. "We'll split up for now. I don't think we're in any danger. We can trade information as soon as we're through here."

The women departed, reluctantly. The nine male adventurers, escorted by Kasan and Kagoiano, walked to the rear of the council hut.

Tony sniffed the air. There was old smoke, and smoked meat, and what smelled like cheap tobacco.

The air toward the rear of the hut was cooler. Better cross-ventilation, deeper shadow. The floor was wood covered with straw mats, some of them decorated with stain. He looked in vain for the hidden holo projector. Kagoiano was a projection; Tony had contrived to brush against him. But he couldn't figure how the continuity was handled. Surely Lopez had had to switch projectors at least once, when Kagoiano entered the hut, but the transition was carried off so smoothly that it was unnoticeable.

Which raised another disturbing possibility: that a holo-gram could be substituted for a real person, even a Gamer. Tony was learning respect for Henderson. *Hell of a Game you've got here, friend.*

In the rear of the hut was an alcove partitioned off with a hanging mat. Kasan lifted it aside, and the Gamers entered the new room.

In a few seconds Tony's eyes adjusted to the darkness. The first things to emerge from the gloom were ten small points of light. At length he could see that they were eyes: unblinking, glaring, not-quite-focused eyes that seemed to stare through them all and off to distant and unknowable reaches beyond. A withered and trembling voice said, "Come."

He could see more clearly now. Five old men were seated in a semicircle around a dish of what looked like dried fruit. Chester squatted in cross-legged position di-rectly in front of them. Tony saw that their eyes didn't "track" as he moved, and concluded that he had found an easy way to differentiate between holograms and human actors.

"I am Chester Henderson, and these are my followers," the Lore Master said. "We come to assist your people in any way we can."

Kasan reeled off a string of gibberish, and one of the men answered with his own unintelligible words. The man who spoke was very old, the skin hanging on his body like a coat on a rack, time-ravaged lines eaten into his neck and face until he resembled nothing so much as a sun-dried fig. His features were very African, his skin darker than Ka-san's, darker than almost any 21st century American black. Tony caught the name Pigibidi.

"Gun-Person welcomes you to the Council, Chester. He says that he knows you are a mighty sorcerer, and hopes that with your help the threat to the souls of all people can be averted."

Chester was interested now. His gaze shifted equally between Kasan and the elderly Pigibidi. The old chieftain pulled a piece of fruit from the bowl and chewed it thoughtfully, then spoke again. When he ceased, Maibang interpreted.

"Gun-Person says that for years the people of the islands endured and cooperated with the invading Europeans in the hope that your people would share with them the secret of your enormous wealth. When it became clear that you did not wish us to make contact with the spirits who had made such wealth possible, we knew that you had much to lose if we ever discovered your secret. We knew that whatever the origin of your cars, your planes and gasoline engines, you had gained some part of them by thievery and lies. The people of the islands began a campaign to discover your secrets, the secret to the *rot bilong kako,* the path the cargo travels from God to men." Kasan paused, and Gun-Person talked in his native language for another minute or two. Kasan sank down into a squat as he listened. Kagoiano and the rest of the Gamers followed suit.

Kasan Maibang spoke. "We joined your churches, learned of God and Jesus, your names for our deities Manup and Kilibob. We prayed to Jesus-Kilibob for cargo, and received nothing. We worked as slave labor on your plantations, and learned the Pidgin english that you taught us to speak. We built roads, changed many of our native customs, and many ceased to own as many wives as they

could feed, all that we might at last be given the secret of
Cargo. All was useless, and in the process many of our old
gods turned against us, thinking that we had abandoned
them. We were a people without a culture, abandoned by
our gods, and denied the secrets of yours."

Kasan paused, his dark face screwed up in concentration as he apparently hung on Pigibidi's every word. "At
last we determined how the foul imbalance had happened. God-Manup had always intended for us to receive
the cargo, but the Europeans had, with sacrifice and
prayer, won over to their cause some of the minor gods
who were in charge of addressing and distributing the
cargo. They changed the labels on the packages to the
names of white men. We knew what was happening now,
but how could we bring it to a halt?

"The great battle that you called World War II provided
us with the opportunity that we needed. Many of our
young men joined your forces against the yellow Europeans, the Japanese. During this time it became possible
to kidnap several of your men and officers, attributing their
disappearance to field casualties." Pigibidi was grinning as
Kasan spoke. "We . . . entertained them for several days.
Some for weeks. At last, shortly before they gave up their
ghosts, they also gave up the secret of the cargo. We know
now that the ceremonies must be spoken in proper, not
pidgin, language. Sacrifices of pigs and fruits are desirable,
as are other things that even you might not know.
Paramount is the holy sacrament, the sacred fluid that
binds you Europeans together, that infuses your bodies
and spirits, that is given to children when they need suck,
and to the old wise ones before they close their eyes for the
final time." Kasan's voice quavered with religious ecstasy.

Chester mused for a second, then shook his head. "Wine? Milk?"

"Those too have power. But I refer to the rare and precious substance you call Ko-Ka-Ko-La."

Chapter Eight

THE BANQUET

The Lore Master stared, then spread his hands in acquiescence. "You've found us out."

"We used our newfound knowledge to open the Road of the Cargo, and in the year 1946, began to regain some of the power that had been stolen from us." Pigibidi spoke again, some sadness in his face. "For a time," Kasan said, "we had everything we hoped for. Do not look at our village now and think that you know the way it was then. White soldiers came to take away our Cargo, but the gods were with us once again, and we killed them all. We drove the Europeans from New Guinea, and lived in peace with our neighbors. We, the Daribi, were first to know the secret of the Cargo. We ruled the other peoples of the land, but we did not kill or enslave them. We even made them gifts to ease their hunger and want.

102

"At last, our sorcerers began to divert even the Cargo intended for the Europeans, and still your people could not stop us. We had grown too strong. And we grew in power and in *mana* until the black day on which we grew too proud."

"What happened?"

"We stole your greatest and most powerful Cargo. The feat drained their strength from the *tindalos,* the ghosts and gods who serve us. A rival tribe had stolen a case of the precious Ko-Ka-Ko-La. At the last moment they used their own knowledge of the *rot bilong kako,* the Road of the Cargo, to divert this tremendous gift to themselves. Our loss cost us much honor and much *mana.* Today our enemies rule most of the tribes of this land. We and the Agaiambo are the only remaining free peoples. Soon, very soon, our enemies will be strong enough to destroy us for defying them. Afterward they will extend their rule to the other Ocean Peoples, and from there to the entire world, and when they rule the world they will crush all other religions. Your gods will die for lack of worshippers."

Chester shifted his posture and rubbed his bony knees to get some circulation back into them. "If the entire world is trying to stop them . . . how can they resist?"

Kasan spoke a few words to Gun-Person, who spoke in reply. The guide turned to Chester. "Your people do not know that our enemies have removed themselves from the physical plane of your world. They have turned the world, our world, inside-out, and nothing can come here unless a path is opened from within. My people opened the path for you."

Chester closed his eyes to think. Without opening them, he said, "That would explain the altered shape of Chambri Lake."

Oliver spoke. "It would explain why the water was salt instead of fresh."

"Ah hah."

"Yeah. I didn't think of it at the time, but the lake was salt. So it wasn't Chambri Lake. It's the Pacific Ocean . . . in fact, it's every ocean in the world."

"Good, Ollie. Very good. That means our directions are going to be screwed up. We can't trust our compasses. If it hadn't been for the mountains we used as a reference point, we would never have gotten here." His eyes opened slowly. "What was it your enemies stole from you?"

Kasan spoke to Pigibidi, who seemed surprised and disturbed. "Surely you would know better than we? It was large, and we sensed many of your greatest men gathering to see it used. Our sorcerers sensed it when it began to move, and we took hold of it and guided it toward us. But it never reached us. We do not know its size nor its weight nor its shape nor its color. But it would have brought us immense power, and now it is in evil hands."

Chester nibbled at his lower lip. "World War Two. Hum. Could be . . . a prototype thermonuclear bomb? But the war was already over . . ."

Maibang shrugged.

". . . All right. What exactly do you hope we can do for you?"

The chieftain conferred with his council, while Kasan listened. Presently Kasan said, "Tomorrow night is the full moon. There is to be a sacrifice of a woman plucked from the seas, in a place sacred to your God, an Anglican mission far to the west. If you can stop the ceremony, you will weaken our rivals and gain precious information from the woman, who has lived among them for a month. She can tell you how to reach their stronghold, there to steal back the mighty Cargo which they stole from us, which we in turn stole from you. You must do this thing, for the sake of all living souls. We will give you guides and other help, but the trip will be dangerous. Many of you will die. But there will be rich reward as well."

Chester looked at Maibang, a tiny smile playing over his lips. "Well, we're here, and I guess we're ready. One more thing. Who are we fighting?"

Maibang acted as if he had been struck with a live wire. Too rapidly to follow, he babbled out a string of words to Gun-Person, whose face grew ashy with fear. "No! No can say!" Pigibidi said, his first English words since his initial invitation to "Come."

Chester frowned. "Why so coy? Why can't you tell us who we're fighting?"

Maibang shook his head. "Very bad, very very bad. This tribe is our enemy. To use their name would be theft. To use anything that belongs to another without his permission is very bad *mana.* You Europeans never understood that. Perhaps that is why you lost your power at last."

"Something like copyright violation? What about the Agaiambo? You used their name."

"They are allies. They will be helping you on your journey."

Chester nodded. "All right, we're in. We'll need some more information, and we'll need provisions, and a couple of guides. I assume you'll be staying with us, Kasan? Good. Is that it?"

"Only this, O Great Sorcerer. Tonight we will feast your people as a sign of our gratitude."

"How many people are you having for dinner?"

Kasan repeated the quip to the chieftain, who sat in stony silence. Kasan shrugged. "I guess it loses something in translation."

"Don't we all." Chester hauled himself to his feet. "Well, let's meet the ladies and swap data before dinner." He made a slight bowing motion to Gun-Person and left the hut, brushing the room-divider mat carelessly aside with one hand.

Gwen and Acacia stood somewhat apart from the other women, watching the Men's Council hut while preparations for the feast went on around them. The feast would be real. Rich mingling smells of roasted pig and yam were thick in the air.

A pit had been dug in the village square, and had been lined with coals. Alternating layers of leaves, pig meat and various vegetables had then filled the pit. Men poked holes in the layers with long spears to provide heat flow.

"That smells just *too* good, Cas." The blond's nose crinkled in delight. "I can't take any more. I'm going to go right over there and dive in."

"I'm afraid they might not pull you out. They'll just divvy you up with the other—I mean, with the pork. Ahem."

Gwen's fingers drummed on her hips. "Could you run that past me again, Ms. Spindleshanks?"

"Oh, no, I think that one is happy right where it is. Ollie! Tony! Over here."

The men made their way to the waiting ladies. "Come on," Acacia said after a firm hug, "let's find a place to sit down."

Oliver asked, "Won't Chester want to debrief you?"

Gwen stamped her foot. "Oh, *forget* Chester for a minute. Let's have our *own* debriefing."

He considered that. "Done. It's not cheating to compare notes privately."

They strolled past the thatch huts to a small stand of trees in view of the main square. They watched the preparations for the feast, and Tony laughed. Acacia pillowed her head against his shoulder as they sat, and nudged him with her small fist.

"What's so funny, cowboy?"

"I'm just wondering how much of that food isn't really there." He stretched luxuriously and dropped one arm around her and pulled her closer. "You know, I've almost stopped wondering which of the natives are real."

"Glad to hear it," Acacia murmured, playing in the grass with the toe of her shoe. "Anyone you only see at a distance, anybody engaged in repetitious movement, and usually anyone you see killed violently, is a hologram. Lopez will use as many holograms as possible."

"Why? Aren't holograms expensive?"

"So are actors. Remember, other Gaming parties are going to run this Game. The holograms are part of the package, but the actors have to be replaced every time."

Oliver lay on his stomach in the grass, watching the native chefs. He asked, "What happened to you ladies whilst we were riddling with the savages?"

Acacia wagged a finger at him. "You first."

Oliver and Tony obliged by telling everything they could remember. Gwen and Acacia listened intently, and finally agreed that they had received much the same.

"Trappings were a little different, though," Gwen mused. "There were three old women. One was in a trance the whole time. A younger woman translated for us. She's supposed to have been to missionary school as a girl."

"They brief these actors pretty well." Tony plucked a

straw from the ground and stuck it playfully in Acacia's hair. "It seems they can answer anything we ask."

Acacia laughed. "Don't be too impressed. I'm pretty sure Kasan wears a transceiver under that bushy hair. Whenever he stops to pray, or talks gibberish to one of the 'natives,' or scratches his ear, he's talking to Lopez."

"Is that legal? I mean, doesn't that put us in a vulnerable position?"

"Not really. The I.F.G.S. is watching Lopez pretty closely. I think Lopez considers himself clever enough to destroy us, and Chester particularly, without cheating."

Oliver sniffed the air. The rich aroma of roasting vegetables and pork had drifted up to them. "Ummm-um. Have you ever been *very* glad your name isn't Goldberg? It sure feels like dinnertime." He started to get up, then hesitated. "What time is it, anyway?"

Acacia dug into her backpack, bringing up a disk watch set in an antique silver dollar. "I've got six-fifteen. Why?"

"Oh, just my devious mind. It's an hour and forty-five minutes before the Game closes down for the night. We're about to be treated to a banquet. Nothing drastic has happened for, oh, call it five hours. We're all pretty relaxed. Do you follow me?"

Gwen looked gloomy. "Oh, Ollie. Sometimes I don't like the way you think. I hope you're wrong."

"So do I." Acacia's hand was straying over the hilt of her sword. "But I wouldn't go Banco on it. Eyes open, troops."

The serving plates were attractive silvery disks with the word "Chevrolet" stencilled on the side. Ollie laughed and nudged Gwen. "Hubcaps."

Gwen nodded and pointed a chubby arm toward the

nearest hut. "Look at that window. What's a glass window doing in a New Guinea village?"

Oliver squinted, scratching his head. "You know, I didn't notice that before."

"I think it's a truck windshield. Take a closer look around this place. A lot of it is patchwork like that."

He began to see what she meant. The thatch roofs of several huts had been finished with canvas, and many of the natives' knives seemed jerryrigged from flattened tin cans. Most of the spears were bamboo, but a few were thin steel tubing with nastily sharpened points. Incongruously, the roofs of a couple of the huts sprouted broken remnants of television antennae, and come to think of it, weren't a few of the women wearing skirts made of parachute silk?

"Echoes of a Golden Age," Ollie said soberly.

There were roast pork, yams, and leafy vegetables only S. J. could name. Although the meat had been tended largely by the women, it was divided and served by the men. Larry Garrett, a Cleric almost as dark as the natives, passed around a hubcap full of steaming maize. It was golden, delicious, and its kernels dripped with some sort of liquified fat. Garrett told Oliver, "If Lopez keeps feeding us like this, I don't care *what* he hits us with."

"Amen to that, Brother." Oliver muffled a belch. "Pass me the beer, will you?" Garrett handed him the big gourd. The beer was warm and flat, but Oliver quaffed it with evident pleasure.

The Gamers squatted or sat on the dirt and ate and talked and laughed. Some of the natives were eating too, but many just stood back and watched. Oliver had waved away the offer of lukewarm raw milk. "No, I really don't think I'm ready for pig milk, thank you." The native waiter had pretended not to understand and passed on. It was probably cow's or goat's milk, Ollie thought, but you never knew . . .

Some of the warriors were pushing something out on a platform. A massive television set with a broken screen. Gun-person walked slowly out of his hut and raised his knobby arms. First the natives, then the Gamers, fell silent.

He spoke for almost a minute. Then Kasan stood and translated. "Pigibidi wishes to demonstrate his own magic to the magicians here gathered, that they might see what once was, and understand." Polite applause greeted this announcement, and Kasan waited it out. "Once this box brought us pictures and sounds from all over the world, yes, even beyond its edge. Our enemies have rendered it worthless, except when our great chief uses his own strength to animate it. See now his greatness."

Pigibidi squatted on his heels, and began to chant, shuffling his feet in a strange rhythm. Now his chanting grew strong, now it dropped so low that they couldn't hear it at all. Slowly he uncoiled from his squat, mouth opened so wide that his facial wrinkles seemed to radiate outward from it like the rays of the sun. A gurgling howl rose from his throat. Tendons and veins stood out in bunches from the old man's neck as the howl reverberated from huts and trees.

In the bowels of the dead television set, merely a mid-twentieth-century flatscreen model with shattered tubes and a crusted interior, a light began to grow. It pulsed like the mating glow of a firefly, shifted from red to orange to bright yellow, and the yellow curled from inside the set as a tongue of flame might leap from a fire, and there was suddenly a flat bank of opaque amber fog at least five times the size of the set.

The old man rolled his head in great circles. His eyes

became glassy, his body trembled as if shaken by wind or cold. But he danced on.

Now the ground itself shook with the force of his incantations, and as it did, shapes formed in the smoke, dark winged shapes that seemed to wobble to the rhythms as they flew. There were perhaps a dozen small shapes within the cloud, flapping their wings with seeming awkwardness, darting and climbing, becoming more solid by the second.

Gun-person screamed and fell to the ground, twitching like one helpless in the grip of an epileptic seizure. He foamed at the mouth and clutched helplessly at the air, fingers crooked into talons.

From the corner of his eye Oliver saw Chester go taut, an instant before the first of the giant hornbills emerged from the smoke.

"Weapons!" Henderson screamed, his voice all but lost amid the screams of the villagers. Then the birds were among them. Three of the Gamers were already swathed in green light and fighting back.

Mary-em was the first to attack. She whipped the halberd off her back and assembled the threaded handle just as a wickedly long beak snapped at her. She hit the ground and rolled, and as the bird wheeled clumsily for another pass she gutted it. Its death-squawk sounded like a maniac laugh as it plunged to earth.

"One down!" she cackled triumphantly. She took a firmer grip on the halberd. "Here, birdie, birdie . . ."

A hornbill swooped at Tony. The Thief stood paralyzed with shock. The bird flew right by him. "What the hell?" he said to nobody in particular. Acacia pulled him to the ground, none too gently.

"Listen." Her voice was a terse hiss. "You're a Thief, so they're going to have a hard time seeing you. But your skills won't help the rest of us much right now, so just stay out of it, okay?" She jumped to her feet and joined the fray.

Tony stayed on his stomach and watched her go, his expression ugly.

Eames, the massive warrior, stood with his back to one of the huts, and three wall-eyed black children cowered behind him. One of the hornbills swooped in from the air while another approached on the ground, waddling forward and thrusting its three-foot beak at him with a noisy honking sound. Eames thrust at the airborne bird first, and as he did, the one on the ground bit at his wrist. The green glow around his hand immediately went pink. Eames said, "Damn!," and hastily switched his sword to his left hand. As if sensing his increased desperation, the birds began to worry him more boldly, taking turns to draw his attack, then pecking at him.

The grounded bird prepared to lunge for his neck as a bolt of red flame struck it in the side. Immediately it caught fire and flopped away trailing smoke and the smell of singed feathers. Eames took advantage of the moment's diversion to skewer the other bird when it flapped back in for a bite. It cawed in pain and expired.

Wiping his forehead with the back of his hand, Eames looked around for his benefactor. Alan Leigh ran over. "Are you all right?"

Eames nodded. "Just caught me one on the wrist. I'll get one of the Clerics to fix it up as soon as the fight's over."

"Good," Leigh said sincerely. "I don't want you out of the Game too soon." He spun around and ran toward Gwen and Oliver, who were protecting the unconscious Gun-person.

Bowan the Black had taken a stand at the far end of the

roasting pit. As a hornbill swooped, honking, its brown wings beating the air like those of a condor, he called fire from the pit, engulfing the unfortunate fowl.

Chester and Gina stood back to back casting glowing spears of light. Several of Gina's missed, but those that scored shore off wings and heads. Chester's beams were deadly accurate.

Most of the Clerics and S. J., the Engineer, hid beneath one of the huts. This wasn't their work. When an inquisitive bird thrust its beak beneath the building and poked around for them, S. J. used a makeshift spear to keep it away. The bird, angered, squawked to its companions and several of the monstrous hornbills joined it. They butted and slammed into the hut. The walls shook.

"It's collapsing!" S. J. screamed. "Everybody out!"

As the last body squirmed out from underneath, the building's supports gave way; an entire side collapsed, and the rest of the building followed it down.

Gamers ran in all directions.

Across the courtyard, Maibang fled from an attacking hornbill. He was too slow. As its claws gripped his shoulders he screamed in pain and terror. "Please! Help me!" The bird flexed mighty wings and pulled Kasan into the air.

Bowan gaped. "Chester! We're losing the guide!"

"The hell we are. Gina! Bowan! Join hands with me!" Maibang's thrashing feet brushed the roof of a hut.

Hastily the three linked up, and Chester intoned solemnly, "We three meld strengths, we three meld minds. Demon of the air we find blocked before and bound behind."

The hornbill reacted as if it had run into an invisible wall. Brown feathers flew as it beat its wings helplessly, trying to escape the grip of three mighty wizards.

Chester smiled with grim satisfaction. "Return unharmed that which is ours, and you may flee with your life, thing of evil."

Whooping with frustration, the bird at last opened its claws, and Kasan fell butt-first through the straw roof of a hut. Straw flew as if a bale of hay had exploded, but when the dust had settled the guide limped into sight with a huge grin on his face. He waved his hand and Chester waved back, screaming at him to lie low.

Most of the remaining birds were wounded and dying. Acacia had finished one off by the roasting pit. She gave it a shove with her foot. Her foot went right through it; but a split second later the corpse rolled over and landed with a satisfying thump and a spray of embers and ashes.

The remaining hornbills were dispatched with a minimum of problem, and soon all was quiet on the Melanesian front.

Natives emerged from their hiding places to see what the powerful strangers had wrought. Only a few of the Daribi warriors had stayed to fight, and several of these were dead.

Chester raised his hand. "Any fatalities? How many injuries? Auras, please." Everybody promptly glowed green, except for Eames, whose wrist glowed scarlet, and Larry Garrett, who had a scarlet glow all down his right leg. "What happened?"

Eames explained his own wound. Garrett had been hit by a support (foam plastic) when the hut collapsed. Chester sighed, but seemed not totally dissatisfied. "Okay, we've got two minor casualties. Gwen, you weren't in that action, so your energy should still be up. Let's have a reading on Gwen's healing aura and see if she can handle both wounds." Gwen's green aura slowly shifted to a warm gold, twinkling like a field of stardust. "Good. You heal them now, and you'll have a full recharge by morning."

"Right, Ches." She raised one hand. "Hear me, O Gods—" The golden glow concentrated around her right hand, then lashed out to bathe both wounds. The red glows died. "How about that. The gods can be right cooperative sometimes."

"Thanks, Gwen. Okay, people, we've only got a few minutes until close-down for the night. Good day, everyone. Lots of points. We'll get some treasure points tomorrow, I'm pretty sure, so you Thieves and Engineers don't worry. Everybody gets their share." Chester looked around until he spied Kasan. "Get over here, Maibang." The little guide skipped over with a prankster's grin plastered across his face. "I'm not going to ask you how you managed the business with the bird. I just want to know if Gun-person's mind is snapped for good, or what?"

Kasan managed to look serious. "Grave damage, yes, very bad. He had been helped to his resting place. Perhaps in the morning he will be able to help you, but I'm afraid that he is dying, and the men's council will not speak to you unless he recovers, or dies, in which case they may choose a new spokesperson, who will decide whether or not to cooperate with you. I'm afraid you are on your own, now."

"Not quite, my friend. You're coming with us." Chester thought for a second, then asked, "What about the women's council? Will they speak to us?"

Kasan seemed to ponder that. "Yes, yes they might. But in the morning." Maibang noticed Oliver with his arm around Gwen. He spoke sternly. "It is not proper for those of the opposite sex to sleep together before such an undertaking."

Oliver was incredulous. "Jee-zuss. We're *engaged!*"

"It would not matter if you were married. Please. If you do not follow the rules of our people, the women's council may not aid you. Further, they may forbid me to accompany you on your voyage."

Chester waved deprecatingly at Oliver. "Go along with it. All bets are off after eight anyway."

Gwen hugged her man to her, and whispered something in his ear. He reddened noticeably, and pecked her goodby, and moved to join Chester and the other men.

Acacia took Tony's hand. It was cool and unresponsive. She looked into his face with playful concern. "I'll meet you by the banana tree, *hombre*."

His lip curled with ill humor. "I thought I was supposed to stay out of trouble. I'm only a Thief, after all."

She stepped back from him, holding both of his hands, and searched his eyes. "Hey, Tony, I was only trying to help you. I was talking about the *Game*, Fortunato!"

He squeezed her hands back, but there was little affection there. "Yeah, well, you were so busy slaying dragons that I guess you didn't have time to notice that you were coming on a little strong. I mean, I might like to play too." There was hurt in his voice, and Acacia didn't know what to say.

"Hey, Tony, I'm sorry, really. Listen—"

He thrust outward with his hands and shook his head defensively. "File it, Cas. I'll be all right. You just can't keep telling me to take everything seriously, then suddenly tell me it's just a game. I didn't get to do a damn thing today, alright? I got to watch everybody else play hero while I lay with my face in the dirt. I don't know what that would feel like to you, but I felt pretty shitty, alright?" He reached out and stroked her gently on the left cheek, then turned and walked away.

Acacia watched him go, her mouth hanging open, jaw working as if trying to find something, anything to say. Words wouldn't come.

Gwen tugged at her arm. "Come on, Cas, let's check out our bunk space." Numbly, Acacia nodded and followed.

One of the village women showed them to their hut. Gwen, Acacia, and Mary-em laid their bedrolls down one side of the woven-reed flooring; Gina and Felicia down the other. Acacia said nothing as she watched her mattress inflate.

A callused palm slapped her heartily across the back. "Man problems?" Mary-em boomed cheerfully. "Don't worry about your boyfriend, honey. He's just got first day jitters, that's all it is. Just hunt him down after lights-out and give him a little bit to calm him down, and he'll be all right."

The little woman chucked her under the chin with a playful nudge that nearly lifted Acacia from her feet, but the dark-haired girl managed to keep smiling. "Right, Mary."

"Right? Of course I'm right. Mary-em sees all, knows all. You take it from me." And she waddled away humming a verse from "Eskimo Nell" that dwelt on the amorous advantages of six-month nights.

Acacia grinned in spite of herself, and lay down on her bedroll, gazing at the ceiling and waiting for Closedown.

And approximately thirty seconds later, without noise or fuss, the natives outside the door turned transparent and faded gently away into the night.

Chapter Nine

KILLED OUT

Albert Rice unlocked the front door of the R&D complex and stepped aside. It was 9:15 P.M., and Rice had just twenty-two minutes to live.

His public smile was in place, but Ms. Metesky and the Lopezes never saw it. There was a bite in Richard's voice. "It may be that you don't quite realize just what three-tenths of a second's delay can do to the Game, the Gamers, and *me*."

"Welles and Chicon are thoroughly competent," Ms. Metesky said placidly. "They'll have it fixed long before morning."

"They'd better. They'd drowning well better. It wasn't my programming, Metesky. That bird didn't drop right away, and Panthesilea had to stand there with her *foot* out in the middle of a *battle!* And Bowan had to repeat himself before he got his fireblast . . ."

They passed outside. "Thank you," Ms. Metesky said to Rice, and stepped after them, adjusting her wire-rimmed spectacles as she went, frail hands trembling a bit from the cool air. Rice locked the door behind them.

As the door slid shut his smile faded like a happy-face drawn in a puddle of mud.

He was thinking, *How could anyone give a damn about three-tenths of a second, anyway? Lopez was a cocky little shrimp who liked giving orders. Talked funny, too. Prissily precise even when he was being nasty. Always: "Excuse me, do you think you could assist me with . . . ?" Or, "May I have a tracking badge, please? I'd like to stretch my legs a bit, and I don't want anyone to get nervous." Always with that phony politeness: phony, because the correct answer to every such question was, "Yes, sir."*

Time to start rounds. Rice hopped the elevator to the third floor and thumbprinted the timeclock as soon as he stepped out.

On the third floor were many of the model-building shops. Working in steel, aluminum, wood, fiberglass, styrofoam, molded plastic and many more exotic materials, the wizards of Dream Park designed in miniature the rides and attractions of the future. Structures first produced as computer-drawn holograms would one day become foamed steel or the absurdly delicate-looking carbon crystal fibers. Rice enjoyed the occasions when he worked the day shift and could look in on the shops, hear and feel the vibrations of lathe and press and drill working their wonders, smell the burnt-plastic tang from the molds as a new concept was given solid life.

But now the shops were empty, the building deserted except for a few techs in Game Central on the second floor, and a few of the late workers in the Psych and Engineering sections on the fifth.

He checked every door and peered down every hall-way, checking the shadows, checking the nooks. He re-membered a tale about the niece of one of the lathe workers. She'd hidden in the building until after close-up, then managed to get into one of the molding shops. Secur-ity found her five hours and twenty thousand dollars worth of damage later. In the course of her spree she had some-how interfaced a roller coaster and a human anatomy model. The results had been so interesting that it inspired the *Mr. Digestion* ride sponsored by Bristol-Meyers in Section I.

She ended up with a spanking and a college trust fund. But a guard had lost his job.

Corridors branched and split, and Rice followed them all, checking every inch before he was confident enough to thumbprint the time clock *clear* and take the elevator to the second floor.

Even while remaining cautious to check every cranny for security breeches, he still took time to cakewalk. He glided from side to side with graceful speed, ducking imag-inary blows. *Cakewalk.* Typical name Griffin would give a fighting move. Strange man, Griffin. Tough but soft. Al-ways encouraged gentleness in his men, always wanted them to give the tourists the benefit of the doubt.

Rice approached the vaultlike door of Game Central's control room, where the Lopezes worked their magic. He pressed his palms to the door, then, almost timidly, his cheek. He felt its metallic smoothness, and the purring vibration from the machinery within. He stood there for a while, and whispered, "Playing God." His expression, soft for a bare moment, hardened to a frown and he walked on. Next to the control room was the Dream Park override, where Larry Chicon and Dwight Welles supervised the technical data being fed into the Dream Park computer system. This room had a shatterproof plastic window, and in the interior dimness there twinkled a few tiny red and white lights.

Next came the chamber where Metesky and the other officials checked the events of the game to insure that all was conducted according to the rules of their crazy organization.

The hallway threw his footsteps after him as he reached the last door and doubled back. Working during the day was good, but Rice liked the night too. Nobody around, no oddballs to deal with. Plenty of time to think, to remember.

If he dwelt on it, Rice could remember visiting Dream Park when he was ten years old. How long ago that seemed. Twenty years seemed like eternity. At the same time it seemed that he could reach out and touch the head of the little blond boy with the perennial sniffle. And now he had grown up to work at the great illusion factory.

Come with me, little Albert, Rice invited himself as he summoned the elevator. *Come with me and peek behind the dreams. See the computers and cameras. See the gears and oilcloth and plastic struts that make the magic. Then squeeze the last tears out of your eyes, mix liberally with the fractured fairy tales of youth, and try to mold the resultant mess into an adult who can stand on his own, and damn well fend for himself.*

A flicker of a grin played on his mouth. He could fend for himself, he could fend himself right into a gravy job here at the playground of the world. There was room at the top for him, for anybody who knew what cards to play. Dream Park's business was lies, and little Albert knew all about lies. Some of them meshed so tightly together in the mists of years past that he could no longer separate them from reality.

Illusions . . . Just why exactly was it that only his father had brought him to Dream Park? Daddy said that Mommy was sick and had to go away for awhile. But there had been the one phone call in the motel room, when his father screamed, "Emma!," over and over into the telescreen, and mother's face had been cool and distant until a man's voice in the background called her away. Daddy had cried into the darkening screen, tears streaking his strong, handsome face. And when the tears dried, he had taken young Albert by the hand and the two of them had gone to Dream Park for the second day of a four day vacation.

The last three days of that vacation were more fun than any Albert could remember, except that down underneath the smiles and laughs he remembered a grown man crying into an empty screen.

Illusions.

When the two of them returned home, mother was there with kindness and warmth, but afterward she was gone more frequently. Whether to go to "the hospital," "a relative's," or a "job seminar," the result was the same, the aching loneliness he could feel emanating from his father like waves of heat.

One day Albert came home from school and his father told him that mother was leaving for good, and that the boy had to decide which of them he wanted to live with. Albert had opted for his father, and within the space of six months watched a vibrant, vital man become old and broken. It wasn't hatred that he felt for his mother, for her little gifts and concerned phone calls, it wasn't resentment. In a strange way he was almost glad that this thing had happened to the man he loved most in all the world. Young Albert knew that he had learned an invaluable lesson; that all there was in this world were lies and dreams, and that was just the way it was. *Thanks, Mom.*

He stepped out of the elevator at the first floor, and stiffened almost immediately. Something . . . what? a sound? yes, a sound, the last hiccough of an echo in the hall, and Rice became very cautious.

Rice looked both ways down the hall and saw nothing. He toyed with the idea of calling it in. Had he really heard anything? Walls do settle in an old building. The hall was perfectly quiet, but Rice relaxed only slightly. He walked out, almost on tiptoe, and turned left toward the secretarial pool. Passing a mirrored light panel he was almost amused to see a slightly crouched shape, the semi-snarl on his lips somehow incongruous beneath the soft blond hair.

No sound. Nothing. Nuts. He made himself check the doors on the ground floor; office space mostly, and easier to clear. Past the administrative section there were some filing closets, but nothing valuable, really. He glanced at his watch: nine twenty-seven, and eighteen minutes until the next check-in. Time for a little break. Past the filing cabinets was the first floor break room, with sandwiches, coffee, and a few small tables.

Rice let himself in and flicked on the light. Oh yes, there was a new soft drink dispenser. He pushed his Cowles Industries charge card into the slot and punched the lemonade button. An eight ounce plastic pouch dropped into his hand. It felt cold and shapeless, like liver straight out of a meat drawer. Rice preferred bottles or cans.

He worked the nipple loose and took a long swig as the arm fastened around his neck.

Lemonade sprayed from his mouth and choked in his throat. The arm tightened. Rice gagged, doubling up, lemonade running from his nose and down his face, his hands flailing ineffectually.

He forced his head to the side, getting his throat into the

crook of his attacker's elbow, so that the strangling forearm no longer crushed his windpipe. Then he fought: an elbow to his assailant's gut followed by an identical blow to the other side which brought a satisfying *whoof* of painfully expelled air. But instead of letting go, the attacker jumped up and wrapped both legs around Rice's waist from behind, squeezing the ribs until they creaked. Rice felt his sight wavering and threw himself backward, trying to smash a head between himself and the floor.

There was a grunt, and the pressure eased as they both hit the floor. Rice clawed at the strangling arm, gasping a precious lungful of air. With renewed strength he punched back over his shoulder and felt his fist graze flesh. Encouraged now, he punched and elbowed until the grip began to give, then braced himself and started to rise to his knees. If he could do that, he could gain the leverage to throw his weight back against the edge of a table. He made it to one knee and was moving his right into position when his knee landed squarely on the pouch of lemonade. It popped open, and he skidded on the wet, losing all balance to tumble face-first back on the floor.

His attacker landed in the middle of his back, driving the remaining air from tortured lungs. Belly-down on the floor and thrashing, Rice felt a strong forearm slide back across his throat. Another arm clamped across the back of the neck for added pressure. Bleeding darkness boiled up around and within him, but with an enormous effort of will he pushed the ink clouds back and got one arm under himself. He began to push with arms drained of strength, his lungs aflame and his temples throbbing a bass beat of pain. He tried to scream, to hiss; dry croaking rattled in his throat as his vision blackened and he heard his own thoughts as a faraway call: *ohmygod ohgod, please, just one more sip, one spoonful of air please please* . . .

"Get Bobbick here. Now." Griffin spat it at Melone, the pudgy guard who worked the top three floors of the R&D building. Melone backed out of the room. He was glad of an excuse to leave. He had never seen a dead man before. And Rice was inarguably dead. A hologram might have shown an unconscious man gagged and bound hand and foot. But to share the same space with Rice was to feel the presence of death. It lay still and muggy in the air. His eyes were closed, head crumpled to the side like the head of a doll, blond hair somehow reminiscent of a wig fitted to a mannequin.

Griffin stooped for a closer look. Rice's hands had been tied behind his back. No, correct that: his wrists had been bandaged together with surgical tape, and his thumbs had been bandaged separately. Tape had been wrapped twice around the ankles; more tape covered his mouth. Rice sat with his back against the soft drink machine, head slumped to his knees. Griffin gently took Rice's shoulder and eased him upright. There was a shallow indentation in the thin metal, precisely where Rice's head would have been, were Rice sitting up.

Griffin jumped reflexively as footsteps entered the room. "Sorry, boss, did I—?" Millicent Summers winced at the sight of the dead man.

"He's dead, Millie. Listen, I called you and Marty because I'm going to need some extra eyes and ears, okay?" She nodded jerkily. "I want the CMC doctor over here in fifteen minutes. I want a complete security sweep of the building. I want to know about anything unusual going on in the line of projects."

"There's the Game in Gaming A, Griff." Her eyes were fixed on Rice, and he could tell she was fighting to remain calm. Griffin felt a certain bizarre satisfaction in finally finding an hour when Millie wasn't totally awake and alert.

"Right, Millie. I need to know if anything has been tampered with, or if any security seals have been breached. I don't think whoever did this really wanted to kill Rice. If I'm right, it was supposed to be theft, so that's where we start."

Millicent nodded again, her eyes still watching Rice's corpse. "Get going, Hon," Griff said gently. "I'll handle things here."

She tried to smile. The result was hideous. She gave up and backed out of the room. Griffin heard her break into a run in the hallway.

Griffin examined the room, trying to reconstruct events. Clearly, Rice had lost a fight here. Knowing the guard's wiry strength, Griffin thought he must have been taken by surprise. That could mean several things: being jumped from behind, attempting to restrain an intruder of unexpectedly high physical skills, whatever. Chairs had been knocked over. There was a half-dried puddle of lemonade near Rice's feet. His right knee was stained.

A mental replay of Rice's file was in order. 30 years old, blond, 5' 11", 170 lbs. Ex-Navy man, submarine service. Spent six years there, and left with an honorable discharge. Two years of college, then three years of odd jobs, and finally Cowles Industries. Both parents alive, mother somewhere in Minnesota, father an out patient at a geriatric center. Fairly well liked, but didn't socialize except for the company mixers at CMC.

Griffin sat down on one of the undisturbed chairs. He rubbed his eyes with the palms of his hands. Wasn't there something else? Oh, yes. His apartment in Cowles Modular Community had been vandalized. He had declared no losses, and no investigation had followed. Perhaps—

"Bobbick is on his way, Chief." Melone was back, face

reddened as if with exertion. His eyes studiously avoided the corpse against the soft drink machine.

"Right. You stay here until Marty arrives. Have him coordinate a report for me. The legal department needs in on this." Griffin scratched the wiry fuzz under his jaw. "I need to check into something, but I think an emergency meeting should be set up with Harmony. Buzz me whenever that's ripe, would you? Oh—I know I don't need to tell you, but I will anyway. Don't touch anything that's been disturbed."

Griffin's mind projected a quick layout diagram of the R&D center as he waited for the elevator. There had been a complete security check on all of the alarm units only the week before. Griffin had participated; he knew that it had been thorough and accurate. It would take hours to check over each unit for traces of bypass or tampering, and he would have those results by morning, but there was one possibility that he could investigate right now. It was a long shot, but Griffin had long since learned to check into those little nagging doubts.

The elevator took him down to the basement. When the door opened a night light came on. Alex flipped on the main lights.

There was no sound except the hum of generators, low in the background. Griffin walked to the stairwell, moving between rows of storage boxed and plastic-wrapped maintenance gear. He stooped at the door of the stairwell, checking the lock. There were no external signs of damage or tampering, but a check of the record tape would tell him if the magnetically-encoded lock had been opened within the past few hours. With the right kind of careful preparation, a thief need not have forced the lock.

He crossed to the service shaft on the other side of the room. It was three feet from the ground and sealed with a circular steel door. He climbed the short ladder that led to it and examined the surface of the door. There were a few smudges, but maintenance personnel had been through the tunnels during the day's Gaming. In fact, substantial restructuring of Gaming Area A was going on right now, but the men and machines performing those tasks would be brought in through one of the environment dome's side panels.

But this tunnel . . .

Griffin flipped out his wallet and tapped it on. "Patch me through to Maintenance, please." There was a moment's buzz, during which Griffin turned up the collar of his light jacket; the basement was chilly.

A beep sounded, and a woman's voice came on line. "Yes, Mr. Griffin. How can we help you?"

"I want records of all egress and entry into Gaming Area A service shaft, um," he glanced at the yellow numbers stencilled above the portal, "eighteen. It leads into the Research and Development building."

"G. A. 18?"

"Right."

"One moment, please."

While the line was dead, Griffin found himself hoping that he was wrong. How could they have overlooked this? It was inexcusable, and understandable at the same time. Why guard against Gamers? He knelt by the base of the stairs and looked carefully. There were definite smudges of dirt, and a tiny shaving of green leaf.

"Mr. Griffin?"

"Here."

"G. A. 18 was used once today at 4:30 P.M."

Griffin held his breath. "What was the reason?"

"Pressure check in sector twelve, apparently. That's one of the lines that feeds the artificial lake."

"Then there was no need for the technician to go topside?"

"No, I don't believe so. There's a Game on right now, you know. All of the work was accomplished in the tunnels."

"Right." Griffin thought quickly, weighing factors. "When that technician comes in in the morning, please have him verify that." He signed off and folded wallet and transceiver away.

He looked again at the smudge. The steps, like every other accessible inch of the Park, were cleaned daily. The smudge must be recent. Probably a foot had descended on this ladder in the last few hours. Griffin checked his watch. Eleven twenty. Rice had been found at ten past ten, twenty-five minutes after he missed his check-in.

And where would an intruder find dirt and leaves to step in anyway?

Bet on it: these would be Brazilian plant life.

An elevator took Griffin back to the first floor. The CMC doctor had arrived, a tall thin man who ordinarily wore a warm smile. Now he wore a rumpled and hastily-donned shirt jammed into what could pass for trousers but looked suspiciously like pajama bottoms.

"Dr. Novotney," Alex said in sober greeting.

The thin man said, "Griffin. Listen, I can't do much here. I'll have to take the body to my lab to learn anything. We can't move him until the County coroner comes, or the police clear it, is that right?"

Griffin scratched his head. "I think we can handle this. Dream Park is an independent municipality, and I have the authority to clear it. We're going to have to deal with the

County, but I'm betting that Harmony will want us to keep this as close to the chest as possible."

"We've got the pictures, Griff," Marty Bobbick said. "What a mess."

Griffin was glad he was here. Bobbick would see that things got done if Griffin had to get off by himself to think things out. A nervous tic made Bobbick's pleasantly ugly face squint every time his eyes passed over Rice's body. He chewed a mouthful of gum with near-manic intensity as Griffin talked.

"We need prints. There've been too many people in and out of here for a heat scan to do much good, but try it anyway. I want all the record tapes collated. Somebody wanted something in this building. I want to know what it was. Maybe the development people can tell us. Get hold of somebody who knows what the hell they're about and tell him to join me when I meet with Harmony."

Marty nodded, his square jaw pumping up and down with nervous rhythm. "Got most of that covered already. Millie's on the record tape right now, and the infrared equipment should be here any minute." He counted off tasks to himself and came up satisfied. "Guess that's it for right now, then, except for moving Rice . . . ah, you want him over at CMC?"

"No. Take him to the Park medical center. Better facilities there. Check with the legal department and find out if we can do an autopsy if it's needed."

Rice was being carefully loaded onto a stretcher. Two guards hoisted him away, and Bobbick watched the sheet-covered body go with pained eyes. "Hell of a thing," he said softly.

"Yeah," Griffin agreed. "A hell of a thing."

Chapter Ten

NEUTRAL SCENT

Griffin managed to catch a couple of hours sleep before his scheduled meeting with Harmony. His office couch was uncomfortably soft, but it was better than tubing back to his apartment for a mere catnap. Afterward he shaved and washed his face in his office lavatory.

The face in the mirror was a stranger's. The green eyes, the close-cropped black hair, the massive shoulders, the two-inch scar under the left ear . . . these he knew. But the *vulnerable* look made it a stranger's face. Murder made a difference.

There had been deaths at Dream Park. Coronaries, strokes, a drug overdose or two (one thing he would never understand was people who came to Dream Park to do their drugs. While most people struggled to maintain emotional equilibrium under the sensory overload, there were those few whom even Dream Park's magic couldn't satisfy. Call it evolution in action), and even a few genuine weirdies, like the kid who somehow managed to drown in thirty-six inches of "quicksand" in the Treasure Island Game a couple of years back.

But never a murder. Never. He remembered the still-ness of Rice's face, the tangible aura of *death* that had touched everyone who came into the room. Not here. Not at Dream Park. Things like that didn't happen here.

But they do, and it has. Even here, you can die. And it's in your lap now, he told the frightened stranger. He checked the stranger's shirt for nonexistent wrinkles and checked his sleeve for the time. 4:25 A.M. Five minutes to get there.

Griffin's office was on the second floor of the Adminis-tration complex, a ten story building in the exact center of Dream Park, standing on an island in the middle of the central lagoon that connected the wedges of the Dream Park pie. Harmony was on the sixth. The halls on the sixth floor were empty but for a single forlorn maintenance 'bot whirring almost inaudibly as it sucked up dust.

Griffin let himself into the outer office, past the empty Reception desk, and knocked on Harmony's door. A radio announcer's voice called for him to enter.

The Dream Park Director of Operations could easily have demanded an office on the eighth or ninth floors, among the luxury suites. He preferred to be within easy reach of his staff. The office was not impressive from the outside. Inside, it was a delight. The outer wall was all window, above a magnificent view of the lagoon and sections I and II of Dream Park. The room was high-ceilinged and carpeted with natural fiber. Best of all, and the thing that made it such a pleasure to visit: most of the furniture was made of beautiful, expensive, delicately stained wood.

The mahogany desk was massive, and so was the man behind it. Harmony must have weighed two hundred and thirty pounds, only about twenty of it fat. He was in his late fifties, balding, and wore inappropriately delicate pince-nez. His nose was flat enough to bring water to a plastic surgeon's eye, and his shoulders had that linebacker look to them. Only the voice betrayed the image of overwhelming physicality.

"Griffin. Glad to see you." The tones were cultured in the extreme, every word lovingly rounded, as if shattering the bruiser image were an old and favorite game. Harmony reached across the desk to shake Griffin's hand with crushing strength. "Have a seat, please. We should probably wait for O'Brien."

"Skip's in on this? Oh, right. We need some tech assistance."

Harmony successfully stifled a yawn, shaking his head. "Damnable hour to roust someone from bed, but as long as we had to do it, we might as well spread a little of the grief around, eh?"

Alex laughed and looked out of the window absently. It was still too dark to see anything out there, and he found himself hoping the meeting would last until dawn came to Dream Park.

"Albert Rice," Harmony was saying. "Blond fellow?"

"That's the one."

"Was he a good man?"

"He was reliable and intelligent. He was up for a desk job if his psych profile fit the bill. My guess is that he would have been working over here in a year or two."

Harmony clucked softly. "Seems to happen like that much too often. Well, this whole thing is a mess, Alex. It puts Cowles Industries into a rather sensitive position, and I'm not sure of the best way to handle it. How much have your people learned?"

"Just what you already know. The target was a storage area on the third floor. It may have been something in development for one or more of the new attractions. The whole thing appears to be a case of industrial spying gone sour."

Skip O'Brien opened the door. "Good morning," he said, then shook his head. "I guess there's not much good about it, is there?" He carried a loaded briefcase to the unoccupied chair. "I got together as much information as I could on short notice. Alex, are you sure that that was the only cabinet disturbed?"

"Absolutely. The record tapes on the locks all say that the action happened between nine-thirty and ten-fifteen. The door to the little biochemistry lab in Development on the third floor was opened at about nine-forty. The project file had been rifled, and we believe that a sample vial of some sort may have been stolen."

"Oh, my." It was all that Skip said, but he cracked open his briefcase and began to run notes through a small viewscreen. When he looked up, there were little worry lines creasing his forehead. "I don't think that you have to tell me which file it was. And the corresponding sample vial was missing? Was the file designation 'Neutral Smell'?"

Alex nodded. "How did you know?"

"If you spent your time in R&D, you'd know the talk. There was only one thing in there that might have inspired a theft like this. It was sent down from the big Cowles facility in Sacramento. Really secret. This was only the second sample we've received. No offense to you, Alex, but they were worried that something like this might happen. They don't have to worry about Gamers and tourists, so their security is tighter. Anyway, if someone was after that file, then he was hunting very large game indeed. Poor Rice got caught in the middle." He paused, preoccupation unfocusing his eyes. "I hope that whatever information I can give you helps you catch the bastard."

Griffin jumped a bit at that. He couldn't remember ever having heard Skip curse.

O'Brien noticed. He said, unhappily, "If I hadn't recommended him, Rice might still be alive."

Alex was a handspan too far away for a comforting touch, so he tried to put softness in his voice. "He needed a job, Skip. He wasn't your responsibility, just another ex-student of yours, and you helped him. I don't think he'd blame you for the way things turned out."

"Maybe not. Maybe he wouldn't. I don't like it anyway."

"None of us do, Skip," Harmony told him. "So let's have what you've got. It'll clear the air, and might even enable us to catch the bastard. As you so neatly put it."

"Right." Skip fiddled with the viewer until he seemed satisfied. "Some of this is going to be a bit thick, but I'll try to hold the pidgin Swahili down to a minimum."

Harmony leaned back in his chair and steepled his fingers, eyes half closing. Griffin crossed one leg over the other and canted forward.

"Dream Park deals in illusions both subtle and gross. Gross effects include physical constructions, holograms, most of the sound effects, and so forth. Subtleties are mainly concerned with the results of combining different stimuli in the attractions, the manipulation of time and space in the waiting areas, et cetera. Basically, then, placing the customer in a proper mood to 'correctly' interpret the gross effects. Without the 'immersion period' immediately preceding a ride or experience, the illusion isn't as convincing. This is old stuff. The Disneyland people used to use waiting time to prepare the customer psychologically.

"At any rate, as we learned more about the subconscious effects of various elements of Dream Park, we began to wonder if a more direct manipulation of the subconscious might be a fruitful area for study. Since we only want to use those techniques within the attractions themselves, we didn't have to worry about the existing statutes covering subliminal advertising."

Skip showed them his first real smile since entering the office. "Some of it was almost absurdly easy once we set our minds to it. We started with sounds. Some frequencies in the subsonic range are well known to stimulate uneasiness or fear. We started with the buzzing sound that angry bees make. When we were satisfied that we could produce fear response in more than eighty percent of our test subjects, we went on from there.

"High-speed light flashes were even more effective. In the early days, such techniques could only be used on people watching projection screens or billboards, flashing a message lasting for only hundredths of a second. Our holographic projection techniques take us far beyond that. We can broadcast separate images to two people standing side by side. Effectiveness with this technique isn't where we would like it—only about sixty percent right now—but the flexibility is enormous."

He looked up from his viewscreen, folding the lid of his briefcase down. He had been speaking distractedly, as if one part of his mind were collating information while the other part related it to them.

"Human beings have four basic kinds of sensory receptors. Electromagnetic, mechanoreceptors, thermoreceptors, and chemoreceptors. The rods and cones of the eye are electromagnetic receptors. Mechanoreceptors respond to touch, pressure, et cetera. For instance, the eardrums are mechanoreceptors; they respond to the pressure of sound waves. Thermoreceptors are free nerve endings sensitive to heat and cold. We've done work in each of these areas, with the promise of more to come. We had trouble with chemoreceptors. Taste buds, the cells of the carotid and aortic bodies, the olfactory cells of the nose . . . we couldn't do much with those, so naturally that was where we concentrated our efforts."

Griffin drummed his fingers on the arms of his chair and cleared his throat. "I take it that whatever was stolen was a result of these efforts?"

O'Brien looked sheepish. "Am I going on too much? I thought some background would be useful."

"Go ahead, Skip, there might be something valuable in even the trivia."

"O-kay. Our problems were manyfold: accuracy of the effect, harmlessness of the chemical agent, undetectability, means of distribution, et cetera. We made an abortive effort to trigger the olfactory nerves with sound, but it just won't work. The receptors respond only to chemicals.

"The potential is tremendous, gentlemen. The olfactory nerves are the only ones that connect directly to the brain. The medial olfactory lobe seems to be involved with the limbic system in the expression of emotion. There is believed to be a 'pleasure center' located there.

"As I said, the olfactory cells need a chemical to trigger

them. What they are, actually, are bipolar nerve cells originating from the central nervous system itself. When one is triggered it becomes 'depolarized,' which causes a battery effect, and a current flows. Voila, a nervous impulse. Present theory holds that the molecular shape, rather than the chemical properties of a substance, determines its smell. On the basis of this theory, seven different primary classes of odor have been established: camphoraceous, musky, floral, pepperminty, ethereal, pungent, and putrid. Of course these can be combined. What we theorized is that there are 'neutral' scents, scents which trigger depolarization in the olfactory nerves without any conscious sensation of smell. If we could find the molecular shape which accomplishes this, we would be on our way."

"How many different kinds of response were you hoping to get?" Harmony asked from behind his peaked fingers, eyes still deceptively lidded.

"We weren't sure. Nausea, salivation, sexual behavior, and—"

"Sexual behavior?"

"Everybody triggers on that one. Yes, sexual behavior. As far back as the 1960's two chemicals, copulin and androsterone, were found to be sexual signals in monkeys, and to some extent in human beings. Humans have a more complex set of factors involved in attraction than animals. Many of them are social in nature and no chemical yet discovered can really make up your mind for you." He grinned. "But we're trying."

O'Brien extracted a cigarette from his inside coat pocket and lit it with an unsteady hand. At a glance from Griffin Harmony unobtrusively turned on a tiny fan in the ceiling, and Skip's smoke vanished into it.

"What we did," he began again, "was to use an advanced version of a device called an electro-olfactograph, which registers electrical impulses in the olfactory nerves. We finally found a substance that causes depolarization without conscious recognition of scent at any concentration."

"What was the chemical?"

"I couldn't give you the formula, Alex. I don't know it myself. I can say that it was a highly volatile lipid-soluble chemical, with saline as the carrying agent. Once we had that, the work really began. It was really incredible. This was all about seven months ago. Since that time I've heard that Sacramento has variants that will induce tears, laughter, reflex vomiting, sleep, even something suspiciously like *agape*, brotherly love. God only knows what they'll come up with when they really know what they're doing. At any rate, they sent over a sample for us to test, that and accompanying data. I'm afraid that is most probably the target of our burglary."

Alex asked the question. "What does this batch do?"

Skip turned his palm briefly to the ceiling. "Not sure. That was why they sent us the sample. They felt that our proximity to Dream Park might give us some additional testing options. Preliminary testing indicates that it is a general emotion intensifier. If this is true, and it is a substance as totally harmless as all preliminary testing indicates, it is an incalculably valuable advantage over our competition. The theft of the sample, and of the printed matter, breaks us wide open." He folded his hands in his lap. "That's most of it."

Harmony sat up in his chair and turned to Griffin. "Well, Alex? What do you think?"

"I think I was right. Industrial espionage. How many

people knew the stuff was here, Skip?"

"Maybe five, myself included. Perhaps twice that many in Sacramento."

"Thanks. You saved me my second question. There's a leak, that's for sure. Whether it's electronic or human I can't say now. With twice the people knowing it in Sacramento, it might be twice as likely for the leak to originate there. It would be a neat trick to wait until a sample is transferred here. Then again, it doesn't take a genius to see why I'd rather believe *that* theory." He sighed. "Well. It's happened. I don't believe the damage is irreversible."

Harmony's ears perked up. "Why?"

"I don't think that the thief has left the scene yet."

O'Brien seemed troubled. "The building was searched. If the thief didn't leave the building he must be one of us. The security men, the psychology staff, and whoever else was here."

"A small group from engineering was still on the fifth."

"Right. We were all routinely searched, so the stuff wasn't on any of us physically, but that doesn't help. It could be hidden in the building."

"Might be, and we're checking on that." Griffin nodded, arranging his thoughts. "I don't think that's it, though. I found some traces in the basement of R&D that suggest that the thief came into the building from Gaming Area A. That is the weakest link in our defenses. We have excellent protection on all outer perimeters, but between Gaming A and the basement . . ." He shrugged. "The Gamers are so out of touch with reality that they were never considered a serious threat. But the thief used surgical bandage. Gamers carry medical kits . . . Skip, how long ago did the sample arrive?"

"Three weeks."

Griffin tsked discontentedly. "Maybe still. Better yet
. . . Skip, how long before that was it known that a
shipment was to be made?"

"At least another month."

"*That's* the margin for error we need. That gives plenty
of time for the information to reach our competitors. Time
for them to research our defenses. After they found our
weak spot, they looked for a Game that was running at the
right time. After that, find the aah . . . right, the *Lore
Master* being challenged. Get the names of the people he's
likely to choose, and make your approach from that list.
Complicated, but with seven weeks lead time, not impossible."

"What exactly do you see as the sequence of events
here, Alex?" There were oceans of tension crackling just
beneath the superficial calm of Harmony's voice.

"At approximately nine o'clock last night, one of the
Gamers in Gaming A broke away from the others and
headed toward the northwest corner of the Research and
Development complex, staying clear of any workmen
renovating the Gaming area. This person entered a service
duct and gained access to the lower level of the complex.
He reached the first floor by stairs or elevator. Rice blocked
his path, so he rendered Rice unconscious with a 'sleeper'
hold of some kind, probably an air or blood strangle.
They're easier than nerve strangles. Rice was tied and
gagged, and our intruder completed his business with no
further trouble."

"Rice's death was accidental?"

"I'd think so. Would you bind and gag a dead man? The
important thing is that the killer is still in the Game. If we

move now, we can collect them all before morning and begin questioning.''

Harmony raised a single thick finger. "There are several problems inherent in this situation. First of all, we cannot detain these people against their wills without involving outside law enforcement agencies. They would demand to see their attorneys, and in such a meeting information concerning the drug could change hands. If the thief becomes aware that we know he's a Gamer, before we know which Gamer it is, the drug could be hidden anywhere in the seven hundred and forty acres of the Gaming area. It may already be stashed away, and we might never find it. Then there is the Game itself to consider. We stand to lose a good deal of money if the drug escapes our control, but we also stand to lose approximately—" He consulted a figure scrawled on his deskpad. "—one point five million dollars of our money already invested in the South Seas Treasure Game. Not to mention an estimated twenty-two million in revenue over the next eight years if film, book, programming, and holotape leasing and sales go according to estimations."

Harmony's voice dropped a bit. "Frankly, there's another problem. You are both aware that our water rights and tax privileges are coming up for review next year. If we can isolate our suspect before we call in the authorities, we'll be that much further ahead, without investigating teams crawling over us."

"What are you suggesting?"

"I'm not totally sure. I need to think about this, and we'll need to consult the I.F.G.S. I believe that the Game lasts four more days? Then that's how long we have before it becomes necessary to call in outside help. I believe our legal department can negotiate us that much time. Alex, please meet me back here at nine o'clock, in—" He consulted his watch. "—three and a half hours. You may or may not like my idea, but I think it may be for the best."

Chapter Eleven

GAME PLAN

The world around Alex Griffin blurred like dreams, then sharpened to near-reality, as Bobbick and Millicent fiddled with the focus of the hologram projector. Griffin found himself in the living room of an apartment at the Cowles Modular Community.

The apartments were almost infinitely maleable to the tastes of the occupants. Windows, built-in accessories, raised or lowered ceilings or additional rooms were no problem. Even entire living units could be moved into varying clusters with a minimum of difficulty. Griffin's own apartment presently included a small gym, a large library-study and a sundeck overlooking one of the starburst-shaped pools.

He didn't recognize this one. "What have we got here, Millicent?"

"It's Rice's apartment, Griff," Bobbick answered, chewing the end of a pen. Griffin restrained a snort. Chewing gum, pens, fingernails, Bobbick always seemed to have something in his mouth. He wondered idly if the man's oral compulsion had anything to do with his popularity in the secretarial pool.

The viewpoint backed away from the fireplace for an overall view of Rice's living room. The gas burning fireplace was brick-encased and raised a foot above the living-room rug, which was light brown and high-tufted. There were two shelves of books and what looked like a microcube reader to the right, with wrought iron spider bookends. The other wall was a picture window.

The scene blurred, sharpened. Kitchen . . .

"When were these taken?"

"This was about a month ago, standard shots for our designers to study. We've been wondering if the vandalism in Rice's apartment was all coincidence." Millie hesitated, then plunged ahead. "It's an awful thing to think, boss, but since Rice wasn't shifted to the night schedule until after the vandalism, well, it just seemed kind of strange to us, that's all. We thought we'd look a little closer, that's all."

"Rice didn't report anything stolen . . ." Where did that thought lead? Could Rice have been involved in the Neutral Scent Affair? If he wanted to change shifts, he could have done it with a simple request. That might have been suspicious, so he had a confederate set off the alarm while . . .

Too much, too complicated. And too grotesque. But not impossible.

"All right," he said at last, "just keep me posted on any developments. I need to think for awhile. Let me know when Dr. Novotney comes up with anything, will you?"

Millicent and Bobbick acknowledged and went back to their viewings.

Griffin let himself into his office and plopped into his chair without bothering to turn the lights on. He leaned back and put his feet up on his desk.

They want me to handle this, he mused. *I wonder what Harmony will come up with? I wonder if the legal department can buy us the time we need.*

In the middle of a Game, one of the players had departed and returned unnoticed. What kind of Gamer would do that? Possibly for the first time in his life, Alex wished he knew more about the Games.

The thief would have to have some experience, though. Enough to be able to find that extra time, that opportunity. To count on it. Ideally, he would have played one or more Games in Gaming Area A itself. It'd be in their records . . .

Alex had seen Rice twice in the two or three days preceding the . . . burglary? Accident? Murder? Call it *accident* for the moment. Rice had called in the vandalism forty-eight hours ago. About thirty-six hours ago Alex had seen him for the last time, hauling luggage for the Lopezes. What were his last words? *I'll see you later, Chief.* Right, Rice.

Griffin rubbed his eyes, tried to remember. Rice had thrown a housewarming party four months after coming to Cowles Industries, a fairly drab affair with tons of official-issue smiles and politely inebriated people acting mildly scandalous. There had been a few moments of genuine hilarity, notably Millie and one of the maintenance techs singing a duet of "Baby It's Cold Outside" with the male and female roles reversed. There had also been a tiny tiff of

some kind, between . . . who had it been? Rice and some
buyer from Costuming over something or other. Couldn't
remember.

Griffin's eyes kept wanting to close without permission.
He shook his head to wake himself up. He was losing the
battle when the intercom buzzed. "Griffin," he said automatically.

· "We may have found something, Chief. Could you step
out here for a minute?" Millicent's voice had perked out of
its lethargy.

"Right." Somewhat to his own surprise, Alex was on his
feet instantly. He walked from his office into another shot
of Rice's living room. "What have you got?"

Bobbick rotated the view three hundred and sixty degrees. "There are a few minor changes in this shot. Oh, this
holo was made about three hours ago. Rice cleaned up
whatever mess had been made. Remember that he insisted on handling it all himself, said there was nothing
missing? That may have been a fib. Millie, would you put
on the other shot?"

Reality blurred; then an almost identical picture colored
the air. "This is a shot taken a month ago. See that
statue?" Bobbick pointed out a simple but very attractive
statuette a meter tall. It was of a nude woman reclining on
crumpled cloth, her face a graceful oval. "The statue isn't
in the later shot."

"It isn't?" For an instant Griffin was uninterested, then
suddenly he remembered. "The argument at Rice's party
with that lady from Costuming."

"Mrs. Kokubun." Millie sounded positive. "She really
wanted to buy it from him, made him a good offer, too."

"Right." Griffin remembered now. "He begged off for
some reason or other. Didn't he make the statue himself?

Something about the 'last relic of a misspent youth'?"

"It's nowhere in sight now," Millicent said. "We looked."

"Maybe it was broken," Bobbick murmured.

"Could be. Why wouldn't he make an insurance claim, then? He had a roomful of witnesses who could verify that he was offered a stiff price for it. If it was destroyed by the vandal—"

"No," Bobbick interrupted, "I mean maybe it fell over accidentally."

"Hmmm. I see what you mean. It's fairly low to the floor on that shelf, but I could see it happening. It's a horizontal motif, though, so it wouldn't be easy to just knock it over. If it did fall . . . probably wouldn't shatter, not in that carpet. It's worth looking into." Griffin looked at his watch. *"Eight-fifty?"* He smacked his palm to his forehead in mortification. "I didn't even know I'd fallen asleep. Let me wash my face, I've got to be back in Harmony's office in ten minutes. Well done, people, keep looking." And he disappeared into his office while Millie and Bobbick counted softly to each other. At the count of thirty, Griffin exploded out still pulling on his coat, and was gone.

There was an ironhaired woman in Harmony's office. It took Alex a moment to place her. "Ms. Metesky," he said with an unconscious bowing motion. He took the chair next to her, nodded his greeting to Harmony. "Where are we?"

Harmony brooded before answering. "Alex, I'm still not sure how this is going to hit you."

"If it's a good one, I'll go with it." Alex crossed his legs and sat back. *All right, let's see how much trouble I'm in . . .*

"It goes like this. Until the South Seas Treasure Game breaks up, we have all our suspects in one place. They don't know that we've narrowed our search to Gaming A. Our legal department has notified me that we can proceed on our own initiative as long as all suspects are made available for questioning after the Game is over. Ms. Metesky understands the severity of the situation, and has already spoken to the Lopezes concerning my proposal. To save the Game, they have consented."

"To what?"

An ironic smile tugged at the corners of Harmony's mouth, and his voice was more soothing than ever. "I want you to join the Game, Alex. It is scheduled to last another three days and some hours. We hope that in that time you can identify the killer, and perhaps even find the missing sample. Of course you'll get special compensation for this unusual duty, but I'm sure that the main attraction will be the chance to handle the situation ourselves."

Oh, brother! Still, crazy as it sounded— "It sounds better than just turning it over to the State Police. I never liked that."

Harmony was delighted; his face and hands became animated to the point of nervous tic. "Good, good. We'll insert you into the Game as Dream Park's optional player. In this context, your fantasy identity is more important than a cover story about your outside life, and we'll have one drawn up for you. The Lopezes will keep us informed of their game plan, and so we'll know where and when to insert you into the Game, hopefully within the first few hours of today's play. Metesky, you work for us, so I expected you'd approve our request. How did the I.F.G.S. representative react?"

"Myers didn't like it. He felt that the Game was more

important than, as he put it," and Metesky's voice became an unexpectedly and wickedly accurate imitation of Myers' painfully precise diction, " 'a little petty thievery.' He hardly seemed to understand the importance of solving the crime." She looked down at her folded hands as she said, "When they've been at this too long, they forget that dying can cost you more than points. Maybe that's *just* what some people want to forget . . . In any case," she looked up, "Myers agreed to extend the sanction of the I.F.G.S. after I guaranteed minimum disruption of the Game, and threatened to close the Game instantly if he didn't."

"So the Game is on."

"Afoot," Griffin said softly. "I'm going to need a briefing on Gamesmanship, although I assume Lopez won't be trying to kill me off . . . ?"

But Metesky was shaking her head, her gray locks rippling around her shoulders. "I'm afraid that's out of the question. You will have the same chance of being killed out of the Game as any other player. To conduct this in any other way would be disruptive to the Game, as well as a dead give-away to the other players. You will play as a novice, and we'll give you a set of characteristics that will serve you fairly well. The rest will be up to you. If you are forced out of the Game, I imagine we'll have to shut it down at once. The Fantasy Gaming Society will withdraw their sanction if there is any tampering with the odds of a Game, and the Lopezes won't run it without I.F.G.S. support, so there you have it."

"Just great. I have to stay in the Game and solve the crime at the same time." He closed his eyes tightly. "I'm going to need a transceiver to stay in touch with my staff. Any new developments might be more than professionally interesting."

Harmony seemed confused. "What do you mean by that?"

He couldn't really have missed that point, could he? Alex said, "We've been assuming that Rice died by accident. If he didn't, or even if he did, and our thief becomes aware that he's being hunted for murder . . . well, I could lose more than experience points." Griffin seemed on the brink of saying more, then shook his head and stood up. "It's nine-thirty now, so the Game's been going for ninety minutes already. I think I'd better get ready. Where do I go from here?"

"Gaming Central for costuming and briefing. As soon as Lopez makes a kill, we will insert you into the Game." Harmony pushed himself up from his chair and shook Griffin's extended hand. "Good luck, Alex. We're counting on you."

Alex waited until the office door had closed behind to release a soft, amazed whistle. "Of all the cockamamie ideas I've ever heard . . ." Then, that one moment of doubt voiced and behind him, he headed for the elevator, his mind filled with variables and unknowns.

Chapter Twelve

OVERVIEW

Myers was adamant. His little black eyes focused down to points. "All right, the snake was justified. I still say that the bird attack was uncalled for, beyond anticipation, and possibly a non-organic part of the Game structure you are building."

Richard Lopez regretfully pulled his attention away from the Game, secure in the knowledge that Mitsuko could cover any problems.

"Listen, Myers, I run my Games by the book. Melanesian magic is naturalistic. What I mean by that is that its structure is designed to explain natural phenomena: crop shortages, disease, weather peculiarities, luck in hunting, and so forth. They explain all of this with a series of myths concerning gods and spirits. Some of them were once men or animals, but in dying they became operative on a higher plane. Human beings gain power through wealth, knowledge, age, social position, or the help of spirits.

"*Now:* Pigibidi was the most respected elder in the village, and *therefore* a powerful magician. Clearly the village is under assault by unnamed enemies. Clearly the enemy is skilled in sorcery. Pigibidi, an old man, went into a dancing frenzy intended to impress the visiting wizards and warriors. He pushed himself too far and weakened himself physically, and that weakened his psychic powers as well. He himself formed one of the most formidable barriers against outside attack. When he passed out, the Daribi became vulnerable. The rest of it follows from that."

Myers was unimpressed. "And you think that Henderson should have followed that line of reasoning?"

"Not at all," Lopez said in a voice he usually reserved for children. "How many people were killed in that attack?"

Myers frowned. "None of the Gaming party, but . . ."

"No buts. How many were seriously wounded?"

"None, but I don't see . . ."

"You're supposed to see, dammit! Myers, don't you find it unusual that there wasn't even a serious wound among the whole lot? It was a warm-up. Henderson needed an opportunity to blood his group, and I need to teach him some of the rules of my universe. Don't worry. When the real fireworks start, any nasties I come up with will have clear precedent in prior Game encounters. There will be no valid protests from Mr. Henderson, I think." Lopez turned back to his console.

As he did, Mitsuko visibly relaxed at her controls. They each had their own keyboard, and individual sets of foot controls for the viewfields. Within easy reach were additional controls that regulated conditions in the control room itself. At the moment, a single hologram floated above and slightly in front of the central control board.

It was the Daribi village. All of the Gamers were present, and packed to go. The council of elders was present, along with the blanket-swaddled Pigibidi. Richard cocked his head, and Mitsuko nudged a sliding indicator, and the sound rose to audible levels.

"—leaving now," Henderson was saying to Gunperson. He seemed chipper and alert. Maibang was at his elbow, wearing khaki shorts and shirt and carrying a backpack.

Pigibidi, a sickly figure nursed by two young attendants, spoke a string of unintelligible words filled with long vowels. Maibang translated. "He says that he is dying. He must tell you something that he feared to say before."

Chester pursed his lips speculatively. "Can't his enemies get to him in the hereafter?"

Lopez immediately bent forward and whispered into the goosenecked microphone projecting from the top of his keyboard. "Tell him that Pigibidi's ancestors are strong enough to protect his spirit, if not his body."

Maibang scratched his ear. "Although the powers of our departed ancestors are limited upon this plane, they assure the soul of Pigibidi a welcome resting place among the heroes. In life, he fears only for the village. In death, he needs fear nothing."

"I see."

Mitsuko diddled a dial and Pigibidi's face broke out in a sheen of sweat. He was in obvious torment. Saliva drooled from the corner of the wrinkled mouth, and when he coughed there was a deep-seated moistness to it that was decidedly unpleasant. He tried to sit up, and the two young men helped him. His mouth framed words in English.

"You find . . . find them. They . . . Foré."

There was a gasp from the assembled villagers, and Pigibidi's body shook as if a string of firecrackers was exploding in his stomach. Chester Henderson called to the other Gamers. "Do not say that word! Don't mumble it, don't whisper it. We can't use that word during Game time!"

His attendants tried to steady Pigibidi, but they could do nothing. Their leader howled in torment. His eyes rolled back into his head until they were glistening white orbs shot with red and yellow. He bit through his lower lip; blood trickled down his chin.

Someone whose back was to the camera pointed an unsteady hand at the dying Pigibidi's abdomen. It was collapsing from within. As it did, the trickle of blood became a torrent. His muscles locked in a final spasm, and he was dead.

A mournful wailing filled the air. The villagers began falling to their knees to clutch at the dirt in sorrow. Kasan Maibang remained standing, his dark face darker still with pain and rage. "This will be avenged. The spirit forces of our enemy have eaten Gun-person's liver, but we shall slay them to the man." He raised his arms in invocation, voice quavering with holy wrath. "Hear me, men of the Daribi! These brave and powerful strangers come to fight our fight for us. They will need bearers, guides, and friends. Who among you will come with us to help?"

Mitsuko leaned to her mike. "Let's not get too dramatic, Harvey. Just say the lines."

Maibang scratched his ear, doing a good job of hiding a grin. Mrs. Lopez covered the microphone and giggled.

Myers asked, "Harvey?"

"Harvey Wayland. Isn't he good? I found him in a student production of *Illuminatus* at USC eleven years ago. We use him as often as we can."

In the projection field, three strong young men had joined the ranks of the Gamers. They were dressed in native garb of woven fiber. Chester was questioning Maibang, but as if he already suspected the answers. "Why the birds last night? Why did Pigibidi die like that?"

"We are in a continuous battle against the forces of our foes," Maibang explained. "The elders of our people are our first line of defense. Gun-person was our greatest power. When age and exhaustion sapped his strength, the barrier was breached."

Chester nodded. "And the liver? What could do that? Some kind of worm?"

"No. Very bad thing. Izibidi. Ghost people."

"Ghosts. 'bidi' suffix means person or people . . ." Chester was talking to himself. His voice rose to more audible levels. "Our enemies can control the spirits of their dead?"

Maibang shook his head. "Not control. They are allies. They cooperate."

"Do the spirits of your dead cooperate with you?"

"They may, if the call is strong enough. I have the knowledge, but not the power."

"Then we'll get along fine. We have the power, and I'm getting the knowledge a little piece at a time . . ." Henderson's voice was drifting away again, and Gina's hand on his shoulder pulled him out of it. "Right, hon. All right, let's clear out of here before something uncuddly pops up. Mary-em, I want you up front with me. Ollie and Bowan in the rear. The rest of you, eyes open, I think the gloves are off."

The troop shouldered their packs, and with a last backward glance at Pigibidi's hideously twisted body, moved off in an orderly line. As soon as they were out of sight, Mitsuko's private viewscreen flashed to a patch of jungle, where the Gamers were coming into view. Richard's screen stayed with the village. At a flick of his finger, Pigibidi's body, the two retainers, and the silent elders vanished. He spoke into the mike. "Attention. This portion of the Game is over. Those of you who are scheduled for the Agaiambo sequence should report to makeup immediately. The rest of you, thank you for excellent performances." The two dozen 'native' men, women and children gave themselves a round of applause.

Silent electric trams buzzed through the underbrush, and workmen bustled out to dismantle the village. About half the actors got onto trams, which moved them quickly away. Some of the others began walking; others waited for the second run.

The holo dissolved, and Richard Lopez spun around in his chair to face Myers. "Our first chance to kill somebody comes in about forty minutes. We've got to get them closer to the swamp first." He drummed his fingers against each other. "You know, I've got this Game stocked with some of the nastiest surprises we've ever come up with, but this is too much like murder, somehow. I don't like it."

"There's no reason for you to feel like that." Myers was soothing. "Accidents, those with positive or negative results, are always part of every Game. If the odds are shifted a bit this time, another player will have the advantage of the counterbalancing good luck. I promise that the Game won't suffer."

Richard looked at the bald man curiously. "Official nitpicker of the I.F.G.S. that you are, Myers, I'm surprised that you agreed to this screwing about at *all*, let alone as

calmly as this." He fingered his small beard reflectively.
"Last year when Henderson threw a tantrum about a few
little snow vipers, you were the first one to start waving the
rule book in my face, screaming infraction. When I was
cleared of any fouling, you were instrumental in forcing me
into a face-to-face with the aforementioned Loremaster, in
the interest of 'fair play.' Why are you now playing lap dog
for Dream Park?"

Myers purpled a bit, and Mitsuko threw her husband a
worried glance. Myers said, "Shall I call Ms. Metesky and
tell her that you find Dream Park's terms unacceptable?
She would halt the Game immediately, of course. This
would be inconvenient and embarrassing to all concerned,
and, I might add, expensive to you. Exactly how much of
your personal capital is invested in the South Seas Treasure Game?"

"A lot," Lopez conceded. He looked up to Myers from
behind beetled brows. "I'm relieved to find you so interested in my welfare."

Myers bristled. "I've said all that I need to say—"

"More," Lopez corrected him gently.

"I'm going back to the observation room. Goodby,
ma'am," he said to Mitsuko. She turned and flashed him a
brilliant smile, which he could not make himself return. He
departed, spine rigid.

Mitsuko reached out her left hand to her husband, and
he took it warmly, chuckling to himself. Then his expression sobered.

The control room door opened again, and Metesky
entered. "My goodness, what did you say to Myers?
There was a storm cloud following him out of the room."

"I'm afraid that my husband expresses displeasure
perhaps too skillfully."

Lopez looked sheepish. "I didn't really mean to be nasty with Arlan. I just dislike people messing with my Games."

"I know, Richard. I'm sorry, but there has been a murder."

"Dammit, there are a hundred murders a day in this state, but only one Game a year. Why can't they leave me alone to do my work?" He sighed. "All right, all right. I'll cooperate. You'll get your sword fodder."

"Thank you, Richard."

Metesky folded a cot out of the wall and sat, fascinated. Richard and Mitsuko were far more interesting than other Game Masters, most of whom were either sallow scholars or ex-Gamers so deeply immersed in their fantasy worlds that their motivations were nearly incomprehensible, and their conversations completely so.

But like any professionals at the top of their field, the Lopezes were exceptional. Bright, imaginative, personable and often irascible, Richard contrasted with his wife, the better known of the pair. Mitsuko was always reserved, never displaying more of her talent than necessary. As people, they were interesting. As Game Masters, they were spellbinding. Metesky had watched them conduct the hornbill attack. During these sequences, when the computer-animated holograms had to attack and respond in the most lifelike of fashions, the Lopezes were one mind with twenty fingers. The illusion they created was complete: no one ever seemed to notice that only two or three of the birds were actually attacking at any moment; the rest were in the air, in a holding pattern. It was marvelous the way Richard would take a bird out of its automatic figure-eight and bring it to life with the sure hand of a master puppeteer, flying it with double-toggle controls and foot pedals.

It was like watching a duet on a synthesizer keyboard. With something close to awe in her heart, Metesky watched them.

The group had been trudging through the bushes for some time before the terrain began to change. The bushes gave way to vines and creepers, and the soil was becoming damp and sticky. Maibang chose their path more carefully now. He and the warrior Kagoiano were in the lead, and they looked worried.

Chester's voice crackled into the room. "Gina! Let's have a sweep of this area. What exactly do we have here?"

Richard sat back and whispered to Metesky. "Chi-Chi can always pick up on a Magic request faster than I can. I'm not totally sure how she does it." He glanced into the hologram. Gina was swathed in green, and her eyes were closed. Mitsuko listened carefully to Gina's invocation.

When her fingers touched the keyboard they fairly disappeared into a pink blur, the keys beeping softly at machine speed as she fed her request into the computer. A shadow-image of a steel locker appeared floating before Gina, and vanished a few seconds after she opened her eyes.

The Loremaster nodded. "Good. We're very close to something interesting. I want Garret up front, we may need a Cleric." A dark face separated itself from the rest of the group.

"Are we going to need protection, Chester?"

"Some of us might. We'll need to recover that chest, whatever it is, and that probably means an Engineer. If it does, he'll need protection all right."

Richard muttered to himself about the sharpness of the holo image, and when Chester called for a trail indicator, the Game Master handled it personally. He manipulated the image of the chest until it was translucent but dead clear. The image floated ahead of the group and led them to a stand of trees growing in moist, spongy earth. The trees were thin-boled, with spidery branches and sparse leaves. The roots twisted about on the surface for a few feet before disappearing underground. The chest image sank into a tangle of roots.

Chester looked at the patch of trees speculatively, and raised his right arm. "Reveal to me hostile or malignant spirit forces!" His green glow expanded to a field twenty meters across, and in its light there were dim, writhing shapes, little more than wisps of fog. They retreated from the light.

"Right," he muttered. "S. J., front and center." There was a whoop, and the youngster materialized at Henderson's shoulder, breathing heavily. "We have some treasure to recover, and it's between those trees. What do you suggest, Engineer?"

Grinning, S. J. walked quickly around the stand; probed into the soil with his boot toe; nudged the roots. "I don't think it would take long to dig through this stuff. These trees aren't from New Guinea, that's for sure. They look like something from the Matto Grosso. My bet is that the Army didn't spray them with fungicide before they planted 'em. They look like they have root rot."

"Would you try to stay in character, please, Engineer?"

Richard Lopez gritted his teeth. "Little bastard. We'll have to cut that out of the final tape. I'd *love* to kill him out of the Game right about now."

Metesky's voice was sharp. "We can juggle the odds in the computer, Richard, but you can't choose the victim. You just have to see which way it goes."

"I can wish out loud, can't I, Metesky? That S. J. character just rubs me the wrong way."

S. J. had broken a folding shovel out of his pack, and

was digging industriously. Eames, never one to miss a chance to flex his muscles, chopped away at the exposed roots.

Chester watched them dig. In the control room, Richard lounged back in his chair and watched Chester think. Neither spoke, until the Lore Master softly said, "Garret . . ."

The Cleric quickly crossed himself and dropped to his knees in prayer. Mitsuko's fingers flew over her keyboard, and an instant later a soft, golden glow surrounded the young Engineer.

S. J.'s shovel struck metal, and Eames got down into the hole to help. They shifted the remaining soil with their hands. With a gasping wrench they tore it free. Chester stalled them for the few seconds that it took to cast a Reveal Danger spell on the corroding steel chest, and when the glow showed only green, he told them to go ahead. Richard heard a certain reluctance in his voice. He smiled.

Jimmying the rusted padlock was easy for S. J., who seemed to have brought a tool for all occasions. He set the blunt folding edge of the shovel against a screwdriver-like implement and pounded it into the thin line where the halves of the lock met. It split into three pieces, and the Gamers cheered. Taking a cautious step back, the youngster lifted the lid.

"All right," he breathed. "Guns."

There were four holstered handguns, two rifles and at least a hundred rounds of ammunition. There was also what looked like Army-issue canned food: turkey rolls, Spam, and tinned pound cake. S. J. was ecstatic. "Cargo! Yee-hah!"

Even Chester seemed pleased. "Very good. That's not

a lot of points, but it's definitely a start. S. J., we're going to intensify the protective field around you while you test them."

"Gotcha, Chief."

"Gwen, would you please add your prayer to Garrett's?" She had scarcely nodded before the green glow appeared around her, and the golden glow around S. J. deepened until it seemed that he was in the center of an amber gem.

He picked up a revolver, worked its action a few times, and thumbed in a cartridge. He sighted carefully on a tree some twenty meters away, and pulled the trigger. There was a deafening report, but no puff of dust from the tree. Frowning, he loaded in two more rounds and pulled the trigger again. The same loud bang, and no sign of a hit.

"Ah, S. J., what is your character's coordination rating, anyway?"

"Lousy. Eleven. That's why I'm an Engineer. I'll try a closer tree."

This time dust puffed from the tree trunk. This was hardly surprising; he'd fired at point-blank range. "Okay, who wants this one?" Tony's raised arm caught his eye. He handed the revolver over butt first.

Next he extracted the rifle from the box. "M-1," he murmured. "Nice." He worked the trigger a couple of times, then loaded in one of the bullets and sighted on a rock ten meters away. He squeezed the trigger.

The gun roared and flamed, and there was the zinging sound of a ricochet. S. J. ducked instinctively. "Jesus—"

The air in front of them shimmered, and a ghostly image of Garret appeared. Chester cursed venomously and Garret groaned, looking at the shimmering red splotch spreading on his shirt.

"Aw, *shit!*" he said with real feeling. His legs buckled under him and he sprawled in an untidy heap, mouth open, eyes rolled up in his head.

"Nice fall," Richard muttered. He tapped two keys.

Garret's hologram double crooked a spectral finger to him.

"Wait a minute," Chester said. "Gwen, do you think you have enough for a saving spell?"

The blond girl's cheeks plumped with worry. "Right now? I'm not sure. If that was a natural accident, maybe. If there were spirit powers involved . . . I'll try." Unhappily, Gwen raised her arms and began her invocation. "Hear me, O Gods. Harness my strength and give this man back his life. By the powers which are mine to wield, I ask this." She sank to her knees and bowed her head, eyes closed.

Lopez nodded, smiling respectfully. "Well done. I wonder if it will work." He watched Mitsuko feed the request into the computer. Electrons danced; a random number was selected and matched against two logged Wessler-Grahm numbers, Garret's assigned stamina and Gwenevere's power level . . . Lopez shook his head as the rosy aura around Garrett faded to a sooty tinge in the air. "No good. Sorry, sweetheart." He tapped a key.

Garret jerked at the shock from his neck tab. He rolled over and stood up to confront his *tindalo*. "Well, I guess that's it, huh? Guess I didn't last too long in *this* Game." He started to say something else, and it would have been bitter. Gwen squeezed his shoulder with one soft hand, and he turned to follow the somber ghost. The two figures left the projection field.

Richard's face was no happier. Metesky saw a flash of deep resentment before it was submerged behind a neutral mask. One dark slender finger played with the end of his mustache, and his eyes were half-lidded. "All right. You've got your killing. Put the watchdog on, and let me do my work."

The Dream Park liaison stood and started to leave. "Metesky!" he yelled at her back. "Tell the watchdog that if he screws with my Game, I'll kill him out of it so fast his nose will bleed, and hang the consequences!" He saw her silent nod, and spun his chair back to the console.

Mitsuko watched Metesky leave, heard the door sigh shut behind her. Then she flexed her fingers gently and went back to her work.

PART TWO

Chapter Thirteen

ENTER THE GRIFFIN

"We can't use these guns, Chester." For the first time in the Game, S. J. looked unhappy. "They've got to be jinxed. If what's-her-name . . . Gwen couldn't save Garret, there has to be magic involved." His blond hair was limp with sweat and greasy with dirt. He looked tired and discouraged.

Chester tapped his foot in impatient rhythm. Unconscious of Gina's hand stroking his arm, he stalked angrily to the chest and glared in. "We paid blood for these things, and we're going to have them. Maibang, front and center." He snapped his fingers angrily.

Maibang, his khakis blotched with sweat after the march, appeared at Chester's side. Henderson thought carefully before speaking. "Now listen. We know that Gwen couldn't reverse the accident, but she was temporarily drained by the protective field she cast for S. J. We

169

need to disarm this booby-trap, and I don't want to try one
of our spells until I know the alternatives. I remember
reading something about your magic. There is a ritual,
something about a table, but I can't remember it. Do you
know?"

"I know the table ritual. Which of my people would not?
I don't know if it will be enough."

"We'll try it anyway." Chester looked around at the
thirteen Gamers and the three natives, nodding when
there were no objections. "All right. Kasan, what do we
do?"

Their guide scratched his head. "We need a table, first,
and a clean white cloth, and some gifts. Food is best. And
flowers, of course."

"S. J.?" Chester said without looking at the youngster.

"Covered, Chief. I can whip up a three-legger in a few
minutes using branches."

"Good. Dreager, help him. As for the gifts, I think that
the gods have already provided that . . ." He picked up
one of the cans of tinned meat.

The table was crude, but serviceable. Dark Star had
donated a white skirt, which was spread as a tablecloth.
Gwen's candles, normally used for exorcisms, burned in
the center. Bandanas and knives and spoons from various
backpacks made do as place settings, napkins and silver-
ware. Arrayed upon the table were all of the cans of food
from the buried chest, two of Oliver's tropical chocolate
bars, some beef jerky from Dark Star's larder, and flowers
gathered by the rest of the crew.

"We are ready to perform the *bilasim tewol*," Chester
said. His voice held no trace of doubt or uncertainty.
"Kasan will assist me, but it is my power that beckons.

Hear me O Gods, hear me Jesus-Manup. We strive for your people. I know that our actions are righteous in your sight. Do not let our brave priest's death be a useless one. We are desperate with need, yet we destroy vital supplies to demonstrate our faith."

On cue, Bowan the Black said, "Fire!" The aura around his right hand blazed from green to red; flame shot forth to touch the table. Like the Biblical burning bush, the jerky and chocolate and aging tin cans blazed up without being consumed, and without scorching the robe.

"We have shown our faith. Give us now that which we need to harness the strength in these weapons." Henderson was still speaking when the air began to shimmer. Three ghosts took shape: translucent caucasians in jungle camouflage uniforms. Their faces were pasty, and one of them bore a gruesome open slash along the side of his face, a machete wound, perhaps.

"Who are you?" Chester demanded imperiously. There was a moaning crackle of sound, and one of the three worked its mouth without words. Finally noises came from the withered throat.

"We're . . . your kind . . ."

"Americans, yes. How did you die?"

The one with the machete-scar answered this time, coughing out his words in jerky phrases. "We died to take . . . the Cargo back. You'll die too. All of you. You . . ." There was a pause, and the pale and whiskery dead mouth worked wordlessly until sound stuttered forth again. "You don't know what you're up against."

"Help us," the Lore Master demanded. "You must. Give us the guns."

"The guns were ours—" The gaping slit in the spirit's face began to bleed dark sludge. "But the Foré stole a secret weapon. It might have beat . . . the Japs . . . if it hadn't come so late. Now the Foré have it. We were sent with guns to take it back. Guns! No damn use against magic. We died in this . . . stinking jungle . . . but in our last breaths we cursed the guns. Cursed them . . . so that they'll kill anyone who uses them."

"Remove the curse. We need them. With them, we will win you your vengeance."

The spirits seemed to confer with each other, then Machete-Wound answered their request. "You're being . . . stupid. You'll see. But we were . . . stupid too. You can have your . . . heroes' deaths. Take the guns. Kill as many Foré . . . as you can . . . before you die . . ." The spirits faded with the voice. A final "Give 'em hell . . ." hung in the vacant air.

Chester cast a precautionary "Reveal danger" spell before giving the go-ahead. Gina was sympathetic. "You forgot to check the guns themselves, last time, Ches. After the outside of the box showed green you didn't worry about it."

"You're right. But that's the last easy point Lopez is getting from me, you can count on that!"

Tony and S. J. carried handguns now. Kagoiano had one of the rifles, and Dark Star carried the other slung over one freckled shoulder. The other two handguns were packed neatly away. "Let's move," Chester called out, and the column moved on.

McWhirter slapped the pistol at his side heartily as he moved up next to Oliver. "You know, I feel like a new man with this thing on my side. Um—the bullets aren't real, are they? I mean, those shots looked awfully real to me."

Oliver seemed a little irritated. "No, they're not real. But it's still not a good idea to set one off next to somebody's ear. Even a blank can hurt your eardrums."

"Right." He watched Gwen's hand find its way to Oliver's arm, and jealousy showed in his face. His eyes flicked back toward Acacia, who guarded the rear with Alan Leigh.

Ollie caught it. "You know, those bullets aren't real, but I know something that is, and you're playing with it right now."

Tony pursed his mouth. He didn't need to ask what the chunky warrior meant.

"Listen, Tony—"

"Fortunato, thank you. You're Oliver, I'm Fortunato, right? And we're off to steal what sounds like an atomic bomb, an experimental one at that. All crazies in *this* camp."

"Go ahead, play games with her feelings, Tony. She may have hurt your feelings last night, but it wasn't on purpose, and she thought she was doing you a favor. You're hurting her on purpose."

Tony brushed a springy branch out of his face as he walked, and said, "The ground's really getting marshy. We'll have to watch for quagmires."

Oliver was disgusted. "All right, *Fortunato*. I just don't see how your *macho* could be wounded all that badly."

"Watch out for snakes."

Gwen released Oliver's arm and stretched out a hand for Tony. He skittled out of her reach, but he was grinning now. She stuck her tongue out at him and snuggled back up against Oliver.

Tony set his long chin bravely and dropped back in line to where Acacia kept vigilant watch, her hand never straying far from her sword. She pretended not to notice him.

"How goes the rear guard, Panthesilea?" he asked nonchalantly. She made a noncommittal sound, studiedly looking the other way. He matched strides with her for several steps, trying to read her expression. "Listen, hon, I'm sorry about last night." She flickered an eyelash in his direction, and he was encouraged. "My pride just got hurt a little, that's all. Hey, it's hell being a man. The burden of carrying my ego around everywhere I go is enough to make me old before my time. Hey, Panth, at least look at a poor soul when he's humbling himself before you."

"I don't think you can keep up with us on your knees, so just keep walking. I guess I'll get over it." The frost was thawing, but there was still a distinct coolness in her voice.

"Believe me—mind if I take your arm? I mean, it's not doing anything right now, and looked kind of lonely—I'll make it up to you. Tonight, if you'll let me."

At first there was no real response, then he felt an answering inward pressure from her arm. "Is that right?"

"You bet. Moonlight, soft breezes, and a warm bedroll. Mosquitoes courtesy of Cowles Industries."

She raised an eyebrow skeptically. "Not like last night, eh?"

"So I was off sulking in the bushes. Sorry about that. You weren't in *your* hut last night either."

"Well, in case you haven't noticed, there are some very attractive men on this expedition." She fluttered her eyelashes at him. "*Very* attractive. Some of whom know how to treat a lady."

"When they can find one—just kidding. Aw, Cas, you know I can't handle this kind of thing very well. What say we call it a truce."

"Agreed." She slipped her hand down to his, and squeezed, feeling a little knot of tension dissolve in her stomach. Her newfound feeling of relaxation brought an automatic smile to her face, and Tony pointed at it.

"Now what's that for?"

She gave him a little-girl laugh, wishing there was somewhere that they could go to curl up together and get it out of their systems.

"By the way," Tony said thoughtfully, "Where *were* you last night?"

A shout from the front nullified that question. Tony's hand found its way to his holstered pistol in a blink, and he had to run to keep up with Acacia, who was in motion instantly.

The ground was extremely moist, now, and every footstep sank an inch into the muck. Reeds and fernlike plants abounded, and in the areas where water had seeped out of the ground to form puddles, islands of green scum floated. Someone shouted, "Help!" up ahead, and Tony realized that he had heard that cry twice before, too faint to register consciously. Another monster? An attack by the Foré, whatever the hell *they* were?

He almost bumped into Acacia's back, so suddenly did she skid to a halt. She was bent over, trembling, and at first he was afraid for her. Then he heard the laughter and knew it was all right.

A man was stuck up to his waist in quicksand, or the Dream Park equivalent thereof. He was big, with thick shoulders and neck. *Another jock warrior*, Tony bet himself silently. The man had close-cropped red hair and an unsaintly look of irritation on his face. "Get me the hell out of here, will you?"

Chester was laughing, hands on knees, standing as close to the quicksand as he dared. "Well hello there, stranger. I've been expecting you. Who exactly are you, and why should we trouble ourselves to rescue you?"

"I'm the Griffin. I'm the best Thief in the world."

"Excuse *me*." Dark Star tossed her head, bouncing her

short brown hair. "And just how do you think you deserve *that* title, Mr. Titanic? Leave him, Chester."

"Now, now. Let's have no quarreling over matters of rank. We're all equal here, except me of course. Still, her point is well taken. On what grounds rest your claim to greatness? Hurry, now, I do believe you're an inch or so shorter than you were a minute ago."

The man looked down at his waist and grimaced. "Well, I stole the Emerald Eye from the sacred statue of Katmandu."

"Not bad. Anything else?"

The man shifted uncomfortably in the muck. Tony reflected that the stuff must itch like crazy. "I filched the Silken Bellows from the temple of Kosell the Wind God."

"My. That must have been exciting." Chester covered a yawn. "If you've never done anything bigger than that, we may have to lend you a snorkel."

"All right. Last try. I have the only existing black market print of *Star Wars.*"

"Woops." Chester paused respectfully. "A slight anachronism, seeing as we're in New Guinea circa 1955 or so, but the point is well made. We'll get you out, S. J., you've earned a rest. Where's our other Engineer? Let's get Rudy Draeger out here."

Draeger, a short stout man with a bulky backpack and a sunburn-red complexion, hustled out and began taking mental measurements. His voice was a squeak. "No really solid trees to use as a pulley, so I'll need some help with the line. Eames, would you be kind enough? Thank you."

Eames looked miffed to be thanked before he had consented, but he stepped forward and took the end of the thin nylon line Draeger offered him. The chunky little man threw the other end to the trapped Thief, who wound the end of it round one wrist and held on with the other hand.

The procedure was clumsy but effective, and with an obscene sucking sound, he came free of the mire.

The Thief wiped his leather trousers partly clear of mud and smiled cynically. "I guess after an introduction like that I'd better be worth it."

"He's a mind reader, Chester," Dark Star sniffed.

Chester hushed her with a look. "You aren't who I was expecting, so I assume you're a guest of the Dream Gods?"

"Well put. I can promise to pull my weight, though."

Dark Star scratched one of her stubby ears. "Do you expect us to share our supplies with you?"

"Ray of sunshine, aren't you? It so happens that I know the location of a substantial quantity of supplies." He paused for effect, then added, "Including a couple of six-packs."

All reservation dissolved in that instant. Oliver shook his hand heartily. "Glad to meet you. My name's Oliver. What's yours?"

"Griffin."

"All right, Griffin. Let's find your supplies and break for lunch."

Chester looked at his watch, then squinted up at the "sun" that burned on the inner surface of the covering dome. "If I were a sundial I'd say it was three o'clock or so, but I know it's only eleven-thirty. Somebody's collapsing time on us and I wonder why . . .?" The last words were almost under his breath, and Chester shook himself back to alertness. "Fall in with Mary-em. She'll protect you until we see what you can do."

"*Her* protect *me*?" There was an incredulous edge to Griffin's voice, broken off as small strong fingers dug into his arm.

"Come on, handsome. If Mary-em has to nursemaid

somebody, at least you've got a decent body to guard."
She crinkled an eye at him speculatively. "Naw," she said
finally.

Griffin tried to fix a friendly, or failing that, at least a
neutral expression on his face. "Well, let's go."

"Let's."

"The goods are about a hundred meters that way—" he
pointed toward a slightly less marshy stretch of ground,
and the Gamers headed in that direction, eagerly.

"My name is Acacia," the dark-haired girl said, sitting
down next to him. "But you can call me Panthesilea."

"A chrysanthemum by any other name . . ." he
grinned at her, and downed a forkful of pork and beans.
His feet were bare, socks and shoes laid out in the sun to
dry.

A lantern-jawed man with shaggy black hair staggered
up the slope with a beer in either hand. The foam plastic
"cans" had been suspended in a shadowed pool of water,
and were pleasantly cool . . . cooler than the water, in
fact. The newcomer said, "I'm Tony McWhirter." He
tossed a can to Acacia, who caught it neatly. "Dark Star
and I are the other Thieves on the expedition." He
plopped himself down next to Acacia, sighed with con-
tentment, then ducked as she playfully sprayed him with
beer foam.

Griffin asked, "Have you been on many of these?"

"Nope. This is my first one. The lovely lady dragged me
along. You?"

"My first time too. I supervise Gavagan's Bar. It's one of
the Dream Park restaurants. That's what got me in."

"That old demon wanderlust got to you, huh?"

"Something like that. These people kept stumbling into

the place, dirty, exhausted, grinning all over their faces. I finally had to find out what it was like." Griffin was quoting the real Gary Tegner almost word for word. He knew Gavagan's well enough, and he'd found the time to talk to the Gavagan's Bar manager for nearly half an hour.

He'd been very busy these last few hours. Someone else had packed the backpack he had found waiting with the beer. Presently he'd have to search through it, to see if anything had been forgotten . . .

Tony regarded Griffin's shoulders and arms casually, noting the way small muscles bunched and writhed in the man's forearms as he turned his fork. "You know, I would have thought a man like you would want to be a Warrior."

"Don't like blood. I like skulking about in dark corridors, and outwitting the forces of justice. You?"

"Thief is what my Wessler-Grahm came out to. As a fighter, I wouldn't have lasted more than a minute against the oversized turkeys yesterday."

Acacia laughed and touched Tony's arm lightly. Oliver chimed in. Griffin scooted over a couple of inches and patted the ground next to him. Oliver sat down, followed by Gwen. Griffin asked, "How did you do?"

"Against the big birds? Not bad. I didn't kill one by myself, but I crippled two of them, and somebody else finished them off. Not a whole lot for my individual points, but the group points will be good, so I'm not worried about it. I'm worried about my little darlin' here." Gwen snuggled her back against his; she was facing the other way, pretending not to listen to the conversation. "She hasn't really had a chance to strut her stuff yet."

Now Gwen turned around. "Don't worry about me. What about Tony and Dark Star? There hasn't been any call for Thieves at all."

"Aha." Griffin chewed for a bit, then explained. "I've been wondering why she came on so strong. Really attacked me."

Acacia agreed readily. "Yes, you're probably right. This expedition has been a field day so far for Warriors and Wizards. Not too shabby for Engineers either. I think Dark Star is worried about her points." She tsked condescendingly.

"May I assume that you and the lady in question aren't on the best of terms?"

"We aren't on any terms at all. I just don't warm to her, that's all. Don't know exactly why, except that I seem to remember something about her cheating in a Game." Acacia seemed suddenly alarmed. "Don't tell her I said that, though, okay?"

"Scout's honor."

"I could be wrong anyway."

There was a cry from a group of Gamers a few feet away. Gina Perkins was dragging something that looked like an old-fashioned set of sleepers. It rustled like snakeskin.

Gwen tugged Oliver to his feet and they ran over to inspect the thing. Tony followed a second later. "Oliver and Gwen," Griffin said to Acacia, "those two are pretty well inseparable, aren't they?"

"Absolutely. Why do you ask?" She licked the last bit of gravy from her stew can.

Griffin stood up and stretched lazily. "Oh, I don't know. Maybe I think she's kind of cute." He extended a hand to her and pulled her up.

"She's adorable," the dark girl granted. "But is she really your type?"

"And who might be more my type, hmm?" If Griffin had

been standing four inches closer, they would have been kissing.

Acacia turned and pointed to the woman who had found the curious artifact. "Oh, I don't know. How about Gina?" She smiled at him over her shoulder. "She's with Chester, but she's been known to forget that. I hear." She started toward the group of Gamers, and Griffin followed close behind.

Business first, Alex. He shut his grin down to a bare smirk.

At first he couldn't believe his eyes. Unmistakably, Henderson was holding up a complete human skin: hollow, dry, dark brown, flapping in the air like long underwear hung up to dry.

"What the hell is *that?*" Griffin asked.

"Either random magic, or . . ." Henderson was thoughtful. "I seem to remember something about a legend of men who shed their skins . . ."

S. J. looked at it closely. "Oh-oh." His head snapped from side to side. "Where are our bearers?"

Kogoiano stepped forward promptly. So did Kibugonai, a short stout man with flat features.

Chester bellowed, "Nigorai! Nigoraiiii!"

Maibang shook his head with regret. "I'm afraid that you are holding Nigorai in your hands."

Henderson started, then examined the skin more closely. When he came to a tiny white scar over the left eyehole, he nodded. "I suppose the revolvers he was carrying are gone too."

A quick search confirmed it. "Then he was a spy, a . . . a member of the enemy impersonating a Daribi." He wiped a thin hand across his forehead, and Alex could see that the Lore Master's hand was trembling.

"Faked out again," Acacia whispered at his shoulder. "We've lost points, and now the enemy knows we're coming. He was a spy." He started to throw the skin to the side, then stopped. "No. I'm not going to be stupid again. When lunch break is over I'm going to scan both of our bearers. I'm also keeping this skin. It may come in useful." He folded it carefully and put it in his pack.

As the crowd drifted back to their lunches, Griffin found himself wondering about the only man in the group larger than himself. Eames had sandy red hair and freckles; he looked boyish, and his massive musculature provided an interesting contrast. He seemed to be alone. A single man in the group could have slipped away last night.

Griffin stood with his back to Eames, trying to pick up bits of his conversation with the slender man with the receding hairline and brown braided hair. Leigh, that was his name, Griffin remembered it from the dossier he had studied before joining the Game.

Alan Leigh trailed his hand appreciatively over Eames' shoulders. "You look a little tight there. Muscles need massaging, maybe?" There was a minimum of leer on Alan's face; perhaps his chipmunk cheeks were a bit more in evidence than usual. Out of the corner of his eye, Griffin saw Eames was flinching.

"Look, Alan. I told you last night. It's not that I don't like you as a person, I just don't get into it like that. Really."

Leigh sighed. "What a waste. I could be a big help to you in the Game—"

Wrong thing to say. Eames became palpably hostile. *"Under what circumstances?"*

He was about to say more, but Alan picked up on the feeling and wagged his head. "No, I don't mean that. Really." He smiled sheepishly. "Anyway, we still have three nights left, and you know where to find me."

That was as much as Griffin felt like eavesdropping on, and he turned away. Most of the Gamers had finished eating and were preparing to leave. Griffin had tagged eight Gamers as couples: Chester and Gina, Dark Star and that "Bowan the Black" character, Oliver and Gwen, Acacia and Tony. Acacia seemed to be looking around. All of the other players were singles, and were therefore to be considered first.

Except that the comment about Felicia "Dark Star" Maddox was very interesting. Something to keep an eye out for, while most of the wackos kept their eyes open for dragons and such . . .

Chapter Fourteen

THE WATER PEOPLE

The ground was mushy. Water lapped over the laces on Griffin's boots. Twice he had to stop to shake the water out. The realism was hard to fault. He half-expected to find leeches on his ankles. "Goddam Gamers," he muttered. "Why couldn't this have been a desert game? Or a nice mountain?"

"What was that, Griffy?" a gravelly voice sang in his ear. He shuddered. "You can call me Griffin, or Griff."

"If it makes you happy, but I like Griffy better."

This was insane. He was being nursemaided by a fifty-year-old battleax of a midget who carried a nasty halberd on her back, and continuously sang snatches of dirty songs. If a man had called him "Griffy", teeth would have flown like popcorn. In Mary-em's case, he wasn't sure whether it was amusement or caution that kept his dander

184

down. The woman was as solid as the warrior she pretended to be.

Henderson called the column to a halt. They had
reached the edge of a waterway that stretched in three
directions as far as he could see. It was choked with plants
and floating debris, and subtle disturbances of the surface
suggested living things within. Griffin shuddered. *Realism.*
Henderson conferred with Maibang out of his hearing, and
Alex went back to Mary-em.

"I take it you're a long-time Gamer."

"Oh, yeah."

"How many of the Gamers do you know?" he asked
nonchalantly.

"Y'mean before this Game started?" She scratched her
head thoughtfully. "Well, Chester an' me are old buddies.
Hell, I wetnursed him through his first stretch as a Lore
Master."

"How long ago?"

"Seven years. A jaunt into the Hyborean Age to steal
the Serpent Ring of Set from the finger of Thoth-Amon."
She gave a harsh bark of amusement. "Now *there* was a
pretty bit of thievery for you."

"Difficult, was it?"

"You wouldn't believe it. Chester lost three-fourths of
our party, but the Game Master was penalized by the
I.F.G.S. for running an excessively nasty game."

"I wouldn't have thought you would complain about
anything, Mary."

"Mary-em, Griffy."

"That's Griffin, Mary-em."

There was something moving on the marshy water.
Boats? Boats. Several rude canoes were floating toward
shore. They shimmered and wavered like things of myth,

their pace as slow as the setting of the sun. By now the entire party was standing at the edge of the water, and Griffin peered out, hands shadowing his eyes from the reflected glare of the Dream Park sun.

There were six of the canoes, all large enough for more than the two apiece who were paddling them.

"What's this?"

"Looks suspiciously like transport, Griffin."

"Where are we going?"

She gave him her kindest shut-up-and-see smile and then ignored his question.

Henderson waved greeting to the approaching boatmen. There was no response, and even from a distance Griffin could feel Chester's body go tense. The Lore Master raised his thin arms and performed an invocation. Green light enclosed his body, then streamed across the water to envelop the canoes. When they reflected only green, the Lore Master relaxed and dissolved his spell.

Now the oarsmen were closer. They seemed dead-eyed and unnaturally quiet. Even their paddles were silent as they dipped into the lake.

The lead canoe nosed into the gooey excuse for a shore. Its occupants exchanged greetings with Kasan.

"Do you know him? Our guide?"

Mary-em looked at him curiously. "Not before the Game. Why?"

Griffin cursed himself silently. These surroundings were affecting his professional judgement. He could *not* just line up suspects and quiz them. "I just had the feeling that I'd seen him somewhere before. Funny."

"Why funny? He's bound to be a professional actor. Now will you kindly shut up and let me enjoy the Game?"

She gave him an affectionate elbow-nudge in the gut. Griffin gasped for breath.

She was one of the three. Chester Henderson, Alan Leigh, Mary-Martha Corbett: the three who had explored Gaming Area A on previous Games. Drown it, he *had* to ask her questions. But he didn't have to like it.

Henderson called them all around him. "These folk are the Agaiambo. They are our next link in the chain, and will take us to our rendezvous. Split into groups of three, and get ready to board the canoes."

"You and me?" Griffin asked Mary-em playfully.

"Try getting rid of me, Handsome."

They joined Rudy Dreager, the plump Engineer who had pulled Griffin from the quicksand. They piled in between two silent boatmen.

The paddlers crossed a stretch of clear water, then turned into a channel choked with green and yellow vegetation. It looked like a stagnant canal in the last throes of nutrient strangulation, the vines and roots growing so fast that they kill themselves and the entire eco-system of the waterway.

The going was painfully slow. The lead canoe halted at frequent intervals so that the front paddler could saw vines with a long-handled knife. At last Griffin began to relax. He leaned over to speak to Mary-em, who was humming tunelessly, her sharp little eyes never ceasing their side-to-side sweep of the vegetation.

"How did you get into this, Mary-em?"

"Regular little psychiatrist, aren't you? What do you do on the outside? I mean for work. Very few people can make a living out of prying into other people's business."

"I'm supervisor for Gavagan's Bar in Dream Park." The

lie came surprisingly hard. Masochistically, he forced himself to elaborate: "Most of my job is keeping the food and the service up to par. R&D does the special effects. But letting a customer bend my ear is part of the job too. What about you?"

"Well, I retired myself at thirty-five."

Griffin whistled. "Good going." He trailed his hand in the water, until he remembered the vague stirrings he had seen at the bank of the main body, and pulled it out quickly. "How did you manage that? Lose a toe on the job?"

He felt her tense, and wondered what nerve he'd scraped. "Nothing so dramatic, sonny. Just a little principal called Modular Economics. That means that instead of getting a lot of money for doing one thing, you get little chunks for doing different things well, and you're your own boss. It's flexible, fun, and free. The three F's."

"Sounds good. What do you do well?"

"If your ears were a little dryer I might be convinced to show you. If, however, you mean what do I do for money, I'd have to give you an alphabetical listing."

"A few highlights would do."

"Did you grow them muscles just so you could survive being nosy?" She tickled him, and he coughed to cover his broken giggle of surprise. "I do guide work for rock climbers in Yosemite, and I teach Kendo—"

"You *what*?"

"Let's see. I do a little philately, sculpt bonsai trees half-well, and have been known to pick up a few bucks sewing costumes for Gamers. Want more?"

Griffin swallowed hard. "Jesus. How many of those things do you do well?"

"The Kendo and the rock climbing, mostly. The rest I just picked up."

Alex nodded. He was wondering what such a super-woman was doing playing fantasy games, like a kid . . . but that was obvious enough. Didn't R&D have something on the boards that would let someone like Mary-em play as a statuesque blond? Yeah, he'd heard something about distorted holograms: a process too expensive to use, so far, that would let a man play as a woman or vice versa, or as a dwarf or a giant . . . but he wasn't about to mention it to Mary-em. She'd feed him her halberd.

After what seemed an interminable trip, the canoes drew into a less choked patch of water. Now instead of travelling single file, the five canoes spread out abreast of each other. Presently they pulled up to a rude dock with wooden moorings sunk in the muck.

It didn't look like much, but it was indisputably a village. The foundations were tree trunks that rose out of the swamp five or six feet, and the wooden platforms set atop them looked as stable as any paranoid schizophrenic.

Griffin tied their boat up next to one of the dwellings, and they waded soggily and carefully ashore. The boatmen followed unsteadily, as if walking on ice skates. When the men reached land, Alex could see why; their feet were hideously deformed, scarcely more than misshapen clubs.

Looking around, Alex found that all of the boatmen were similarly crippled. Most were using their paddles as crutches.

He chose not to ask what was going on. A detective should spend some of his time detecting.

They were being led to a central platform. It was set on

firmer ground than the dozen or so thatch-roofed houses grouped around it. Like the others, it too rose several feet above the ground, perhaps to discourage alligators from basking on the front porch. People were coming out of hiding, women and children and older men, and a small contingent of spear-carrying warriors. All were club-footed nearly to disability.

As they reached the central platform, Griffin watched the nightmarishly long shadows of their hobbling companions and suddenly realized that it couldn't be later than two o'clock. But the sun was nearly set! He checked the watch on his cuff. It was quarter past two.

What were the Game Masters planning for tonight, to be bringing the night so early?

The Gamers were directed to a wooden ladder, and one at a time they mounted it. The two bearers waited below.

"Please," Maibang was explaining softly. "The Agaiambo are a boat-people who spend most of their lives in and on the water. They venture onto land rarely. Over the years their feet have shriveled away to what you see. But they are a proud, fierce people, and great allies in our fight. Pay them the respect due to a warrior people who have resisted evil at tremendous cost."

There was a muffled clumping sound, and the ladder shook as it was mounted. A face rose over the edge of the platform, a face incredibly aged and weathered. Only the eyes seemed truly alive: chips of diamond stuck in a withered black apple. The man was supported on one side by a walking stick, and on the other by a woman scarcely younger than he, her empty and wrinkled breasts swaying pendulously with each uncertain step. She helped him to a sitting position but remained standing herself. She held his hand with what Griffin interpreted as protective affection.

The old man mumbled, rubbery lips twitching with palsy, and as he did a thin streak of drool ran glistening to his chin. The woman spoke. After a minute of halting dialog, Maibang translated. "She says that her man is sorry not to greet us in strength, but he is very tired, the fight is not going well. The village of the Agaiambo is too close to the lands of the enemy, and the assaults come more frequently now. The end is near."

The old man experienced a facial spasm, and his lips pulled back from brown stubby teeth. With an enormous effort of will he controlled himself, and mumbled again to his woman. She repeated his words aloud, and Maibang translated. "I am not the leader of the Agaiambo, he says, for the leader has been dead for a week. We placed him in his ku, his exposure coffin, so that the rain and the sun might return his flesh to the earth, and speed his spirit on its way to Dudi, the village of the dead. But our enemy, who had brought death to him in the form of the dreaded Bidi-Taurabo Haza "

Chester interrupted. "Pardon me. I don't mean to be rude, but I may need to know about that. What is this Bidi-Tar-whatever? I know that 'Bidi' means 'man' . . ."

Maibang relayed his request to the old woman, who gave a lengthy reply. "It is the man-ripe-making snake. If you meet its eyes you rot from within."

Chester nodded, murmuring, "Tropical twist on the Gorgon legend."

"Please," Maibang insisted, "this is important. In four days he died, badly swollen and already nearly putrified. His body was placed on the ku. Two days later, he was half rotted. The flesh hung loose on his bones—"

Next to Griffin, McWhirter groaned. "Good Lord. Is this
really necessary?" Acacia had her hand over her mouth.
She looked a little green herself.

"But then his eyelids opened, and in the empty wet
sockets there burned a terrible flame, and the man who
had led us came down from the ku, and with the strength
of ten he decimated us. Not fire, nor spear, nor knife could
slow him, and he killed all who came within his grasp. At
last, desperate, we bound his limbs with snares, cut him in
pieces, and threw the pieces into the swamp. Even that
was not enough, for one of the arms came out of the
swamp and tried to re-enter the village. One of the great
lizards who haunt the water's edge caught the arm and
devoured it."

McWhirter looked dyspeptic. Griffin hid his amusement.

"This is why we are so weak, he says. We have under-
gone many such assaults in past years, and each has taken
its toll. We would not have survived even as long as we
have; but this village is situated on ground holy to both
your gods and ours. Years ago, missionaries came to teach
us of God and Jesus. Not far from here they built a place of
worship. Because we of this village helped supply materials and what labor we could, they blessed our land and
our boats."

The old man had been mumbling to the woman as
Maibang spoke, and she relayed more information to
them. "But now," Maibang continued, "we fear that our
protection is weakening. We know that strange things
have been happening at the old Anglican mission, and that
tonight a sacrifice will take place there, on the altar of your
God. They will desecrate the holy place, and end our
protection. We will be doomed. We are not strong enough

to stop them. You are strong. You have powers. Your world is at stake as much as ours. It is in your hands."

It was slow in coming, but it was there: an almost tangible crackle of emotion in the air, a feeling of shared *purpose* that ran through the adventurers like an electric current. And strangely, unmistakably, Griffin's heart speeded up by a few beats, and he found himself thinking: *this sounds like fun.* Then he remembered who he was and why he was here, and pushed these thoughts aside.

"We can do it. Count on it," Chester said grimly. "Tell Maibang how to get there, if you can't supply us with a guide."

It was very dark now, but a full moon was rising, and it would soon be light enough.

The last few hundred meters the adventurers had traversed as quietly as possible. Griffin watched Mary-em for his cues. The dwarf-woman was deadly serious, her halberd threaded and in hand, tilted against danger from any direction. Alex was aware of the inadequacy of the dagger in his belt, and wished for one of the stolen guns. Fortunato seemed at home with his Smith & Wesson, and Dark Star had unslung her rifle and was carrying it at port arms as she traveled.

Whatever else he might think, these people were taking their Game seriously. The Griffin would too, if he wanted to survive long enough to find Rice's killer.

The progress of the line had ceased, and they were bunching up. Henderson came back down the line. "We're near the mission," he told them briskly. "I sent Oliver and Gina ahead to scout for us, and we can't move in until we know what we're up against. I'm sure they've got guards and fortifications, and probably a ghastly or two." He glanced significantly at Dark Star. "If my hunch is right, we'll have some action for our Thieves. You'll have to brief Fortunato and Griffin, honey. You're our only experienced Thief."

Oliver broke through the line, breathing shallowly. "It's up there, all right. And it's not empty. Looks as if there are about two dozen natives, and maybe one boss man. I don't see the sacrifice, but they're preparing for it, no question."

"Weapons?"

"I saw spears, mostly. Knives, a couple of bows, and two guns. No machine weapons."

"Good. Gina?"

"I took a read on the area, and there's plenty of magic, all right. At least two priests fifth-level or higher, and one vibration I don't like at all. I think that was one of the . . . Enemy, and if they're all as powerful as him, we're in trouble."

"Stow that. We can handle them. What does the lead man look like?"

The redhead pursed her lips thoughtfully, trying to remember. "Strange. Animalistic. Leather loin cloth, long fingernails and toenails, very dark. Looked like his hair had been shampooed with mud. Very strong aura, and even though I was shielded, he knew I was there."

Chester grunted. "Any link with the sacrifice?"

"Slight. She's in there, and she's plenty scared, I can tell you. Chester, we can't try a frontal assault, they'll kill her, and she's our only link to the Enemy."

"Got it. You're right, of course. Good work, hon. Did it tax your energy much?" The green field glowed around Gina, and Chester judged her aura with a practiced eye.

"You'll do. When the assault begins, team with me."

"You talked me into it," she grinned, snuggling against him.

He pretended not to notice. "It looks like we are going to need the Thieves. Gina's no slouch, and if her shielding wasn't good enough to slip past them, then no one but the Thieves can do the primary work."

Despite himself, Griffin felt a bubble of excitement percolating its way to the surface. "What's our mission?"

"Rescuing the fair maiden, of course."

Chapter Fifteen

THE RITE OF HORRIFIC SPLENDOR

At the edge of the clearing, hidden behind a broad-leaved tree, crouched three Thieves. Two were novices, and their hands and foreheads were damp with expectation. One of these was blue-eyed with shaggy black hair; he carried a pistol and dagger. He wore dark pants and shirt, and his face had been blackened with charcoal. His name was Fortunato.

He hawked and spit quietly, too near the boot of the second novice, a huge man who moved with disquieting ease, who squatted on his haunches with the relaxed endurance of an Outback Abo. His hair was red and cut short. His thickly callused hands were curled loosely

196

around a twelve-inch poniard. He called himself the Griffin.

The third Thief held a subtle but powerful influence over the others. She was not what one would call pretty, except perhaps by the light of a lonely campfire. Her lips were too large; they glistened momentarily as she wet them with the tip of a pink tongue. Her ears sprouted like semaphore flags from under her short dark hair. Now they were straining to catch any slightest sound. Only her eyes might honestly have been called beautiful. Within them was a swirl of tiny reflected lights, oilfires floating in a whirlpool. Her eyebrows arced together like markings on the face of a bird of prey. Her entire body was canted forward like a runner awaiting the gun. Her name was Dark Star.

Before them was spread a strange and barbaric panorama, one which assaulted every sense. Lean, dark figures twisted in rhythmic movement, as the sound of wooden drums and reed pipes mingled beneath a bloody moon. Maibang, their dark wiry guide with the quick eyes and the ready tongue, had said that this was originally an Anglican church. No living man remembered clearly the day that the forest creatures arose and slew the missionaries; but since that day, no sane man came within a spear's cast of those vine-mottled walls. So much blood had soaked the ground that the very souls of the priests cried out in agony at any footfall.

The church, crumbled and in jungle-moist disrepair, was small, not much more than living quarters for the long dead occupants. Services were held in a roofless chapel, an open area covered with ancient and rotted mats, where two hundred at a time might kneel together in prayer.

The roofless chapel now hosted a ring of frenetic dancers. Another ten or twelve natives, scattered in an outside ring, swayed silently to the beat without moving their feet. In the middle of the area was a frame of timbers lashed in the form of a vertical "X".

"If she isn't out here, then she's got to be inside the church building itself—" Dark Star's breath caught in her throat, and she pulled her companions back further into the bushes.

The figure that came out of the building was a strange one. He looked more beast than man. His nails were talon-long and sharp, his canines were filed to points, his hair was a shattered wasp's-nest of mud and sticks. He glared around the clearing, looking right past them, and spoke sharply and hurriedly to the dancers. They took handfuls of grain from little leather pouches at their waists and began to sow it.

Griffin nudged Fortunato. "Most of their attention is focussed in front of the building. Shall we try the rear?"

Fortunato's grin split the stained blackness of his face. "What about it, Star? Will we need a distraction?"

"Only to get out alive. Now listen, both of you. We need to work our way around to the other side of the church, and we have got to do it *quietly*. Follow me." She shifted the rifle from behind her shoulder and held it across her chest as she crouched. She ran lightly through the bushes. At intervals of five meters Griffin and Fortunato followed.

They made it to the other side of the clearing and stopped, surveying. Dark Star nodded, and they scurried across the fifteen meters of clearing to the back of the church. The rear wall was half again as tall as she. "Boost me," she whispered to Griffin. He bent and linked fingers for her to step into, and straightened up. The Thief caught the edge of the roof and pulled herself up until she had both elbows resting on it. With a final push from Griffin, she was up.

Fortunato helped Griffin up, and the big man returned the favor. Fortunato was panting heavily. Dark Star sent him a dirty look, and he tried to quiet it down.

Years of rain and weather had reduced a once sturdy roof of thatch and timbers to rotted weakness. They were able to crawl along the main supports without much risk, but the tilt of the roof made it a tricky business. The sound of the music and stamping feet drowned any noise they were making. If they didn't shake down too much dust on the people within, they would be all right.

Dark Star shinnied up the slanted center beam, bracing her feet in the thatch. Griffin and Fortunato followed. She halted a couple of meters from the top, drew her knife, and slit a peephole in the woven straw. She had to saw at some of the stronger fibers, but accomplished her task without noise. Griffin followed suit.

The room below them was dimly lit, but in the flickering light of a single torch it was possible to make out four figures. Two men stood with arms folded, bracketing a woman who lay bound on a pallet. Above her loomed the mud-haired man who had directed the dancers. At this range they could make out slitted cheeks stained with fresh blood: self-inflicted ritual wounds, probably rubbed with dirt or manure to create permanent scars.

The girl was blond, and her clothes, now tatters, had once been expensive and beautiful. Griffin couldn't see her face clearly, but her body was small and sweetly shaped.

Dark Star's toe nudged Griffin's ear, and he glanced up. She gestured, cutting the air with her knife. Griffin made a circle of forefinger and thumb. He liked the idea; the thatch roof seemed to be made of two sturdy mats joined at the center beam. If they slit it where it met the beam, they would be able to drop through onto their enemies.

Quietly, they cut. The moonlight made their task easy, and only the pulsating sound of the drums promised doom. Once, one of the guards below glanced up, and they stopped cutting until he turned away. Griffin looked back at Fortunato, who kept the watch for them. The Thief rubbed at the charcoal around his eyes and waved back dutifully.

Dark Star was preparing to peel the roof back when the door of the chapel opened, and several warriors filed in. The girl moaned as they hoisted her to their shoulders. They carried her out.

Griffin heard the lady Thief curse venomously. He understood how she felt. So *close* . . .

Two guards remained in the room after the others left. Griffin tapped Dark Star on the foot. He pointed down. "All right," she whispered, "give it a—"

A patch of air in front of her face glowed red. "Gary," she said, breaking character, "your blade is still live. Sheath it and unlock the handle."

Griffin looked at her blankly before he remembered the admonitions given to him by the referees in Gaming Central:

1) No live blades during personal combat. All edged weapons have detachable blades, with simple holo projectors in their hilts. All sheath sensors must confirm lockdown before combat sequences can begin.

2) No physical contact allowed, and no blows may be aimed at joints, groin, face or neck except with hologram blades.

3) Minor infractions will necessitate halting of the game and awarding of penalty points. Major infractions will automatically terminate the Game.

Alex pushed his poniard into its holder until he heard it click. Then he twisted the hilt a half-turn, and it came free. An eight-inch glowing blade projected from it, and he passed a finger warily through the field. The red glow before Dark Star's face dissolved, and she gave him the go-ahead.

But the Griffin's own face felt like it was glowing in the dark. Jesus, a Dream Park Security Chief had been that close to slicing up two actors! Great publicity there, O Griffin! . . . hell with it. Griffin ripped the roof open and dropped into the room.

The guards were taken unawares. He landed almost on top of one; his knife plunged bloodlessly into his back half a dozen times. The native collapsed. The second one tripped over the corpse of the first, and as he flailed to the ground Griffin cut his throat neatly.

The big Thief shook his head. "Swordfodder," he muttered.

Dark Star dropped from the roof, followed by Fortunato, who nearly twisted his ankle. She looked around at the damage, and gave him a grudging nod of approval. "Pretty smooth for a first-timer. What do you do for an encore?"

He ignored her and moved quietly to the door. "We don't have much time. They're getting ready to do it now."

She peeked out at the wooden frame, where the European girl was being anointed with a mash of crushed grain and pig blood.

"Fortunato," Dark Star said, pulling the blackfaced

Thief to her, "do you think you can hit a man's throat at fifteen meters?"

"I can try. My Wessler-Grahm is seventy-nine for dexterity, and beyond that it's up to the computer. The gun might be better."

"No, save the bullets. Use the knife."

Fortunato twisted the knife hilt free, and now he held a glowing blade.

"We'll have to time this just right . . ."

The music outside grew louder. Swirling and capering, the scarred and mud-haired high priest moved around the girl and jabbed at her with a blade chipped from black glass. The others moved back to let their leader dance, hypnotized by his movements. He was fairly foaming at the mouth now, scuttling from side to side like a rabid crab. He drew a knifeline of blood on his own stomach, then writhed forward, rubbing his belly against the girl's and smearing her with blood.

Griffin couldn't see the captive's face from this angle, but he could see her body stiffen and jerk away. The high priest grinned lasciviously and did it again, more slowly, and this time her wail of misery rose quaveringly above the throb of the drums. He raised the knife high, and—

"*Now!*" Dark Star hissed. Fortunato's hand flickered in a short arc as he mimed throwing the blade. A glitter of silver flashed from his hand to the priest's throat. The priest gagged, hands flying to his neck, and blood drooled from between writhing lips.

"Bullseye!" Fortunato shrieked delightedly. Before the word was out of his mouth Griffin was out of the doorway and streaking to the side of the captive. There was a brief moment when their eyes met, and the gratitude and awe in

her face were glorious. Fortunato was at his side in the next
instant, and they faced the charge side by side as Dark Star
untied the girl's bonds.

The first man in thrust a spear with a glowing point at
Griffin. The Thief sidestepped, grasped the haft firmly, and
twisted. The man somersaulted and landed on his back.
The second man in got the glowing point in the stomach
and collapsed, howling. A quick glance at Fortunato
showed that he had acquired another glowing blade and
was holding two natives at bay.

Dark Star had the girl loose. She thrust her to the center
of a protective triangle formed by the three Thieves. Two
men rushed her. One went down before Dark Star's knife.
She sidestepped the other's wild swing. He sprawled to the
ground, and she finished him from behind.

Suddenly the mass of natives pulled back into a ring,
and several spears were raised to casting height. As they
prepared to throw, there was a marrow-rending screech
from the rear. The natives turned *en masse* to meet the
new threat, but it was clear from the first that they were
unequal to the task.

For Mary-em had arrived. The little woman charged like
a berserker, her glowing halberd tilted before her. Her
leather armor was caked with dirt and her face was grubby
and scratched, but the gleam in her eyes was effervescent.
A dozen warriors and wizards charged behind her.

Gina's power staff whined and piped its song; lightning
leapt from the tip as she played and danced amid the
slaughter. Panthesilea wielded her sword with stunning
speed, fighting her way to Fortunato's side swiftly, pursing
a kiss at him before turning to stand shoulder-to-shoulder
in the fray.

The natives fought to the death, every one of them. Spears, knives, and corded muscles glistened in the torch-light as the battle raged.

Oliver the Frank moved in a cautious circle around his opponent, native spear matched to glowing broadsword. The spear's luminous tip grazed his stomach as Oliver twisted aside, thrusting his own weapon in the next instant. The native's spear jerked up, and Oliver had to acknowl-edge a deflection. The two men withdrew to the ready position, attention focussed totally on each other. Oliver faked high and went for the knees. As the native warrior tried to block he overreached and Oliver looped the blade up and into the ribs. Howling, his foe went down holding his stomach.

The battle was almost over, natives lying dead and broken everywhere. Suddenly the Lore Master yelled for their attention. He pointed to the roof of the church.

Lurching along its edge, knife projecting from the hol-low of his throat, tottered the priest. His eyes were glassy, and half-dried blood shown on his chest as he looked down at them.

His lips twitched back from his teeth in a ghastly carica-ture of a smile, eyes alight with a hatred stronger than death. He opened his mouth, and gurgling whispers bub-bled forth.

"Back, everyone!" Chester screamed unnecessarily. They retreated from a patch of air shimmering in the square. "Get the girl and let's get out of here!" Chester yelled, but by that time it was far too late: the shimmering patch cut the girl off from everyone but Eames and Leigh, who stood over her alertly.

"What do you think, Chester?" Gina asked, panting.

"Reveal Barrier!" he yelled. A bolt of green flashed from his hand into the glowing area and dissolved it.

"Illusion! It was a stall—"

The jungle behind them shook with the sound of branches snapping and popping. The ground shook with an ominous rhythm, and Eames swept the girl into his arms, carrying her to the center of the Gamers. They formed a ragged half-circle facing the jungle, and waited.

There was a collective gasp as the thing lumbered out of the trees into the clearing. It was huge, the size of the church building, with a snakelike head attached to a greyish, roughly spherical body. It had dozens of short stubby legs that moved more like cilia than jointed appendages, and carried it toward the Gamers with frightening speed. The mouth was strange, shocking. It was no bigger than a man's mouth. It was lost on that vast face.

Chester watched its approach cautiously. He saw the thing glide up to one of the fallen natives. Its mouth expanded like an awakening Morning Glory, exposing gums lined with row after row of small sharp teeth. It hunched over the body and slurped it in halfway, and chewed.

Chester backed away. "We don't want any part of that thing. Let's clear out of here."

Fortunato called, "Chester?" and waved the heavy revolver he was carrying.

"Try it," Chester commanded. "The rest of you, get going!"

The Gamers began an orderly retreat. The creature finished the native and glanced up. Its mouth pursed hungrily. It followed, fast.

Fortunato/McWhirter stood braced with his legs apart,

arms stiff, both hands wrapped around the gun butt. He fired twice, quickly, and paused to observe the effect.

Two small pucker marks on its smooth front were not bleeding; in fact, they were closing. It hadn't slowed at all.

Tony fired again, more carefully, aiming for its eyes and mouth. He fired until the gun was empty, then ran like a Thief, with the creature too close behind him.

The orderly retreat became a rout. Kasan Maibang led them to a path through the bush wide enough to travel double-file, and the wave of Gamers stretched out into a line. Tony McWhirter's sprint had cost him; he was exhausted. He ran like he was about to fall over at every step.

Chester ran with Maibang. "What is that monstrosity?"

The little guide's reply was wheezed between clenched teeth. "It is called a Nibek. Our enemies called it to avenge themselves."

The Lore Master looked back. The trees weren't slowing it. Timber was smashed into bits by every shrug of that massive body, and still it gained, a disturbingly human snarl decorating the tiny mouth.

"Damn it!" a voice screamed from the rear. He looked again, and saw who it was, at the tail of the column: Mary-em, her legs too short for real speed. Another few seconds and the tiny mouth would expand to swallow her—

"Leave her," Maibang said urgently. "In the time it takes to eat her, we can be far up the trail—"

"I should feed you to that goddam thing," Chester raged. "She's mine, damn you, and that Nibek can't have what's mine without a fight." He pivoted and raised his arms. "Hear me, O Gods—" The green glow surrounded his body, and when he yelled the sound was like roaring thunder. "Gather to my side, my children of light and darkness. This spawn of Hell shall not have us."

Fortunato was hugging a tree, gasping. To Alex he wheezed, "Acacia says . . . Thieves don't fight well. Better hang back."

Eames had joined Mary-em, and the Nibek drew up short, hissing. Its scaly head weaved slowly to and fro; and one eye was missing, shot away. Panthesilea and Oliver joined them, blades out and ready. Behind them, Gwen knelt in prayer, casting a sparkling white aura around them.

Gina and Bowan the Black slipped to the right, flanking the thing. Chester went left.

It attacked. On its first pass Mary-em stabbed at its remaining eye, diving out of the way so that its answering snap only grazed her. She had missed. Eames slashed at it, and the Nibek swung its head around too swiftly for the Warrior to escape. He stumbled back as his aura flashed red. The monster's mouth began to expand, and only Oliver's blow to its legs turned it back around. Oliver backed up until he was against a tree, and the Nibek's mouth smiled as it came in for the kill. The white protective field around Oliver glowed more intensely, and the thing gave its warbling cry of frustration when it couldn't get through.

It turned its attention to Gwen, who still knelt in prayer. She kept her eyes closed until it was almost upon her, then turned her palms outward, and the full power of her inner strength blasted into its face. It reared back, blinded.

From his side angle, the Lore Master unleashed a bolt of such intensity that the night became red-tinted day for an instant. Draeger tried to bat the Nibek with a large branch, and as the monster recoiled from Chester's blow, it smashed into the Engineer. Draeger's aura went bright red, fading to black.

But now the Gamers were better organized. The Nibek bit at Gwen while Bowan seared it with flame. Tony had reloaded and was firing into the beast. The brush itself crackled and smoked, but the Nibek's hide only crinkled under the assault. Griffin hurled his captured spear, and it went through the creature's head completely. Though greenish blood pulsed from the wound, it lived on.

"Its brain must be in the body! Magic users! Closer in now!"

Gina stood almost in the midst of the smoking brush and hurled her power into the creature's side. It struck a tree in its agony, and a mass of flaming branches fell, striking Gina squarely. She yelled her rage as her aura went red and then drained to flickering black. Chester saw it, and his face went sick. "Bowan! This is no good! This thing is too strong, it's killing us! I'm going to try for a split attack!"

Bowan set his balance and redoubled his efforts, a fountain of flame pouring from his fingertips.

Chester threw his arms wide and intoned:
"Hear me now, oh Lords of Light!
Knowing that I fight your fight.
I care not what the spell may cost,
Let your servant pour forth—frost!"

From the tips of Chester's fingers gushed a stream of white particles that struck the Nibek opposite the side bathed in fire. The thing's mouth quoited out and it screamed as its skin split down the spine, exposing bone and red meat.

Now the Nibek was in real agony. Bowan changed his attack and sent his fire arcing over directly into the wound.

It crawled in diminishing circles like a half-crushed beetle. Now the warriors moved in, slashing and stabbing. It was eyeless and nearly legless, and still trying to run, when the Gamers hacked it apart.

The survivors leaned on each other or against trees, panting, looking around them.

"Auras!" Chester yelled, and they flashed on. There were six red-tinged glows, and three black. Two black auras were solid; Gina's still flickered.

Chester sounded exhausted. "Gwen. See what you can do for Gina. We've lost the others." The Cleric nodded, touching Draeger sadly on the shoulder as she trudged past him to Gina's side.

Draeger was incensed. "Just what do you mean, 'lost the others'? Aren't you even going to *try*?"

Chester extended his hand in sympathy, and the angry Engineer knocked it aside. The Lore Master said, "Listen, Dreager. Gwen's only got so much power, and she's already used up a lot of it protecting Eames and Oliver. If she tried to help all three of you, she'd run out of juice. She couldn't help anyone then."

Draeger snorted, his reddish complexion growing ruddier. "Well, then only one of us can be saved, right?"

"One," Chester said quietly.

Draeger walked up close enough to rub belt buckles, and stuck his nose almost into Henderson's mouth. "So how is it that *she* gets to live? What's the matter? You don't play fair to anyone who isn't laying you?"

Chester's voice wasn't loud, but everyone heard him. "Draeger, you are dead. All the way dead. Didn't you feel the jolt? Your *tindalo* is standing right behind you, see?" The stout Engineer turned and looked, and shuddered as he saw his misty-white translucent twin crook a spectral finger at him. "If you were as much a Gamer as the other man the Nibek killed, who had the class to quietly bow out, we might have been saved this. Since you ask, though, I give Gina consideration because she is a competent Magic User, while you are a second-rate Engineer without enough sense to leave the fighting to the fighters." Draeger sputtered, trying to get out a reply, but Chester cut him short. "And, Draeger, in answer to your implied question: I suspect that if I *had* spent last night with you instead of Gina, I'd be even happier to get your dead ass out of this Game."

Draeger looked about him at a ring of unsympathetic faces. He spit into the dirt. His ghost was moving away, and he followed a few steps, then stopped, his fists clenched. "You'll be sorry for that, Henderson. I swear to God you'll be." Then he ran into the darkness.

Chapter Sixteen

REST BREAK

Gina sat on her bedroll with her knees drawn up to her chest. The campfire popped. Ham and beans simmered next to the flames; the smell was delightful, compulsive.

"We had a couple of serious accidents and three fatalities today," Chester said. "We'll need a replacement Engineer, and we need another Cleric to take up the slack for poor Gwen. I know where we can get both of those in one package, so we're set there. I'm worried about our points, but the Nibek was no pansy monster, and the I.F.G.S. has to give me credit for that, so it should balance out." Gina nodded. She seemed half asleep, but Chester didn't notice. He sighed and rubbed his eyes with the palms of his hands. "I think we're running a little to the good right now, and in a Game like this, that's the best we can hope for." Gina rested her head against his knee. "I'll bet we see Dreager again, though. As a zombie. Even so, how much damage can he—"

Griffin watched and listened, unobtrusively, leaning against a tree trunk with his arms folded. Strangely, he was tired. Real fatigue, as if he had spent the day fighting real monsters instead of holograms.

Like the others, he had stripped off his backpack and collapsed to the ground, whooping with delight. And why not? It was all good fun . . .

He shook his head. Business. Stick to business. He looked around at the fifteen people in the camp. Twelve were Gamers; the others were the Rescued Maiden and the actors who played Maibang and Kagoiano. Unobserved, he faded back into the trees until the campfire was barely visible.

The transceiver in his wallet hummed as he punched it on.

"Griffin here. Marty? You there?"

"Right on it, Chief. We've already interviewed the three Gamers who got killed out. We've even voice-stressed the first one . . . what was his—oh, yeah, Garret. The other two have agreed to do it tomorrow. And they're all staying on as guests of Dream Park."

"Your sunny personality, no doubt."

"Oh, no doubt. The unlimited Experience pass might have had something to do with it. I mean, not only go to the head of the line every time, but *free* too? Garret says he's going for the Guiness record on the Gravity Whip."

The laughter felt good, a release after the day's tension. "I've picked up some interesting things myself. I think we can clear Alan Leigh. He was busy last night trying to seduce Eames, one of the warriors."

Alex wasn't particularly surprised at the short pause,

and then the discomfort in Marty's voice. Bobbick, like Melissa and much of California, was a product of the post-quake religious revival. Sexual conservatism still was less the exception than the rule. Though Gamers made their own rules . . .

But Marty was a professional, and he asked a professional's question. "Can we scratch Eames too?"

"No. He hasn't done much Gaming, so he's not high on the list . . . but he turned Leigh down. He could have been alone at least part of the night. If Leigh came after him, he could find that Eames had moved his bedroll to avoid a sticky situation. But Leigh wouldn't have started a seduction if he wasn't planning to stick around and enjoy it. I suspect that we can rule out Henderson too."

"Why?"

"Think about it. We never took the Gamers seriously as a threat because they're so into make-believe. Henderson lives and breathes for the Game. It's his whole ego, and it pays off well in terms of power and fame. He strikes me as the kind of person who wouldn't risk that for money. This is mostly hunch, but as long as I'm out in left field, we might as well exclude Gina too, because they spent last night together. I'm inclined to think of this as a solo job for now. Of course it *could* have been a team effort, one partner supplying an alibi for the other. Hmm . . ."

"What is it, Griff?"

"More grief. Check the Alternate waiting area. It's as close to the edge of Gaming Area A as R&D is. Could one of the Alternates have gotten into 'A', then doubled back through the service duct? It does seem we've got a blind spot for Gamers. Psychologically, we just never considered them to be any kind of threat."

"I'll cover it."

"Good. Now let's give me something more to look for. Have you got a map of Gaming A?"

"I've got a dozen. We've been marking them up."

"You're ahead of me, then. Okay, mark out the killer's easiest routes to Gaming Area A service shaft 18—"

"He only had one good path. He had to go around a piece of papier-mache mountain. Griff, we should put TV screens on these transceivers. I could show you."

"One path: good. Now get Lopez or somebody to tell you what the killer *had* to see on his way to G.A. 18. Something he knows about that the rest of us don't."

"Lopez may not be happy about giving forewarning to a Gamer."

"Dammit, we've got a *murd* . . . yeah. Be as persuasive as you can."

Marty sounded skeptical. "Sure."

Millie's voice came on line. "Chief, I've got some information for you."

"Anything earthshattering?"

"Shattering, no. Interesting, yes. Rice apparently died of suffocation some time after he was tied up. We think he regained consciousness before dying."

"Why?"

"The bandages on Rice's thumbs and wrists were heavily abraded. He must have been rubbing them against the concrete floor, trying to get loose. The gag blocked his mouth, and evidently his nose was stopped up."

"Whew." Griffin shook his head in the dark, feeling a tremor run the length of his body. "That's a hell of a note. Killed by a cold. That's really crazy." He ran his hand through his hair, trying to focus. Fighting dragons was exhausting. "What else?"

"Well, that missing statue was either stolen, or is in the

hands of someone outside of Dream Park. No one knows anything about it. Rice made it in his second year at the University of Oklahoma. One more thing. Kokobun, the lady who tried to buy it from him, said that it felt hollow."

"Hollow. All right."

"This gets even trickier, Chief. Skip O'Brien did a check on Rice's psych profile, and the computer record has definitely been tampered with."

"In what way?"

"O'Brien says that the original report he filed when Rice first came to work here indicated that Rice was too much of a loner for office work. He just didn't fit into a team effort. *Now* the file shows him as having highly developed communication skills, a higher frustration tolerance, and his military IQ has been upped ten points."

"Well well. This is definitely getting strange. Somebody was grooming Rice for a desk job. Maybe an important one. Millie, find out if Rice put in for a transfer to another department, will you? Or if anyone requested his transfer. Keep working on any leads you can, and thanks, good work, people. I'll be back in touch. Beep me if anything urgent comes up, but remember, I might not be in a position to answer."

Bobbick's voice came back on the line. "By the way, Griff. We've all been following the adventures of the infamous Griffin, and I must say that you looked great out there against them savages."

He laughed, and Millie joined in. She said, "When you chucked the spear at that monster, you looked so *serious*, Chief. Have you been leading a double life, maybe? By day a meek, mild-mannered security honcho, by night an avenger of evil—"

"Let's not go overboard, gang. I'm glad you're enjoying

yourselves, but we've got business. I'll ring you tomorrow."

The transceiver blipped as Griffin closed and pocketed it. Griffin steepled his hands over his nose and breathed deeply. From where he stood with his back against a vine-shrouded tree, he could hear sounds of merriment from the campfire. The voices were tired but happy, and as he listened, Mary-em began to croak out a song.

"It was good enough for Odin,
Though that croakin' was forebodin',
Till at last the Giants rode in;
Still it's good enough for me!"

He wanted to smile but couldn't. *Business first, Alex. Business. There's a killer and thief to find before you can relax—*

"Gimme that old time religion,
Gimme that old time religion,
Gimme that old time religion,
It's good enough for me!
Montezuma liked to start out
Rites by carrying a part out
That would really tear your heart out,
And it's good enough for me."

No, he couldn't relax then, either. There would be paperwork and conferences. Then court appearances and depositions. Then a complete redesigning of the security procedures at R&D. Then—

He shook his head. *Keep this up and you'll start thinking that all you do is work your ass off, go home and crash, back to work, sleep for a few hours, work . . .*

Well?

"Hi," Acacia said, materializing out of the dark. The beige denim safari outfit she wore was appropriately

stained by the day's activities, and she looked tired. But
tired or not, she had pinned back her flow of dark hair, and
it framed her face beautifully.

"Hi, yourself." A smile wormed its effortless way onto
his mouth, and he moved a half-step closer to her. "What
brings you out here?"

She gave a mischievous giggle. "Well, Tony wanted to
sing, and I got bored. And a little lonely."

He perked an ear in the direction of the fire, and picked
up McWhirter's thin but pleasing tenor beneath Mary-em's
roar:

"—Old time religion,
It's good enough for me!
  It was good enough for Kali;
  Though embracing her is folly,
  She'd be quite an armful, golly!
  So it's good enough for me."

"What about Eames? Did I notice some knowing smiles
passing between you two?"

"That was for last night." She leaned against the tree,
shoulder to shoulder with him, and stretched luxuriously.
"It was no big thing, really, mostly talk. He's not as much
my type as I thought he was."

"What is your type?"

"Aha. That is what they used to call a loaded question."

"What do they call it now?"

"An unnecessary one, given that I'm out here in the
woods with you." She smiled uncertainly, searching his
face. "I don't know about you, Gary."

"What don't you know?"

"Well, I can't help getting the feeling that you'd rather
watch than participate. You like to stand aside and observe."

He cleared his throat. "Is there anything wrong with that?"

"No, not really. It's just that there's something about you that I like, and I get the feeling that you're not getting as much out of the Game as you might be."

"What am I missing out on? I mean, I'm having a ball."

She frowned at her boot-toes. "You've got this attitude, and I can't put my finger on it. You go through the moves, enthusiastically, even, but there's something businesslike about it. As though you're afraid to have too much fun. I bet you take your job very seriously, don't you?"

"Oh, I guess so. I see what you're driving at. But why would someone who's afraid to have fun work at Dream Park?" He ran his finger softly along the side of her neck. "Or join a Gaming party?"

The voices floated to them:

> "It was good enough for Dagon,
> A conservative old pagan
> Who still votes for Ronald Reagan,
> And it's—"

"Since I don't know anything about you, I guess it's all right if I make a few wild speculations. It seems to me that Cowles Industries is a perfect place for someone who likes their fun vicariously. How often do you actually use the facilities?"

"Not very often," he admitted, "but . . ."

"And I bet you've got some job with a killing amount of responsibility, don't you?"

"Oh . . . hell, maybe so. Running a restaurant is as much work as you want to make it," he quoted Gary Tegner, too woodenly. (Then he remembered answering, "Come to think of it, so is being a Security Chief.")

There was a flicker of disbelief in Acacia's eyes, quickly

hidden. "I would have figured you for a different kind of job. And actually, I wouldn't think that coming on this expedition was your idea, either. You don't really fit in, Gary. Did your doctor tell you to do it for your health, or what?"

"Tell me," he said, putting his arms around her waist and locking his fingers together. "If I promise to try to fit in and have some fun from now on, what do I get?"

She answered him.

"You know," she said, pulling just far enough away for her eyes to focus on him, "there was even a bit of business in that kiss."

"Well, maybe I mean business."

"I just bet you do." She kissed him again, longer this time, and hotter. When she broke away, her questions were temporarily subdued. She ran her hands along his chest, feeling the hard muscle, and the questions flared again. "You know," she said in a near-whisper, "you don't really add up, Gary, but I like you."

"Why?"

"Because you ask too many questions, that's why. And damn few answers. Which means that behind the big strong silent man routine there is the kind of little boy I like." She snuggled up closer to him. "How long has it been since you told that little boy that he's worked hard enough, and it's all right to play for awhile?"

He shrugged uncomfortably. *About ten minutes. Damn!* "I guess that's why I'm here. Maybe it has been awhile." He tried to kiss her again, but she turned her head slightly to one side so that he grazed her cheek.

"Gary, you use kisses to get away, not to get closer. You don't have to say anything to me, but ask yourself how long it's been. And if you feel like talking to me, I mean really talking, you know where to find me." She kissed him with a strangely subdued energy, and disengaged his hands from her back, and walked back toward the campfire.

Griffin watched her go with mixed emotions: relief at being free of her prying, and a little confusion at the sadness he felt. She had no right to pry into his mind or his life. He wasn't there for her pleasure, or even his own.

"It was good enough for Isis:
She will help us in a crisis,
And she's never raised her prices,
So she's good enough for me!"

Quietly, hands in pockets, he joined the Gamers at the campfire. There was a lull in the singing, and the pork and beans were dished out. Eames came balancing two plates. He carried one of them to the small honey-blond girl who had been the captive of the Foré, and sat down beside her. Alex had seen her dossier. Her name was Janet Kimball, and like Harvey "Kasan Maibang" Wayland, she was an actress participating for straight points and a small percentage.

She was perched on a rock, listening intently to Alan Leigh. Her ragged clothes were covered with a black cloak from Bowan's pack, but even in her state of disrepair she seemed totally at ease.

"—wanted to see how the other half lives," Leigh was saying, "so I signed up as an actor in Muhammad Porter's Slaver Game. "Your objective is to free your fifty purchased tribesmen from the frigate *Tante Marie* before it reaches market in New Orleans, and without causing the crew to drop their cargo overboard—' "

"I watched the tape. Yes, I remember you now. Brrr."

Leigh nodded complacently. "I made a *good* slaver. Suave, evil, ready to sell my own mother if she'd been the right color . . . Come to that, you'd fetch a fine price anywhere, my dear." He allowed his gaze to linger on Janet's exquisitely shaped legs with obvious relish. For that moment Alan Leigh *looked* evil, and Janet looked like she liked it. Then he broke the spell by consuming a fat forkful of savory legumes. It blurred his voice somewhat. "So who exactly are you supposed to be, Janet?"

"*Lady* Janet, if you don't mind. I'm a British noblewoman, captured by foul natives on my way to Australia."

"Were you ravished?"

"No," she said wistfully. "I rather think they hoped I was a virgin."

"No chance of that, huh?" Eames put in.

"I wouldn't have put it quite like that, Mr. Eames . . . ah! There's one of my brave rescuers now!"

Griffin nodded acknowledgement. He squatted in front of her with a plate of beans balanced in his lap. "You're well worth the saving, too." She curtsied where she sat, and he went on. "So you're going to lead us to the dreaded Forè, eh?"

"Yes. Just don't mention their name during the Game unless you're ready to die. I can, because they gave me permission. I supposedly spent three weeks among them, while they waited to sacrifice me under a new moon." She turned to Leigh. "I find barbaric customs *very* stimulating."

Leigh leaned close to her. "Madam, beneath this civilized and cultured exterior you will find the heart of an absolute beast."

She seemed fascinated. "Teeth and all?"

"Especially teeth. Perhaps you'd like to see my horns sometime . . . ?"

"Warriors are a lot more basic and earthy than wizards," Eames sniffed. "I'd think you'd be a little more attracted to my type."

"Yes, you'd think so, wouldn't you?" Leigh said warmly. He and Janet giggled without malice.

Eames was growing increasingly frustrated. "Listen, Janet, would you like to go for a walk?"

"Love to," she said, gazing into Alan's eyes. "Shall we?" And the two of them left the campfire.

Eames stared after them, biting his lip. "I'll be damned. Who'd think she'd prefer a faggot to a real man?"

Griffin politely said nothing. Eames looked at him, challenging. "What do you think?"

"I think she's a Gaming groupie. She went after Alan because he has more I.F.G.S. points than you do." It might even be true, Alex thought.

Eames grunted, somewhat mollified. "Yeah, that must be it." He gave Griffin a "just-us-men" smile. "You know, you can't ever figure women out."

"No, I guess you can't." Griffin directed his attention mightily to his rapidly cooling food. To Eames's verbal sallies he merely grunted his replies. The warrior lost interest and grumbled away into the woods.

Alex let his mind following an earlier track. *Leigh has a good many Experience points. Leigh played a previous Game in Gaming Area A. And if Leigh noticed, some time last night, that Eames was safely occupied with Acacia, then . . . but would he count on Acacia keeping Eames occupied?*

Mary-em bounced down next to him. "How ya, Gary?"

"Doing pretty good. Feel a little tired, I guess."

"Big strong man like you?" she cackled. "I would have thought you'd wear out the lot of us."

"I just haven't slept well for the past couple of days," he said truthfully. "That always tears me up."

"Well, get some rest tonight, you'll need it soon enough."

"How so? These things don't seem so tiring. Nobody's fallen over yet."

"And the real fireworks probably start tomorrow. Lopez has just been testing us. By tomorrow night the last of the replacements will be in, and that's when we'll get hit with everything in the book."

"But why should that be so tiring? It's just a game . . ."

She looked at him incredulously. "Take a look around you, sonny. Do these people look like they've been playing a *game*?"

He did look around. And Mary-em was right. Fatigue was etched into every face, dark rings under eyes and noticeable trembling in fingers and hands. He focussed for the first time on the amount of touching and cuddling going on around him. Tony and Acacia cuddling in the shadows, Bowan and Dark Star touching each other with almost embarrassing intimacy, and Chester snuggled with Gina in their double sleeping bag. Oliver and Gwen had retreated from the campfire altogether.

It *was* a little like a battlefield, he realised. The highly charged sexual atmosphere was no mere tease, and anything but casual. The immersion into a fantasy world was total; the exhaustion was real. The real need to reach out and touch . . .

Where did it all fit together? And how did it relate to him, and his problem? He looked at Mary-em, who was waiting patiently for his response. There was no electricity in her face now, but there was poise, and purpose. How did she fit in?

"You're right. It doesn't feel like a game. But it sure isn't real life. So what is it?"

"It's not that simple, Gary," she said, and he realised with a start that he had never before heard her speak softly. "It's a little different for everyone." Her eyes twinkled at him, and he was startled again to find himself considering her attractive. "Mostly, it's just fun. What you bring is what you get, sonny. Now, me, I do some pretty wild things all the time. Some of these folks never do anything more exciting than talk to a filing computer. So they come for straight out adventure. Some come for the Game challenge. You know, chess with living pawns. Puzzles. Some come for the people. I mean, when you're into Gaming as deep as this, sometimes it gets hard to find friends who don't think you're from Mars. That's all too simple, really. It's little bits of all of the above, different for every Gamer." She chucked him under the chin. "That's what makes it fun. So think about it. I think you'll make a hell of a Gamer when you figure out where you fit in."

She waddled off to her sleeping bag and zipped herself halfway in. The bag rustled, and she started handing clothing out, making a neat pile by her head. Griffin felt a sudden and inexplicable wave of affection for her; he fought an urge to hug her goodnight. Instead, he deposited his dish in a grimy pile and found his own backpack.

He was within touching distance of half a dozen sleeping Gamers. No aspiring killer would try anything with so many potential witnesses nearby. The Griffin unrolled his superlight, heat-reflective sleeping sack, wishing for a moment that it was plain cotton. He slipped into it and took a final look around. All was quiet, all was peaceful, except for the half-formed questions that raced through his mind in unending circles, like dozens of tiny dachshunds chasing their tails.

With a supreme effort of will he pushed the questions out of his head and settled down to rest. He heard crickets in the bushes. He was wondering whether those chirps were live, or just more Dream Park magic, when his mind fuzzed out in sleep.

Chapter Seventeen

THE LAST REPLACEMENTS

The dream was too vivid for comfort. It began with the Nibek chasing Griffin through the halls of R&D, and ended with the creature cornering him in the first floor lounge. A spear materialized in his hand, and Alex threw it into the monster's head. It screamed thunderously and collapsed to the floor, melting into the form of Albert Rice, trussed and gagged and sitting dead by the drink dispenser.

"I'm sorry. . ." Griffin found himself saying automatically. A small crowd of people materialized, *tsk*ing the still form of the guard. A little gray-haired lady waved a disapproving finger at Alex. "He may not have been well balanced at the end, but he was a fine, upright boy," she said.

Someone in a snowy-white doctor's smock spoke with Bobbick's voice. "I knew the lad well, and *he* wouldn't take this sitting down . . ."

And just before the morning mists dissolved into the sounds and smells of breakfast, a third voice whispered, "Believe me. He was for real until he got his back up against it. Believe me . . ."

"Hey there, sleepy-head!" Acacia grinned at him, squatting to look into his face. Griffin parted gummy eyelids and groaned aloud. "What's the matter, tough guy?"

"That's simple, Cas. This sleeping bag doesn't go over too well with my water-bed body."

"Well, how would some bacon and eggs go?"

"Fresh eggs?"

"Absolutely. Kibugonai showed up this morning toting a cache of fresh eggs, bread, and orange juice."

"Me for cargo." The last niggling speculations about his dream were swept away by the sudden hollow in his belly. "What time is it? How long till Game time?"

"About an hour. Come on and eat. Kasan says that there'll be a place to bathe up ahead." She sniffed under her arms, dubiously. "Frankly, I need it." She bounded up and made for the next bedroll, where S. J. lay curled into a compact lump.

Griffin yawned. He split the velcro seal and rolled out of the bag. His legs felt a little sore, and he massaged life into them with the practiced edges of his thumbs. Breathing deeply and slowly, he stretched out to touch his toes and twisted to each side, feeling the circulation return to the muscles in his back. He finished the warm-up with a few slow push-ups, then got to his feet.

The mood of the group was highly charged again. A night's sleep had refueled their fantasy engines. Alex remembered the nuzzling going on yesterday evening, and wondered whether sleep had much to do with it.

Henderson was holding court against the bole of a tree, munching a sweet roll while balancing a plate piled high with eggs and fresh bread. Kagoiano served Alex his breakfast, and the security man ambled over toward Chester to eavesdrop.

"What did you think of last night's opposition?" Bowan asked between bites of egg.

"The natives?"

"Typical orcs," was Chester's answer. "It's really a shame nobody has figured a more realistic way to conduct personal combat. Dream Park is too worried about injuries and lawsuits. So no rough stuff—"

"Orcs?" Griffin asked.

Henderson was brusk. "Generic term. The old role-playing games were overrun with these little beasties out of *Lord of the Rings*. They were ridiculously easy to kill. Now it's a nickname for swordfodder in general. Okay?" Griffin nodded mutely. "Now, Lady Janet is going to lead us as far as she can. She was blindfolded much of the time, but believes she was kept on the water somewhere. Is that right?"

"Certainly." Lady Janet's head was pillowed contentedly on Leigh's shoulder, but her voice was brisk. She was into her part. "I'll tell you everything I know. I have an excellent sense of direction."

"I'm sure you do. We have another clue." Chester pulled a black-bladed dagger out of his belt. "Considering that it was the focus of last night's ceremony, we can count on its being important. Does anyone recognise the material?"

"Obsidian," S. J. piped up. "Volcanic glass with a composition similar to rhyolite."

"Right," Chester said, smiling approval for once. "And the significance?"

"No opinion. What good is a glass dagger?"

"It tells us that the people we're looking for probably live near a volcano. So what we're looking for is a body of water not too far from a volcanic region. Kasan can help us there. We should have our two replacements pretty quick, and then we'll be back up to full strength. I have an almost perfect group now, and when the fun really begins we should be working together well. Yes, Tegner?"

"Who will the replacements be, and when exactly will they join us?" Griffin asked.

Henderson's gaze was inquisitive. "Have you ever been a cop? Or maybe a reporter?" Alex shook his head negative, cursing silently. "Well, they're the Braddons, Owen and Margie. I don't know exactly when they'll show up, but it will probably be within the first hour or so of play. Yes, McWhirter?"

"Do you know what our points are like? I mean, how are we doing?"

Chester didn't look totally happy with the question. "We've lost three people and taken some wounds. We've made a lot of kills, recovered a load of cargo, and rescued Lady Janet. There are other factors involved, but for right now we're ahead. I don't want to discuss how much ahead we are—things can change too fast in a Game like this one, so I don't want you to feel either cocky or discouraged. Any more questions?"

There were none. Henderson gestured expansively. "Then go and prepare, children. The fun begins in . . . thirty-five minutes."

Tall, slender palms outlined a patch of lower growth. The crescent-moon-shaped border trailed off from the campground like the tail on a Q. Inside was more tropical jungle, making the "good luck sign" anything but obtrusive. Alex had had to get S. J. to point it out.

As Alex pushed through the palms, the vegetation within the border became ghostly, revealing a tiny rectangular structure. No Gamers were waiting their turns, praise the Lord, and he'd be invisible to anyone outside the border of trees.

It was very basic inside. Toilet, washstand, towel dispenser.

"Marty?"

"Yeah, Griff. I can barely hear you."

"I'm in the restroom, and there's no window. I'd rather not be overheard, so I'm keeping my voice down. Let's make this fast."

"Okay. What's new?"

"Some new Gamers coming in. Husband and wife, named Braddon."

"I'll check them out. Griff, the Alternates spend all their time watching the Game and looking for details and taking notes and discussing strategy. That waiting area is pretty crowded. I don't think anyone could *count* on a chance to get into Gaming A without being noticed."

"Good. Have you talked to Lopez?"

"Yeah. He doesn't pressure worth a damn. I managed to get him to look at our map. He pointed out *two* paths around the mountain to the exit, G. A. 18. Lopez says both paths would take the thief past a piece of a big airplane."

"Which piece? Wing, cabin, tail? How big?"

" 'Piece of a big airplane.' When I tried to get more he told me to get drowned."

Hell. "All right, so if we get to a big airplane I'll watch everybody's faces. Thanks. Anything else?"

"Nope."

"The Griffin, signing out."

Griffin was paired with S. J. as the group waited for the Game to begin. All bedrolls were stowed, all backpacks shouldered and balanced. The sun shone faintly through the dome that covered Gaming Area A, but the morning was already warm, and the rich aroma of moist jungle greenery was heavy in the air.

At precisely eight o'clock a new sun peeked over the mountain range to the east, sending bands of soft red tone through the scattered clouds dancing above the crest. The old sun faded out. The air filled with the sounds of birds and rustling life. To Griffin's eye even the trees seemed to stand a little straighter.

"All right, people, let's move out!" Chester called, and in pairs the column headed toward the sun.

S. J. kept stride with Griffin by picking up his step until he was almost skipping. The pathway was broad enough for the youngster to shadowfight in zigzag patterns, slicing at the air with his knife. He pulled a slender branch from a tree and skinned it down to a wand. He flicked it like a whip at branches and insects.

Laughing aloud, Griffin tapped him on the shoulder. "That's not exactly stealth you're practicing there."

Breathing a little heavily, S. J. spoke without turning around. "Nope. Don't need it."

"Why not?"

"Lopez won't hit us with anything too nasty until our two replacement Gamers have joined up."

Griffin scratched his chin, his fingernails scraping on stubble. "How do you figure that?"

"Easy." S. J. took a couple of lunging thrusts with his wand. "Lopez wants to catch Chester with his pants down. He's not going to take any chances to give Henderson a legitimate beef to take to the I.F.G.S. Getting some of us killed out now might do that. If he wants to get us when we're short he can afford to wait til tomorrow, when we get no more replacements. That way Chester can't squawk. See?" He finished his lecture with a vicious swipe at a butterfly. It evaded easily.

"You know a lot about Gaming, don't you?"

S. J. nodded vigorously. "I'm the best. Even if nobody knows it yet."

"Do you spend a lot of your time Gaming?"

"Not like this. I mean, there's never been anything quite like this before. Even the ordinary Games only come along every couple of months. The first run-throughs, anyway, and they're the most fun. I do a lot of home Gaming. I'm linked up to about five Games: three American, one from Japan and one in the United African Republic. That last one is weird. Uses Hausa mythology. I tie into them a couple of times a week, see how far the other Gamers have pushed the expedition, enter my own moves, and see what happens. Sometimes we arrange for all players to be on line at the same time, so the Game can go on for hours and hours. One of the American Games is a solo: you're playing against the computer, so you can play forever if you like. In general I like the group Games."

"Why?"

"Gets me ready for Dream Park. I'll be a Lore Master one day. I want to know how units interact."

Units. Did he mean Gamers? "You've put a lot of thought into all of this, haven't you?"

"Sure have." S. J. popped a fly out of the air with the tip of his stick. The mutilated insect flopped to the dust and buzzed around in circles. S. J. made an unhappy face and set his heel on it. "I never expect to hit the darn things." He brightened and added, "Must be gettin' better, huh?"

"I guess so. Tell me. What do you do when you're not Gaming? I mean, is this your only social outlet?"

"Why do you ask?"

Griffin shrugged noncommittally. "You seem to put a lot of yourself into Gaming, that's all. I don't know much about all this, and I just wondered how high a price you pay for . . . well, excellence. Is that reasonable?"

Now it was S. J.'s turn to hunch his shoulders. "I guess so. I've heard all the stuff about people who are into fantasy being reality shuckers. Or maybe it's reality that shucks us. I dunno. Anybody can see that a group of Gamers has more than the average proportion of Bizarros. But I don't think Gaming made them that way. Now me . . . I'm still in school, so I've got the academic trip to worry about. I've got a part time job, so that uses up time too. I guess a lot of the energy that's left over goes into Gaming."

"What does that do to your social life?"

"What's a social life? I mean, do you think I'd be Big Man On Campus if I didn't trot down to Dream Park, or spend my evenings in front of my console? Heck. Most girls think I'm in free fall. Where else but around Gamers could I possibly find someone I have anything in common with?"

Griffin chuckled. "Any success there?"

"Some times more than others. This trip, zip." His face lit up. "But I have hope! The Game is yet young."

"Does it make you unhappy to see other people pairing off if you're alone? I felt a little left out last night, for instance. I would think that a war game could be a lonely place sometimes."

"Yeah. Especially at night. When I find a girl who Games, though, I'm going to start getting her into these things. Until then, I'll sneak my thrills when I can get them."

"Meaning?"

S. J. contrived to combine mystery and childish glee in the same smirk. "The night has a thousand eyes, Mr. Tegner."

"Meaning?"

"Nothing, unless you're vulnerable to blackmail."

"Being deliberately vague?"

"You betcha. I'm allergic to pain."

The mountains were noticeably closer now. The troop was tramping through regions less like green hell and more like densely shrubbed foothills. The ground was no longer mushy, but hard-packed dirt giving way to rocky ground. Soon they were winding their way past huge moss-encrusted boulders and under the lip of a sheer cliff. Looking back, Griffin noticed that perspective had changed; the jungle behind them seemed to be lower than the path along the cliff face. As they wended their way into the "mountains" Griffin lost sight of the jungle several times, and each time it came back into view it was smaller and lower.

They continued to climb. By contrast with the stark rock walls around them, the trees and thick brush had been downright cheery. After a long stretch with nothing to look at but granite, they broke through the first set of foothills into another stretch of greenery.

The trail led down into a meadow marked with huge twisted trees, green and greener still from the vines that swarmed up into their branches. Flowers exploded from the vines, red and violet fantasies that looked ripe enough to pluck and eat. The meadow was ringed with tumbled rock, but at the far end it was fenced by the rise of a mountain. From halfway up the mountain face tumbled a cascade that sparkled like blue diamonds in the sunlight, and where waterfall met ground it formed a small lake.

Two people waited on the shore.

More cautiously now, the column wound downward. Griffin saw the white aura glow around someone near the front, and tongues of green flashed out in all directions, then vanished.

No danger on the trail. Chester let the line hurry a little. Alex began to smell the moisture in the air, to feel the coolness of the lake, to sense what it would be like to plunge into its depths. Previously ignored, the grittiness of dust-encrusted underclothes and the strong soupy smell of an unwashed body became jarring irritants.

He found himself breaking into a run. Around him Gamers were abandoning backpacks and outer clothing. The two strangers on the bank beckoned them on with lazy smiles. Griffin had almost reached the water when Chester yelled, "Hold it, dammit. We're going to have to test that water first."

The group grumbled, but waited for the go-ahead.

Chester strode over to the newcomers and greeted them happily. "Margie. Good to see you." The lady was in her early sixties, judging by her hands and neck, but as well-preserved as a woman could be. When she stood it was with a grace that would turn any man's head, and her figure was still trim and firm. Her hair was gloriously gray, rippling softly down to her shoulders and not much further. "And you, Owen. Sorry to make you wait."

"It's okay, Chester," the man drawled. He looked to be Margie's age, and carried himself well. He stood with a trace of stiffness, and he stretched like a big gray cat. "Margie and I can always use a little time to sit and watch the water gurgle."

The Lore Master smiled. "The water's safe, then?" They both nodded. "Don't mind if I test it myself, do you?"

"Not a bit, dear. Don't drain too much of your power, though."

Chester gave her a tolerant wink and spread his arms. "Hear me, oh Gods . . ." His aura flicked into place. "Reveal danger!" The lake lit up in clear green.

"We're safe, children. What the hell—I declare a break. Let's have some fun!"

Mary-em whooped and stripped her chunky body down to the buff, dove into the water without even testing the temperature. Leigh and Lady Janet were next to strip and dive. Eames, still in his underpants, wiggled a toe in the water, grinned with hollow bravery, and took the plunge.

Soon the entire group was splashing and playing. Griffin stood on the bank alone, chewing his lip. Acacia swam over to him.

"Hey there, big fella. Come on in and play." She splashed at him with deadly accurate aim.

Griffin caught himself peering through the water for a better view of her. "Aren't the cameras still on?" Bobbick and Millie must be having a wonderful time . . .

Acacia gave him a raspberry. "Don't be silly. We're on break now. The Game is suspended for half an hour. Are you coming in, or am I coming out to get you?"

"Not that that's a bad idea, but . . ." Griffin balanced one-legged to pull off his shoes. He sat down to pull his pants off.

Acacia's appreciative whistle echoed across the lake. "My my. Just *look* at those legs." She swallowed water and coughed it out, laughing.

"Inherited 'em from my mother," he growled. From now on he'd spend more time on his sun deck. He seemed to be wearing flesh-colored briefs. "All right. Here I come." He jumped in with a resounding splash.

The water was cold and sweet, and varied from two to four meters deep. Griffin forgot his embarrassment and let his whole body wriggle with pleasure. He dove down to the lake's sculpted stone bed, running his hands along it, watching air bubbles leak from his mouth and wobble up to the surface.

How long had it been since he last dipped in a pool? The only possible answer was: too long. He spent fifteen hours a week exercising, but it was all work-related. At this moment Dream Park and Alex Griffin's work seemed worlds away.

He arced back up to the surface, barely avoiding Owen Braddon, who was backstroking across the pond. Not swimming as fast as (for instance) Bowan the Black, nor looking as pretty—he was easily thirty years older than Bowan, and the small pot belly ruined his streamlining— Braddon clove the water with a clumsy enthusiasm that made him a joy to watch.

Griffin sank beneath the water as a weight landed on his shoulders from behind. He came up sputtering.

"Guess who?" Acacia yelled, and pulled him back under. This time he grabbed one of her legs and wrestled her down. Her giggles sent a stream of bubbles frothing from her mouth as she kicked out and caught him firmly in the chest, breaking his grip.

She swam quickly away, and Griffin followed. He

watched the sun play on the muscles of her long, light brown legs as she tried to outrace him. Acacia glanced back over her shoulder, *eeked* to see him so close behind her, and dove under water again. Griffin gulped a lungful of air and followed.

Turbulence clawed at him, water and bubbles forced their way into his nose and buffeted his face. Then the water was calm again, and he realised that they'd swum through the waterfall.

There was eight meters of space between the rock wall and the cascading tons of water, and Acacia waited for him there. He swam to her, taking her into his arms playfully. Her body was slippery in his hands as she jumped up and licked the tip of his nose. "Very kinky," he said, glancing through the waterfall to the Gamers beyond. Nobody was paying any attention.

"Only mildly so, *hombre*." She locked her arms around his neck. "Hey, mister." She arced her eyebrows conspiratorially. "Ya wanna fool around?"

"I'm not sure I believe you," Griffin said, nuzzling her.

"Believe this, then." She kissed him fiercely, lifting her body to him, and Griffin found that one part of him believed her totally. They rolled in the water, blinded by mist and roar and water, aware only of each other. Mouths locked and bodies pressed tightly together; they were a tiny, tangled pocket of heat in the roiling cold.

When they broke, she pulled a few inches away, eyes glowing, huge, breathing a little shallow. "Now *that* was communication, mister."

"Yesss . . . I thought I heard something there. What was it saying?"

She hoisted herself tantalizingly high enough to look him squarely in the face. "Me want."

Griffin's hands steadied her hips, adjusting, and they both took a sharp inhalation—

"Well. Is this a private party, or what?"

Griffin and Acacia broke away from each other. Tony McWhirter was treading water about three meters away. A grin was frozen, lifeless, on his face.

Acacia flushed guiltily. "Tony! I, uh . . . thought you were . . . well, I—"

"It's pretty clear that you weren't thinking about me, so save it, Cas."

The dark haired girl shook her head disbelievingly, her hair spraying droplets in all directions. "Tony, don't be mad. You said it was all right if we each had our fun—" She turned pleading eyes to Griffin for an instant, and he backed away from her. Acacia swam over to Tony and tried to link her arms around his neck. He shook her loose.

"Yeah, well that's true, and it's certainly worked out well for you, hasn't it? I mean, with every available woman sewn up, and four or five loose men running around, you've had plenty of opportunities to bat those lashes and wiggle your hips. Then, if things didn't work out, well, old Tony's always available, right?"

"Tony, it isn't like that—" Again she tried to hug him, and he pushed her gently away.

"No, Cas. It's all right. I just don't think it's fair that every time you do this to me, everyone ends up thinking I'm the villain." He turned and dived and was gone beneath the waterfall.

Griffin swam over to her, although he didn't try to touch her. She watched Tony go, and some of the vibrancy had gone out of her.

"I'm sorry," Griffin said, not knowing what else to say.

She didn't look at him. "I'm sorry too." Her voice was

painfully flat. "I think maybe we had better get back to the others."

Through the rippling vertical sheet of water, the retreating figure of Tony was indistinct and growing smaller with each stroke. Acacia started to speak but the words wouldn't come at all.

Griffin followed her out through the thundering turbulence. He had let his mind stray from business. He wasn't here for fun. And the more he thought about it, the less it seemed that anybody else was, either.

Chapter Eighteen

SNAKEBITE CURE

Griffin was pulling his boots on when Mary-em slapped him on the shoulder . . . gently. That startled him. "Hey, Gary. Did you know this Rice guy? The guard?"

Griffin didn't let himself react. "Rice? I dunno. Does he work in Dream Park?"

"He did. Owen and Margie were telling us about it. Seems he got killed in the Research building a couple of days ago. The whole place was buzzing with it when they were being prepared for insertion this morning."

Griffin kept his eyes on his boots. "Hmmm. Maybe I did hear something about it. I'm sorry. Last week was really hectic." He pulled the laces tight and tied them. "I wasn't paying much attention to gossip."

"Well, I just thought maybe you knew him. Maybe he ate at your restaurant now and then?"

"It's likely enough. What happened to him?"

She jabbed him with the tip of a short strong finger. "I thought maybe you could clear that up, handsome. Ah well, get your pack on. Playtime's over." She waddled away whistling tunelessly to herself.

Well, that solves one problem, Griffin thought. He had considered dropping a comment about Rice's death into a group discussion, just to see if anyone flinched. For the role of the thief he had too many suspects; and nobody seemed to be acting like a hunted killer. Now the news was out, and he could sit back and watch the results.

It seemed likely that the killer didn't know the guard was dead. The Griffin's prey might well believe that Rice woke up with a headache and a sore neck. That would make it a game, a complex exercise in ingenuity and daring. But *murder*, that would be different. The Gamer who had chuckled privately about his marvelous coup might now begin to show signs of panic.

And who *was* left as suspect? Well, high on the list were Bowan the Black and his lady, Dark Star. Mary-em, S. J., and Tony McWhirter had no apparent alibis for Thursday evening. Neither did Oliver or Gwen. All of the other Gamers were covered, assuming that those who had already been killed out agreed to submit to the voice stress analyzers.

Unless . . . Acacia? Was she covered for the *entire* night? Pride be damned, the lady seemed uncommonly interested in the Griffin's past. *And my body. Damn Fortunato! Did he have no sense of tact?*

Come to think of it, what about Kasan Maibang? He was in the Game at that point, and would have to account for his actions like any Gamer.

And what of the workmen who entered Gaming Area A

to change the sets? Could one of them have sneaked away from the others . . . ?

"Holy mother of mercy," Griffin whispered bitterly. This was quickly getting out of hand. He would have to have Bobbick check *that* for him as soon as possible.

He stood, breathed deeply and shouldered his pack. The line was forming again, but this time he had a new partner: Acacia. She stood next to him, waiting for Chester's call to move out. She didn't speak.

"Hey, lady. Who's not communicating now?"

Her smile was faint. "I'm sorry, Gary. Do you mind if I walk with you?"

"I'd like that. Things aren't good with the boyfriend, eh?"

A sigh. "On and off. Off right now. I don't really feel much like talking. Do you mind? I'd just kind of like to walk with you." She looked up at him, and for the first time he saw no strength, no assurance in that beautiful face, only confusion and loss.

So Griffin walked with her as Chester started the column on its way. Together they wound their way into the mountains, silently sharing the sights and moods of the day.

Together they huddled beneath the branches of a gnarled dead tree as the Foré sent a storm against them. *Dora,* the spirit of nature, raged in the sky and in the earth, and dark clouds gathered, spitting splintered lightning into the mountains. Protected by the Clerical power of Gwen and Owen Braddon they still shivered in the cold rain. The wind plucked at them, and torn brushwood tumbled through the air at frenzied speed. When lightning struck, the ground trembled ominously, and rocks began to fall.

It seemed that half the mountain was falling on them:

waves of mud, a hailstorm of boulders. They saw the earth open and swallow one of their bearers. Before the storm was over Acacia and Griffin were cuddling for warmth, still unspeaking, shivering as they held one another.

". . . costing us *time!*" Henderson muttered, while Mary-em bellowed a song into the storm.

"I have a magic Wizard's staff, I think
            it's really swell,
Whatever tries to slow me down, I blow it
            straight to Hell—"

They could barely hear her, and nobody would join her. She desisted.

When at last the rain stopped, and the storm clouds boiled away into vapor, the Gamers crept out and looked anxiously into the sky, shaking water from their hair and bedrolls.

Acacia kept her eyes on the ground as she straightened herself up. She was barely audible as she answered Chester's roll call, and Alex watched her, worried.

Only Kagoiano had been killed, which left eighteen people in the Game: the fifteen players, Lady Janet, Kasan Maibang and the bearer Kibugonai. As soon as everyone had their breath back, they continued on.

After another mile of silent companionship, Griffin finally asked, "Does he do this to you often?"

"I don't know who's doing what to who, right now. Hell, maybe I am too bossy. Maybe I do play around too much . . ."

Alex chose to ignore the implied question. "Come on, Acacia. Yesterday you were telling me that I needed to get more involved in the Game. Okay. So do you, now."

"You're telling me to ignore the fact that the man . . . that someone I love has been hurt through my actions? I can't do that."

"Then go talk to him."

"No," she said softly. "I can't do that. Not yet. We might be able to talk later. We've had this problem before, and it's always worked itself out. Before. Maybe tonight we'll be able to talk." She looked up at him with the same pleading eyes he had seen under the waterfall. "I hope you don't think that I'm a tease, because I really do like you. I just don't think that you and I should take things any further than they've gone."

"I can understand that. Really. Listen. Let's just forget that all of this happened, all right? If you help me believe that I'm a Thief out to steal back precious Cargo, then I'll help you remember that you're a beautiful Warrior heading for the fight of her life. How does that sound?"

She creased her neutral expression into a smile and said nothing.

The route they traveled was turning green again, but now the trees and bushes seemed stunted, twisted, as if the soil itself contained alien nutrients. No branches bore leaves, but strange golden fruit hung from them, and Griffin wrestled with the temptation to pluck and taste one.

He couldn't explain it, but somehow he *knew* they were being watched by hostile eyes. He found himself thumbing the hilt of his knife and whistling tunelessly, nervously, his eyes roaming the crags above and the occasional gullies below.

The other Gamers were restless too. Alex caught Tony McWhirter looking back at them. Tony's eyes shied away when they met Griffin's. He seemed not resentful, but afraid.

"What do you think, Cas?"

"I feel it too. Something's happening. It'll be soon." She shivered, and drew her sword, holding it at ready though there was no visible foe.

Fear. *That* was what he felt, pure fear, something on a level he couldn't touch intellectually, something more primitive than reason.

Up ahead, Chester called the line to a halt. The mass of Gamers grouped around the Lore Master in a ragged semicircle.

Chester raised his hand for silence. "We all feel it, so I don't need to tell you that there is danger up ahead. I think we're nearing Cargo. What form it will take I haven't a notion. If we have to break the line for combat, let's see mixed couples. Try to pick someone of a different guild to stand with now. We can't afford to lose two of any category. Let's try to spread the damage. All right? Anyone who needs to exchange partners, now's the time. S. J., up here with me."

The youngster whooped and raced up to stand next to the Lore Master. Some of the players scrambled around, but Alex and Acacia stayed together.

The path narrowed and led through a slit in the rock wall. Owen Braddon, a Cleric, provided a gentle white glow to protect and illumine their way as they passed through a long, roughly triangular tunnel. The tunnel was cool and dry, but there was slippery moss underfoot. When it opened out again, there was a collective sigh of relief.

They were on the other side of the mountain now, heading into a wooded area filled with clumps of disturbingly twisted trees. They seemed to be on a plateau, and Alex watched Lady Janet point to another range of mountains beyond, and saw Chester smile.

One tree stood apart from the others, its branches spreading in all directions for a radius of a dozen meters. Looking at it, seeing the unhealthy brown of its mottled limbs and the manner in which its roots crawled snakelike along the ground before burying themselves, Griffin felt fear again.

Chester stopped the group with a raised hand, and walked toward the tree a few paces. He studied it carefully, then came back. "S. J.," he said brusquely, "I think that this one is for you. We've got Cargo."

"Subsonics," S. J. nodded. "I can feel it. Okay, we've been lured and warned. How do we handle it?"

"I'm not sure . . ." Chester was watching the tree with a practiced eye. "The Cargo won't be buried *under* the tree. That would be too much like last time . . ." He watched the branches swaying in the wind. "Wait a minute. The air currents here aren't strong enough to move the tree that much."

"Look at the shadow, Chester." S. J. pointed.

The tree's shadow was behaving even more strangely. It weaved, out of synch with the movements of the tree. The shadow-branches strained out, spectral fingers pointing towards . . .

"The cairn of rocks." About twenty meters from the tree stood a pyramidal pile of large stones.

"S. J., Margie, Eames and Griffin. Come with me. The rest of you, stay back."

The quintet of Gamers walked slowly to the pile. Chester halted them, and walked forward and around in a wide circle. At one point he stopped, backed up a bit, then turned and came back to them. "All right. S. J., you and Eames take the far side. Margie, you and Griffin work this side. Let's get some of these rocks cleared away so we can see what we've got."

Alex thought he saw a guilty wince crease Chester's face when S. J. answered with a perky, "Yes, chief!" and

bounded around to the far side. Something wrong here
. . . but what? Alex bent to the job of clearing the rocks.
Margie, as an Engineer, had to help supervise, but at her
age she could scarcely be expected to move the small
boulders herself.

He grunted, rolling away a stone. "What do you think
of . . ." He heaved another aside. ". . . of this Game? I
mean, so far?"

"Heavens. I've hardly had a chance to get into it. I'm
hoping that I have a chance to rig something really interesting before too much longer." .

"Don't you get points for everything you do in the
Game?"

"Of course, but it's more fun to do something elaborate.
Besides, the Gamers vote for bonus points at the end, so it
never hurts to be flashy."

Chester's voice cut in on them. "Don't worry, Margie.
You'll have plenty of opportunity to show your stuff."

"I certainly hope so, dear." She stepped around toward
the other side of the five-foot heap. "S. J.? How are
you—?"

Chester moved quickly around to intercept her. "Let's
keep our teams divided until—" Griffin watched, suspicion chewing at his nerves. Margie ignored Chester and
walked smoothly around him to the other side. Chester
took another step, turning. His legs were crossed when a
rock rolled under his feet. As he stumbled, he grabbed at
one of the rocks on S. J.'s side—

From his angle, Griffin saw only a small white snake with
red and yellow trim slide out of the pile. Chester's face
went slack and pale as he saw it, and paler still as it
expanded its hood and reared back hissing. "Kill it!" Henderson whispered in a ghastly quiet voice, his eyes riveted
on the reptile.

Alex hurled a stone at it. The snake disappeared.

"Damn." Chester said it with intense feeling. His face, already pale, had taken on a yellowish cast. "Oh, *shit*."

Margie helped him to his feet. "What is it, dear? The snake didn't touch you, did it?"

"It didn't need to. Oh no . . ." He seemed dazed and disoriented. Gina had broken away from the rest of the Gamers and was beside him, steadying him. "Don't you see?" He spread his arms wide. There was a pale yellow glow all around him. "That was a *bidi-taurabo-haza*. I'm *dead*, Margie. I'm walking dead."

By now the mass of Gamers had broken ranks and were grouped around him. Acacia pulled Alex to the side. "Did you see what happened? Why the hell didn't he scan that pile for danger?"

Griffin lowered his voice. "He knew it was there. He tried to kill S. J. and Eames out of the Game. He got caught himself. Rough justice."

"Whew. So Chester finally got caught." A leashed chuckle. "I wonder how he'll get out of it?"

Gwen stood by the rock pile, concentrating with her eyes closed. Her aura glowed around her, then spread to envelope the heap. It too glowed white, fading as Gwen opened her eyes. She glanced around at Chester. "It's clean now."

"Great." He crooked a finger impatiently at the rest of the group. "All right, let's see what we have here." He motioned Gwen and Owen to his side. "Pool your strengths. Do you think you can save me?"

The two Clerics meshed aura for a few moments, then shook their heads. The older man clasped Chester on the shoulder. "I'm sorry, Ches. It's too strong for us."

The king was dying. Was that check, or mate? Griffin asked, "What does that do to us? Is the Game over?"

Chester flagged a hand impatiently. "No. Something *that* deadly, that struck without warning? And even worse, a snake? Not after the hell I raised about the snow vipers, he's too eager for a clean kill. No . . . " Henderson's gaze unfocussed, and he scratched his side reflectively with a bony thumb. "No, I think our Mr. Lopez has prepared a way out for me. He's having another of his little jokes."

Bright red hair streaked with dust, and one slender arm scraped from wrist to elbow: Gina had moved a good many rocks very quickly. "We're almost finished, hon." She picked up her power staff and brushed it off. "What happens next?"

"We wait and see, Gina." The Lore Master reached out an unsteady hand for her, and when she took it he pressed it desperately hard against his cheek.

He looks like he thinks he's dying, Griffin thought. *He looks like he is dying. How can he let a game do this to him?*

As the rocks were pried loose or rolled away, three wooden boxes surfaced. Faded stencilled letters showed, and the Gamers began to laugh.

Chester walked over to the others and, in spite of himself, began to smile. Still partially covered by pebbles and dirt, there lay three battered cases of Coca-Cola.

"Well, children, this is our way out," Chester said. "I hope." He motioned to Kasan, and the guide jogged up without hesitation.

"Yes, oh dying bwana?"

"Are your Cargo gods strong enough to save me from this disease?"

"Oh, most assuredly, Mr. Henderson. The only real concern is what the gods may want of you in return for your life."

Chester seemed only mildly surprised. "You mean the undertaking of the quest is not enough?"

"Oh, no. You do it more for the sake of other Europeans than you do for us simple island folk."

"All right. Scan these boxes, ah . . . Owen and Bowan. We don't want any more screw ups just yet."

The pile glowed white and green, with no hint of red. Chester said, "Open them."

Margie produced a slender crowbar and, with an economy of movement that was delightful to the eye, she levered slats from a box. S. J. and Oliver attacked the others.

Each box contained twenty wasp-waisted bottles of caramel-colored fluid. Warm.

"All right. We're going to have to appeal to the gods of Cargo. That means we need to be as high and holy as possible. For this group, I'm afraid that means about three bottles each."

Kasan held up his hands. "Ah . . . none for me, bwana. You can count me out of this one."

Kibugonai deferred also, as did Lady Janet. "I'm allergic to caffeine," she said sweetly.

Chester sighed. "Then it's four bottles each. Let's get started."

Griffin sat cross-legged next to Acacia in the semicircle. Gwen and Owen were at the hub, the opened boxes of Coca-Cola at their sides.

"Hear us, Jesus-Manup. Hear us, God-Kilibob. Hear and observe," they intoned slowly. Gwen opened a bottle and passed it to Owen. Owen gave it to Alan Leigh, Leigh passed it to Mary-em; it passed down the line until it reached Chester at the far end. Gwen continued opening bottles until all held twelve-ounce containers of lukewarm cola.

"We accept this thy sacred fluid into our bodies in thy names . . ."

Griffin gagged it down. "I don't *like* soda pop," he whispered to Acacia. "I don't drink this junk."

"Shut up and glug," she whispered back, not bothering to hide her grin. "You've got to."

Griffin finished his, and passed another bottle along. "What if I have diabetes?"

"Then you can have your implant adjusted after the Game. Drink," she commanded. Ollie handed him his next twelve ounces.

Griffin drained it, stifling a heartfelt belch. Then he reconsidered and eructated with vigor. The echoes were fearsome; they seemed to go on forever, down the line and back up.

After the fourth round, moans could be heard from all corners. Tony looked green and had hiccoughs. Alex sympathized wholeheartedly.

"Who's ready for lunch?" Mary-em's question raised a chorus of vile suggestions.

Owen and Gwen finished their drinks, and sat amid a heap of empty bottles. "We are ready. Hear us, oh gods—" The air above the entire group began to shimmer with electric white. Owen lowered his voice. "All join hands, please."

Owen and Gwen faced each other, interlocking fingers as they closed their eyes.

The aura jumped and crackled, a bird's nest woven of lightning. The air sizzled with power. Griffin squinted against the glare. His skin crawled. The ground itself trembled.

A thunderous voice split their ears, a sound that echoed to the far mountains and back. "Yes, my children," the voice said with tremendous deliberation, each word rounded and perfectly enunciated. "I know what you wish of us. Yes, your leader may be saved. He shall pick five among you, quick-witted and wise, to compete for his life. If you win, his life will be returned to him. If not . . ."

The voice faded away, and the dancing glow lifted.

Chester definitely looked more yellowish. He rose unsteadily to his feet. "Leigh, Acacia, Oliver, Gina, and . . . Griffin." He gazed at Alex speculatively. "Something tells me that you might answer questions as well as you ask them."

Confusion ran unmasked on Alex's face. "Questions?"

Acacia took his arm comfortingly. "Don't worry. I think you'll do fine."

The sky rumbled above them, and clouds began to mass. Like soapsuds floating in a whirlpool, they swirled together, directly in front of the sun, eclipsing it. Darkness fell, and stars glowed above them. Then it seemed that the very fabric of space was twisting and torqueing, tortured by forces beyond imagination. The stars were rippled aside as the sky tore open. Soft, pale blue light pulsed beyond the edges.

From the region beyond the sky came a tiny shadow that growled noisily, growing larger by the second. Now it was plainly visible, an olive-drab Army-issue helicopter with its engine at full throttle. It hovered above them, then set down on the grass twenty meters away. A dark man in a smart white uniform hopped from the door and ran to them carrying a clipboard.

He saluted Chester smartly. "Mr. Henderson? I believe that your representatives are ready?"

"Yes," he said, looking warily at the helicopter. "Where are you taking them?"

"To heaven, sir."

Chester pointed. "In that?"

"Surplus cargo, sir. We don't waste anything. And now, if your people are ready? Yali is waiting."

"Yali? Who is Yali?"

The man with the clipboard clucked disapprovingly. "He is your intermediary. Certainly you don't think you can get an appointment with God on such short notice? Be happy for a chance to speak with His district Manager. Are we ready?"

"One moment." Chester spoke softly and hurriedly to his five representatives. "I remember a little about the New Guinea heaven. It was very European. Don't let that throw you. The important thing is the questions. Good luck."

Gina reached out for his hand, and he took it for a moment, squeezed, then let it fall. "We won't let you down, Chester," she promised. He nodded silently, his grin a lopsided slash.

The Gamers followed their host into the helicopter. The door slammed shut, the engine revved, and in a cloud of dust it lifted off and vanished into the wounded sky.

Chester watched the crack seal shut, swallowing them. "Now it's wait," he muttered. "It's just wait."

Chapter Nineteen

NECK RIDDLES

"We will be arriving in Heaven in approximately three minutes," the man with the clipboard said. He had already taken their names down in a precise hand. His name was Gengai.

There was nothing to see but dense blue fog which strobed light. Leigh sat across the aisles from Griffin, elbows balanced on knees and chin balanced on fists. Griffin leaned toward him. "Well? What do you think we're in for?"

"Some kind of test of wits. Neck riddles, probably."

"Neck riddles?"

Acacia bumped him on the shoulder with her palm. "Neck riddles. In olden days, a convicted felon was sometimes challenged to answer a series of riddles. If he won, he gained his freedom."

"Sounds like a good deal. What did the local king get out of it?"

"Jollies, mostly. Imagine a poor half-starved and half-flogged-to-death prisoner standing in chains at the Royal Court riddling for his life. Sometimes the prisoners did have something to lose. Hanging versus burning, for instance."

"How does that apply to us? It's only Chester's neck on the block this time."

"It's everybody's. Without a Lore Master to lead us, we don't stand much of a chance. Lopez knows that, and he knows we know it, and believe me, he'll take advantage of it."

The blue fog cleared, and there were white clouds above and ahead of them. One billowing cloudscape bore a classically boxy-looking two-story house. As they "climbed" to the level of the cloud Griffin felt his load of Coca-Cola become buoyant, and knew that the 'copter was actually losing altitude.

They landed. The door swung down for them. The five Gamers stepped down into knee-high white fog. The surface underfoot was spongy. The house nearby had white clay shingles and bamboo shades on its windows.

Strains of vaguely martial music drifted from within. Griffin recognized the overture to Bizet's Carmen. He hummed along, wondering where the insanity would end.

At the door they were greeted by a European manservant in coat and tails, who bid them enter with Old World formality. Gengai led them through a narrow hallway plush with white carpeting. Not a stick of furniture marred the path, so that when their guide turned left into an open doorway, Griffin was unprepared for what he saw.

The room was opulent. The ceiling was lost in distance;

the walls seemed to go up forever. Two of the four walls were covered in bookshelves, a third wall was an enormous world map. The fourth was hung with reproductions of classic works of art. Griffin recognized a Picasso, two Dalis, a Frazetta. Frazetta? Well, why shouldn't God borrow from the future to decorate his rooms? But the paintings didn't really complement each other . . .

The room was furnished with wrought iron chairs interwoven with wicker and padded with leather. The total effect was fabulous and slightly off-center, as if the designer was only partially familiar with the culture he was imitating.

They took chairs near the center of the room. "I don't like this," Acacia said. "It's too polite. We're supposed to be lulled."

Griffin drummed his fingers on the chair's arm. He could pick out titles on the shelves, and they were the same bizarre hodge-podge as the chairs and the paintings. There was a set of *Encyclopedia Britannica* next to five years of *UFO Quarterly* bound into leather volumes. One whole shelf was filled with books in an *International Classics* series of some sort. Directly below it were paperbacks in plastic envelopes. The effect was mildly disorienting.

He should be trying to remember riddles. He couldn't. As a child he had never been tempted by riddles.

Footsteps in the doorway. Griffin found himself straightening self-consciously in his seat. He refused to go so far as twisting around to see who was there.

"Good afternoon." The man's voice was cultured, studiedly so. The footsteps came closer, and the figure passed into his peripheral vision and to the wall map. "I trust that it *is* afternoon on Earth? Ah, good. And your trip was comfortable? Fine, fine."

He was a middle-aged black man, larger and stronger than most New Guinea natives. He wore a tropical shirt and razor-creased white plantation pants. He clasped his hands behind his back and fairly pranced from side to side, personal energy radiating from him like waves of heat.

"I am Yali, and I would like to welcome you to Heaven. I hope you will enjoy your stay." He laughed heartily, as at a private joke. "Yes, I most certainly hope you do. After all, some of you may stay forever. It is a nice place, actually, one of those infinitely rare situations where one is rewarded commensurately to one's efforts. Surely that is Heaven by any man's definition?" Again the vastly amused guffaw.

"Now that we are all friends, do have lunch with me, won't you?" Yali clapped his hands, and two beautiful dark women haloed in pale auras wheeled in twin carts laden with food.

Oliver ran his tongue lightly over his lips. "I hope this isn't a trick. Suddenly I am famished."

"Me three," Gina echoed.

"No tricks," Yali assured them. "Please. Enjoy."

The two carts locked together, and flaps folded out from the sides to form a buffet. . . of Spam, canned pineapple, crepes, rice, meat loaf, corned beef, and sliced white bread.

Acacia leaned close to Griffin. "It looks as if this whole place was designed by pulling random pages out of 1950's women's magazines."

"Frightening, isn't it?" Griffin chose a light meal, refused a charitably offered Coca-Cola, and returned to his seat.

Yali bounced up and down on his toes, grinning, and Griffin paused in mid-bite, a piece of a children's rhyme running through his mind. . . . *And welcome little fishes in with gently smiling jaws* . . .

Yali was unable to restrain his enthusiasm any longer. "I do not wish to interrupt your meal, but just as your mouths must be fed, so must your minds." He tapped his head with a forefinger. "Do you all agree?" There were no dissenting opinions, and that was enough for Yali. "I am sure you are wondering who I am, and how I earned such a position of honor in Heaven."

"All right, Yali, consider us mystified." Acacia ate while she listened.

"I was born in the Ngaing bush area of Sor, a member of the Walaliang patriclan and the Tabinung matriclan. During World War Two, Europeans came and promised my people that if we fought the Japanese we would be given all of the things that the Europeans had—electric lights, automobiles, metal tools, tinned meat, and so forth. Naturally we were excited.

"Understand that my people had lived a satisfying, happy existence before the Europeans came with their guns and missionaries. They told us that the reason we were denied sophisticated technology was that we were descended from Ham. Ham, as you may recall, was Noah's son, and after the flood he laughed at his father's drunken nakedness. I'm not terribly familiar with Judeo-Christian myth patterns, but I believe that Ham . . . no, it was Ham's son Canaan, was cursed to be a 'servant of servants' unto his breathren. Well, being evil and natural slaves and all that, we weren't fit to have the secret of Cargo, were we? So my people tried to conform themselves to the dictates of the Church, and we helped the Europeans build roads and plantations, and we dutifully marched off to war.

"I was one of those who fought. I died in the jungle, and because I was a brave and virtuous man, I went to Heaven. Here I learned that God—not *my* God, nor *your* God, but

God nonetheless—had always intended that we receive our share of Cargo, and that the Europeans had been diverting our goods for their own purposes."

Leigh asked, "And why didn't the Almighty put a stop to it?"

Yali smiled benevolently. "Because in his infinite wisdom, He perceived that this was merely a skirmish between people of different cultures, and that in time all inequities would be rectified. And indeed this is happening now. My people have learned the Cargo secret and are using it for their own enrichment. I, due to my familiarity with both New Guinea and the European—"

Acacia interrupted. "Where did you get your knowledge of Europeans?"

"Ah, an excellent question. Basic training for my army unit was carried out in Australia. There I was appointed Area Manager and given substantial training, including a thorough course in grammar. God, as you may have heard, has little patience for slang, colloquialism, or Pidgin English. Naturally, as soon as the political situation in Melanesia is back to normal, the natives will be able to address me in their own tongues. For the sake of continuity, however, it is now convenient to take messages in English. Paper work, you know. We're swamped with it."

Griffin asked, "Heaven doesn't have computers?"

"No." Yali moved up to the wall map and fingered a switch. "Have you been wondering just where we are? After all, theologians have debated for centuries over the exact location of Heaven. Some have said that Heaven can be found beyond the stars. Some say it exists in the heart of Man, and others claim that it does not exist at all, that God is dead, or at least unemployed."

Griffin stifled his laugh. "But you know otherwise?"

"Absolutely." The flick of a switch turned the wall map transparent. "And it is my pleasure to reveal to you the true location of the Hereafter." Beyond the transparent wall was a vast white cloud deck. A hundred meters out, a hole punctured the fluffy white. The hole was about twenty meters in diameter, and ladders rose from beneath, resting against the edges. Light- and dark-skinned angels climbed up and down, carrying packages.

"Heaven is situated directly above Sydney, Australia. Naturally this opening is not visible to the inhabitants of the city. We sometimes sub-contract with Australian manufacturers to create Cargo for us. Some of our angels are presently exchanging goods with a jewelry company which is building a golden throne."

Acacia raised one lovely eyebrow. "Is this for Him?"

"Oh, no. It's for me. I asked Him if He'd like one Himself, and He said that it was just about the ultimate in kitsch." Yali flipped the switch and the picture-window became a map again.

"But I'm sure that we have more interesting things to speak of. Matters of life and death. Philosophical things. For instance, can any of you tell me what a dozen rubber trees with thirty boughs on each might be?"

At first Griffin didn't understand; then he felt the sudden tension in his companions. It had begun.

Oliver looked at the other four Gamers as if checking to assure his right to answer. He cleared his throat. "That would be the months of the year."

"Quite right, young sir. And have you a question for me?"

Oliver considered. "Yes, I think so. It's in the form of a

rhyme:

> As I went over London Bridge
> I met my sister Jenny
> I broke her neck and drank her blood
> And left her standing empty."

The stout warrior looked at Yali challengingly. "Tell me, who was my sister?"

Yali rolled his eyes to the ceiling. "Such a fine meal you've just enjoyed. Would any of you care to share a bottle of wine with me?" He grinned maliciously at Oliver. "Rest assured that it won't be the same bottle our friend drank atop that famous bridge."

Oliver looked only slightly chagrined. "Close enough. Jenny equals gin, not wine."

"Ah . . . quite." Yali pulled a chair up and sat carefully, crossing one leg over the other with exaggerated care. "It is said among my people that some things are improved by death. Tell me, what stinks while living, but in death, smells good?"

Griffin's mind raced as he tried to come up with an answer.

"Oh, come now. Surely such clever minds as yours won't find this too consuming a problem." Yali smiled smugly.

Leigh raised a tentative finger. "Ambergris. From whales. They stink while they're alive, but when they're dead, you can make perfume from the ambergris."

Yali seemed delighted. "Very clever. Very clever indeed. Unfortunately we simple island folk rarely traffic in expensive perfumes. The proper answer is: the pig. I believe that you people were treated to one of the succulent creatures two days ago? Such a delicious aroma when roasted. But perhaps you feel I was unfair. Would you care to ask me a question in return?"

The sorcerer thought hard for a minute, then said, "All right. Riddle me this: what goes through the door without pinching itself? What sits on the stove without burning itself? What sits on the table and is not ashamed?" He said it all in one breath, and as he waited for his reply he panted slightly.

"Excellent. Let me think . . ." Yali scratched his ear. His eyes slid shut. Was he getting hints from Lopez? Griffin didn't want to believe it.

Yali's eyes flew open, and his mouth formed an "Aha!" oval. "Could it be the sun? Yes, I rather thought it might." His eyes rested with gentle malice on Alan Leigh, who squirmed uncomfortably. "We may have further business later, you and I. Now . . . who is next?"

Acacia glared at him. "Let's hear it, Yali."

"So eager. Let me think . . . what have we for the headstrong young lady? Ah, I know. What work is it that, the faster you work, the longer it is before you're done, and the slower you work, the sooner you're finished?"

The laughter in Yali's face was totally unreflected in Acacia's. She beetled her brows and twisted a curl of dark hair around and around on a forefinger . . .

"Miss Garcia, I'm afraid I must insist on an answer."

"Ah . . . weaving a basket? The f-faster you do it, the more mistakes you make, and the more likely you are to have to redo it . . .?"

"Such inventive minds we have here today. No, I'm afraid that the correct answer is 'roasting meat on a spit'. Don't you see, the faster you turn it, the slower the meat cooks. And of course, the slower you turn it, the faster it cooks. Isn't that just a corker?"

"A corker." Acacia's eyes were half-lidded, and there

was an umber flush to her cheeks. Alex could almost smell the sulphur bubbling in her words. "All right, 'Yali', try this one.

> Whilst I was engaged in sitting
> I spied the dead carrying the living."

She tossed her dark hair back with a flip of her head. "What did I see?"

Yali closed his eyes and hummed. He drummed his heels gently against the white floor. He scratched his ear.

"Mr. Yali," Acacia said curtly, "I'm afraid I must insist upon an answer."

He glared at her. "Quite right, Miss Garcia. Could it be a stretcher? A stretched hide carrying a wounded man?"

"What an ingenious fellow you are. And so quick with your reply. A pity to disappoint you. I'm afraid that the proper answer is a ship. A vessel made of dead wood, carrying living men." She curtsied in her seat, and Yali smiled wanly.

"Well, that helps your side a bit, but you're going to need more. Who's next?"

Gina, who had been lost in thought, perked up. For the first time, Griffin found no trace of a dreamy cloud in her expression. Even the fire in her hair seemed to blaze brighter. "I'll take it."

"So. Try this: 'I know a word of letters three. Add two, and fewer there will be.' "

Gina buried her head in her hands and moaned. At first Alex was worried, then he listened more carefully to the sighs and realised that they were phony.

"Oh my," she said finally, wiping her eye clear of a nonexistent tear. "The answer wouldn't be 'few', would it?" Her bright red eyebrows arched, and her face screwed up in an expression of mock-concern. Yali nodded unhappily. Gina hitched her chair closer, teeth showing whitely in her smile. She resembled nothing so much as a cat on the hunt, and Alex found himself silently cheering her on.

Her voice was warm honey. "I have a little old question for you, dear. I give you a group of three. One is sitting down, and will never get up. The second eats as much as is given to him, yet is always hungry. The third goes away and never returns." Her smile became beatific. "Who are they?"

Yali seemed very displeased. He rose from his chair and click-heeled across the room, blank-eyed, mumbling to himself. Ultimately he turned on his heel to face them. "Yes, yes, I know, time is against me. I admit I have no answer."

"Oh, I'm sorry. The correct answers are Stove, Fire, and Smoke. We're even again," Gina said sweetly.

"So you are, and you have one player left to go. Mr. Tegner. Or do you prefer *Griffin*?" There was a peculiar gleam in Yali's eye, and Alex knew that Lopez was having his little joke.

"In this context I prefer *Griffin*," he said.

"Very well, Griffin. There is a saying you may have heard in your business:

Whoever makes it, tells it not.

Whoever takes it, knows it not.

And whoever knows it wants it not.

Can you tell me what I speak of?"

Alex brooded. *In your business.* What did he mean by that? As the Griffin, the Thief? As Gary Tegner, restauranteur? Previous riddles had referred to food . . . Or as Alex Griffin, Dream Park Security head? Nice wide range of choices, there.

Whoever makes it, tells it not. Why? Something illegal or immoral? That would fit the Thief *and* the Security Chief. Good. *Whoever takes it . . . whoever knows it.* If you know what it is, you don't want it. A restaurant owner might take black market meat if he didn't know what it was. Do you "make" black market meat? Or bad meat, meat that wouldn't pass honest inspection. *Pass?*

"Excuse me, Griffin, but I'm afraid I need an answer now."

Get a hunch, bet a bunch. "Counterfeit money."

Yali's expression went dull. Acacia reached out a warm hand for Griffin's and squeezed affectionately.

"Well. Right you are. And do you have a riddle for me?"

Alex had finally remembered a riddle. "Do as I say, don't do as I do. Say boots without shoes."

Yali's eyes unfocussed. His lips moved, silently repeating Alex's words, while Alex sweated it out. Presently he said, "Boots."

"Drown!"

Yali's teeth flashed like sudden lightning. No, he *hadn't* been sure. "Well. We're exactly even. Five for you, five for me. Unfortunately, that leaves you where you started, with Mr. Henderson's life dangling by the proverbial thread."

Oliver folded his hands neatly in his lap, and squared his shoulders, but the way that he chewed his upper lip before answering betrayed his nervousness. "What happens now?"

"I am going to ask one more riddle, a tie breaker. If your team's selected representative can answer it, Mr. Henderson lives. If not, he dies."

Oliver was indignant. "But that's not fair! You can make the answer as ridiculous as you like, and if we don't get it, that's the end!"

"Quite so. I recognise the intrinsic uncertainty in such a
contest, so I will offer you a side-wager. If any of you will
put your own lives up as a stake, I will accept it. In other
words, if you win, everyone lives. If you lose, Mr. Henderson lives but one of you dies." The five were silent.
"Well?"

Griffin was thinking, *I can't! I'm not a self-centered
coward, I'm a detective. I can't!*

Leigh stood, drew in a deep breath and exhaled noisily.
"I got us into this. If I hadn't blown both points we'd have
won. It's only fair that I be the one."

"Bravo, Mr. Leigh. Such bravery. Such sacrifice!"

"Such bullshit. Let's get on with it."

"Quite. For your life, then:
    Who makes it, has no need of it.
    Who buys it, has no use for it.
    Who uses it can neither see nor feel it."

"Repeat that, please."

"You should listen more carefully, especially since the
answer has special significance for you—" and Yali repeated the riddle. Griffin found himself holding his breath.

Leigh was stalling, his puffy cheeks drawn with tension.

Coffin, Griffin realised suddenly. *Coffin. Coffin, you
idiot!*

Desperately, Leigh blurted, "A prosthetic leg for a blind
child?"

Yali shook with silent mirth. "What an imagination. You
will certainly be welcome here in Heaven. No, it's a coffin,
Mr. Leigh. Don't you find that dreadfully appropriate?"
Yali stretched his arms hugely, happy to have claimed at
least one victim. "Well, unless you'd like to play more
games, the rest of you may return to Earth. Mr. Leigh and I
have business."

Gina stood and took one of Alan's hands in hers. "Thank you," she said sincerely. "You didn't have to do that."

His mouth twitched, trying to form a smile. "Yeah, well, I might have done it better."

There was moisture glistening in his tear ducts, and Gina kissed him softly on the mouth. "I'm proud of you anyway," she said.

Acacia hugged him from the side. "Ditto, Alan. Don't worry. We're going to win this for you, kid."

"Yeah," said Leigh, staring into the wall, his face doughy and lifeless.

Gengai appeared at the door. "We're ready to leave now," he chirped.

"Wait a minute!" Griffin found his voice ragged. He took Leigh by the shoulder. "Thank you, Alan."

The Magic-user managed to nod his head in acknowledgement. "It's all right. Go on, get out of here. And win it!"

"We hear and obey, O mighty mage." Gina kissed him again, on the cheek. "Watch us. It'll be worth it."

The helicopter drifted away from Yali's cloud. Looking out, Griffin could see a string of white factories on adjoining clouds, white puffettes rising from their smokestacks as they busily churned out Cargo. Angels with multi-hued parakeet wings fluttered here and there carrying loads, and a heavenly choir performed Handel's Messiah in full-bodied SphericSound.

But all that Griffin could really see or hear was Leigh's face, red with the effort to hold back tears, and a cracking voice that said, "And win it!"

Suddenly, unaccountably, that was all Alex wanted to do.

Chapter Twenty

THE SEA OF LOST SHIPS

It was 1350 hours by the watch imprinted on the cuff of Griffin's denim shirt. The group had been back on the march for an hour and a half.

The line wasn't jolly. A grim singularity of purpose could be seen in every face, heard in every terse word. Mary-em had tried to get songs going, but the efforts had died stillborn. Finally she gave up, her tanned and wrinkled face puckered with discontent.

Their trail wound them steadily deeper into the mountains, and this, in part, may have contributed to the sense of sobriety and unease. Griffin found himself gazing up into the crags with a chilling and undeniable feeling of approaching doom. Unbidden, images of death and decay sprang into his mind, and he shook his head, irritated and upset.

Subsonics and subliminal imagery? he wondered.

Lopez psyching us out? Maybe. Griffin had known it from the first: this was a blood duel.

Acacia walked next to him, her hand occasionally finding his for a few moments, squeezing then releasing. As if she too needed the reassurance of physical contact. He took comfort in knowing that his strange mood was shared.

Although the path was broad, Alex found himself wandering over to the edge to look into the gorges below, now mostly shrouded with mists. There was no wind, and it didn't feel any colder; but it *looked* cold. Alex gave in and put on his windbreaker.

Acacia was mumbling under her breath.

"What did you say, Cas?" He tried to force warmth into his voice and it came out sounding just that way: forced.

Reflexively, she moved closer to him and took his arm. "Nothing meant for human consumption, that's for sure." She shivered. "I really am getting uptight, and I don't know why. We haven't taken really heavy losses . . . yet."

"Yet?"

"The replacement period ends tonight. Tomorrow and the day after we'll get hit with heavy artillery. I know it."

Alex thought about that. "Is there any way to minimize the impact?"

"Yeah. Don't make mistakes. You can see how easy *that* is. There are just too many ways to die in this Game. Think about it: how have we lost people? Riddles, monsters, natural hazards, gunshot . . ."

"You know, that doesn't sound like you, Cas. Where's the get up and go?"

"It got up and went. I *know* I'm acting strange, dammit, and I don't really understand it, either." She kicked a pebble out of the way, dark eyes following it as it skipped across the road and vanished over the edge: not falling, but suddenly gone, kicked beyond the hologram illusion of a misty chasm at their feet.

"Listen. What if I told you that if you keep your chin up you'll get a surprise tonight?"

"Gary—I told you that we shouldn't take things any further. There's been enough trouble."

"I'm not talking about trouble. Just a little harmless fun."

"Harmless, huh? Fun? Just what do you have in mind?"

"Everything but."

"But what?"

"But taking things any further. We can go as far as we went, can't we?"

She squinted an eye at him. "And what about Tony? If we're off alone together somewhere *not taking things any further,* we might as *well* be screwing."

That word was a jolt. Alex thought it over. "You're right either way. Okay, either we don't go off alone at all or we take things wherever they go. How's that sound?"

"Indecisive. Gary—"

There was a sudden jolt as the line came to a halt. On a ledge seven feet above the trail, there stood a slender dark figure. At first Alex was reminded of Millicent: the short, tightly-curled hair, the delicious figure and the skin tones were all similar. But this woman was nearly a foot taller than little Millie, and Millie would never have been found in that bold, challenging stance.

She wore buckskin boots and beige leather pants with a copper-buckled belt. She wore a red vest over a beige blouse, and carried a businesslike dagger in a fast-draw sheath high on her left side. The knapsack on her back rode as if weightless. She stood fists on hips, legs spread apart and braced firmly. Alex found her beautiful. His lips pursed into an automatic whistling position.

"Who is *she*?" he asked Acacia.

"I think I saw her at the Gamer selection proceedings, but I don't know the name or the rank."

The tall woman jumped down from the ledge. A miniscule wobble spoiled the illusion of a perfect landing. Chester greeted her. "Holly Frost, I presume?"

"You've got it, lover. Second-level Thief, first-level Magic User, and generally excellent lady." She dusted off her buckskins by knocking them against each other. "And it looks like I arrived just in time. What have we here, a zombie march? I don't see a bright face in the bunch. What the hell, maybe I should join the other team—" She turned as if to walk away, then turned over her shoulder and smiled slyly.

"On the other hand, since I obviously have no competition here, maybe I should stick around, accrue a few points, steal somebody's old man . . ."

There wasn't a sound from the other Gamers, although a few mouths hung open in shock. Then Mary-em pushed Bowan out of the way and waddled over to Holly, gazing up at her like a demolition man examining a condemned skyscraper.

"Think you're pretty hot, do you, treetop?"

"I know it, grandma."

Mary-em drummed her fingers on her waist for a few moments, then her crinkled face split with a grin. "It's high time we had some new blood. These lackards are slacking off already. Think you can roust things up a bit?"

"Or know the reason why."

"Good enough." The little woman stuck out a grimy hand, and they shook. "Name's Mary-em, but you can call me Mary-em."

"Done." Holly looked at Chester. "You're the man. Let's get this show back on the road!"

In spite of himself, Henderson's tired face lit up, and there seemed to be new bounce in his step. "All right, group, you heard the lady. Let's do it!"

"I want her with me," Mary said. She glared at Bowan. "Why don't you find yourself another perch, sonny?" She pulled Holly in next to her. "You better be able to sing, honey, or I'm going to intimidate you half to death."

Holly slapped her on the back. "Do you know 'Friar Malone'?"

Their mood was infectious. Soon the entire line was moving at a brisk pace, singing a tale of the unlucky *personna* of an unskillful Gamer of bygone days.

"Through dungeon and city
Both ugly and pretty
Went the brave lawful Cleric named Friar Malone.
He whirled his warhammer
'Gainst the vampire's glamour
Crying, 'Down with the Demon Undead, Undead, oh!' "

Alex noted that Acacia's expression was no longer strained, and he was happy. It seemed that everything was right again, that the mission would be successful, that—

How *could* he have forgotten Rice? None of this was real; not the mountains, nor the mists, nor the warm arm of the woman at his side, nor the happiness he had felt a moment ago. But Rice was real; Rice's bound corpse was real.

And the Gamers sang with no sign of grief:
"But a Succubus found him
And in her lair bound him
And became the foul death of brave Friar Malone.
Now his ghost stalks the barrow
That he tried to harrow,
Crying, "Down with the Demon Undead, Undead
Oh!' "
But death had been real for Rice, and Griffin would not
forget it again.

The trail wound down out of the mountains, cramping
them between masses of granite. Presently it rounded a
tight turn, and Griffin and Acacia stepped out of shadow
into a view of sand dunes and ocean.

Acacia gave a low whistle, and Alex felt her hand tighten
on his. The Gamers had stopped and spread out.

Downslope was a semicircle of bay. It must have been
deeper once. The line of Quonset huts along the sandy
shore had once been Navy docking facilities. The docks
were high and dry now, and the buildings deteriorated,
and the harbor must have been two to three meters deep.

The water was littered with boats and pieces of boats,
broken airplanes both military and commercial, ruined
machinery of every description. Angular shapes halfway to
the horizon might have been the bows of luxury liners sunk
almost beneath the water. One of the military aircraft had
the grinning jaws of a shark painted on its nose, others
showed a fading red sunburst. There was even one
boat—about ten meters in length, standing on its keel as it
leaned against its rotting dock—with swastikas embla-
zoned on its flank.

The killer had crept past a big airplane on his path to

Rice and the neutral scent. Now, which Gamer was giving undue attention to the mired and broken airplanes? Trouble was, *everyone* was intently studying the harbor, except the Griffin, who was fruitlessly studying them.

"Now what in the world is a Nazi patrol boat doing in the Pacific?" Holly Frost murmured to Acacia.

Chester was conferring with Maibang. Acacia called, "We want in on this, Ches."

Chester nodded agreement. "That sounds fair. Let's gather round, people." The Gamers crowded around the Lore Master, and he tapped Kasan on the head. "You're on."

Kasan Maibang was nodding to himself. "I have heard of this place, but never seen it. Have you, Lady Janet?"

The small blond nodded her head, then shook it. "Not actually *saw*, but I think I was brought through here on the way to the Mission. You know, for the sacrifice?"

The little man's eyes were bright, and his grin managed to convey mystery and menace at the same time. "I think that the lady may be right. In truth, this place smells of evil, smells of our enemies. This is the Sea of Lost Cargo, where our enemy lures European transportation and robs them."

"I want a close look at those buildings," Chester said. "Then . . . What's the matter, Fortunato?"

McWhirter had been shaking his head as he studied the harbor. "They don't look quite . . ."

"The ships and planes? Most of them are holograms. Why not? We can't get to them anyway. There won't be more than one or two solid mockups." Chester pointed. "Like that Nazi ship. Stands out, doesn't it? Almost whistles for our attention. I think we'll search there next. Very carefully."

Gina sidled up to him. "Danger, Ches?"

"You can bet half your points on it. We'll split into groups once we're down there. One group goes in, one guards." He glanced at Holly. "Well, lady, we get to test you out a bit early. Are you up to it?"

She said nothing, but licked her lips eagerly. Mary-em fairly vibrated in place.

Alex nudged his companion. "Looks like Mary-em's met her match."

"That'll take some doing. We'll see."

The Gamers spilled downhill. Griffin felt vaguely surprised to find that the incline was real. Curiously, he was more disoriented than he would have been if *everything* had been illusion. He looked above himself, at the mountains they had just crossed, and wondered: *How much of that was real?* And didn't know.

His unease vanished with the childish pleasure of running pell-mell down the slope, always just on the verge of toppling forward. Behind him, S. J. dived into a roll and tumbled to the bottom, whooping. He sprang to his feet, shook the dirt from his hair and adjusted the straps on his backpack. "Wow, that was fun!" He ran halfway up the slope again and tumbled back down, bouncing to his feet like an elf shot out of a cannon.

When everyone had reached bottom, Chester began ticking people right and left. "S. J., Oliver, Panthesilea, Griffin, Dark Star, and . . . Holly Frost. You come with me. And Maibang. The rest of you stay with Kibugonai and Lady Janet. We're going in."

"Well all right," Holly said, her face deadly serious. Her eyes gleamed as they roamed the aged buildings that lined the docks. She and Griffin were the tallest people in the group, and she gravitated toward him naturally. "You're the Griffin," she said, appraising him. "I saw the spear cast you made on the Nibek. Not bad at all."

"Mildly spectacular. Your name's Holly? This is Panthesilea."

Acacia smiled at Holly with an edge of challenge. "This is your first big outing?"

"My first 'first run'. I've done my share of straight Gaming." The tall black girl noticed the way Acacia moved closer to Alex, and clucked loudly. "No need to get possessive, honey. I haven't even decided if I want him yet."

Acacia couldn't seem to decide how to react to that comment. "As soon as you make up your mind, clue me in, will you?"

"You'll be the second to know." There was a broad flash of tooth, and Holly pivoted on her heel to investigate the other members of the group.

"I'm not sure why," Acacia said softly to Alex, "but I think I like her. Or I don't. One or the other."

"What I love about you is your absolutely fearless self-appraisal."

The Gamers moved in two clumps toward the docks. Bowan the Black's "Reveal danger!" generated only a wash of green light. Nothing threatened them, then . . . except the passive danger of the rotted wood they walked on.

The years had not been kind to the long arc of wood-and-concrete docks, nor to the quonset huts and smaller wooden structures. But Griffin noticed anomalies. Every line and cable was neatly coiled, ready for use and rotting in place. Winch machinery was rust-free, oiled and polished. A riveted metal tank on stilt legs showed freshly painted letters:

AIRCRAFT FUEL

"Chester, this place isn't abandoned."

"I know, Griffin. We'll have to watch for the owners

coming back. And ask ourselves why this place isn't guarded. Meanwhile . . . that building?''

No need to point. Everyone had already noticed that one particular Quonset hut. It might have been built yesterday. The metal gleamed. In the walk that led to the front entrance, some of the wood planks had been replaced.

Gina cast another *Reveal Danger*. Nothing.

The first team went in. The rest hovered at the entrance, ready for emergencies.

It had been the Administration Building. Wooden walls had blocked it off into cubicles with desks. Most of the partitions had been torn out. The desks were still there, but most of them had been lined against one long wall. But the papers and coffee cups and ash trays were still on the desks, some neat, some messy; and the desks had been dusted. The great expanse of concrete floor had been swept recently.

The floor was cluttered with . . . well, stuff. As if children had played here, Griffin thought, while the teacher was gone.

There were big, sweeping patterns drawn on the concrete: a good representation of the dockyard and shoreline, in green paint, and an airfield overlaid in brown paint on the bay itself. There were a dozen malformed little figurines made from gourds and tubers and wood. There were flocks of toy ships and airplanes, a rich variety of them. Some were crude representations with bamboo hulls or gourd fusilages and wings of clipped leaves; but other craft looked like they had been bought in American toy shops, or built for the offices of naval and air force officers. A ''table ritual'', candles and clean tablecloth and fresh flowers and cans of corned beef and Spam, had been carefully arrayed on a big desk with four desk chairs around it.

"A cargo cult magician's workshop," Holly Frost said. "If we desecrate this place, we'll put them out of business for awhile."

"Yeah," said Chester. "Maibang, how would we go about. . .? Skip it." He went to the big front entrance and shouted, "Margie!"

"Chester?"

"See if there's any fuel in that tank we passed. Find a can and fill it up. Take Eames. The rest of you, start tearing up the boardwalks for wood. Desecrate be drowned! We're going to burn this place."

"Chester?"

"Yeah, Griffin?"

"We don't want a bonfire advertising our presence."

"I know that. We'll set up the fire and touch it off just before we leave."

Oliver and Dark Star moved among the desks, looking for anything that might turn up. S. J. began arranging a bonfire with wood handed to him through the entrance. Tony called from a far corner of the building: "Chester? Two cases of Coca-Cola."

"Save a bottle for each Gamer. Smash the rest," Chester directed. Tony began smashing bottles with his gun butt.

Presently Eames and Margie were back with three big gasoline cans. Margie was glad enough to relinquish her heavy can to Griffin. He began splashing the fluid across the painted map of harbor and airfield.

It didn't smell.

He splashed a bit on his hand and sniffed at it. Nothing. He touched his tongue to it.

Water?

He looked up—and half a dozen Gamers were looking at him in disgust. Griffin continued distributing the "gasoline". He felt like an idiot. Of course Dream Park wouldn't permit a huge bonfire in Gaming Area "A". The fire, when it came, would be a hologram.

The small Nazi ship leaned drunkenly above them as Chester's group stood looking up. The remaining Gamers followed to within twenty feet, and stopped. They were well trained.

The ship didn't look all that stable.

"Forward bow," S. J. said. "I bet if someone gave me a lift up I'd find a rope ladder, and—"

"No need," Chester told him. "There are hand holds set in the side amidships. You can do the honors as soon as I make a scan." He raised his arms and chanted his incantation.

Griffin found himself looking around at the others instead of watching the emerald fireworks. Someone else wasn't paying much attention, either.

Dark Star was pretending to watch Chester, but she was carefully rubbing something out with her foot. He watched her slow, subtle grinding motion, almost as if she were putting out a cigarette. Then she shifted her balance to one foot, locked her hands behind her back, and waved the inverted fist back and forth.

Alex glanced back. Bowan was watching her hands intently. A signal, then. Signalling what?

When the green glow faded, S. J. mounted the metal ladder and climbed aboard. "All clear here, Admiral," he called, and disappeared from view. Dark Star was fourth in line to board, and Griffin arranged to be last.

"Just a second," he whispered to Acacia. Unobtrusively he wandered over to where Dark Star had been standing. Rubbed almost into oblivion, but still discernible, was an immense footprint. It was all he could do to stifle a yell of surprise.

He scrambled up after Acacia, enjoying an excellent view of her trim posterior. She helped him on board, and he drew her firmly over to the side.

"Acacia, why would you hide a clue?" Acacia looked puzzled, and he rephrased. "What I mean is, if you saw a sign that indicated danger to the group, would you have any conceivable reason for not telling the rest of us?"

She thought about it. "Well . . . I'd be lowering the chances of survival for the other players. That would mean fewer people to divide the group bonus with. *If* we won."

"Hmm . . . is that all?"

"Well, if you were the only one who knew what was coming, you'd have a better chance to prepare a plan of action. You'd look really good once the feathers started flying. I guess you know that the Gamers vote a special point bonus for Best Player. Then there are points for bravery . . ."

"Any monetary incentive?"

"Only indirectly. When you've accumulated enough points to be a Game Master or Lore Master, then you can start making money." Her words held an unspoken question.

"I'll tell you later. Just keep on the lookout for a big monkey."

"Say what—?"

Oliver came for them. "Come on, guys. Things are hotting up."

Acacia reached out and stroked Oliver's chin, feeling the three-day growth of beard. "You look terrifically fierce, amigo. I bet Gwen loves it."

He playfully brushed her hand off. "Come on," he

grinned. They followed the warrior into the cabin, where most of the Gamers were busy searching. Griffin noted that Dark Star cast frequent worried glances out of the windows.

A steel door stood open in the back of the cabin, and narrow metal stairs led down into darkness. Maibang climbed out of the gloom, followed by Chester.

"I think we may have something," he said, waving a roll of paper. "We found it wedged behind one of the engines." They cleared dust and twisted scraps of metal from a table top and spread out the scroll. Chester arched a single thin eyebrow. "A map . . ."

S. J. was squeezing his head between Chester and the table, and his little brown eyes lit up. "Aerial survey map, chief."

For once Henderson seemed undisturbed by Waters' enthusiasm. "Significance?"

The Engineer turned the map upside down, and flipped it backwards before placing it right side up again. "Don't seem to be any markings here . . ."

Chester was tracing a line with his forefinger down what seemed to be a river. The map covered a mountainous region, readily recognizable as New Guinea. "Pre-Inversion," he murmured. "Anybody see anything interesting here?"

Alex scanned the map carefully from across the table, differentiating the greys and blacks into jungle and plain. "There's a blank area about the size of a dime right *there,* in that mountain range."

Chester's gaze followed the pointing finger to a pale circle amid a patch of jagged lines. "Maybe someone dripped coffee on it? or water?"

Alex ran his finger lightly over the surface. "Nope. Paper's not rough there. I think that's our clue."

Henderson nodded ungrudging admiration. "And I think that you're right. Well then, *if* it's a clue, then . . ." He paused, scratching the three-day stubble on his chin. "If our Illustrious Enemy doesn't appreciate anyone speaking their names, then just maybe they don't like anyone to *find* them, either. A spell intended to make them invisible just might backfire with a photograph, leaving a blank area like this."

Acacia was still puzzled. "But why a German boat?"

Chester waved it off. "Visual contrast. It tells us where to go. It is in context, though. German spy planes and high-altitude cameras would have been ideal for supplemental fly-bys in World War Two. Just a matter of cooperative technology. Kasan, do you recognise this area?"

The little guide hemmed and hawed for a minute, then nodded his head. "And look here, *effendi*. We have a large body of water. That would fit with what Lady Janet told us."

"Good, good. Where is this?"

"Hmm . . . I believe there is a volcano in here, but I can't find it. It may be hidden in the blank spot."

"May be?" Chester seemed skeptical.

"Let's not expect too much from a poor native guide, *kimo sabe*," he said modestly. "Trust me. It's there. And if . . . *since* it's there, I think we have here a half-day's march, along the coast, then inland."

"Excellent. Progress at last." Chester scooped up the roll and curled it, folded it once and stuck it in his backpack.

Holly Frost sniffed the air. "Let's have a danger read,

Boss Man. I don't like this setup too much."

"You're first-level magic. You handle it."

"Much grass. Hear me, oh gods!" She tried to spread her arms imperiously, but her knapsack was ill balanced, and she had to shift it on her shoulder. She was totally unembarrassed. "Reveal Danger!" A green cloud enfolded her. One edge of the cloud swirled with crimson light.

Chapter Twenty-One

THE HAIAVAHA

The mood in the cabin changed instantly. Oliver was the first to drop his hand to his sword. "Methinks it's time to split," he said, peering out of the cabin.

"Right you are," Chester agreed. "Women and Lore Masters first." He was out of the cabin in three elastic steps. "Hustle, people," he called back, scrambling down the ladder. "I'm getting a tingle. It's coming, and it's big."

They bolted after him. Dark Star looked grim, edgy, and Alex found that worrying. He pulled Acacia to the side. "Get ready. Remember what I said."

"Big monkey time? Monkey shmunkey," she grinned, drawing her sword. "Just give me something to cut, and I don't care if it's King Kong."

That, of course, had been Griffin's first thought. "They wouldn't *really* hit us with King Kong, would they?"

"I should let you sweat, asking a question like that. Of course not, dumbo. This is New Guinea, not Skull Island. Different mythos."

"Just asking." Alex followed Oliver down the ladder. He felt the vibrations as soon as his feet touched the dock. He lifted his arms to help Holly, and she fell back against him.

"Now normally I get along just fine, handsome, but in your case I'll—"

He felt her cheek, against his, grow taut. "Holy hell. *Griffin*—"

Alex spun around, and gasped. Two hundred meters away, a light plane of some kind was taking to the air, in pieces. Water surged, and the dock shook with the impact of the waves. A sound that started in the bones and radiated outward, only belatedly recognizable as a bestial snarl, grew in intensity until it hurt their ears. They glimpsed a dark, vaguely manlike figure rising above the water, then sinking again behind a capsized ocean liner. The liner trembled, and the grinding wheeze of shredded steel filled the air.

Oliver flashed a glance at Chester. "What do you think, Ches? How do we tackle it?"

The Lore Master was peering out over the junked vessels with tiny frown lines crinkling his forehead. "We don't even know what the hell it is. All I know is that that mother's *strong*." He squeezed Gina's hand hard, and she flinched. "And angry. Honey, how much time do we have before curfew?"

She lifted a naked wrist. "No watch."

"Just about fifty minutes," Griffin volunteered.

Chester considered. He looked worried. "I don't really want to tackle that thing tonight. We're all a little tired, and

I think that Lopez is counting on that. Well, I'm going to surprise him and back off."

Bowan the Black, face set in a mask of frustration, pushed his way past Oliver to protest. "What do you mean, 'back off'?"

Chester snapped, "What would I mean, Bowan?"

"I can't believe I'm hearing you right. This is the second time you've had us turn tail, Henderson. It doesn't look good on my record."

"How would being on the receiving end of a massacre look on your record?"

Dark Star had sidled up next to Bowan. She said, "You may not think we can handle it. I do." She turned to the others. "Anyone else? Shall we do a quick vote?"

"It'll have to be quick," Chester said. The thing was wading toward them now, leaving a white wake. A river of water flowed from its fur. Smaller than King Kong, but much larger than a man, it seemed a cross between an ape and a boar, with a boar's tiny eyes, long snout, and jutting white tusks. Wet, the fur was almost black; but the lank dry fur of its head and shoulders was red, with bright orange and yellow-white tufts. Its arms were disproportionately long; the hands were underwater as it waded straight toward them. Chester said, "We're short of dithering-time. Okay, I vote we run for it."

Oliver ground his foot nervously. "Sorry, Chester. I've gotta back Bowan on this."

"Okay. Gwen?"

She held onto Oliver silently. The body language was clear.

"Alright, who else?"

Griffin had chosen. "Follow the Lore Master. Run, but keep looking back. We might learn something."

"I agree," said Margie. Owen nodded.

S.J. seemed very unhappy, one thin hand in front of his mouth, brown eyes darting back and forth before he finally moved next to Chester.

He knows something, Griffin told himself. He caught Acacia's eye and motioned her toward him. She gritted her teeth, but she came.

Holly Frost was watching Griffin with the barest of smiles pursing her lips. The wheels turning in her head were nearly audible. She stepped toward Chester, who nodded his appreciation.

"Alright," he barked, "no more time for fence-sitters. Decision time, people." Eames joined Bowan. Tony moved to join Chester. Acacia tried to establish eye contact with Tony, but he ignored her.

Mary-em grinned rakishly. "Now normally, I love a fight. But I'll stick with my buddies this time." She linked arms with Griffin and Holly.

Chester took a quick count. "That does it. Outvoted, Bowan."

The black-garbed figure gripped Chester's arm and spoke low. "Let me try a spell, Chester? Please? You can start the rest running."

Chester's eyes focussed on the oncoming monster. Abruptly he nodded. "Try it if it's quick." His voice rose. "Not much time, people. Gina, put a firebolt into that Quonset hut. The rest of you, head for the slopes."

Bowan had turned to face the bay. He breathed deeply, readying himself, and raised his arms.

Gina called on the gods. Flame lashed from her staff. The Navy Headquarters building whooshed flames from doors and windows.

Bowan's voice was impassioned.

"Oh gods of Darkness, grim and cold,
Deliver us from Evil's hold.
Destroy this ape, whate'er it be,
And transfer all its power to me!"

At the sound of the last line, Chester's head jerked around. "What—?"

Green light formed a halo around Bowan. Green light reached toward the monster in a narrow spear of destruction. The monster snarled and waved a black-taloned fist. The bolt touched its face . . .

And fire lashed back along its length, as if green light could burn like gasoline. The halo enclosing Bowan flashed from green to yellow-white. They heard the *whuff* of the fire catching, and then Bowan screaming curses from inside a tremendous candle flame.

Bowan ran out of curses. He stepped out of the flame and looked upslope, to where the Gamers had stopped to watch. "Chester?"

There was pallid light around him now; even his robe seemed white, and his face whiter. Behind him the great flame stuttered and died away.

"You've got to help me, Chester!" Bowan called.

The boar-ape walked up onto the dock. Bowan flinched violently, but it passed Bowan as if he did not exist.

The Lore Master glanced from Bowan to the advancing beast. He screamed, "No time, Bowan. You're already dead! Look behind you!"

Where flame had engulfed Bowan the Black, there stood a neat conical heap of ash with black bones protruding.

Dark Star tried to run to the slain magician, but Chester

caught her by the arm. "Can't afford to lose you too. Get up the incline, dammit!"

The monster took one more step towards the fleeing Gamers, then turned ponderously toward the blazing Quonset hut. It disappeared behind the building.

Chester's eyes widened as he watched a plume of firelit smoke sucking itself back into the building's doors and windows. The flames went black—black!—dwindled and were gone, leaving not so much as a soot stain on the corrugated metal.

"Double damn," Chester whispered. "Now *that's* a trick." Then, "Oh!"

He fished into his pocket and pulled out a teardrop-shaped crystal, clear as ice, with a blood-red spider frozen in the center. He pointed it at the monster. "Hear me, oh gods! I request a tracer, a mark by which to find this beast on the morrow!" His aura flickered with strain, but the talisman lit from within, the spider crawling sluggishly to life. "Got you," he grinned at the monster, dropping the crystal back into his pocket. "And tomorrow . . ." He turned and ran, ignoring the dying sound of Bowan's voice, the milk-pale *tindalo* still standing with arms outstretched, screaming:

"Damn you, Henderson! I'll get you for this! You wait, coward . . ."

Alex sucked air as if he'd been underwater too long. The ache in his chest was only just beginning to subside. Next to him, Mary-em was bent double, coughing, her ruddy face even darker than usual. These last five minutes he had run while pulling Mary-em along by her sword harness.

The monster had only given up the chase after the lot of them were totally exhausted. Henderson was on his side in the grass, wiping sweat from his face with a wet, dust-crusted sleeve. Gina lay sprawled beside him, her eyes closed, breath rasping in her throat.

McWhirter was up and spreading his pack. The Gods knew where he found the energy. He'd been ahead of Alex all the way, even before Mary-em started to fall behind.

S.J. balanced on his knees, dry-retching. He shook his head and looked at Dark Star venomously. Between coughing fits he was mumbling words that Griffin had to strain to hear: "I knew it. I knew I should have blown the whistle on those bastards. I knew it . . ."

Professional reflexes triggered. Griffin rolled over and stood up, though his head spun. He walked over to S. J. Waters and hovered above him. Waters looked fearfully up into a big black shadow.

Griffin dropped to his haunches beside the boy. He kept his voice low and matter-of-fact. "Tell me all about it, or we both talk to Henderson."

"W-what do you mean?" S.J.'s expression made the protest pitiful.

"If I can't get it out of you, maybe Henderson can. You were spying on Bowan and Dark Star. What did you see?"

Waters seemed to weigh his options. Griffin gave him some time, then started to stand up.

"Wait! Griffin, if Henderson finds out—"

"He won't. Not if you tell it straight."

"Sit down before someone notices!"

Griffin sat.

"All right. The first night of the game, everybody was hopping into the woods for some nookie. Hell, man, I just didn't have anything better to do."

"So you played peeping tom. You followed them. Why them?"

"Oh . . . Bowan's such a . . . I mean, the way he acts,

you can't *imagine* the mighty sorcerer with his pants off. And Dark Star, why would anyone chase *her*? I just wondered about them. So I followed them.

"The only thing was, they weren't interested in fooling around. They cut across the Gaming area to where the workmen were setting up props and testing the holograms, and they spied. I just spied on them. The workmen turned on the giant monkey and ran it through its paces. I saw Bowan and Dark Star go into a whisper on it, and then they both scampered back to the Daribi village. They've been waiting for that thing to show up ever since." S. J. laughed. "They must have thought it was just a poor man's King Kong."

His face had finally lost some of its beet color. He hunched his shoulders. "Really, that was all there was to it." His eyes pleaded, and suddenly Griffin felt sorry for him. "Please don't tell Chester, huh? Honest to God, I wasn't trying to cheat. I was just lonely and thought I'd have a little fun. Please?"

What S.J. had said seemed to fit the facts. And it helped. Griffin patted his shoulder comfortingly. "I won't say anything. You just stay out of other people's business, okay?" The Engineer nodded with all the sincerity he could muster. Griffin stood, walked a few paces away, and flopped.

Acacia got unsteadily to her feet and walked over to join him. He held out his hand to her; it was clammy and cold with condensing sweat. Her face was streaked with sweat and what looked suspiciously like tears. She hugged him, and said angrily: "God, Lopez made us pay for that."

"For running?"

She nodded. "Can you imagine what that rout is going to look like on tape? I wouldn't want to be Chester right now."

Mary-em's face turned angry. "What was he supposed to do, Acacia? You saw what that hairy freak did to Bowan."

Acacia sank to the ground and stared at her feet.

They looked like the aftermath of a disaster. Alex was in good condition, but it had been no picnic for him. The damnable thing, the haunting, humiliating thing, was the way Lopez had toyed with them. The monster had remained just close enough to keep them running, and far enough back that they wouldn't turn and make a stand.

Henderson was waving the group together with an unsteady hand. "Kasan!" he bellowed. He looked around for the guide. Kasan was having trouble getting up.

"All right, Kasan. What was it?"

The little guide kept one hand on his chest and swallowed air before trying to speak. "I have no clue, bwana. There are many such creatures known to us—"

"Clues? I'll give you clues. That critter's fur was the color of fire where it wasn't wet." Henderson stopped to pant, then: "When Bowan tried to steal its power, it burned him crisp. And we saw it make a fire burn backward. Aren't those clues? Its power is fire. What kind of fire demon have you got for us?"

"Ah. Now I believe that I know what that creature was. The legends of my people speak—"

"Cut the bullshit, dammit." All heads swung around to face Dark Star, who was wiping the wet from her eyes with the side of a clenched fist. "I just want to know what killed Bowan."

Henderson gave her a warning glance, and she bit her lower lip, furious.

Even Maibang seemed a bit upset. "I was saying that we have a legend that might apply. The Haiavaha—"

"Nobody gives a good goddamn what its name is. *What was it?*" She was shaking now, her voice rising almost to a scream. Chester crossed to her in two strides and took her by the shoulders.

"Now you listen to me, lady. You and Bowan wanted to have at Jumbo back there. In fact, you wanted it so damn bad that it really makes me wonder. I didn't like it then, and I didn't like it when Bowan gave us his little prepared incantation. Frankly, I don't think he's good enough to come up with that off the cuff. Do you get my drift?" She tried to turn away from him, but his slender fingers bit into her shoulders without mercy. "Now you and I both know that I can't prove anything. But so help me, if you don't shut up and let the rest of us play this Game the way it's *supposed* to be played, I'll see to it that you join Bowan the Black."

The other players seemed embarrassed for them both. Dark Star nodded her head silently, a single teardrop drooling down her puffy red cheeks. Maibang cleared his throat politely. "Um . . . I was saying that my people have a legend about this creature." Chester had finally released Dark Star, and had turned to face Maibang. "It is said that centuries ago, Man was forced to eat his meat raw, and lie helpless in the darkness of night. He was denied the secret of fire. Fire was the sole possession of the Gods, who felt that such a gift was more than mere humans could safely control."

Chester had his mind back on the Game. "Was there no fire at all on Earth?"

"Ah, that is where the Monster comes in. Fire could be found in but one Earthly place, the lair of the dread Haiavaha. Whether itself a minor god, or merely a watch-dog for the gods, was not known. But when men shivered in the cold, the Haiavaha had warmth. And where men depended upon the coming of dawn to rescue them from the clutches of night, the Haiavaha had somehow gained possession of a small piece of the sun, and kept it burning in its cave.

"Many men died trying to steal the secret. Then one night a dog was beaten and chased away from the camp for stealing a haunch of pig and insulting the cooking-woman. Its master shouted that it could not return unless it could redeem itself. The dog found the cave of the Haiavaha, and, seeing that the creature was asleep, snuck in and stole a burning branch. The monster woke and came after the dog. It ran for its life, the fire burning its mouth horribly. Dogs have not been able to speak since that night. But it escaped the Haiavaha and brought fire to the village."

"And ever after Man has had fire. I can guess that much. But if this is the Haiavaha, what does it want from *us*?"

Maibang shrugged. "Possibly it is still angry."

Chester propped himself on his elbows, thinking. "What about the way it made the fire burn backward?"

"Our legends do not speak of that at all."

"But in that case . . ." A smile spread like a slow dawn over Chester's long face. "It's still there to be stolen. Right. You know, it's a pity that dog couldn't talk when it got back to the village. You'd've stolen It by now."

Maibang was grinning too. "I believe we would at that."

The Lore Master seemed to be vastly pleased. "Well, it's a damn good thing that I put a tracer on the Haiavaha. Tomorrow we'll hunt that thing down." He stood, stretching. "Now, people, let's pitch camp. Uncle Lopez should be providing us with dinner any time now. I think we've earned ourselves a little party. What say?"

A ragged cheer broke out, and the Gamers fell to un-packing. Griffin spread and adjusted his sleeping bag, let the mattress inflate, and flopped.

A moment later he was pulling himself to his feet. *Business.* He looked around; nobody was paying attention to him. He sauntered towards the trees. Acacia glanced up and saw him, a mischievous smile curling her lips.

"Hey there, big fella. If you want to wait a minute, you can have some company."

"Modesty forbids, my dear. My kidneys are floating, and an audience freezes the faucet." She laughed, and nodded, spreading out her sleeping bag. Next to his. Alex thought warm thoughts.

Chapter Twenty-Two

THE ELECTRIC PIZZA MYSTERY

As soon as he was into the woods he fished out his wallet and flipped it on. "Switchboard," a reedy voice called.

"Patch me to security. Bobbick. This is Griffin." Alex put his back to a tree and tried to think. Somehow it was difficult to forget the Foré and the Haiavaha and concentrate on the reality outside Gaming Area 'A'.

Bobbick's voice was the link he needed. "Hi, chief. I know you've been busy. That's some pretty rough play."

"I'm not sure it's play at all. Listen, what have you got for me?"

Bobbick didn't answer for a second, and Griffin thumped the communicator gently. "You there, Marty?"

"I'm here all right. I just don't like having to say this. Oh, man. Griff, we've definitely got murder on our hands."

"Christ," Alex muttered. He sank his weight back into the tree and waited.

"Novotney confirmed it. We knew that we had death by suffocation, but there was a possibility that Rice had a cold that blocked his nasal passages. You know how he was always sniffling."

"Yeah."

"Well, there just wasn't enough mucus to block the passages."

"I think I can guess the rest. Someone knocked him out, tied him up, gagged him and held his nose shut until he died." He slapped his forehead with the palm of his hand. "Oh, dammit. I knew there was something I was trying to remember."

"What's that?"

"Last night. That damn dream. 'A fine, upright boy.' 'He wouldn't have taken this sitting down.' Oh good *Christ*, of *course* it was murder."

Bobbick sounded confused. "Ah . . . I'm not sure I follow you, chief . . ."

"Listen. Rice's wrists were abraided. We know he was struggling when he died. How the hell did he end up in a sitting position?"

"What?"

"Sitting. Sitting, dammit. He was sitting up. If he had been thrashing around, he should have ended up lying on his side, or on his back, or anything. Do you realize how unlikely it is for him to just accidentally end up in a sitting position?"

Bobbick inhaled sharply. "I see what you mean."

Griffin brooded. "I'm going to need to think on this some more. What else do you have for me?"

"Good news, bad news, and worse news. First, we've

established the whereabouts of the 'A' workers the night Rice was killed, and all of them are clean. Likewise for Maibang. Everyone who took the voice stress test passed with flying colors, but—"

"Alan Leigh?"

"He's clean. I thought you'd cleared him."

"I had some second thoughts. But if he passed the voice stress . . . what else?"

"This Orville Bowan—Bowan the Black is his listing— anyway, he's refused the lie detector. When I told him we'd have to abort the Game, he laughed and said it would serve Henderson right."

"Yeah. I guess that doesn't surprise me. Forget him, he's clean."

"Great!"

"So are Dark Star and S. J. Waters."

"Sounds like you're making progress. Who's left?"

Griffin had to count on mental fingers. "Ollie Norliss, his lady Gwen. Not prime suspects, but not in the clear, either. Ah, Tony McWhirter and Acacia Garcia." He didn't like having to say that, but it was true. Masculine vanity aside, why *was* she sticking so close to the Griffin? "And Mary-Martha."

"Mary-Martha Corbett?"

"That's the one. I'm not sure about her. She's been in Gaming A before. Pulling a little bit of industrial spying off might just amuse her. And that about does it."

"Okay, one more thing," Bobbick said. "Millicent did some back checking. She was curious about Rice's college life. She got hold of the Sulphur University newspapers for his residency. Guess what?"

"What?"

"The face on the statue. We found it. It belonged to one

Sonja Prentice, a co-ed who went to school with him. Griff, she committed suicide just two months before Rice left college. Now, what was her statue doing in Rice's apartment?"

"Alex mulled it. It wouldn't be *that* startling a coincidence . . . "No opinion. I wish we could ask Rice."

Griffin returned to the campground to find that Kibugonai had ferried in a case of cold beer, and Maibang was lugging a crate into the inner circle. When they levered it open, Gamers broke into unabashed applause.

There were loaves of hot garlic bread and six tremendous wheels of pizza with varied toppings.

Owen Braddon smacked his lips. "You know, there's one thing about Lopez. He may fry you or drown you, but he'll never let you starve."

A line formed, and disintegrated in laughing wrestlers, and re-formed.

"There had better be one in there without anchovies," the Lore Master laughed, "or I'm gonna lodge a complaint." He seemed cheerful enough, considering the beating he had taken today. Was he *that* sure of tomorrow's target? or was it just good politics?

Griffin joined the line. He tried to find the spot inside him that hadn't been shaken by Bobbick's news. The smile he wore was strictly off the rack, and it wouldn't hold long against Acacia's prying.

He took a lion's portion of pizza and snagged two beers. Acacia joined him at his bedroll and leaned back, propping her plate between knees and stomach. She munched noisily, totally unashamed.

Alex managed to talk around a mouthful of pizza. "I'm not sure, but I think that this is my favorite part of this

whole nutty business." His hunger had teeth in it, and the
cold brew tasted unbelievably good. Acacia mumbled
something that sounded like agreement, and that was
good enough for him. He watched Margie and S.J. finish
setting up the campfire, and let the warmth sink into his
bones. He was happy. He had found that untouched spot.

Some of the conversation around them showed nerves
frayed by fatigue, but the air of grateful relaxation was
contagious. Lady Janet seemed to be enjoying passing
around the garlic bread. Alex wondered if it was an excuse
to check out the eligible men, now that Leigh had been
killed out. She curtsied saucily in front of him, smile a
touch too predatory for his taste. "Hot bread, m'lord," she
said in her sexiest voice. "Sweeter than a virgin's kiss."

"That's what I like. Service with a simile." He couldn't
help but notice that Acacia had moved an inch closer to
him as Janet made her play. "I'll go for the bread, and I'll
take the kiss on faith—" But she had served Acacia and
passed on.

Desert stars shone in clusters, sharp and bright on the
black dome of Gaming Area A. The night was windless. A
full belly moved him even further into an intoxicatingly
mellow mood.

Acacia nudged him. "You know, I can't put my finger
on it, but you're both more uptight, and more relaxed than
you were yesterday."

He flared at her. "*Will* you stop analyzing me for just a
little while? You make me feel like a bug in biology class.
Where's your dissecting needle?"

"I've got sharp teeth, if that would help."

The anger had flared and vanished with no trace remaining. Alex chewed the inside of his mouth and tried not
to smile. "Now you, young lady, are what is properly

known as a tease. Has anyone ever told you that?"

"And has anyone ever told you that you've got beautiful green eyes? I mean, talk about character. They damn near match the green peppers on my pizza."

Stifling a guffaw, he tried to edge away from her. "Whew. Just what is into you tonight?"

She ran a finger down his arm, her face deadpan. "Do you mean right now, or what am I hoping for later . . .?"

Alex fell back on the sleeping bag, laughing helplessly. "Punchy," he gasped. "Fatigue toxins. I think I like it."

The Gamers ate like starved wolves. Many had already finished. Holly and Gwen were swapping lines from songs on the far side of the fire.

Without a wind to stir it up, the fire burned slowly and steadily, only an occasional pop from an exploding green branch stirring up the ashes. Alex slipped his boots off and moved his feet closer to the flame. He looked around, noting that a few people were missing from the circle. Henderson, Gina, McWhirter, Eames, and Lady Janet. Ah-ha. What kind of little party was going on out there?

Holly dragged Gwen up to the fireside, and broke the air with a loud cough. "Hey, listen, people. How many of you know that we have a celebrity in our midst?" A few boozy cheers egged her on. "This young lady actually has a couple of Nashville albums, and I want to get her singing for us." Mary-em in particular led the shouting approval.

Gwen looked terrified. "Uh . . . I only sang backup on a few tracks. Ollie?" She swallowed hard, eyes begging him to get her out of this.

Ollie didn't notice; he waved her on. "Go on, Gwen! Hey, people, she's really good!"

There was something in Gwen's eyes that Alex didn't like at all, a touch of genuine fear that touched him deeply.

Part of him wanted to tell everyone to leave her to hell
alone. He restrained himself. *Don't be conspicuous, O
Griffin. Don't make waves.* Wishing he were someone
else.

Mary-em jumped up, grinning ear-to-ear. "Oh, come
on, honey. Holly an' I'll help you through it. Do you know
'The Fighter's Lament'?" The Gamers roared their approval, and Mary-em linked arms with Gwen, Holly on the
other side, and began to croak out a tune, Gwen's high,
sweet contralto finally wavering from an unwilling throat:

> "I once had a sword, or should I say, it once
>   had me.
> I just picked it up, oh what a sword, it was plus
>   three.
> Its Ego was twelve, a fact of which I wasn't aware;
> Then I tried to leave and I found that the sword
>   didn't care; oh . . ."

Gwen's voice faltered, but the Gamers, most of them
roaring along to the tune of an obscure 20th century
ballad, didn't notice at all.

> "I walked through the halls, wasting my time,
>   nothing to find.
> Then I turned a corner, and then I said, 'Oh no!
>   Undead!'
> The thirty-two Wights saw me coming and started
>   to laugh;
> And I closed my eyes as my sword started hewing a
>   path; oh—"

Gwen abruptly tore herself away from the other women
and ran from the firelit circle with her hands covering her
face. Ollie gaped in astonishment. He rose and ran after
her.

Holly and Mary-em were shocked, and Mary-em started

to follow the sobbing girl, but Holly linked arms with her tightly, holding her, forcing her to sing on.

> "And when I awoke, I was alone, that sword had
>   flown.
> Now I use a club; isn't it good . . . no-ego wood."

Mary-em disengaged herself from Holly and looked up at her. At first she didn't say anything. Then, "I'm really not sure that this was a good idea, Holly."

Frost laughed. "Oh, come off it, Mary. Who could have known the little thing would be so skittish?"

"I could have. You could have. We could have listened. She *said* she doesn't sing in front of an audience—"

Holly stepped back and regarded her uncertainly. "Well aren't we being a little goody-good this evening? I didn't notice you defending her." The two stared at each other for a tense moment, then Holly turned on her heel and walked away.

Oddly, the other Gamers had noticed little. One clump was singing. Another surrounded Owen and Margie, who were speaking of older, wilder, looser Games. "—Doors that could open anywhere in space and time. One afternoon we were running the Khronal Dungeon, and we opened a door and found ourselves looking out into the living room where we were playing. One of the characters shot the Game Master with a crossbow bolt, and the whole Dungeon disappeared!"

More beer was being consumed, the last of the pizza was gone. Couples were breaking away from the fireside to find privacy. But Mary-em seemed, for the first time that Griffin had seen her, totally unnerved.

Eames wobbled out of the woods, a beer in his hand, plastic smile stretched tight across his face. He leered at

Mary-em and she folded her arms, tucking her hands in her armpits. "What are you staring at, Eames?"

He laughed. When he spoke it was in the ingratiating tones usually reserved for idiots and children. "What's a matter, huh? Isn't she feeling himself tonight?"

The other voices died. Griffin felt danger tightening in the air. *Are we all going crazy?* He wanted to scream a warning. Then Acacia's hand was on his neck, stroking him. It felt very nice, very comfortable, and suddenly he could do nothing but watch.

Let it happen, he thought. *He's an asshole anyway . . .* He shook his head like a drunk going down for the third time and wondered *what the hell was in that beer?*

Eames said, "You know, Mary-em, I don't like you at all. You are one of the homeliest, most ridiculous little witches I have *ever* laid eyes on, and I wish—"

Mary-em's fist shot out like a piston, almost level, catching Eames squarely in the groin. He whoofed air and doubled over, swinging a wild reflexive haymaker. Mary-em went under it and came up, snatched two handfuls of Eames's hair. Both of her feet left the ground as she rammed her knees into his face.

Eames shot upright and stumbled back with his face covered in blood. Back into a corner of the fire. He did a ragged hop, trying to stay clear. Then his mind gave up trying to guide his body, and he did a slow spiral to the ground, onto his knees, then flat on his bloody face.

Mary-em looked at him, and tears began to stream down her eyes. She wiped at the streaks with a chubby hand, then walked unsteadily to her bedroll and collapsed into a ball, sobbing.

Everyone stared, then, embarrassed, turned back to

their own little groups and couplets. Griffin felt a vague urge to get up and do something, but once again Acacia's hand dissuaded him.

"Don't worry," she said, her mouth close enough to his ear for him to feel the heat in her breath. "They'll both be all right."

He tried to find surprise, indignation, any emotion more appropriate than the one that was starting to stir. "All right then. What's on the agenda, more songs?"

She took his face in her hands and brushed his lips with hers. "*Se algunos juegos para mayores, hombre.*" She whispered.

Griffin spoke little Spanish, but the message in her eyes needed no translation at all. He had trouble finding his voice. "Let's go play Pathfinder, shall we?"

Her smile was hot enough to scorch. She rose, then bent and demurely collected her bedroll. She glanced up and said with half-lidded eyes: "I think we may need this."

He felt giddy, dizzy, and not totally sure of what he was doing as he nodded, gathering his own bag under his arm. Together, the two of them walked into the darkness and kept walking until the campfire and its noises were far behind them.

Acacia kissed him gently, almost shyly. "Here?"

He spread his sleeping bag down in silent agreement. They linked the inside edges together and sat next to each other, eyes locked wonderingly. "I didn't . . . I really didn't think that this was going to happen, Gary." She shied away an inch, and he reached out his hand.

He knew what he should be saying, and he forced his thickened tongue to say it. "It doesn't have to if you don't want it." He tried to mean it.

"We both know better than that . . ." She seemed to

want to say something, but he stopped her by leaning forward.

The kiss seemed to go on forever, and what logic was left in Alex's head dissolved together. His blood seemed to fizz. She held him, and he could feel her nervousness.

"Help me, Gary. I don't understand it. I don't. I want you, but I don't know what's happening to me." There was no strength in her voice. She sounded like a little girl . . . but her skin was smooth and hot, and he couldn't stop touching her. Excitement and wonder burned in her eyes as he helped her off with her clothes and she clung to him, fingers digging into the muscle of his shoulders. When at last he pulled the bag over them both and took her in his arms, she closed her eyes, murmuring only "Please, please, Gary . . ."

Gary. Not Alex. He paused, unsure, gazing into eyes that were afraid. He felt the fire that roared in his mind and body and from somewhere gathered the strength to pull away. *Something's wrong here. She's not—The crazy way the others were—Lopez wouldn't drug us, but—*

Then she rolled hard against him, and the questions were wiped away as they began to move together. The same fear, the same wonder he felt was in her eyes too, but there was something more now, something that began to build until at last it clouded his vision. And for a while, in that moment without time, there were no longer two people who strove and sought, there was only one body with four limbs that found a rhythm of its own.

When the everlasting moment was over, when he held her and she buried her face against his chest and cried, he stroked her hair and looked into the darkness surrounding them both, and doubted his sanity. *I can't be feeling this,* he thought. *I can't.* But the words rang hollow even to him.

Presently the force took them again, with equal power, as if the whole universe were moving in them, irresistably. Afterward he held her, and she held him, and together, without words, they waited for morning.

Chapter Twenty-Three

BLACK FIRE

Birdsong woke him. Real or recorded? Alex opened gummy eyelids and looked into the face of the woman sleeping in his arms. He watched her for a bit, almost holding his breath. Her breathing was slow and even, and she wore a slight smile. A smug smile?

Unbidden, his brain called up vivid tactile images of last night. *My God*, he thought, disbelieving. *That was one hell of a powerful experience!* He watched her face, tenderly, and wondered when she would wake up. Then more memories intruded.

Eames' malice, Gwen's fright, Mary-em's tears. They fell into a pattern.

Neutral scent.

Why didn't I see it?

Because my brain was running on neutral scent. And it activates emotions already there . . . omygod.

He shook Acacia until she stirred and clung to him, making baby-sounds, her lips curled in a satisfied smile. Her eyes opened. They seemed huge to him, and it was all he could do to merely smile in return.

"Morning, handsome," she yawned. She snuggled closer to him in the bag. "You certainly know how to treat a lady."

"Wish we had time for thirds."

"Well?"

"I'm starting to remember things. We'd better get back to the others. We could be facing a disaster."

He wriggled out from between the bags and stretched, the cool windless morning air sweeping away the remaining cobwebs. Acacia watched, the bag pulled up to her neck, as he pulled on his pants. "You sure we have to get back?" She still seemed half-asleep.

Alex nodded and pulled his sleeping bag from atop her. She shivered and yelped, scrambling for her clothes. She was saying something to him, but he wasn't listening. *Why? Why would a thief waste something so valuable on a vicious practical joke?*

Not until she threw her arms around his neck did he snap alert. "Hey there, you. You're strange. I mean really odd, but I like you anyway." She bunched up her sleeping bag and tucked it under an arm.

She had to run to keep up with him, and some part of him felt sorry that he didn't have more to share with her. But sorry or not, he had to deal with something far more urgent: the thief knew who he was. He must have used some of his stolen flask of "neutral scent" to put The Griffin out of action while . . . while what? What was the thief doing last night?

The campground was a mess. Gamers littered the ground. S. J. had gotten sick on himself. Mary-em lay on her side beneath a twisted old tree, far from her sleeping bag. Dried tears streaked her face. Owen and Margie lay close to the ashes of last night's fire, half out of their zipped-together bags, both naked, their clothes piled untidily about them.

Adrenalin-doped blood pounded in Alex's throat. *Too few. Where are the rest?*

Eames? Alex spotted the Warrior curled up with Captured Princess. *Check.*

Chester? Slumped sitting up, with his face between his knees. And Tony was splayed out near the Lore Master's feet, snoring loudly. His twisted sleeping bag must be half strangling him. Red scratches laced his cheeks.

S. J. Waters: in his bag, sleeping like a baby. Gina: missing. Now what was Gina doing away from Chester? Maibang and Kibugonai: missing, maybe getting breakfast. What tendencies in an actor might be accented by "neutral scent"?

Gwen? Ollie? "Cass, do you see Ollie or Gwen? Or Maibang?"

"Maibang left when the Game broke off last night. Gwen and Ollie generally go off in the bushes anyway . . ." But she looked worried now. "I'll go after them."

"Good. Anyone else you find, too."

Acacia pushed off into the Brazilian plant life, calling.

Chester Henderson's head jerked upright. He wiped his eyes clear with the back of his hand and looked about him. The sense of something seriously wrong came home to him, and when he saw Alex he frowned. The Lore Master pulled himself up and paused a moment to balance. "All right, Tegner. What do you know about this?''

"I don't know much. I know we were all crazy last night, and I don't think it was the beer.''

Henderson still seemed woozy. He jumped up and down a few times to get his circulation going, and surveyed his Gaming party. "What a mess. If Lopez spiked those pizzas—'' He shook his head. "That's too crazy.''

He reached down to shake Mary-em's shoulder. Griffin took his cue and woke up Eames, checking the big man's face for damage. There didn't seem to be much more than a badly split lip. Eames winced the first time he tried to move; then got up, moving like an old man, and went over to Mary-em. They sat down together and spoke in low voices.

By now most of the Gamers were awake and moving. Neutral scent didn't leave a hangover . . . not a physical hangover, anyway. Gina came wobbling in out of the woods, and Griffin cocked a curious ear when Chester went to meet her. The Lore Master reached a hand out to her, stroking her red hair, and she huddled at his chest. "Are you all right, Gina?'' She nodded wordlessly.

"I really don't remember much. After you got into logic puzzles with S. J. I just wandered off.'' She could tell that her answer seemed to bother him. "Really, Ches. I wasn't with anyone. I just wanted to be alone.''

Chester nodded, stiffly, and moved away to wake S. J.

Ollie and Gwen and Acacia emerged from the woods. All three seemed subdued. Acacia moved up next to Alex to whisper, "You were right. Bad vibes. Could have been something in the pizza?''

"I doubt it.''

"Or the bread,'' she said, looking toward the Captured Princess. But Janet too had that bewildered look: *Was it really me doing that?* Acacia shrugged. "Just this once, I wish the cameras stayed on at night."

"Damn right," Alex said. *It would have nailed the bastard early, saved me this trip . . .* Did he really want that? *Would have saved Rice*, he thought, sidestepping.

Even the Braddons were stirring now. Owen's eyes popped wide, and he disappeared into the bag like a snail into its shell. He must have signalled Margie from down there; she blinked, looked down into the bag, then looked around her. Her eyes rolled—it looked like self-mockery—and she was sliding down to join her husband when Gina took pity on them, threw somebody's sleeping bag over them, and began shoving clothes in under the edge.

Chester Henderson bellowed, "All right, enough is enough! I'm not sure what happened last night, but I'm sure that one of you thinks it was hysterically funny." There was no answer. "But it's not going to stop the Game. Roll those sleeping bags! The Game starts in twenty minutes. When it does, we move!" His eyes darted around him. "Breakfast or no breakfast," he added, and then he saw Maibang and Kibugonai coming with the robot carts. His relief was vividly obvious.

They trailed up into the hills, following Chester, who was following a small spider embedded in crystal. Margie chattered as if the pressure of words was too much for her. "That's *never* happened to me before. Not even when I had the figure for it. We just . . . seemed to forget there was anyone else around. First we were just talking . . . talking about all the good times . . . the skiing, and the Games, telling each other stories . . . it's surprising how much we still have to tell each other, isn't it, dear?" She glanced at her husband, who nodded brightly. Owen

Braddon wore a fatuous smile and a dazed look, but he walked like a king.

"And then we were pulling each other's clothes off. It was rather nice," Margie said wistfully. "And it felt like nobody was looking anyway . . ."

"I was just scared. I never had a case of stage fright like that in all my life," Gwen Ryder said. "I heard Ollie calling, but it must have been half an hour before I stopped running. And then—" She stopped.

"Yeah. Then *I* needed some reassuring," Ollie said. "What could have done so many different things to us? I never heard of anything like it."

"Me neither," Tony McWhirter said. His clothes were a mess, slashed by thorns and drenched in mud. He was shaken, and defensive. "I don't know what it was that scared me like that. I just ran until it wore off."

"It could put some of us in mental hospitals next time!" Acacia's snarl faded to a thoughtful frown. Suddenly she grinned at Alex and stopped talking.

The line was bunching up. The little cluster at the tail rounded a clump of trees and found the Lore Master staring up a slope of bare rock, toward a cave mouth. "In there," he said. "Back up a bit, troops. Walk soft. Dark Star, Fortunato, Griffin, Margie, Gwen—"

Flat on their bellies, the six watched the cave mouth. Chester kept one eye on the crystal. "The ghastly hasn't moved for a couple of minutes. Probably asleep. We'll have to risk it, but we can make it a little safer.

"Gwen, do you see that notch in the rocks to the right of the cave mouth? Margie? Good. It looks big enough to hold you both. So. The rest of you, you're going in. Steal what you can find, but we're particularly interested in

whatever that ghastly used to snuff our fire. If you're hurt,
or if you need an Engineer—"

"Check," said Dark Star.

"Remember, you're Thieves. Don't try to fight that
thing."

"Not likely. If Bowan couldn't handle it . . ."

Chester looked irritated, but he only nodded. "Margie,
you and S. J. uproot a bush big enough to cover that cleft.
You Thieves may want metal containers for what you have
to steal. Get 'em out of your mess kits." He glanced at the
crystal and said, "Still hasn't moved. Okay. Get moving."

Margie and Gwen were in place: hidden, assuming the
Haiavaha was too stupid to notice a bush that sprang up
overnight. Much closer, the Thieves were flattened against
rock next to the cave mouth.

Next to Alex, Tony McWhirter wiped palms on his torn
trousers and grinned crookedly. "Nerves."

The cave seemed pitch black. Alex whispered, "Any
ideas?"

Dark Star didn't answer at once. She studied the approach, and finally tapped him on the shoulder. "I have
the highest rating here. You'd better give me the first
shot." Without waiting for agreement, she crept around
the side of the rock and was inside. An aeon later her hand
and wrist reappeared, and gestured.

Griffin went. He sensed Tony moving in behind him. He
paused a moment to let his eyes readjust to the gloom.
Gradually he recognised what he was hearing: breathing
from within, deep and slow.

The outlines of the cave revealed themselves as his eyes
sharpened, and he looked around carefully.

The cave seemed to have been hewn from rock by hand or claw, not by the forces of nature. As Dark Star flashed her shielded torch he saw chunks of stone that looked as if they had been pulled forcefully from the walls, and deep, wide scratch marks.

"I think someone's been sharpening his claws." Alex heard his whispered words echo faintly from the walls, and wished he had been silent. McWhirter bumped into him from behind, muttered an apology.

There was light ahead, perhaps around a bend in the cave. It was so dim that at first he thought it was a reflection from Dark Star's torch.

She had already shut it off, though, and depended on night vision and feel to guide her. Alex found the going easy if he stayed a few paces behind her. The footing was rough, but not treacherous, and he only stumbled once. As they neared the corner there was a squeaking sound, and a shadow whined past his ear, followed by two more. Bats.

The sound of breathing was clearer now. The light must be around the next bend. Dark Star reached out her hands and made contact with both of them. "All right. This is it, and we can't make any mistakes. You remember what this bastard did to Bowan. It sounds like it's asleep, but it might be playing possum."

"Can it see us? I thought that Thieves were just about invisible." McWhirter was still nervous.

"Just about isn't enough. Maibang didn't specify, so it probably doesn't have outrageous hearing ability, but be careful, all right?"

Griffin followed her around the corner, trying to control both breathing and footsteps.

They had come into a sizeable cave. To one side the wall

had crumbled into big and little boulders: potential hiding places, if they got that far.

The Haiavaha was here. He was asleep, all twenty feet of him, curled up like a drowsy wolf, in a nest of clean white bones. A trough surrounded him, a circular moat grooved into the rock, perhaps eighty feet in diameter and two feet wide. A fire burned in the near arc of the trough, a single column of flame that cast the only light in the room.

There was something else, too . . . Alex rubbed his eyes. Directly opposite the dancing flames, night-black tongues of shadow danced in imitation. It might have been another fire, save that it ate light.

Alex edged closer, on his belly, until he could look into the trough. Logs and brush were piled in the trough, halfway around the ring. The fire was eating the wood, leaving red coals and then ashes behind it. The bed of ashes stretched around one hundred and eighty degrees of arc, then . . . of course. The black fire was burning its way around the circle and leaving chunks of wood behind it.

Tony laughed, stifling it quickly. The Haiavaha stirred in its sleep, and Dark Star snarled soundlessly. They crept around the trench, toward the black flames on the far side. Alex put his lips against Dark Star's ear and whispered. "How much of this do we want?"

She didn't answer. She took the lid off her mess kit and, holding it with her bandana, gingerly waved it over the shimmering ashes. When she was sure that nothing drastic was going to happen, she shoveled out a lidful of ashes with a black glow playing over them. She began to fill her soup pot.

Alex scooped only ashes. *Save some ash to feed the black fire later*, he caught himself thinking, and added: *It's probably too late to save my mind. Bobbick and Millicent must be having a wonderful time watching this.* Tony scooped up black-glowing treasure hurriedly, casting worried looks behind him. At first Griffin wondered what the problem was, then he heard it too: a muffled sound not unlike popcorn popping. A fusillade of gunshots from outside.

Dark Star tugged urgently at Alex's shoulder. He followed, on his belly, and was into the rubble of fallen rock before he dared look back.

The Haiavaha was stirring. It uttered a roar that quaked the cave, sending bats fleeing from the roof and shaking down dust.

McWhirter joined them in the rocks. Presently he noticed that his hands had a pale red glow. "What the hell?"

"Frostbite, you idiot," Dark Star hissed. "Here." She tugged his scarf from around his neck and wrapped it around his pot. The black fire within popped and sucked up light.

The Haiavaha was awake now, and had pulled itself erect. Its pig eyes roamed the cave for intruders, and Griffin's hand sought his knife. The thing looked right past them as shots and yelling filtered into the cave. It stalked away, growling.

Tony watched it go. "They're going to need help out there."

"Forget it. Just do your job right here." Dark Star checked to be sure the coast was clear, and scampered back out to finish filling her pot. Alex paused once to use the soup pot to scoop ashes—he had no need to protect his hands—and was on his way. He was first to reach the cave entrance.

Margie and Gwen met him there. The sound outside
was horrifying, the din of battle mixed with the unearthly
vibration of the Haiavaha's roar. Gwen was edgy, impatient. "Enemy attack. They've got guns. How'd you do?
Anyone hurt?"

"We found a kind of reverse fire, anti-fire. Tony got
frostbite handling it."

Tony and Dark Star emerged. Gwen called up her aura
and played it over the red glow of Tony's hands until it was
gone. "Anyone else?"

"Not here."

Gwen nodded and was running downslope. A Cleric
wasn't needed here; she wanted to join the battle. Dark
Star put a hand on Alex's arm. "Give me that," she said.
"Just ashes? Good thinking, O Griffin. Fortunato, give
your black fire to Margie. I'll need an Engineer to help keep
it going. You two can go fight. Meet us later, if you live
through this. Say . . . up there where the trees peter out.
How's it sound?"

"Sensible," Margie said. She and Dark Star started
uphill around the cave, moving slowly, careful of what
they were carrying.

Griffin and Tony followed the curve of the cliff face until
they could see what was happening.

Half of Henderson's group were pinned down under a
Foré crossfire, but two of them—it looked like Ollie and
Acacia—had managed to escape the trap, and had closed
to sword range with their foes. There were Foré corpses
scattered about the clearing, and at first Alex didn't understand.

Then the Haiavaha stood up. It had a screaming Foré in
one hand, and its mouth was smeared with blood. It

looked around wildly as gunfire found it, and tore into a small pocket of the mountain folk with horrific results. They scattered and disappeared into the trees.

Not until the sated Haiavaha was climbing back toward its lair did the two Thieves come cautiously down from their perch. Chester was waving his hands, calling the rest in.

Alex felt out of breath. "Jesus Christ. What happened?"

"Right after you left. Two parties of the enemy were waiting, and they got Eames before we even knew they were there."

"Dead?"

"Wounded pretty bad, I think. Gwen is tending him." Chester noticed their empty hands. "What did you get?"

"Reverse fire, just like you thought. Dark Star and Margie are upslope tending it, waiting for us. I'll take you there."

"I sure hope that this was worth it. It has to be. They captured Maibang and Janet." He pointed a long finger. "At least now we know where we're heading."

In the distance, perhaps three miles away, was a volcano. It appeared extinct but the leveled top was unmistakable. "Nobody even saw it until I cast a Reveal Danger. And it wasn't on the map. So that's where they are, all right. Gwen!"

The blonde raised her head. She was crouched over Eames. Shimmering white light reached from her aura to the wounded man. Eames watched miserably as shimmering red spread across his shirt from the blotch left by the jelly bullet. She had not noticed the pale, translucent figure patiently waiting behind her, wearing Eames's face.

"Come on, Gwen. Sorry, Eames."

Eames surprised them. "No sweat. I had a good run. Will you tell Lady Janet I died nobly? And . . . I may be seeing you again." The *tindalo* moved away, and Eames followed, but swerved once to pat Mary-em's shoulder.

Chapter Twenty-Four

AMBUSH

Margie and Dark Star were tending a huge fire . . . and a patient.

Maibang seemed cheerful enough, considering. His legs were stretched straight out in front of him; they had been splinted with the split halves of a sapling. He winced every time he moved. "They broke my legs and left me," he said. "They may have hoped you would try to carry me and be slowed down."

To Alex's eye Maibang's legs showed no sign of misuse. *Like the aviation fuel*, he thought. *You just accept it and act on it. But there goes our guide . . .*

Chester had come to the same conclusion. "We don't dare slow ourselves down that much. Sorry, Maibang. We'll make you as comfortable as possible. What about Lady Janet?"

"They will sacrifice her to the egg. Chester, can an airplane really lay eggs?"

"No."

"Well. Our enemies think they have an airplane's egg. They're trying to hatch it in the volcano, as I told you. I expect the sacrifice will take place at night."

Margie said, "Good. That leaves us time for the fire to burn down."

The flames were already burning less fiercely, turning to yellow-white coal. Margie showed Chester the black fire unburning on a flat rock, with Alex's pot of ash next to it. "I thought we might want a great deal of this anti-fire. It must have some purpose, mustn't it? So we'll need great deal of ash."

"How long, Margie?"

"An hour, I'd say. Then we can rake any remaining coals out of the ash, take the ash and move on."

Chester looked wistfully toward the volcano, the site of the Foré stronghold, a mile and a half away now. "And we don't even know what black fire is good for. All right. Rest break, troops!"

Gamers began dropping their packs immediately. You learned that *fast*. And . . . the bonfire vanished, sound effects and all.

Chester bellowed, "Hear me, Oh Gods! It's a rest break, *not* a time out! Put the fire back, Lopez!" The bonfire reappeared. "All right. Griffin—" The Lore Master stepped up next to Alex and put a companionable hand on his shoulder, with enough force to turn him away from the rest of the Gamers. His voice level dropped. "You know something, don't you?"

Alex thought carefully, and nodded.

"Just who are you, Griffin? What the hell is happening to my Game?"

"I wish I could tell you. I think I can guarantee that you'll know by tonight."

Henderson studied him, his face holding a meld of subdued hostility and curiosity. "If you can't tell me who you are, can you tell me what happened last night?"

"All right. I owe you that much. We were all the victims of an experimental drug. Stolen. It's harmless, but powerful."

Trying to look casual, Chester forced his voice to remain calm. "But *why*? If this is one of Lopez's stunts—" His voice held no conviction. "Why?"

"I'm not sure. It could even have been an accidental spill. But it wasn't Lopez, and it wasn't done to damage your Game."

The Lore Master's slender fingers formed fists. "I'd still like to get my hands on the son of a bitch."

"You'll have to stand in line. The orchestrator of last evening's orgy of emotion has got quite a bit to answer for." Chester's eyes shone with questions. "I'm sorry. That's all I can tell you."

The trail was easy to follow. Dozens of pairs of feet had beaten the scrubby underbrush into the dirt, marking a path that led almost straight towards the volcano. Griffin and Chester were in the front of the line.

They had left with heavier packs. The contents of Gwen's and Kibugonai's backpacks had been parcelled out among the other Gamers. Those packs were stuffed with wood ash. Everyone but the Warriors was carrying a cookpot of black fire.

There were fourteen people left in the line, including

their one remaining native bearer, Kibugonai. The flat nosed New Guinean marched directly behind Alex, talking to S. J. Waters.

"What does your name mean, anyway?" S. J. asked the bearer. "Something like 'terror of the battlefield', or 'finder of yams?' "

Kibugonai shook his head. "It means 'Bitten by a pig'. My mother had a terrible fright the week before I was born—"

Alex cut in. "Have you ever been near this region before? Or do you know anyone who has?"

"Never. None dare intrude upon our enemy. Those who do . . ." Kibugonai shrugged. "There are many ways to die."

Many ways to die. Bandage a man's mouth and then hold his nose shut . . . The thief who stole the 'neutral scent' must have seen the havoc he had caused. What if he had decided to take advantage of it by slitting a throat?

It would have been a mad act. The Game would have ended immediately if the Griffin had been found dead. But he could have done it, and some Gamers were mad, and some thieves too; and knowing he had been that vulnerable made Alex's flesh creep.

They crossed a rise; and where it dropped away one could see the mists of low clouds in a wide, deep gorge. It was spanned by a suspension bridge; but the wooden slats that formed the flooring were worm-eaten and weather-worn, and they were bound together with tattered vines. In several places the boards were broken through or splintered to uselessness.

There didn't seem to be another way across.

Chester sent S. J. across to mark boards that wouldn't hold his weight. Somehow the boy made it across without crashing through. He dropped his pack at the far end and sat hugging his knees, shaking, watching the others crawl across.

They moved on hands and knees, one at a time, trying to avoid the boards marked with Xs, while the bridge danced in the wind. Clouds boiled evilly below the broken slats. The pot of black fire was taped to the small of Griffin's back, an icy spot on his spine. He found it easy to tell himself that the floor of Gaming 'A' was probably a foot or two below him. It didn't seem to help.

The trail remained steep for another hundred meters, then turned into a decline. A large expanse of sparkling blue sea was visible from the first bend, as was the jutting rise of the volcano, now half a mile away. The path was only wide enough for two abreast, and Griffin was glad: it discouraged bunching, and this looked like prime ambush territory. In fact . . .

"Chester, how about a 'reveal ambush' spell?"

"I can see what you mean." He raised his arm. "Hear me, oh Gods . . ." His green aura surrounded him. "Reveal Danger!"

Red light tinged the thatch of trees a hundred feet ahead. Chester grinned. "I'm not sure who you really are, Griffin, but you're not bad. Let's catch 'em with their pants down. Mary-em, Oliver, Griffin, Acacia, Holly and . . . Gina. Split into two groups and work your way through the brush. The rest of us will keep going straight to draw their fire."

Mary-em sidled up next to Alex. She seemed very quiet, and he rubbed her shoulder. "How do you feel, lady?"

She gave him a friendly elbow, but there was no juice in

it, and she knew it. "A little tired, Gary." He knew that it
had to be true, but it was still shocking to hear her say it.

"Well hell. If you're tired, who's going to watch out for
me?"

She smiled up at him from her four feet nothing. "All
right, handsome. For you, I'll tough it out."

He grabbed her hand and set off through the bush
before the positive mood could fade. Gina was with them,
but Alex walked Point, trusting that any nasties in the
underbrush would be more visible to a Thief than a Warrior or Magic-user.

Something touched Alex's shoulder, and he jumped. It
was only Gina's power staff. "I'm getting a reading," she
mouthed silently. He nodded understanding and slowed
down, keeping eyes and ears open for clues.

And there they were. A group of eight Foré clustered
behind a bush by the side of the road. Two of them had
guns, five of them bladed weapons, and one was bur-
dened with an odd apparatus, reminiscent of primitive
scuba diving gear.

"I think that's a flame thrower on that one's back. Wide
angle and high lethality. Not good. The guns are a lot
easier to deal with. Can you run a psychic message to
Chester?"

Gina frowned. "It'll cost me a lot of energy, but I can do
it. Hear me oh gods! Give me communion with our leader.
Your humble servant begs this boon."

Mary Martha pulled her halberd from her back and gave
the blade a half-twist, disengaging it and triggering the
hologram blade. Her nut-brown face turned happy again.
"Now this is what I need." Griffin followed her example,
preparing his weapon.

"Chester's ready." Gina fingered her staff eagerly. "He says for us to go for it."

Mary-em started to edge foreward, but Griffin stopped her. "I don't like that flamethrower. I want to try taking it out with a throw. My agility score should be high enough." He stood to a balanced position and drew his arm back as he had seen Tony do it at the wrecked mission. He snapped it forward, hiding the knife as he did, and watched the holo projection flash quick as light toward the man with the flame thrower. It buried itself in his neck.

Mary-em was howling and jumping, her halberd cleaving the air. She reached their enemies before the gun men could turn around, and her blade passed through a skull effortlessly. Crimson spattered in the air.

The sounds of combat were echoing from the other side of the path now, and a bright streamer of flame rose in the distance. Griffin wrenched a spear from the first Foré who came at him and the man flipped with the motion; Griffin buried the hologram spearhead in his vitals. Gina yelled "Look out!" and Alex ducked as something sizzled by his head. The Sorceress gestured with her staff and two Foré clutched their heads and toppled.

A dive and roll, and Alex had a rifle, courtesy of Mary-em's first victim. The Thief came up firing and took a bright red spear wound in the shoulder as he downed another opponent.

Shocked with the speed of the encounter, he looked around to see that all of their enemies were dead. Gina tested her aura and it flickered a pale green: she shook her head worriedly. "I don't have much left. We're going to have to be careful."

Alex rolled over one of the dead, and took another surprise. The man was dark enough; the sun had burned his skin almost black. But his features were oriental. "Jesus. What do you make of this?"

"Wasn't New Gunea occupied by the Japanese during World War II?"

"I don't know, Mary-em . . . I guess so, yeah. Check the others."

"No time. We've got to help our own people. Here, Gary, take the flame thrower."

Alex liked that idea. He peeled the tank off the back of the dead man and slipped his arms through the straps. He fired a test burst into the trees. It worked fine, except that some of the fireburst streamed to the side, just under his elbow, into the pot of black fire at his waist. He flinched violently.

Gina said, "Better give me that. It seems to attract fire."

Alex handed her the pot. "All right, let's do it."

The three of them scrambled down to the path to find the Foré in retreat. Holly Frost was on one knee squeezing shots off in steady progression, protected by Chester's white energy shield.

Dark Star was in a swordfight. The last desperate Foré was trying to reach—Lady Janet!—who was trying to climb a rockslide and getting nowhere.

S. J. saw what was going on. He threw one of his carefully prepared antifire bombs: ashes and black fire wrapped in a big leaf. It exploded against the Foré's head in a puff of darkness. The half-black, half-oriental face glared pure disgust at S. J. before his backhand swing nearly decapitated Dark Star.

"Well, that didn't work," S. J. muttered, and leapt at the Foré's back. The native whirled, and Dark Star skewered him.

Flame arced out of the bushes towards the Gamers. It

looked like it was going to cremate them, until S. J. hurled another antifire bomb. The firestream vanished into the puff of blackness, just above their heads. Griffin answered it with a burst of his own, and there was a bloodcurdling shriek as a flaming Foré ran spastically from the brush to finally lie twitching and blooming oily smoke in the road.

Henderson seemed ecstatic. "That's it! That's what the black fire's for. Okay, we've got 'em on the run, now let's finish it!" The Gamers yelled their agreement and chased after the fleeing enemy.

Every few hundred feet one of the Foré would stop and try to shoot or chuck a spear at them, but all were mercilessly picked off. Bursts of flame ended magically above their heads. They had reached the base of the volcano itself; the Foré were circling left, trying to stay hidden within the tree line.

Gwen Ryder called, "Griffin! Dagger wound! Hold up and let me cure that." She picked her way toward him. "It'll affect your agility—"

An oversized Foré rose out of a bush, impossibly near, grinning like a thief. The huge machine gun in his arms must have weighed almost as much as he did. He took a moment to brace it against the tree behind him.

Alex yelled, "Duck!" and fired the flame thrower.

The machine gun roared and thrashed as if trying to escape its master. Then Alex's firestream engulfed the man, and the bullets stopped. But Gwen looked down, horrified, at six red blotches lined across her chest.

Alex was standing, cursing, when the sound of another gunshot slapped his ear, and the flame thrower tank jerked against his back.

He fought to pull the straps loose. "Tony!" he yelled at the nearest Gamer. "Anti-fire! Quick!"

McWhirter didn't seem to hear; he watched wide-eyed as the tank *whoofed* into flame. It was still in Griffin's hands as it erupted. He screamed, "Anti-fire, God Damn it!"

Heatless flame glared white around him, blinding him. He flung the flame-thrower gear into the bushes. He was still embedded in flame. In Game context, he must be covered with gasoline. He threw himself to the ground and rolled to try to put out the flames. Waiting for the metal disk at his throat to shock him dead.

S. J. threw his last prepared bomb and struck him squarely on the back.

There was a snakelike hissing sound as frost and fire vied for his life. Then the fire winked out and left him in a cloud of sawdust.

Alex got up. He looked for Gwen . . . and saw two Gwens, one very pale, one haloed in black. The darker Gwen doffed her pack and set it down carefully. Frankish Oliver was standing open-mouthed and paralyzed. She winked at him, and pointed at the pack, before she moved off behind her *tindalo*.

Ollie groaned. He turned from the other Gamers and buried his face against a warm boulder. Acacia moved up beside him, put her hand on his shoulder. He brushed it off. She hesitated, then left him.

Alex saw Chester looking at him nervously. He looked down and saw red and black flickering on his hands and arms. He felt strange: ready to faint. Tony wouldn't meet his eyes.

"Am I dead?" I didn't *feel* a shock . . .

Owen looked him over carefully. "Chester? It would take a lot of energy, but I think we can do it."

Chester watched the last of the Foré disappearing in the distance. To their right was the steep, rocky slope of the volcano. "Damn," The Lore Master said. "That's two already today. Maybe three. And the Game's only been on for four hours." He wiped his palms on his fatigue pants, staining them dark with sweat. "This is going to be murder. All right, try to save Griffin. We can spare the energy. We're going to need every man we've got."

Alex relaxed as Owen bathed him in gold light. It felt like a stiff shot of whiskey taking effect . . . as if deep wounds were actually healing. A wonderful thing, imagination. He stood up with new energy flooding his veins.

Tony McWhirter said, "Sorry. I froze."

"Don't do it again," Alex said briskly. It was a subject he would raise again, but later. Meanwhile, it would be best not to depend on Fortunato's good will.

Chester and Ollie were hunched down next to each other, with Gwen's backpack between them. Yes, of course: Gwen had thought to leave them her backpack full of ashes. *Win the Game.* Alex couldn't hear the conversation, but presently Ollie wore one of the evillest smiles that Alex had ever seen. On second thought, Alex didn't need to have heard. It undoubtedly had something to do with getting Lopez's balls in a basket, a sentiment he could sympathize with wholeheartedly.

Chapter Twenty-Five

THE EGG OF THE AIRPLANE

Chester Henderson must have been running on rage. He forged up the slope of the volcano as if it were level ground, his head swinging from side to side in Gamer's paranoia, seeking the next attack. Lady Janet stayed just behind him. Being kidnapped hadn't done her any obvious harm, Griffin thought. He managed to keep up, but he needed his breath. The rest of the Gamers were strung out halfway to the base of the cinder cone.

"Stop a minute," Chester directed. "God help us if we're spread out like this when the enemy hits us."

They stopped and flopped against the cinder slope, fifty meters or so below the volcano's lip. The line began to close. Chester asked, "Janet, what *exactly* did they say? Could they have been talking for your benefit, or Maibang's?"

Lady Janet shook her head. "They'd already left Maibang. They were boasting, getting up their courage. They bragged about the power of their ancestors' *tindalos*. They swore to defend their Cargo until all of the European thieves are dead, or all the Foré. They . . . they bragged about what they'd do to you. One of them offered to give me your . . . private parts," she said with evident distaste. "*That* was for my benefit. Partly."

"But they were going to fight."

"They meant it. They were egging themselves on."

"Then where are they?"

Lady Janet shrugged.

She'll be one hell of an actress, Alex thought. *She'll be too good for Gaming. Will she give it up?*

The Gamers bunched up around them. Acacia dropped with her back against Alex's knees; but her head was up, alert for the next attack. The enemy had last been seen hiding among the trees at the volcano's base. Where were they now?

Chester stood up. "Everybody got his breath back?"

They charged up the last fifty meters to the rim, each screaming his own war cry. At the lip of the crater they paused, feet skidding in the loose rock.

A few wisps of steam floated within the bowl, obscuring part of the view, but the crater seemed as deserted as the slope. Nothing human showed at all. Chester ordered, "Ollie, Gina, stay here with Lady Janet. The rest of us are going in."

Crevices in the rock vented more steam as Alex slid down into the mists. The rock was loose enough to make him cautious, but the incline wasn't as severe as he had feared. Digging in with his heels stabilized his balance.

The body of water at the bottom was not much bigger

than a pond. It steamed gently. He caught Chester's eye. "Still no defenders."

"I don't like it either."

"Here!" Owen called, and Alex turned to see the older man scrambling towards something dark and egg-shaped. Alex checked sideways and up towards the lip for visitors again, and followed Braddon.

As the shape became clearer, Griffin felt a chill. The fins attached to the blunt end said "bomb" so clearly he could almost hear it tick. The others had caught the same message; their headlong rush slowed to a cautious advance. At last they stood in an uncertain semicircle about the bomb.

It was darkly corroded metal, a pointed cylinder. The flat rock it lay on had been positioned like an altar and draped with white cloth: a parachute. A glass jar held fresh flowers . . .

Even S. J. looked a little disconcerted. "What in the world do we do with this, Chester?" He edged closer to it, to within five feet, but still couldn't bring himself to touch it. "Can we carry it out? This baby has to weigh two or three hundred kilograms. Margie?"

"I wouldn't know how to move it, Chester. Across flat ground, maybe . . ." Her eyes lit up. "Wait just a minute. How did the Black Hats get it in here in the first place?"

"Good thinking. It had to be magic." Chester walked around the bomb in a decreasing spiral, fascinated. "I don't know if we have enough power, though."

Tony was giving the bomb plenty of room. "Maybe we don't want to fool with it at all. Maybe Lopez just wants an excuse to blow us all up."

But S. J. had moved in closer, and now he was actually touching the smooth surface, eyes closed as if trying to sense its internal workings. "Chester . . ." he murmured.

Then louder. "Chester! Why can't we just extract the plutonium and take that with us? It's got to be almost as valuable as the whole damn bomb. And lots lighter."

"Jesus, Waters. You want to fry us all? Or did you bring a ton of lead shielding?"

"I thought maybe the black fire?"

Chester hesitated, then, "No. Radiation isn't fire."

"He's got the right idea," Tony insisted. "We don't have to steal it. Wreck it. Make it useless for the Enemy."

Chester shook his head. "Good common sense, but our mission is *theft*."

"But *look* at it! We'll never move it!"

"Magic," the Lore Master said. "I'm not sure I like it, but it's the only way out that I can see. It'll take everything that we have, and by the time we've got it out we'll be down to the dregs of our magic."

Gina carefully walked closer to the bomb, nose twitching. "The heat and steam, Chester. That thing could be pretty unstable."

"Maybe leaking radiation, too." Acacia seemed almost reluctant to say it. Instantly the Gamers shied back a few feet.

"Alright, then. We need a continual Danger scan on this while we try to move it. Margie, you and S. J. work out a way to lower it once we get to the lip."

"Damn," Margie cursed sedately. "I broke another fingernail."

"Try keeping your fingers out of the knots," Waters laughed, cinching the line tight. They had rigged guide ropes around the bomb that ran up to the crater rim. With luck, they would turn the moving job from an impossibility to a mere back-breaking task.

Chester had sent Acacia up to the top to substitute for Gina, who had entered into deep meditation with Chester in preparation for the attempt. When they rose they both seemed hollow-eyed and deadly serious.

Tony was making them all nervous, the way he kept watching the rim. "With luck we could get it almost to the rim before the Enemy jumps us."

"We'll get warning," Ollie told him.

· "We'd still be afraid to let go of the bomb, won't we? While they're killing our three scouts!"

"Lopez doesn't make it easy," Ollie granted him. "Wish you'd stayed home?" Tony didn't answer.

Chester called, "Are the lines tight?" He moved into position beneath the bomb without waiting for an answer. "The rest of you, get on the lines. As soon as the Reveal Danger spell is in force, start pulling, gently but evenly. Gina and I will do what we can. We're well ahead of schedule, troops. If the Gods—" and he lowered his voice to growl through his teeth, "—and Lopez—" Gina nudged him, and a faint smile finally cracked through his mask of fatigue, "—are willing, then we will taste victory today."

Griffin got into position on line, directly behind Owen. "Do we get a prayer from the Padre?"

Owen tested the line, grunting. "Good Lord, help us move this mother. Amen."

"Good enough."

A weak green glow surrounded the shape of the bomb, growing slowly more distinct. Chester and Gina stood erect, faces shining with sweat—from exertion, or the heat?—and down the middle of the emerald wave they projected came a darker thread of green. It pulsed and sparkled within the lighter hue like a vein of green blood, and when it touched the bomb the casing trembled.

"Now!" S. J. put his back into it even as he called the stroke, and Alex bent to the task, feeling good to have an understandable physical task in the midst of the make-believe.

The rock beneath the bomb crackled and flakes of it fell away, sliding down the slope towards Chester and Gina. Henderson had closed his eyes, and his hands were out-stretched. The green darkened and more rock slid away. McWhirter snarled and heaved; his long gymnasium mus-cles stood out like an anatomy diagram. The bomb shifted and rose several centimeters, and the Gamers loosed a cautious cheer.

Owen's foot slipped a fraction, and he had to move nimbly to catch himself. He turned his head and grinned at Alex, then yelled "Pull! Pull!" His mood was infectious and suddenly the whole group was laughing and sweating in the steam.

The pale green aura blinked and went red.

"Hold it!" Chester's voice was frantic, and the tension left the lines so fast that the bomb almost slid back down the incline.

S. J. crept closer to the bomb, and swallowed hard. "It's ticking . . ." When he turned to look at them all of the color had left his face. The bomb's red aura was darkening smoothly toward black. Part of his head went dark as he leaned close. "Chester . . . I think it's gonna blow . . ."

Shadow had entirely engulfed the bomb.

Henderson was incredulous. "An *atomic bomb?* He can't do this! Just what the hell does Lopez want from me? There's no way—wait a minute." Alex could see wheels turning behind his eyes. "The black fire. Everybody empty your pots onto this thing! Margie, you're carrying ashes? Dump it. It'll stop the priming charges. Who else has black fire? Or ash? Who's got Gwenivere's pack?"

Dark Star and Holly still had anti-fire, and they snatched
up their packs and dumped them out, fingers shaking with
excitement as they searched for the makeshift firepots.
Ollie dumped the ash from Gwen's pack onto the corroded casing. The blackness began to spread through the
ash.

"S. J., Margie, heap it on while—*what the hell are you
doing?*"

Waters had pulled a leverage bar out of his pack, and
way prying at a hatch in the nose of the bomb. "We can't
just pour the stuff on, chief. We've got to try to stuff it as
close to the primer as possible—" His voice was shaking,
and his skinny arms jerked almost spastically as he fought
with the panel. The ticking stopped.

Griffin hesitated only a second, then rushed to help.
"Get out of here, Gary," S. J. panted. "I can do this
myself."

"Stop trying to be a hero, friend." Griffin yanked the bar
from S. J.'s hand and squeezed it into the narrow crack,
leaning his weight against it. Distantly he heard Chester
telling the others to clear out. The door popped open. Alex
sniffed. Odd—

"Thanks and *get out*," S. J. hissed, grabbing the bar
back.

"No sooner said . . ." Griffin slapped the Engineer on
the back and hightailed it. The gravelly surface of the slope
gave that stomach-sinking two-forward-and-one-back
traction of a sand dune, but Alex sprinted anyway. Wondering why they ran. He had sniffed cordite and hot metal.
The primer had already gone off; the bomb's explosion
was retarded only by the black fire. How could they outrun
an atomic explosion?

Just below the volcano's lip, he looked back.

S. J. was still shoveling anti-fire and ashes into the hatch, and had pushed Margie away. She said something to the boy that Alex couldn't hear, and Waters snapped at her. She ran stumbling up the slope. Owen went down after her, to help her the last several yards to the top. They both arrived gasping.

And that cleared the volcano, except for Waters. "Run, you little idiot!" Henderson bellowed, and Alex was surprised to hear his own throat echoing the words.

Tony McWhirter was already a good way down the slope, hauling Acacia behind him by one arm. Alex heard him shout back at them: "Come on!" The others were bounding after him, and Alex joined them.

He was halfway down when a voice called from above. "Keep going! Keep going!" He looked back over his shoulder and saw S. J. at the rim of the volcano, just as the airplane's egg hatched.

It outlined Waters with a halo of light and flame. The ground shook as if a giant's palm had slapped the earth, and then the sound came.

Alex lost his footing and tumbled, falling across a split rock that began to gush steam. He fell into Holly Frost, who frantically tried to regain her balance before cascading with him in a rolling heap. Everywhere geysers of steam erupted from the ground, and he managed to roll around them more by instinct than thought.

By the time he reached the bottom he was totally out of breath, unnerved, elbow-skinned but otherwise alive. He got to his feet and dusted himself off, coughing, looking for bodies to count. Miraculously, there were no black auras.

Then he remembered, and his eyes searched the top of the volcano for a certain young Engineer. It was difficult for him to deal with what he felt at that moment: hope, fear, anger . . . and what else? All of them absurd, all of them real as a cut finger. He saw a plume of black smoke rising, rocks rolling, and nothing else. S. J. was gone.

Acacia read his mind. "He knew he wasn't going to make it, Gary."

Griffin fought with his emotions. "All right, dammit, he knew. But did he know he was dying for *nothing?*"

"What do you mean?"

"He's right, Acacia," Henderson had the same mixed emotions warring on his face. "That was no atomic bomb. Even in 1945, they weren't that small. We'd all be blown to hell and back."

"Well then, what . . .?"

"Decoy, dammit. Another decoy." He watched the smoke churning at the top of the flattened peak. "That crazy little bastard. He's going to make a hell of a Lore Master one day . . ." he shook himself out of it.

Most of the Gamers were back on their feet, although none of them looked too steady. They clustered around Chester like little children around their mother. Numb, disbelieving, and confused.

Holly rubbed a scraped knee. "What now, Ches?" There was no sass in her voice.

"Regroup and rethink. I guess we had better go back for Maibang." He tried to force some life into his voice, but Griffin saw the shallow backward glance towards the top of the volcano and knew what he was thinking: Three down. And the day was yet young.

The brush was blackened and burned away, and great pockets of earth were tarry scorch marks.

"Where did we leave him?" Acacia asked, her voice whispery with ugly anticipation.

Alex could only guess. "There used to be a patch of

shrubs around her, and a group of low trees . . ."

The group was about to spread in search when Dark Star waved her arm. They followed her toward a cluster of black fingers standing up from black ground: charred trees, still standing. There they found Maibang's smoking bones.

Gina sat down and cried. Henderson poked in the ashes with the tip of his toe, as if looking for something, some tiny symbol of victory in the midst of stunning defeat, then he too slumped to the ground and stared off at the horizon, silent and drained.

The Haiavaha. It had found the little guide and had finished what the Foré started.

Chester was muttering to himself, so softly that Griffin almost thought himself imagining it. Ever faithful, Gina came to his side and massaged his shoulder, trying to comfort. He flinched away at first, then began to relax, some of the tension draining from him. The other Gamers seemed to go into neutral, waiting for their leader to unscramble his thinking.

Griffin fidgitted, then plopped down next to Henderson. "Listen," he said, "we need to talk. We have some unsolved logic puzzles here. I don't know any of the answers, but I've got some interesting questions."

Chester didn't look around. "All right. Shoot."

Griffin paused to collect his thoughts. He ticked off questions on his fingers: "First. The bomb in the crater was just an ordinary bomb. Where's the great super-weapon the ghost Marines told us about, the one that was supposed to help win World War II? Second, why weren't the enemy guarding their egg if they valued it so highly? Just where were they? Third, if the super-weapon is hidden somewhere, why wasn't there a second blank spot on the map? Dammit, why was the *first* blank spot there if we couldn't get anything of value at the volcano? Why did Maibang get killed off like that, without any chance for us to save him? I mean, if he's a vital part of the Game, how could that happen?" He paused in frustration. "Or does any of this make sense?"

"It *has* to make sense, Tegner." Henderson ground his teeth together. "Lopez isn't crazy. He can't wipe me out like this without *some* way out. The rules don't allow it."

Henderson scratched a line in the dirt with his toe. "Let's see if we can make sense from this jumble. Let's start with Maibang. Lopez practically murdered him outright. I think we can assume that was orchestrated. It was in the script from the beginning. All right?"

"Why?"

"It means that *we already have the answers.* We don't need Maibang anymore."

"Have the answers? Hell. We don't even know what we're looking for."

"No, but look: Maibang got us as far as the volcano. There was nothing of value at the volcano—of value to us, that is. According to Lady Janet, it was quite valuable to the enemy. So where were they? Defending something *more* valuable, that's where. Defending the *real* Cargo."

Henderson was beginning to smile. Griffin felt the gears turning in his own head as he fought to keep up. "Then we were lured to the volcano because it was *near* the real cargo?"

"Maybe so, maybe no. You were right, there should have been a second blank spot. We examined that map. Was there a second blank spot?"

"I looked. No."

"Then . . . mmm . . . it's in a *bigger* blank spot. The ocean."

"In it? Underwater?"

"In, on, over, whatever. Maibang takes us by the sea road. The volcano is within spitting distance of the ocean. It has to add up, otherwise Lopez has lured us halfway across New Guinea for nothing, and that I don't believe."

"Well," Griffin scratched his head, genuinely puzzled. "What the hell *is* it?"

Chester laughed out loud. "Drown me if I know! Maybe a new submarine, or some kind of spy plane . . . maybe even the one that took the map photos. It could be any friggin' thing, and I don't care." He stood up and stretched, grinning. "I don't care because I know it's there. I can feel it. Tegner—I think we're all going to get some answers before today's over."

Chapter Twenty-Six

THE LAUGHING DEAD

Myers watched over their shoulders as the Lopezes worked.

Mitsuko Lopez was talking steadily into her mike. One of the screens showed troops forming up near shore: eight dark men and women horribly mutilated by makeup, all listening to her instructions in their earphones.

Richard Lopez nodded, nodded, interrupted rarely, while his fingers and feet raced over the controls. Hologram figures danced in response on a second screen, lurching among the dunes and into the trees; vanishing there, to reappear at the shore and begin their march again. They were horrible, these ghosts: long dead and half disintegrated. Some giggled uncontrollably and twitched like marionettes. Richard's lips pursed; his fingers blurred, and Myers watched a long-dead zombie being dismembered by an unseen sword. Richard nodded to himself.

"The woman who's missing a leg and an arm," Mrs. Metesky whispered in Myers's ear. "That's Gloria Washington. She got caught in the Antarctica Ciudad collapse and lost both limbs to frostbite. She took off her prosthetics for the show, of course. She loved the idea, but I'll never understand where Chi-Chi got the nerve to ask her."

Myers said, "Looks like your husband is getting ready to kill them *all* off."

Lopez heard and answered. "Henderson should have kept some of the anti-fire."

"Why are some of the actors giggling like that?"

"*Kuru.*" Suddenly Richard's fingers were flying again.

Kuru didn't tell Myers anything. He nudged. "You can justify it, of course . . .?"

Richard laughed.

Now holograms and fleshly actors marched together, the actors trying to match the lurching walk of Richard's constructs. Richard Lopez turned for an instant. "Myers, it's *there* for justification. Shows I did my homework. Have you heard of *kuru?* The laughing sickness?"

"No."

"Look it up. You get it by eating infected human brain tissue. It causes convulsions and an exhausting, hysterical laughter. The Foré used to get it. Some of our zombies obviously died of it."

Myers's stomach lurched. "It's real?"

"Quite real. Or used to be. The Foré haven't eaten human meat since the last century . . . as far as anyone knows. That area's mostly a tourist trap these days. But about half the women used to die of *kuru,* and a fifth of the general populace. The fighting men got the best parts of the missionaries, leaving the brains and, ah, chittlins for those with less status . . . women, children, the old ones

. . ." Richard let it trail off. On another screen, Henderson was leading his Gaming party down out of the burned area.

Owen Braddon, at the tail, suddenly turned and bounded back uphill. He scooped up a blackened skull and jogged to rejoin the party. The Lopezes turned to each other, grinned, nodded.

Myers was minded to ask; but Richard was talking again. "Can you imagine how long they must have been eating each other if a disease evolved to take advantage of it? It's extinct now. We think."

Griffin watched every bush, every tree, waiting for death. It was going to be bad. Already he could hear the murmur of surf. They must be close, dangerously close . . .

"Penny," Acacia said, and her voice scrambled his thoughts. He knew only that he spun half around, his hands strangling the rifle stock, aiming the gun at Acacia. Momentarily he felt foolish. Then he saw the fatigue in her face, and knew she understood.

The Gamers behind him had no spring left in their step. He could see their fierce determination, but no sign of confidence anywhere.

"What next? What the hell is he going to hit us with next?"

"That's the way to get killed," Acacia said soberly. "There's no 'he' to hit us with anything. Stop trying to play it, and live it." She was exasperated. "Gary, you drive me crazy. One half of you is just dying to jump in head-first, and the other half stands back dunking toes. If you could just stop wondering, weighing, planning . . ."

He managed to find a genuine laugh. "You're a fine one

to talk. We play Twenty Questions every time we say Hello."

"Touché. Maybe neither of us has been very real." Something went out of her voice as she looked up at him. "What if it *had* been for real, Gary?"

"If what had been real? This?"

"Us." There was no overt movement, but suddenly she was closer to him. Not touching, not even looking at him now, but there, and the air was charged.

"We're a little deep in the bullshit to try to sort this out now. Maybe we'll still think it's worth talking about after this is over."

Her eyes probed the bushes too pointedly, and he felt the warmth in the air go away. "Maybe."

Somebody giggled, far ahead.

"What's funny?" he wondered. But Acacia had frozen. The giggle came again . . . hey, that wasn't a Gamer. It wasn't close enough, and besides that, it was *wrong*. It is strained, broken, like the helpless, painful laughter of someone forceably tickled, tickled until the humor was gone, until the nerves beg for release. It made him cringe just to hear it, and it grew steadily louder.

Chester snapped commands. "Oliver! To the rear. Non-fighters to the center of the column. It's coming, so get ready."

They moved forward, slowly.

Alex heard shuffling footsteps. They came in odd rhythm with the laughter. A pained chuckle, then a dragging step. A hiccough of bizarre mirth, and another plodding thump . . .

And the first one appeared. He stood five and a half feet tall, dressed in brown rags. He laughed, and a hideous grin split the blackened face, and the whole body shuddered. In his right hand he carried a machete.

Mary-em measured him. "He's mine." She broke away from the line and walked warily toward him, her blade well in front of her.

Griffin could see her opponent more clearly now. Like the native Alex had ambushed earlier, he showed dark skin and eyes with epicanthic folds. Sure enough, the Japanese invaders must have mated with the native Foré; and the resulting race would have hybrid vigor on their side. As if Chester didn't have enough trouble.

As Mary-em drew close, the man stopped and seemed truly to see her for the first time. He blinked slowly, with gummy lids, and Alex saw how filthy he was. Dirt crusted his face and hands, and the earth looked damp where it clung.

Unbidden, the logical allusion sprang to Alex's mind: ". . . like he just stepped out of a grave . . ."

And that was when the odor hit. *Neutral scent* was Alex's first panicked reaction, almost immediately squelched. This smell was far from neutral.

Once, years before, Alex had bought an old-fashioned fly trap, the kind that catches them in water. One warm July he had forgotten to clean it out for a week, and thousands of flies had fermented in the sun. When he finally went to clean it out, the reek went through him like a brick through sheet glass, and everything in his stomach had crawled the walls.

This was similar. Rotten . . . something rotten. Not meat. Something less *clean* than meat. Something that had been horribly corrupt even in life. Something bottlefly blue on the outside, and pasty green within.

Mary-em was turning green, but now, with a foe in front of her, she moved more surely.

It charged. Mary-em sidestepped the wobbly advance, and drew the blade of her halberd cleanly across its stomach, and whirled to face it again. It laughed and hacked at her head.

Alex yelped with surprise, but Mary-em ducked as if she'd been expecting it. She kicked low and cross-legged, as if smacking a soccer ball, halting an inch from its shin. Its leg gave way, but it slashed as it fell and Mary-em blocked again, spinning like a dancer with a parasol, and with a flicker of her wrists cut the thing on both sides of the neck. It fell to the dirt.

Alex gave her a "thumbs-up" and the little warrior acknowledged him with the barest of grim smiles.

The thing was still twitching. Wounds gaped, but there was no blood.

"Zombie," Chester said. "Our Enemy is pulling out all the stops—" He shielded his eyes and peered down the road, mouth tightening. "Second wave. Panthesilea, Griffin, you spearhead this time."

Griffin surprised himself by asking, "Should we be throwing salt at them?"

"What? No, Griffin, zombies are a different religion. Voodoo. Just fight, okay?"

There were three of the undead this time, moving with rust-stiff joints, faces split into mock-grins. Gagging on the smell, he raised the rifle to his shoulder and fired. Dust puffed from the face of one of the undead. It staggered back a step, then laughed and came on.

The smell . . .! Griffin jacked another cartridge into the chamber and fired again, and again, and the thing fell to one knee. The skin of its face had peeled away like rotted wet parchment. One of its eyes was gone, a moist red socket gaping, the useless eyelid shuttering up and down irregularly.

Acacia wasted a moment staring at the results of Griffin's

marksmanship, then cursed and clicked her sword free of its sheath. The second and third zombies broke toward her, one carrying a machete, one carrying the bayonet off an M-1. They attacked in tandem, and she backpedaled a step to gain time, then dove to the side and slashed brutally at the nearest knee. The creature was hobbled; it fell with a bone-jarring thump. It chittered at her with brown, stubbly teeth and crawled toward her.

The second backed away more cautiously, then smiled. She felt a clammy grip on her ankle, and chopped back to catch the fallen zombie in the head. It howled, but didn't let go. "Drown you! Let go of my—" Kicking and jerking, Acacia managed to evade the second zombie's machete blow and passed her sword through its arm, which went limp. Another backhanded blow and the zombie on the ground released its grip.

Alex stood over Acacia's first victim, holding its machete. "Bullets don't work as well as blades on these things," he said. He peered down the road.

Acacia took the other zombie's weapon. "Just how much damage can they take?" she wondered.

They moved on. Minutes later they could see man-high sand dunes through the thinning trees. This, at least, brought whoops of delight. Alex found himself missing S. J.'s tireless enthusiasm for the Game; he forced himself to make extra noise. He whipped the machete round his head and glowered what he imagined to be a savage grimace.

Mary-em spotted them first. "Company." She tilted her halberd and squared herself, her steps more measured.

They came wobbling out of the dunes, looking vaguely, disturbingly familiar. There were four this time, three men and a woman. They were blocking the path out of the trees. The woman carried a spear of some kind; the men carried the usual machetes.

"Oh, Jesus," said Mary-em, "that's Eames."

Eames's face was a blank mask. He walked at the same dead-steady pace, and there was a huge, bloody wound in his chest. Alan Leigh walked on his right, his step devoid of bounce, expression frozen in death, machete held high.

Acacia started to move in on Leigh, but Henderson warned her back. "Caution, please. We'll keep it at two-on-one as long as we can. Nothing fancy. Just get the job done." He motioned quickly, dividing up his remaining team members.

Acacia and Alex had moved in on Leigh. The zombie wizard seemed to be restraining a bare smile, but the blade in his hand was far from friendly. It flickered in the air, and Acacia made the deflection while Alex chopped at an extended arm. The arm went red, and Alan switched hands moaning. Alex raised his machete again, and Acacia screamed, "Watch out!" He wheeled and ducked in time to avoid decapitation.

His attacker was a giggling native woman, long dead, a great hanging flap of scalp obscuring much of her face. She swung a machete at Alex's throat. Alex ducked and reached for the wrist with both hands. A disarming throw— An instant late he remembered that hand-to-hand was illegal. Too late. The hologram sword-arm passed like shadow through his hands, swung back and slashed clumsily at his short ribs. Red light bathed his side.

Alex broke out of his immobility to slash backhanded with his recovered machete. He chopped away until the creature slithered to the ground and stopped moving. Alex was breathing like a bellows, dripping sweat; he looked around, wild-eyed, for more enemies.

"Griffin!" The high, nasal voice of Dark Star called for help, and he spun about. She and Lady Janet were under attack by a duo of shuffling dead. Both zombies were clotted with dirt; one was in an advanced state of decomposition, and he showed Asian features. Janet had picked up a stick, and seemed able to keep the Asian at bay. Dark Star's forearm glowed red. She had been forced to drop her weapon.

Griffin took a step in her direction, but more dead were emerging from the bushes around them—men and women and half-grown children—and suddenly the entire group was threatened. He saw Dark Star go down with a blade in her neck, and Holly Frost's swift reprisal. Janet had disarmed the rotting zombie, and was using its own machete against it.

Chester had slain three of the monsters with magic. His aura was weakening; he conserved energy by picking up a machete and having at them. Gina used her power staff as a physical weapon. She had little style, but four feet of reach made up for it. The staggering, stumbling Undead women couldn't cope with her extra reach, and couldn't cleave through her staff, and they went down before her in shrieks of painfully sustained laughter.

Oliver had several red streaks on his body, but none of them were in vital areas. Vigor points undiminished . . . Teeth clenched in a fighting grimace, he stood back to back with Margie, who couldn't quite keep the smile off her face as she warded off blows and dealt death. She gave up trying, and seemed to become a demon, her fluffy grey hair billowing behind her as she whirled and slew.

It seemed to go on forever. Alex stopped seeing opponents. They came like waves on the sea; faces formed and faded, grinning and bellowing their hate in choruses of laughter. And always his arm rose and fell, rose and fell . . .

He bore red slashes in half a dozen places, and he waited for the shock to his throat that would announce his death. When the shock came he could lie down . . . but it didn't come, wouldn't come, though the stench of death rose in his nostrils strong and thick enough to choke. Not when he tripped over the body of a fallen Undead and saw that it was Alan Leigh, who winked at him insolently. Not when only Acacia's sharp eye and piercing voice saved him from a zombie attack from the rear. Exhaustion had turned his arms to dead things. The laughter of the dead women was driving him crazy. The sweat rolled down his forehead, obscuring his vision and burning his eyes.

And in Alex Griffin's mind something gave way. It didn't matter that he could see the blades passing harmlessly through each other, that the red slashes were dye or glowing light and not oozing wounds. It didn't matter that the sounds of steel on steel, and steel on rigor-stiffened flesh, were coming from the necklace on his chest. None of that mattered. He was fighting for his life in an alien place, against legions of the damned, and people he cared about were wounded and dying and slaying around him.

He bobbed and weaved among the shadow blades without conscious thought, spinning and capering with a fighting-smile twisting his mouth, and the machete wove a path of destruction. When a red slash appeared on his shoulder he gasped in pain; when a savage thrust brought an enemy down to the dirt, he howled in glee, slashing again and again and again.

And suddenly only Gamers still stood. At least twenty bodies were strewn grotesquely about, limbs tangled in death. Kibugonai, the small man whose mother had been bitten by a pig, was dead. He sat propped against a tree, hands to his stomach, eyes wide and surprised at the cascade of crimson in his lap. Dark Star was face down in the dirt.

And Margie Braddon knelt over the corpse of Owen, stroking his hair and whispering in his ear. She looked up at Chester, her face like thunder. "What now, Chester?"

"I've been counting. We're down to nine, and no Clerics. If we're wounded we stay wounded."

"Ten," said Lady Janet, lifting a machete. The projected blade was bloody.

"Nine," Chester repeated coldly. "We can't trust you." He touched Margie sympathetically on the shoulder. "Whatever it is we're after, it can't be far." Alex could see the fatigue and worry in his eyes, but his voice showed none of it. "Come on. We've got to keep moving."

Margie kissed Owen on the back of the neck. Of all the Gamers, perhaps only Alex saw Owen's hand fumble back to find hers, and give it a reassuring squeeze. Chester rolled the Cleric over and secured the padded bag, and checked to be sure that Kasan Maibang's skull was intact. A few teeth had come loose, and some flakes of black char.

Three pale *tindalos* were coming through the trees. The Gamers didn't wait.

Nine Gamers and Lady Janet moved out of the woods and into the great dunes. Waves boomed ahead of them. Weapons ready, they traced a weaving path. Abruptly Mary-em threw down her pack, flopped against a sandy slope, and gasped, "Rest break, Chester?"

Chester shook his head. "We've used them all up."

He lent her an arm and she shook it off irritably, standing on her own. "I'm not that old."

Griffin rubbed his eyes and said, "I am." He felt as if he had been awake for days. Last night's rest hadn't touched him. Did "neutral scent" disrupt sleep, or was it just the Game? Or Acacia? His vision blurred, and a chill ran through his body. He wanted to curl up in the warm sand. From the look of the other Gamers, the feeling was shared.

But they marched on. Now the sea showed a white-frothed triangle between the dunes.

Alex watched Acacia try for the hundredth time to strike up conversation with Tony. McWhirter's dark-rimmed eyes flashed from her to Griffin, and Griffin felt murder in the air. Acacia gave up and trudged back to Alex, head low.

"Whew. I guess I give up." Her eyes met his, and the self-pity vanished from her face. She tugged at his arm. "Come on, handsome. Let's go get killed."

"Let's."

Griffin watched her as they marched, and saw her rub her eyes three times in three minutes. "Eye trouble?"

"Yeah. Damn, I don't know what's wrong. I don't need to change my contacts for two more weeks."

"I don't think it's the lenses. Listen—" They had reached the top of a dune, the sand sliding beneath their feet and making every step a calf-aching effort. As they crested, Griffin gathered his thoughts, gazing out at the expanse of blue-green water. What met his eyes froze the words fast in his throat.

Chapter Twenty-Seven

CARGO CRAFT

Chester ran up the dune, slid down a step and finished the scramble with the assistance of his hands. He stood, dusting off his pants, and Alex was gratified to note that the Lore Master was as shocked as he was. Awe, surprise, disbelief, a growing hint of laughter—"He's *kidding!* There never *was* anything like that!"

Less than a hundred yards out from shore floated a tremendous seaplane. It looked as big as any flying thing had ever been, short of a dirigible or a spacecraft. There were four lean-looking propeller-tipped motors on each huge wing. The hull was a nearly blank wall with a tiny afterthought of a windscreen on top, a pair of tiny portholes just ahead of the wing, and a tiny door open in the flank, with lines trailing out into the water.

Margie was sitting spraddle-legged, helpless with laughter. "There was. There was," she giggled.

Chester turned. "Margie?"

"It's the Spruce Goose!" And she was off again.

Big airplane. Alex covertly studied the other Gamers. McWhirter and Holly Frost and Gina Perkins, all staring across the water. McWhirter and Gina looked thoughtful, speculative; Holly laughed with her head thrown back. The rest of the Gamers were looking at Margie, waiting.

"Oh my Lord. Let me get my breath. Oh, I hope Owen's watching this." Margie swallowed. "Well. I saw it once, the real thing, long ago."

"Come on, Margie." Chester dropped into the sand, completely relaxed. "This is it. It's got to be. Whatever it is. So what is it?"

"It's the Spruce Goose. Oh, dear. Where shall I start? World War Two? Before my time, dear, but I read about it. There was an industrialist, Howard Hughes; you've heard of Howard Hughes?" Some of them had. "Howard Hughes designed an airplane made mostly of wood because the Allies were running short of metal. It was the biggest airplane ever built, then. Maybe it still is. It would have carried seven hundred and fifty troops."

"So it really was supposed to help win the war."

"Yes. I expcect it was too ambitious. The plane didn't even fly until 1947, at Long Beach. It wasn't supposed to fly then. Hughes had orders to run it across the water without taking off, just for a trial run. Afterward he told the Congressmen that he couldn't hold it down."

Henderson was nodding. "But in this line of history the Cargo Cult magicians got it."

"I expect so. Our present allies must have taken control as soon as it was in the air. They used their magic to fly it from Long Beach to New Guinea. At some point the other tribe took control. And here it is."

"Here it is. But it couldn't possibly have had enough fuel . . ."

Margie shrugged. "Magic."

"Uh huh. Well, that's it. Obviously we're supposed to fly it out of here somehow—"

Gina cut him off with a kind of whispered scream. "Chester. The top of those rocks. There."

From the dune they could see a natural wall of rock that stretched from the tree line out into the water, terminating about fifteen meters from where the plane was moored. Three shadowed silhouettes stood and gesticulated at the seaward end.

Even at this distance there was no doubting *what* they were. Those oversized heads . . . Alex recognized the beaver-dam hair, shaped with the aid of sticks and mud. The clawlike hands, the scarred, greased bodies. The priest at the Anglican mission, multiplied by three. Foré.

Their voices harmonized with the roar of the sea, so that the sea almost drowned them out. But Gina said, "They'll be summoning more Undead." Her voice shook.

A whiff of the wind carried the message: Gina was right. "Stations!" Chester bawled, and the remaining Gamers formed a ragged wedge bristling with machetes.

"Space out more!" the Lore Master screamed. "We have to give each other room! Make for the rock wall!"

But the Foré priests had already been answered.

The Undead emerged from the brush in twos and threes, and the smell was like a gut-split skunk ripening on the road. Alex held his forearm across his nose and held his blade ready. Oliver was to his left, sword high. Gina to his right, spirals of light running along her power staff. Alex felt someone's warm behind wiggle against his, and knew that Acacia guarded his back.

To reach the rock breaker, the Gamers would have to cut through a line of the Undead.

"Advance," Chester said, voice cautious and hoarse. "Slowly."

A dark, pure-blooded New Guinea zombie was the first to reach the wedge, and the first to go down under the blades of Mary-em and Oliver. They had gained another three or four meters before three Undead reached them, two of them women hiccoughing their horrible mirth. The third was the reincarnation of Rudy Draeger, the bullet-slain Engineer.

Once again, something within Griffin, something logical and cool, died without protest. In its place rose a red shadow that yearned to kill. He chopped at Draeger. Rudy moved stiffly but intelligently, and Alex granted him a block, swerving part of his blade to home on the ribs. Draeger blocked again, but Alex's move was a feint, and the dead Gamer howled as a glowing blade slashed his throat. This time Griffin took no chances. He chopped twice more until Draeger's whole head glowed black: decapitation.

Other Gamers were engaged, and Alex wanted badly to break formation and help them; but he held his place. It was their only chance to survive. By slow increments, they had already moved to within twenty meters of the wall. If they could get their backs to it . . .

A machete blade flicked past Alex's ear: someone behind him had missed a block. He turned in time to see Tony McWhirter take a wound in the arm and answer it with a stroke to the knees that sent the zombie tumbling to the sand.

"Move!" Chester's voice could hardly be heard above the grunts and the laughter, but heard it was, and they moved another few steps before resistance grew too heavy.

In the corner of his eye Alex saw Oliver gaping, frozen, eyes wide and puppy-moist, his sword pointing toward the sand . . . Alex spared a glance in that direction.

Trudging with heavy steps, eyes fixed on the rotund warrior with a bloodlust that was more threatening than the uplifted weapon, came Gwen.

Oliver made a half-hearted attempt to block her stroke. It was as if he'd never held a sword before. Her descending blade slipped past his guard easily, and a wet red line appeared on Ollie's shoulder.

Behind Alex, Acacia, temporarily without an opponent, had seen the attack. "For God's sake, Ollie . . . fight back!"

Ollie fought like a man unwilling to strike back. Again zombie-Gwen scored. Her matted blond hair stuck greasily to her face as her arm rose and fell again, her eyes lolling lifelessly in their sockets. Ollie blocked—and missed a perfect opening to her stomach. In a voice so soft that Alex might have imagined it, Gwen said, "Kill me, Ollie. Please."

And Norliss gritted his teeth and slew his woman, plunging his sword into her breast. She went down like a sack of meal, and the Warrior looked sick. Alex took an instant to grip Ollie's shoulder hard. He was relieved when Ollie wheeled to face the next zombie with a vicious stroke worthy of Frankish Oliver.

The Gamers had gained another few meters. Alex grew impatient; he shifted his position in the wedge until he was closer to the lead.

Behind him, Chester used a final bolt of lightning to strike down a zombie, then snatched up a blade as his aura dimmed and winked out. He cursed as he handled the unfamiliar tool, and he attacked clumsily.

Most of the Gamers were wounded somewhere; Alex himself had half a dozen wounds. Margie was unmarked. She had taken to the machete like a bat to warm blood. The Undead seemed unable to deal with her style: imprecise and untutored, but full of crazy energy.

Alex had reached the wall. He set his back to it and yelled, "Re-form!" Chester looked at him with raised eyebrow, then nodded in approval.

The group broke up, hacking wildly at the lunging corpses, and formed two lines against the rocks. The zombies kept to the sand, off the rock and away from the water, and that cut the vulnerable area to two sides, far easier to defend.

Still, they came on, and on. No longer was it possible for Griffin to pause between slayings. The dead piled up around his feet and swarmed to cloud his vision. He was sweating, and the sweat rolled into his eyes, blurring sight. The smell of the Undead, their hideous appearance, and the sound of the laughing, the unholy tittering, were wearing him down.

He saw what happened to Gina. Two corpses menaced her. One was mutilated, a tittering, twitching woman missing a leg and an arm. She leaned on a tall pole tucked under the stump of the missing arm. Her good hand jabbed with a bayonet fixed to half of a shattered M-1 rifle. Gina, fending off a smallish, long-dead man, swung backhand to cleave her open. The woman wheeled; the butt of Gina's machete smacked into her crutch.

Gina froze; she turned to stare. She must have assumed the butchered, half-decomposed corpse was a hologram. The man she'd ignored swung at her neck.

"Gina!" Chester screamed, and Alex saw her buckle to the sand, her aura black as night, and two grinning zombies still slashed at her. Tony scooped up her magic staff desperately. The tool was drained of power, but a night's rest would recharge it.

The line tightened, the eight remaining Gamers clustered about Lady Janet, all of them ragged and wheezing with weariness, arms rising and falling, rising and falling . . .

One face stood out in the press. The shaggy dark brows were whitened, and the glacial blue eyes seemed dulled by death, but it was still Bowan the Black who worked his way toward Chester. The blade in his hand seemed more like a wakizashi, a Japanese short sword, than a simple chopping implement. His target was Henderson. Alex yelled a warning, then turned to his own defense.

Zombie-Bowan snarled and struck. Henderson, clumsy with his edged tool, slithered out of the way and pushed Bowan back to gain room.

But Bowan was out for blood. There was no pause, no lag to give Henderson time to adjust his balance. Bowan spun, and backhanded his sword into Chester's leg. The Lore Master cursed, and forgot all semblance of style, chopping insanely at Bowan.

The former Magic-User was caught by surprise. His aura went red at shoulder, thigh, stomach. He was forced to the ground, where the Lore Master performed butchery.

Next to Griffin, Holly Frost gasped as a red slash spread on her left arm. He deflected a stroke for her while she regained her poise. "Owe you," she said between clenched teeth.

Alex took a wound in the calf, and Oliver a slashed scalp. The animated corpses died in droves; their bodies hampered movement, and now and then one would clutch at an ankle. The action was being forced along the rock spit, toward the sea, toward the Foré priests.

Perhaps they realized it. There was a cry, high and wavering, like the caw of an eagle. The zombie facing Griffin stepped back a pace, and turned.

In shock, Alex saw that the entire mass of Undead had stepped away from the beleaguered Gamers, retreating in a semicircle, toward the trees.

Acacia gasped, "Now what?"

Griffin looked at his wrist. For a moment the watch imprinted on his sleeve seemed foreign, entirely magic, unreadable. Then, "Six minutes to go. We can't follow . . . the zombies, but . . ."

Frankish Oliver turned and began to clamber up the rocks. "We can still . . . get the priests!"

Alex felt that if he stopped moving he would never start again. He pulled himself up behind Oliver, who was not exactly sprinting. Rocks rolled underfoot. He reached the top, to see beaver-dam hair styles disappearing down the other side.

Oliver was clambering along the top of the spit. He stopped. He pointed with his sword, seaward. As Alex came up beside him, he found breath for one word. "Boats."

They stood panting, watching. The three small boats were archaic enough, but they weren't native to New Guinea. There was English lettering on the sterns. Each boat held one Foré priest, standing, and one zombie seated at the oars.

Chester and the other Gamers had found the strength to join them. Together they watched the three boats tie up beneath the door in the flank of the Spruce Goose. The

Foré climbed a dangling rope ladder. Their Undead oarsmen remained in the boats.

And then the sea and the huge plane faded into darkness, though the beach was still in twilight. When Alex looked at his watch it was ten o'clock.

They climbed down from the rocks in time to see Gina rise up to join her *tindalo*. Chester watched her go. When he turned back to them the defeat in his face was impossible to ignore. "He's still dragging it out. Tomorrow. . ."

Acacia swallowed air and clicked her sword into its sheath. Her hair was matted with sweat and sand, and she looked as if she had dug ditches all day. "More likely he's worried, Chester."

At first Chester seemed not to hear her; then he turned. "Worried why?"

"What will the IFGS think about an assault like that?"

He scratched his stubble, eyes worried. "I don't know. We sure as hell had plenty of warning . . ."

Acacia seemed alarmed. "Chester! What is the matter with you? You're on our side, remember?"

The Lore Master sank down in the sand, looking out into the darkness. "Hasn't done you much good, has it?" He turned over, face down. He sounded horribly tired. "Maybe we should have gone back for more black fire. Scatter it in the loam on the forest floor. Rot is slow fire, it should burn backward. Let the zombies come at us there . . . it might have stopped them . . ."

The Gamers shifted around uncomfortably, watching Chester brood.

Alex dropped beside him on the sand. "At least we finally know what we're after. It's right out there on the water, Chester. We even know where to find the boats!"

Chester nodded. He lifted himself on his elbows to glare into the darkness that hid the Spruce Goose. "Make camp," he said abruptly. "Tomorrow's another day. When the priests come back to finish us off, we'll get 'em. Thanks, Griffin. God, I'm tired. But tomorrow . . ."

Griffin dropped his pack. He was unable to find any emotion to hang his fragmented thoughts on. He looked down at himself, for wounds. The red glow of hologram-delivered wounds was gone. The bloodstains left by solid zombie weapons looked like paint. The day was turning unreal.

Ollie dropped into the sand next to him. He mumbled something Alex couldn't quite hear.

"What?"

"I wish it was over." The Thief had to bend low to hear him. "I just wish it was over." He looked like an old man, the muscles in his cheeks slack, jowls hanging. A single tear ran glistening down his cheek.

A pat on the back was the only answer Griffin could find. He moved his pack away, over to a rock large enough to sit on. He huddled there, watching the tides turn off. Eight Gamers left. The Game was, indeed, almost over.

Chapter Twenty-Eight

THIEVES IN THE NIGHT

"Get me Marty Bobbick, please."

"Yes, sir."

Alex sagged against the shadowed back of a dune. The sand was cooling now; it felt good against his skin. He could feel the fatigue, but it seemed apart from him. His mind was racing. The Gamers were camped on the other side, a fair distance away. Alex listened, but tonight there was no singing, no laughter. He heard Margie and Chester talking, but couldn't make out the words.

"Hail the Griffin, slayer of the undead!"

Ha ha. "Go ahead, Marty, get it out of your system."

"Chief, I'm at least half serious. I never *dreamed* these Games could get that rough. If you weren't in top physical shape we'd be carrying you out. How does a sweet little old lady like that Margie Braddon keep going?"

"Sheer *chutzpah*. The rest of us are ready to lie down and die. I'm really worried about Ollie. I guess Gwen needed the points, but the last thing in the world he needed was having to kill his woman. Damn, but at least we know our target now! And it's a whopper, Marty. Tomorrow—"

"It? Not a he or a she?"

He or she? *Oh*. Alex was too tired even to be irritated with himself. "Sorry. Jumped tracks again. It's a he, Marty. You know, I went into this with entirely the wrong idea—"

He heard a faint scuffing from above. A few grains of sand pattered down around him. It stopped almost at once.

Alex rolled over and stood up, without obvious haste, while he kept talking. "I thought we must be chasing an experienced Gamer. Someone who knew the ropes so well that he could find extra time somewhere to creep off and do some work on the side."

"It looks to me like nobody would *ever* know that much."

"Damn right. The better you are, the more you know, the harder you work at not getting killed out. There aren't any ropes to know. Each Game is a whole new ball of snakes." He might have imagined that sound. A gust of wind could have blown that sand down on him . . . but under a dome? Alex felt himself becoming one gigantic ear.

"What are we looking for, then? A novice?"

"Right. And he gave himself away a couple of times." Alex looked up, without turning his head. The shallow curve of the top of the dune had a bump on it. It could be the top of a head. Better not gamble on it. It if wasn't, then a known killer might be coming *around* the dune.

He'd hear boots on sand. Wouldn't he? Alex had left his machete beside his bedroll, and now he regretted it. The Game was in abeyance, and so were the Game rules governing physical combat.

He should have made this call from the middle of a nest of Gamers. Secrecy was meaningless now. Couldn't be .helped. *All right, let's lure him down . . .*

Marty's voice snapped, "Well?"

"He was too tired on the second day. This guy is in excellent condition, and he could barely climb a wall. He'd been up very late the night before. At the volcano, he was *sure* the bomb was a piece of misdirection. While the rest of the team was trying to move it out, he kept looking around. He must have already seen the Goose. And it's too big; it must be a fair part of Lopez's budget. It's an important part of the Game, and we hadn't got there yet. And at the harbor, he was too interested in the planes, and then not interested at all."

Where the hell was he? He could *not* afford to let Griffin speak his name.

"Griff. *Who?*"

Where was he?

"Griff! You all right? Shall I send in help? Griff!"

He'd fooled himself. There was nobody on the dune; he was alone. Nuts. "Fortunato. Tony McWhirter."

"Good enough. Now what? Call the Game?"

But Alex heard a peculiar ragged sigh from overhead.

"I'll get right back to you, Marty." He flipped the wallet closed and pocketed it. "Come on down," he called, and eased his left leg back for balance. McWhirter could still attack, and he might have a sword.

Tony stood up and walked down the slope, leaning slightly backward, plowing up sand. He was unarmed. He stopped several feet away, spread his hands. "I didn't kill anybody," he said.

"You have the right to remain silent," Griffin said. "If you choose to—"

"I know, I watch the boob cube too. Griffin, I didn't kill anyone. The guard almost killed *me*, but I didn't hurt him. I tied him up and gagged him and left him. He was wriggling around, and I thought of maybe using more bandage, moor him to some furniture, maybe. But he wasn't going to get loose quick enough to stop me."

"Nice plan," Griffin said with calculated flatness. "What happened? Did he get a good look at your face?"

"I didn't kill him!"

"He's dead, though. Suffocated. Did you accidentally hold his nose for him?"

Tony dropped into the sand and put his head between his knees. Griffin heard wet sounds. He prudently kept his distance.

"He was still breathing! I . . . oh . . . I cut off his wind till he passed out, but he was *breathing* when I left him!"

"Where's the neutral scent?" Tony looked up hopefully and started to speak. "No deals," Griffin snapped. "It's probably gone by now anyway. You had to have someone to pick it up."

Tony shook his head violently. "He couldn't have found it. Griffin, that's crazy stuff. When I used it on you I had no idea what it would do to *me*. I just went crazy with fear. I must have smashed into *every* tree in Dream Park. There was a place where I was supposed to leave it, but I never got that far. I just got rid of it. I was afraid of it. I was afraid you'd search me."

"Where?"

"I can show you. Can we deal?"

"I'm promising nothing. The only question you need to ask is, how hard is Dream Park going to lean on you? You get to decide that right now."

"Then get drowned! I don't know who was supposed to get it. Maybe he'll find it before you do."

"Have it your way." Griffin whetted his voice to a cutting edge. "But, Tony, even if Rice died of a stopped up nose, it's murder. California law says that if someone dies as the result of the commission of a felony, it's murder. Stand up."

Tony stood. The defiance was gone. "What now?"

"We go tell the others that we're leaving the Game."

The darkness didn't hide the sick dismay on Tony's face. It took Griffin by surprise. "Oh god. This is going to kill Acacia. They won't last five minutes tomorrow."

"You should have thought of that before," said Alex. He sensed Tony's muscles tightening. "Come on, Tony. Playtime's over."

Tony sounded almost hysterical. "I've screwed everything. Everything. Please, Griffin. I can't face them. Please."

"I don't fancy it much either." The brutality in his voice was as much for his own benefit as McWhirter's. "Come on."

You're betraying them to their deaths!

Bullshit. Being killed out isn't dead. Rice is dead.

"Griffin, please! Let's just play out the Game. Give me that much. Just a few hours. Then I'll tell you where it is and turn myself in."

"Don't be silly." *Damn, and we had a good chance of winning, too.*

"I'll show you where I put the neutral scent. Tomorrow."

"I can't make that deal. Come on."

Far too late, Tony jumped him. Griffin leaned aside from his wild swing and kicked him in the shin. As Tony doubled in pain Alex seized a handful of hair and an arm, locking him helpless.

Numb and silent, Tony was steered back to the campfire.

The campfire burned low to the coals, and no one seemed to have the energy to feed it. Kibugonai and Kagoiano were back to serve dinner; their faces were zombie-blank and their death-wounds showed clearly. Lady Janet found the strength to pass around pouches of milk and fruit juice and beer, but her smile was barely lip-deep.

Hardly a head turned as Alex brought Tony stumbling back into camp, until somebody noticed the arm twisted painfully behind McWhirter's back. Chester stood, alarm igniting on his face. He bent his knees twice to get some circulation into them and challenged. "All right, Tegner. Just what the hell is going on?"

Alex released Tony, who stood shivering in a circle of questioning eyes. "Do you want to tell them, or shall I?"

Tony tried to speak, but nothing came out. He gave up and shook his head. Griffin felt pity worming its way to the surface of his mind, and shut his shields down fast. "All right, I'll do it, then."

He had all their attention now. None of them looked at all happy. "Three nights ago, McWhirter broke away from the rest of you and took a private tour. He ended up in the Research and Development department, where he stole a sample of a newly developed . . . invention." No need to give away more than necessary.

Acacia gasped. "My God. So that's where you were that
night." In pain and disorientation she came up to him.
"Oh, Tony . . . no wonder you've been acting crazy. If
only I'd . . . Tony, *why?*"

All Tony did was lower his eyes miserably to the ground.

"That's not all," Alex said. Acacia's look tore at him,
made him wish he had taken Fortunato out of the Game
first and explained later. Or never! "In order to gain access
to the complex, Tony had to subdue a guard. In some
manner not yet clear, that guard, one Albert Rice, died of
suffocation."

Acacia seemed to study him. Then Tony. She said,
flatly, "No."

Alex said, "Well, Tony?"

Silently McWhirter nodded his head, tears beginning to
run down his cheeks, glistening silver in the firelight.

"Then who are *you?*" Acacia's query was delivered at a
scream. The other Gamers seemed transfixed.

"Griffin. Alex Griffin. Chief of Dream Park Security."

Chester looked like he'd looked when the *bidi-
taurabo haza* found him. "All right . . . Griffin. What
happens now?" He reminded Griffin of a man waiting to
hear the results of his biopsy: terrified and fascinated at the
same time.

"Now . . ." *Jesus. Do they have to look at me like
that? I'm only doing my goddam job.* Mary-em sat curled
up on the ground with her face between her knees. She
didn't want to look at him. A hint of defiance burned in
Holly Frost's dark face, quickly subdued. "You know what
I have to do, dammit. Every one of you knows."

No one argued, and he almost hoped they would.
*Come on, you fog-headed fantasy freaks. Yell at me.
Scream. Call me a rent-a-pig. Anything.*

Acacia stumbled back to her place near the campfire. She tried to swallow some beer, but it exploded in her mouth. Ollie held her as she coughed and sobbed.

"That's it, then," Chester said, taking infinite care not to let his emotions leak into his voice. "We're down to six hands now. Tomorrow morning it is." His gaze flicked past Griffin without comment, and settled on Tony. For a brief instant something dark and murderous flared in the depths of those eyes, quickly hidden.

Margie Braddon kneaded her hands together as if trying to scrub something indescribably filthy from them. "*I* had to bring the news in for you. You used Owen and me as couriers, didn't you?"

"Lucky coincidence, Margie. I had to see who might jump when he heard that the guard was dead."

Hope bloomed on McWhirter's face. "Then you weren't sure I knew!"

"It's still murder, Tony. Any death that occurs in the course of a felony is murder. I'm sorry."

"Yeah. So the hell am I."

"Get your things."

There was no sound from the others as Tony walked stiff-legged to his backpack at the rim of the campfire circle. He lifted it with a long, tortured sigh, and slapped the sand off.

In the wavering light, he looked like an old, old man, shadows furrowing his face into antiquity. He was stiff and slow as he walked back to rejoin Griffin. He turned to the other Gamers and whispered, "I'm sorry. God, I'm so sorry. Cas . . . I picked that fight, the first night." She tried to turn away, and couldn't. "Cas, when I saw how tough it was going to be, I knew I had to get it done the first night, before I got killed out, so—"

"Stop it," she whispered.

"I love you, babe. That's all."

Holly Frost broke the silence that followed, giving voice to the idea hiding in every mind. "Hell, Griffin, why can't you wait for a few more hours?"

An absurd thought, but Alex could feel himself becoming defensive. "There's no way I can do that. A man is *dead.*"

"Can any of us bring him back?" Margie tried to shush Holly, but there was no stopping her now. "I mean, why don't you give us a break? I travelled over a thousand miles to be here. Now you're telling me that it doesn't matter what happens to me or any of us as long as you get your man."

"It's my job." Griffin felt himself blushing in the dark. *You're not really leaving them to their deaths. It's just a game!*

Just a game. The joy and the sweat were just a game. The lovemaking and the beer busts and the songs and the tears and the bone-weary exhaustion were just part of the game. And what happened tomorrow, when the Undead and the Foré and Lopez knew what else all came boiling out of the sea and the forest to smash five Gamers, that would be the biggest, shiniest fantasy of all.

Acacia wiped her nose and regarded him. "All right, Alex or Gary or whatever you are. You and I know that what happened between us was a lie." She cut him off when he tried to speak, and maybe that was good. No telling what he would have said. "All right. You don't give a flying fart for any of us. That doesn't hurt me too bad, mister. But I want you to tell me that *you* don't care about what's happening here. That *you* haven't gone out of your mind with the rest of us weirdos. I saw you, Gary—Alex, oh, damn you, I saw what you were beginning to get out of this Game."

He heard the tremor in his voice. "What is it you think you saw?"

"You can't relax, Alex. You're in better shape than the rest of us, by a mile. Why are you as wiped out as we are? Why are you more torn up than Margie?" She leaned toward him, and flinched as one of the coals popped. "I'll tell you why. Because you work so damn hard at everything you do. Because you drive and drive and push until you're about to fall over. And if it's not hard enough, you'll make it tougher on yourself just for the sheer hell of a job well fought. Now you tell me, Alex. Damn you, you look me in the eye and tell me you don't want to stay in the Game just twelve more hours, just long enough to help us beat the pants off Lopez. You tell me you don't care, tough man!"

He shrugged massive shoulders. "All right."

"All *right?* What's that?"

Even to himself, he sounded like a little boy trying to explain something he doesn't understand. "Sure I want to stay. But what I want doesn't matter . . ."

She stared at him. "My God, Alex . . . I thought *I* was hooked on fantasy. Just *why*—"

He snapped, "I'm not here to answer questions, Acacia. I'm not here to have 'fun'. I'm here in the interests of Dream Park, and that's all there is to it."

His prisoner had set down his pack. Tony had long since made his own plea. He was just waiting.

But Chester said, "Griffin. It's in Dream Park's best interests that you stay in the Game." He had turned to face the fire. His voice was low, and very controlled, calculating.

"Don't try to hand me a line of bull—" But Alex knew that he had responded too quickly, too automatically, that he was almost afraid of being shown another way out.

"Tomorrow," Chester said, still facing away, "we are going to be slaughtered. The Game will be over, and will have to be considered one of the greatest debacles in Gaming history. Certainly the greatest I have ever heard of."

"So I'm sorry about your reputation."

"So I'm sorry about Dream Park's investment."

That rang a bell. *Hadn't Harmony said something—* "Go on."

"Don't you know that Dream Park recoups a huge chunk of their money through sales of tapes and books of an Adventure? Through luring people to run through an automated Game, once the bugs have been worked out? How many people are going to want a piece of this one? Cowles Industries will take a *bath,* Griffin." Now he turned, and met Griffin's eyes squarely. "We both know I have ulterior reasons for wanting both of you to stay in the Game. Fine. All I'm asking is for you to take *everything* into consideration. *You* know what it means to you, what it means to the Park. And if you give a damn, what it means to all of us."

Griffin scanned the faces. Eager, tired, waiting for a word from him that would tear everything to hell and gone, or give them a fighting chance. *Just twelve hours . . .*

Christ! What would Harmony think?

Who cares? He's the loon who got me into this in the first place! Still, hadn't Harmony said—"I understand Dream Park's investment is around a million and a half?"

"More, I'd think. Check with your boss. There are resources tied up, interest on loans, advertising agreements—"

"Never mind. Gather round, people. I may need you to talk for me. McWhirter, right next to me." Alex flipped his wallet open. "Get me Marty Bobbick."

Marty was on instantly. "Griff! I was down to hoping you'd remembered to leave a dying message!"

"Marty, I have Tony McWhirter in custody on suspicion of burglary and murder."

"Okay. Good. Tell me where you are and I'll direct you to the nearest exit."

"Not so fast, Marty. See if you can get me Harmony, immediately."

It wasn't immediate. The Gamers sat around him, tense and silent, waiting. Kagoiano, mangled, with edges of bone showing through where the rockfall had smashed him on the third day, brought him a thick sandwich and stood passively until Griffin took it. Griffin forced himself to take a bite, then, suddenly starving, wolfed it.

Ollie said, "Do you know about the Fat-Ripper Specials? They use the same Game, but they cut all the distances by half, and the food is high-protein stuff, and there are paid doctors in the party. Five days rips the fat right off you, and you hardly notice how hungry you are because you're too busy not getting killed. That's how Gwen got her start." He looked anxiously at Griffin, whose mouth was full. "The really good Games sell in places where you wouldn't think there were places. Dream Park stands to lose—"

The wallet spoke. "Griffin?"

"Harmony? Look, if you're asleep, get yourself awake. I've been handed a tricky decision, and I'm passing the buck."

"I wasn't asleep. What's the problem?"

"I've taken Tony McWhirter into custody. He admits to stealing the, ah, materials, but he denies killing Rice."

"Very good, Alex! We'll call Sacramento PD and hand them a nicely wrapped package. Do you have the stolen materials?"

"That's our problem, sir. McWhirter has made us an interesting offer. He'd like us both to stay in and finish the Game. It's only a matter of another twelve hours, and McWhirter will show us where he hid the, ah, materials."

"Game. Yes. Ah, what happens to the Game if you and McWhirter leave it now?"

" 'Worst debacle in Gaming history.' "

"Oh."

Harmony thought it over, and Griffin found that he was holding his breath.

"What if this McWhirter cuts your throat and tries to run? He's killed once. If he perforates a Gamer . . . lawsuits . . . hmm."

"We can take precautions. McWhirter will have a machete with a hologram blade. We'll guard him all night. I'll have Marty seal this place—"

Tony whispered fiercely, "For God's sake put me on!"

Alex handed over the wallet. Tony said, "Mr. Harmony? Listen, I do not intend to run. Where would I go? And I didn't—"

"Just a minute, McWhirter. Have you been warned?"

"I have the right to a lawyer. I have the right to remain silent. If I choose to speak, I can be recorded."

"You are being recorded."

"Fine."

"Are you in possession of materials belonging to Dream Park?"

"No, but I hid them where nobody else is going to find them. I can give them to Griffin tomorrow. Look, Lopez will *cream* us if Griffin and I leave the Game now. And how would *anyone* explain it in Game context? It *kills* the plot line."

"Will the rest of your party trust you not to try to escape?"

"I *swear* it—"

"I want *their* word. On record."

It must have been obvious to all of them: in case Tony perforated anyone while escaping, Harmony was forestalling a lawsuit. One by one they swore they trusted Tony McWhirter's word. Alex spoke last.

"I'm going to lock this place up tight," he said. "A mosquito won't be able to get loose. But I think McWhirter means it. It's going to be a long time between Games for him."

"I can hear the Board of Trustees now. Well, go ahead, and good luck. Oh, and I looked in on you while you were stealing that, ah, black fire?"

Didn't everybody? "Yeah?"

"It looked like fun."

The transceiver clicked—and everybody started yelling. Griffin bellowed, "Quiet!" They stopped. To his transceiver Griffin said, "Security, quick. Marty? Listen. I want airtight surveillance at every exit from the dome. If anyone tries to leave, the Game ends instantly. Don't miss any exits, and don't let someone past just because he's wearing a uniform."

"Chief? You're not coming out?"

"Nope. Neither of us, not till one tomorrow, with our shields or on them." Griffin clicked his wallet shut and looked around. "You're crazy," he said. "You're all crazy, and I'm just as bad. I want a Gamer awake at all times to watch McWhirter, who is going to sleep with his feet wired together. Any objections from anyone?" Not a whisper. "McWhirter?"

He was pathetically grateful. "Hands *and* feet, Griffin, I don't care. Thank you."

"All right." Griffin sank back against the dune. He felt very tired—and light as air. His thoughts finally settled on something. "Henderson?"

The Lore Master still looked apprehensive. "Now what?"

"Eight of us left. All those undead. We don't even have boats. Just how are we going to *win* this mother?"

Chapter Twenty-Nine

END GAME

When dawn broke that final day, there were nine awake to greet it.

Their clothes were soiled and torn. They themselves were scratched and bruised and unsteady on their feet, even with the benefit of a night's sleep. But all of them gripped their tools tightly: swords, machetes, and the magic staff now wielded by Chester Henderson.

Chester stood with eyes wide and nerves afire, waiting for the peep of a double sun that would signal the beginning of the Game.

Alex took no offense that Acacia stood with Tony. She had spent the night with the bound man. Not with someone else, not crying or hating or blaming; rarely touching him, but there.

Holly Frost, her Afro frizzled with sand and sweat, stood

382

next to Alex, a Japanese short sword balanced uneasily in her hand. She studied Panthesilea and Fortunato at a distance, expression carefully neutral.

Tony watched the horizon. He let his eyes sweep back and forth, barely acknowledging the girl at his side for minutes at a time, before relaxing with a great sigh and holding her fiercely to him.

Easy to understand the unyielding focus of his attention. *Play well today, Tony. You won't be back for twenty years.*

Mary-em, Margie and Ollie stood together. Margie had seemingly gained strength during the night, energy from the endless strategy sessions. She and Mary-em grinned at each other and touched the tips of their weapons together in silent salute. Ollie raised his sword wearily and stitched together the rudiments of a smile.

The group formed a rough circle around their campfire, all directions covered. The circle enclosed Lady Janet, who carried a machete. Chester's instructions had been exact: "You don't fight unless you have to. Getting you out is part of our mission."

Facing the woods with a katana held tightly in his massive hands, The Griffin suddenly laughed out loud. *Marty, Millie, Harmony, are you watching? I hope you're enjoying this!*

The second sun rose; the first faded out. Chester watched, critically, as yesterday's wounds bloomed anew on his Gamers and on his own body. The sounds of New Guinea filled the air: birdcalls, the lapping of surf, and a creaking of metal . . .

Low in the flank of the Spruce Goose, a door began to open. A long black arm pushed it back with deliberate slowness. Under a great black globe of hair, a small scarred face leered at them, mouthing words inaudible at that distance. It disappeared inside, and another figure climbed out, stiffly.

It was an Undead, its clothing strips of tattered cloth hanging against dark, ashy skin. It climbed down into the boat and set itself at the oars. Two Foré priests joined it, untied the line, settled themselves. The boat moved toward shore with smooth, steady strokes from their hellish oarsman.

Chester snorted. "Bastards. Only one boat!"

Griffin stifled a sour bubble of gas, tasting his nervousness. The Foré seemed to be looking directly at *him,* leering with a mouthful of filed teeth. Now he could see the muscles in the zombie's back as it guided the boat toward shore.

Ten feet from shore, one of the priests stood in the boat and began to chant loudly. After a time the second priest joined in, creating a melody that made Griffin's skin crawl to listen.

He didn't have leisure to critique the serenade. From the woods came answering sounds: a rustling, scraping promise, fulfilled within moments as the Undead began to line up.

There were at least thirty of them, all armed. As before, the women and children were the worst. They laughed endlessly, bodies twitching with spasms, the laughter blending to hungry growls. Many of the women were bare-breasted, but the effect wasn't erotic. Alex knew that it would be a long time before he could look at a half-naked woman without remembering the empty-eyed zombies of New Guinea.

Among the women and children were grey old men,

crippled and deformed, their frail hands clutching edged weapons. But the front line held the healthy ones, so to speak: a dozen warriors who had died by violence.

Most of them were as dusky as the others, the Foré priests. Two were European. S. J. and Felicia Maddox, Dark Star. S. J. rolled his eyes with zombie fervor. He waved his machete fiercely and grinned from a face ridged and pitted with blast scars. Griffin had to grin back. S. J. didn't care *which* side he was on.

Felicia's face was supernaturally calm, but she led the other zombies.

The boat had beached. The Foré priests disembarked without interrupting their song.

"This is it, people." Chester's voice was loud but calm. "Everyone do their part and we'll get through this. *Shift!*"

The Gamers moved. Before the zombies reached them they had formed a wedge, with Mary-em at the peak. They moved toward the rocks at quick-march.

They stopped and turned when the animated army was ten paces away. Chester raised Gina's staff. His fingers ran across its keyboard. Ruby spirals ran down its length, and light flashed from the tip to bathe the front line.

Felicia caught fire. The zombie screamed a wavering wail that would have torn meat from a human throat, and she fell, smoking and throwing sparks. The two to either side were incinerated as well, but Chester's beam was flickering.

S. J.'s zombie had lurched behind one of its undead fellows, sparing him from the initial blast. In another second the rest of the force had passed the smoking corpses and were on the Gamers.

The dead Engineer went straight for Margie. She almost

stepped out of the circle to meet him, restraining herself at the last moment. She met his downward stroke and growled menacingly.

Griffin kept a measured distance from Holly, and went to work. The blows were coming in a little faster, a little more elusively, and before three minutes had passed two small new patches of red flowed on his limbs. He set his teeth and sent a zombie to the sand with a diagonal crimson wedge creasing his head.

Chester's voice rose above the din. "Keep moving!"

Mary-em screaming and chopping at the cutting edge, the Gamers clove the ranks of the Undead. Slowly at first, then with increasing speed the besieged Gamers won their way toward the Foré priests. The eight defenders were roused to frenzied heights now, as they saw the priests back away and move toward their boat. Mary-em swore foully and burst through the zombie wall, breaking formation to do it.

Her short legs blurred as she charged across the sand, diving at the closest Foré and cutting him down at the legs. He fell to the beach at the edge of the water, and rolled in. The surf foamed red.

The second priest paused a fatal instant to gape at his fellow's fate, then sloshed through the water, pushing the boat away from shore. The undead oarsman sat passively. It had received no new orders.

Tony threw his machete.

(Somewhere outside the world, a computer chose among random numbers—)

The blade made a single revolution and slashed into the Foré's shoulder. He screamed as he clawed back at the evil growth; then kept going, pulling the boat one-handed.

Ollie splashed out with Lady Janet behind him. The

Foré tried to stop Ollie's sword with his bare hand, and failed. While the other Gamers held off the zombies, Janet pulled the boat back toward shore.

Ollie joined her. They had nearly beached the craft, dead passenger and all, when S. J. splashed in and cut Ollie down from behind.

Ollie's aura flashed red. He spun around, and zombie S. J. swung again. In the moment Ollie died, he parried and chopped, and S. J.'s head went black.

Chester shoved Lady Janet into the boat, and helped Margie in after her. The oarsman did not protest as they tumbled it out. Tony piled in and pulled Acacia up, then fended off a slash from a zombie wading in the surf.

After Holly squeezed in, only Griffin and Mary-em were left out, and there seemed to be no remaining room. "Griffin!" Acacia yelled, indicating her lap. Alex yanked Mary-em toward the boat, and she hissed at him. "Get out of here. You *have* to survive, Griffin." She butted him toward the boat with her shoulder.

He pulled at her belt. "Idiot! Swim and hold onto the boat!"

She nodded. They backed into the waves, then swam for it. The boat was moving out as Tony and Holly took the oars; they paused long enough for Griffin and Mary-em to grip the stern.

The terrible minions of the Foré waded into the water now, until it rose above their mouths. And even then they marched on, dead eyes blazing as they vanished beneath the lapping waves.

Margie touched a hand uneasily to her chest as the boat pulled out from shore. She watched the zombies vanish. "They almost made it all the way—"

Mary-em yelped and sank.

"Alex! Into the boat!" Acacia wasn't waiting; she pulled him over the stern by main force. A greenish-black hand fastened on his ankle and he yelled. Tony slashed; the hand glowed red and sank. Alex sprawled into boat, onto the knees of the other Gamers.

Now glistening dead hands gripped on both sides, and grinning dead faces surfaced, eyes unblinking and filled with hunger.

As Tony and Holly rowed, Griffin scrambled off Acacia's lap and chopped at heads and hands. The boat rocked unsteadily as he fought for balance, swinging his sword from a crouch.

A joyful scream cleft the air as they reached the Spruce Goose. Tony tied the line in and helped Holly up. She nodded briskly and pulled herself up the rope ladder and through the open door.

They heard her jubilant shout. "Cargo!"

Behind her Tony yelled, "Look out!" She turned as a gibbering Foré priest hurled a snake at her.

Her hand blurred as she whipped her short sword into a tight S and dropped to the floor. The snake separated into halves and flopped to either side. "Hear me, O—" she had to interrupt herself to roll away as the priest threw another snake. She chopped off its head as it hit the floor.

Her roll took her ankle close to the first snake's severed front end. Dying, it bit.

"*Drown* you!" She stomped at it and stood, lurching toward the priest, who bared filed teeth and hissed vilely. Her aura was blackening from the ankle upward. "Here me O Gods," she cried, "give me *fire!*"

The priest gestured defensively. The flames from Holly's fingertips veered to either side. Holly's wakizashi stabbed through the flame and caught the Foré in the throat.

The Foré fell. Holly, her aura quite black, collapsed gracefully on top of him.

Chester was the last Gamer through the door. He shut it hard behind him. "All right, let's see—" His eyes found the sprawled bodies, and he winced. "Oliver, Mary-em, Holly . . . Christ, what a Game." Then he saw further. "She was right. This is it."

The shadowed walls seemed to curve up and up forever, meeting at an indistinct ceiling. The hold was piled impossibly high with Cargo. Packages of all shapes and sizes filled the hold, in fact blocked it to the very roof.

"Margie. Is your rating good enough to fly this thing?"

She pursed her lips thoughtfully, but didn't answer directly. "Let's find the cockpit."

The cockpit was at the top of a stairway. Its door was slightly ajar, and Alex poked his sword ahead of himself cautiously, then entered.

Footing was unsteady in the relative darkness, but there was light ahead, streaming through the dusty windows. The cockpit was musty with disuse, but nothing seemed to be broken. There were panels filled with antique meters and dials.

Margie followed him in and pointed to the pilot's and copilot's chairs. "That's what I need," she said, and pushed gently past him, swinging around the pilot's seat.

She jumped back, stumbling, and steadied herself against Alex. He turned snarling, blade at the ready, then relaxed.

A mouldered skeleton slumped in the chair. Pieces of cloth stuck to the bones.

"Whew." Margie edged closer to it and nudged it with her toe. "All right. I don't think it's going to be moving around much, now that we've killed the priests." She carefully turned to the other chair, and sighed as she found another skeleton. "Gary . . . Griffin, would you help me get this out of the pilot's seat, dear?"

He trundled it back out of the cabin and to the cargo sections. Bones fell loose; he went back for them.

"How are we doing?" Chester sounded exuberant, and fresh as a daisy. He climbed into the cockpit and stood behind Margie's shoulder. Her hands explored the controls; twisted something. The panel lit up.

She said, "I think that's the fuel gauge. It reads empty."

"It would. *Damn!*" He leaned against the wall, gazing out at the water. "Ah. The fuel dump." He gripped Margie's shoulder. "Remember? At the dockyard, near the headquarters building? Get this thing started up and we'll see if we can get that far."

Margie's hands played over the controls. "I've never flown this model," she murmured, and twisted something. An engine coughed, then roared. The plane began to swing in a circle.

Margie hummed happily to herself. She got another engine started, a third, a fourth. By now all four Gamers plus Lady Janet were crowded into the cockpit, admiring her performance.

The plane finished a full circle. Margie took the joy stick. The plane's curve straightened out. The *Goose* rose on its step and picked up speed, enough for the vertical fin to bite air. Margie turned east along the shore.

"Motors one, four, six and seven now running, Admiral," she told Chester. "The rest are dead, I think, but I'll keep fiddling if you think—"

"Not just now. We don't want to take off. We don't have the fuel for it."

Tony said, "Griffin?"

Griffin glanced at him questioningly. Tony's long face grew serious, and he nodded. Alex shrugged out of his pack and followed Tony into the cargo section. McWhirter went directly to a crate labeled "U.S. Army surplus" and levered it open. He pulled out a couple of handfuls of shredded wood, then lifted a blue cloth pouch. With lowered eyes, he handed it to Griffin.

The pouch had a velcro seal, easily thumbed open. Alex lifted out four sheets of photocopy paper, then a fold of foam cushioning, and from that a tiny vial of thin, colorless fluid. It was only half filled.

"Neutral scent?" Tony nodded. "All right, Tony. If you've played straight with me, I'll do what I can. Which may not be much."

"*Griffin! Fortunato!*"

They pounded up the ladder, into the cockpit, and found that they had reached the Sea of Lost Cargo. The mighty *Spruce Goose* was a terror to navigate here, but Margie accomplished it with elan, and only once did a grinding crash indicate a collision with a smaller, half-sunken craft. "Shit-oh-dear!" Margie said. "Chester, I can't slow down. We'd sink deeper. We might hit something else."

"Then don't."

Margie scrutinized the docking area carefully. "I can get us a little closer, but we'll still have to use the boat, I think, and—" her words died in her throat.

The Undead were waiting for them. At least a hundred

strong, they formed an arc before the fuel dump. A few had marched to the edge of the water and were waving their blades, stiffly.

Chester looked sick. "They'll butcher us when we come ashore. If we ran the *Goose* aground . . . no, we'd never get enough momentum to crash that line."

One of the motors coughed. Margie shut down engine #1, outboard on the left wing. The *Goose* tried to turn, and she pulled it back into line. "Chester, shall I shut down? Or beach the beast?"

"Shut down."

Margie killed the motors. The *Goose* settled. She said, "We may not have the fuel to start up again."

Chester was grinding his teeth. "So *near*. And now we're trapped."

"We've got to try, Chester. What else can we do?" Acacia scanned the line of Undead, and shuddered.

"What time is it?"

Alex looked at his sleeve. "Stopped."

"Eleven-forty," Tony said, without turning from the window.

"Uh huh. The Game ends at one. We've got to beat the Undead, move enough fuel to fly us out, get it into the tanks . . . hell, we don't even know where the tanks *are*. Prime the motors and fly home. Not enough time. It *can't* be enough, not even if we could whip that many Undead."

"That airplane's egg really cost us," Acacia said.

"Yeah. Even so . . . there has to be a way out of this mess. I *know* Lopez."

"Well, I don't see it." The dark haired girl stomped her foot and swore. "Look—if we're going to lose, let's not just sit it out trapped like rats. Let's get out there and kick some behind!"

Margie shook her head. "Chester, there *is* another way."

"What do you mean?"

"The *Spruce Goose* never flew from Long Beach to New Guinea. It's just too far. The tanks would have been dry long before they got there, even if they were full to start with, and they probably weren't. Remember, it was just a practice run."

"Magic." Gears were turning in Chester's head. "But we don't know the ceremony—"

Lady Janet raised her hand. "I do."

"What?"

She smiled, pushing forward until she was almost against his chest. "When those people were holding me captive, I saw them perform their ceremony several times. The spells were in good English. I memorized them."

"Lady Janet, I don't trust you."

Margie swiveled around in her chair. "Chester, she has to be a clue. Why else would she have survived so long in the Game?"

Chester held his head, trying to think.

"They're going to come out, Chester," Tony said flatly. Alien-looking Foré priests had appeared among the Undead, oiled bodies gleaming in the sun. They were directing the launching of boats.

Griffin ignored the boats. Easy to drive through them, if they chose to go that route. "Equipment," he said. "If we've got the ceremony, we've got the equipment too. There's a full Cargo Cult workshop in that Quonset hut. It's a good thing we *didn't* burn it down." He looked out. "The zombies are blocking the fuel, but not the Quonset hut. We can ram right through those boats. The rest . . . well, by the time we got to the Headquarters building they'd be there too, unless . . . unless we run the *Goose* up on the beach. We might never get it loose. Yeah. But it's a chance!"

"No."

"We may have to—"

"No." Chester was smiling, but it was not a nice smile. "I kept looking for the flaw, but I didn't see it till Lady Janet spoke. It's another mousetrap. Lady Janet, have you forgotten the copyright violation rule?"

"By Jiminy, I believe I did," she laughed, and Chester laughed with her.

Alex slapped his forehead, hard enough to hurt. "Some detective. The Enemy's spells are the Enemy's property. We can't use them, can we?"

Tony spun from the window. "Waitaminute!" He shook Chester's shoulder. "It wasn't the Enemy who stole the *Goose. They* stole it from the *Daribi.* So we could use *Daribi* spells if—"

"Yes. Who has Maibang's skull?" Chester searched desperately from face to face as there was no answer. Then Margie raised her hand.

"I got it from Owen, I think." She opened her pack and rummaged swiftly. The guide's charred skull was a pitiful relic, all personality gone; but Chester siezed it like a priceless jewel.

"Table ceremony. Tony, Griffin, rig me a table. The rest of you, I want any remaining rations. Chocolate bars? Salt tablets? Anything that might be accepted."

They set it up in the cargo hold. A warped chest served as a table; they raided a crate of bedsheets for a tablecloth. A few pieces of dried fruit and a lone stick of gum lay on the

cloth next to the black skull. No flowers, no candle . . .
but Chester was grimly pleased.

"The *bilasim tewol*," he murmured, then spread wide
his arms. "Hear me, Kasan Maibang. Hear me, oh Gods.
We destroy the last of our precious supplies that we may
speak with him who was our guide. Hear us, Jesus-
Manup—" The air above the table shimmered, and Chester gestured. "Fire," he commanded, and bare sparks fell
from his fingertips. "Fire," he commanded again, and his
aura tinged red. He ignored it. *"Fire!"* he screamed, and
the table crackled in flame.

The burn-scarred face of Kasan Maibang wavered in
their vision. "I know why you call," whispered the guide,
"but I cannot help you. Only one greater than myself can
save you."

"Who?"

"Pigibidi, the greatest chief of my people."

"Summon him."

"It will cost you *mana*. What have you of power?"

Chester was frantic, tearing at frizzled hair with long
fingers. Then he barked laughter and dumped his pack
out. Almost at the bottom was what looked like a set of
black leather pajamas—the shed skin of a Foré spy. He
placed it on the magical fire.

"It is good . . ." Kasan said, and his face shifted outline
and became the pitted and wrinkled visage of old Pigibidi.

"Pigibidi, Great Chief," Chester began. He licked his
lips nervously. "We are desperate. We must move this
tremendous airplane, and we have no fuel."

The old man's lips moved, and his words echoed in the
hold. "The woman offered you the spell of the Foré. Be
glad you did not use it. One must have permission to use

such magic, and to steal a spell from its owner carries a terrible price."

Chester glared at Lady Janet, who hid a smile. "Pigibidi . . . what shall we do?"

"I will give you the spell you need. If our peoples ever contend again, beware of trying to use it against us."

"No! I swear—"

"A European's promise is worth little. If you have the magical power to lift so vast a machine, I will work the spell for you, that the Foré might be beaten."

"Power. We're out. Pigibidi, there's nothing left! You've got to—"

"I am sorry. Then it is all for nothing."

Chester stomped and swore. "That Lopez! I'll kill him! I swear to God—" He hoisted himself on a crate to look out one of a pair of tiny portholes. The boats of the Foré had reached the *Goose*. Soon it would be over.

The fire burned without consuming, and Pigibidi's translucent visage watched them with the dispassionate calm of the dead.

Alex leaned against the wall of the hold, eyes hooded speculatively. Pigibidi *hadn't* vanished. There must be more. A crate of Coca-Cola? The corpse of a Foré priest? Or— "Chester?"

"What?" the Lore Master snarled. His entire body was shaking.

"Didn't Margie say that Hughes himself flew this thing?"

"That's right," Margie agreed. "He was pilot on that one short flight off Long Beach."

"Well, if that was when they stole it, then it stands to reason that—"

Tony was sprinting up the ladder to the cabin.

"—that Hughes is one of the skeletons," Griffin finished.

"My God." Chester's body calmed down, the excitement flaring in his smile as he realised what Alex was saying. "It's Cargo Cult mythology. And we've got access to the *tindalo* of one of the twentieth century's greatest aeronautical industrialists!"

Acacia retrieved the skull Alex had discarded earlier. "Is this the right one?"

Hughes or the pilot? The bony face grinned sardonically, secure in its anonymity. Griffin said, "Hughes was a millionaire. His clothes would be in better shape—"

Tony half-fell down the ladder, his arms full of bones. "What the hell, we'll use them both! A test pilot makes a perfectly good *tindalo*." He took the other skull from Acacia and set the two at opposite corners of the table, under Pigibidi's hovering face. The flames sparked up.

A Foré zombie had crawled up to the window. It leered at them, pounding with the flat of an ashy hand.

Pigibidi's translucent face nodded at them. It began to speak. "God-Dodo, Jesus-Manup, hear my—"

And his words were drowned in the sound of leviathan engines turning over. All eight propellers ripped at the air. Margie gasped and ran for the cockpit, with the other Gamers in hot pursuit. The *Spruce Goose* shuddered and jerked and surged forward.

Margie scrambled into a seat. A last zombie lay flat in front of the windshield, yelling, hugging the painted wood.

The seaplane rose on its step and picked up speed, nudging aside smaller craft and heading for open water. Margie grinned fiercely as the *Goose* raced along the surface and finally skipped free. They bounced back down, once, with a massive, stomach-churning splash, and the zombie vanished. Then the plane truly found its power and rose from the water with a throaty roar.

Shore and dock fell away beneath them. Jungles and mountains, monsters and dooms, and the gesticulating figures of the Foré were pinpoints to their eyes. As the *Spruce Goose* kissed the clouds the Gamers turned to each other, and there was a swollen moment of silence. Then Alex whooped, and Acacia hugged him, and Tony hugged Margie, and Chester kissed Lady Janet, and the cockpit was filled with laughter and screams of joy.

The Game was over.

PART THREE

Chapter Thirty

THE FINAL TALLY

Hoarse cheering could be heard from within the cabin section of the *Spruce Goose,* even before the Dream Park attendants opened the door to let the Gamers out. Lady Janet was the first to place a foot on the ground. Her legs were wobbly. She shook her head and said, "Wow."

Six more Gamers followed. Holly Frost, last out, bowed grandly to the cast and crew. Chester lifted his arms and cried, "And let's have a big round of applause for the best performance in an expiring role . . . Holly Frost!" Ragged cheers. "And for all the surviving members of the team!" This time the energy ran higher, and the attendants joined in.

Griffin walked at Tony's side. McWhirter's smile was as honest as the others'; it faded slightly when he sighted Bobbick approaching with two security men. He stopped before they reached him and shifted his pack off his shoulder. He brushed a straggling hair off his forehead with a steady hand, then extended it to Alex. "Thanks. You've really been decent about this. I promise you won't have any trouble out of me."

Griffin took it, and was surprised at the ferocity of Tony's grip. "We'll see how it goes, McWhirter."

"All right, Chief. We can handle the prisoner now."

"Thank goodness." Alex shrugged off his backpack and let it thud into the ground. "Marty, escort him to Detainment. Are the County cops here?"

"You know it. We've got a lot to get done here." Marty was steering him along toward a side door, while the other Gamers headed for the main exit. Ahead of them, the two security men guided Tony.

Griffin turned to watch the Gamers leave. Most of them looked back over their shoulders to watch Tony taken away, but no one said anything, until Chester raised his voice.

He sounded tired. "Griffin. You coming to the Tally Party?"

"I'm sorry, Chester. I'm going to be pretty busy." He turned to go, but Henderson raised a beckoning hand.

"You're invited. You earned it. Tonight in my suite at the Sheraton."

Alex waved at him and turned back to Marty. "You're going to have to help me through this. I'm *really* tired." Bobbick made sympathetic sounds.

Griffin caught one last glimpse of Acacia. She had paused by the gate, almost as if she were about to turn around and speak. Then her shoulders sagged with fatigue and she walked on. Tony caught that pause and turned his head away, the remnants of his smile dying altogether.

Griffin watched her go and felt something sharp and hot pricking at his gut.

He handed his backpack to Marty, who took it without comment, switching a wad of gum from one side of his mouth to the other. "Come on, Griff. We've got a car for you."

Alex nodded wordlessly, responding more to nudges than to words. The textured plastic seat of the hovercar seemed alien to him, and he dropped into it hard, as if testing its reality. He leaned back and let his eyes close, his body jolting forward a half-inch as the car started to move.

They were tired, they were dirty, their shoulders sagged under the weight of their packs. They looked like walking dead as they stumbled into the Hot Spot. They stopped, looked about them blearily, and found all tables full.

Alone at a table that might barely hold five drinks, a tall black woman beckoned cheerily. She looked familiar, somehow, Gina thought. She smiled and started that way, tugging on Chester's backpack strap, knowing Gwen and Ollie would follow.

They stacked their packs against a wall. Ollie headed for the Orders window while Chester looked for empty chairs.

"Good Game," the stranger said. "I'm Gloria Washington."

Chester performed introductions. Gina was wondering where she had seen her before. Suddenly the memory dropped into place, and Gina swayed in place, vision blurring.

The tall woman saw it. She snatched an empty chair from the next table over—moving stiffly, a bit clumsily, but fast—and slid it into place behind Gina. "Here, sit down, love. I didn't mean to startle you. I thought you'd recognise me."

Gina sat down hard. "You were missing an arm and a leg the last time I saw you. And the make up . . ."

Chester smiled suddenly. "Aha. The demon undead, undead O! That was a very effective piece of misdirection."

"It was, wasn't it?"

"How did you, um . . .?"

"I picked the wrong time to visit Antarctica Ciudad. I was lucky they thawed *anything*. These prosthetics are . . . well, I can use them, but I've had a hard time getting used to . . . anyway, when Mrs. Lopez suggested this walking dead gig, my doctor thought it would be great therapy. Get me used to the idea." She was slowing down, having trouble getting words out. "That I'm a person who has one leg and one arm. But still a person. You know, I think he was right."

Ollie arrived, carrying a tray. Hands converged on mugs of Swiss Treats before he could reach the table. Gina savored the heat and sweetness in her mouth; her own hunger, suddenly stronger than her fatigue; the moment of revelation. *You're real again.*

She said, "Right or wrong, it was hellishly effective. I couldn't *believe* you weren't a hologram. It was like you came straight out of a grave." She laughed, but it was shaky. "I'm glad we met. It was bothering me." She knocked her mug against Gloria Washington's. "Skoal."

"Confusion to our enemies," Gloria answered.

Alex crumbled a sheet of paper into a tiny ball and bounced it off the wall into the recycler. He wanted another cup of coffee, but it would have turned his stomach into an acid-scarred wasteland.

"What's left?" His voice sounded like a stranger's, tired and thin. A stack of printout paper leered back at him from the top of the desk, and he groaned.

"My God." Numbly, he touched his computer screen to life and asked it for a second printout of "Urgent" material only. As expected, a mere four sheets folded up out of the desk.

One was a synopsis of the McWhirter briefing. It would be sent to all concerned department heads on a need-to-know basis. Griffin nodded as he read. Tony had kept his promise. His description of the woman who had contracted him for the job might do them little good; she'd have changed both name and description.

But they probably had enough information to nail the pick-up man. With the stakes as high as they were, someone *had* to try for the hiding-place.

He initialed the sheet at the bottom and set it aside.

Two pages were a condensation of Park business for the last four days. He set it aside after a brief skim. He and the computer had differed before on what was urgent and what wasn't.

The last sheet was a query into the status of Albert Rice's personal belongings. That needed thought, and a clearer head than the one he carried at the moment.

He glanced at his watch. A quarter to eleven, and time for any sane human being to get some sleep. Hell—why bother going all the way back to CMC? Why not just curl up in the office? He thumbed down the light and yawned until the hinges of his jaw hurt. Every muscle ached for sleep, but a single image remained clear and sharp in his mind.

"Damn you, Acacia. Leave me alone." Her face, that lovely dark-eyed face with the questioning mouth, had been haunting him all day, the most overwhelming reality of four days of fantasy.

He glanced at his watch again, and muttered, "They're probably all in by now . . ." then remembered the early-morning bull sessions of the Game and knew he was lying to himself.

Why fight it? He wanted to go. Tired and irritable and slogged down in a cesspool of work, he still wanted a chance to say goodbye to an unforgetable group of maniacs.

And perhaps one particular lady maniac.

He swung his feet down from the desk and was moving towards the door almost as they hit the ground.

Alex took strange satisfaction in the debilitated condition of the other Gamers. Chester's suite was spacious enough to accommodate the extra couches. Those couches were draped with boneless-looking, bleary-eyed casualties. The suite looked like an emergency ward.

Only the Gamers who had been killed out the day before seemed alive, and the empty beerskins scattered around the room gave even these good reason to look woozy. He caught a strong, sweet whiff of something that wasn't tobacco and ground his teeth, weighing duty against fatigue. No contest. Fatigue won.

He saw Acacia in the corner of the room and headed toward her without haste, letting his ears drink in snatches of talk . . .

A half-familiar voice, jarringly energetic. "No, no, no. The Haiavaha was there because you needed the anti-fire to fight the Undead. You were supposed to ignore the airplane's egg *entirely*. And *why* didn't you go back for more anti-fire?"

It was Richard Lopez, sharing a couch with his wife and—Chester Henderson! The Game Master seemed awake and alert. Mitsuko Lopez listened without comment, her attention shifting as if she watched a tennis match.

"—can't tell *me* that. *You* weren't standing in front of the damned thing," Chester said without heat. He fished absently in a bowl of dried dip with a handful of corn chips, then popped them all into a mouth that had already started to speak again. "Ooo ner thrying . . . You were trying to kill us off and you know it."

Richard shook his head. "Be your age. Where would I *sell* the Game that wiped out Lore Master Chester Henderson?"

"I'm too tired to giggle. You were going easy on us, hey, Lopez?"

"Oh . . . my youthful enthusiasm sometimes leads me to excesses. Mitsuko had to keep reminding me of the money we'd lose if I played too rough. Terrible woman. Always business before pleasure." He and his wife exchanged a quick kiss.

Chester saw Alex, and extended a hand. "Hey, Griffin. Good Game, man. You're not half bad."

A ghost spoke behind him, and Alex jumped. "What happens to McWhirter, Griffin?" *Gina! But she's dead . . .*

"It's out of my hands," he said, glad that it was true. He kept moving; he didn't want to talk about it.

Mary-em, dressed in light green slacks and blouse and looking quite undrowned, was another sight he found startling. She was deep into reminescence with Owen and

Margie and a stranger, a boy in a wheelchair, when she spied Alex pressing through the crowd. "Griffy!" she bawled. From some reserve of human strength she found the energy for what amounted to a flying tackle, setting him back on his heels.

"I was afraid that you wouldn't make it."

Overcome with an absurdly strong wave of emotion for the chunky little woman, Griffin hugged her back fiercely. She stepped back and set her fists on her hips, measuring him. "I may be off my mark, but I think you're gonna be one helluva Gamer."

He raised both hands in protest. "Oh, no. No more for me, thanks."

She snorted derisively. "Like hell." Her grin faded to something softer. "Come'ere, Griffy. There's somebody I want you to meet."

Alex followed her to the Braddons, who greeted him with weary nods. Margie asked, "Did you hear about the frogman, Alex?" He shook his head negative. "Go on, tell him, Mary-em."

The short woman laughed. "Remember when I went under, Griffy?"

"Do I! Jesus. All I remember is, you went 'glub' and disappeared, and a cold hand clamped on my ankle and . . . wait a minute. I felt a *hand*. At the time I just . . . just accepted it. Am I nuts?"

"*You* aren't. That maniac Lopez actually had a guy in scuba gear under the water. He pulled me down and fed me air. I laughed so hard that I almost drowned." She shared their laughter, then pulled Griffin over to the boy who sat in the wheelchair.

On closer estimate, Griffin revised his estimate of his age. He looked closer to thirty than seventeen. His unlined face and thin body carried the illusion with ease at any distance over a few feet.

"Griffy," she said, and there was a tone in her voice, a gentleness and caring, that transformed her face into something lovely. "Griffy, I'd like you to meet my brother Patrick. Patrick—?" Her voice was sweet, low, as if talking to a beloved child. "This is a very important man. This is Alex Griffin, the chief of Security for all of Dream Park."

Patrick reacted slowly, his head weaving in little circles as he raised it to say, "H-hello, mis-mister Griffin." He fought over the last syllable of Alex's name. He raised a frail hand for Alex to shake, the effort of keeping it in the air a heartbreaking thing to watch.

Alex took it in the gentlest of grips. "I'm pleased to meet you, Patrick."

"Y-you're a nize man, mi-mister Griffin. I saw you s-save muh . . . my sister twice." Patrick's eyes lost their dull sheen as they glowed with the memory.

Alex crouched down. "She was worth it, believe me."

"Patrick watched the whole Game." she said, beaming with approval. "He always watches."

Griffin took a hunch. "Did your brother ever Game himself?"

Mary-em nodded, sensing that Alex understood. "Until the accident, yes. Now—" She touched his head fondly, and he rubbed it against her hand like an affection-starved kitten. "Now he just watches his big sister. He can even understand most of what happens."

He looked from one of them to the other, the crippled man/child and the stunted warrior, and the hunch grew solid. "How long have you been Gaming, Mary-em?"

She nodded. "Right again, Griffy. You're definitely detective material."

"That's a relief. Nice knowing you, Mary-Martha." He nodded to Patrick, who watched his sister with worshipping eyes. Griffin softened his voice. "And you too, Patrick."

Mary-em grabbed Alex's arm and wrenched him down, planting a big wet kiss on his cheek. "You ain't shed of me yet. We'll go crazy again, sometime."

"Maybe so." He picked his way across the room to Acacia, who sat with Gwen and Ollie. There was an empty space next to her that no one had filled, and Griffin could almost feel Tony's absence. There were weary smiles in the group of three, and their voices were subdued.

Gwen and Ollie, for once, weren't touching. Somehow it didn't seem to matter. They sat very close to each other, and the affection between them was virtually a tangible thing, making the corner a warm place to be.

As he walked toward them, the blare of the music receded to a dull throb in his ears.

He stood directly behind Acacia, and Ollie's eyes flickered up to meet his as Griffin laid a large warm hand on her shoulder.

Without turning, she said "Hello, Alex." He lit up inside, the weariness vanquished by the magic of her voice.

He sat next to her, understanding who the space was really for. She turned slowly until her soft brown eyes scanned his face, and the edges of her mouth tugged up.

"You know," he said, as honestly as he could, "I've wanted you to say my name for a long time."

Her answer was a meld of warmth and reserve. Only the dark rings under her eyes betrayed a lack of sleep. "I wish that I'd known it." And she waited: a silent question—

Griffin shook his head. "I can't say, Cas. If it's Tony's first offense—" .

"It is."

"*And* he continues to cooperate, *and* if a reasonable doubt exists as to the degree of maliciousness or premeditation . . ." He heard the whistle of air wind its way from his lungs, and felt old. "Maybe ten years. I don't really know."

She was outraged. "And you can't help?"

"Acacia . . ." Jesus. How to say it? "I like Tony. I don't have anything against him at all. But he planned to steal something worth millions. In the process he was guilty of assault and battery to say the very least. If the Park and the State should want to drop him into a hole and pave over the top—why should I say no?"

If a fire in her head had been stroked with gasoline, her eyes couldn't have blazed hotter. He cut off her outburst.

"Acacia. To you, this is someplace you visit once or twice a year, filled with people whose names you never know working overtime to provide your thrills. Now, I'm *not* blaming you. If I were you I'd probably think the same way about this. For us it's—"

"It isn't fair, Alex! He didn't mean to kill anyone. Tony would *never* do that." Desperation seeped into her voice. "I thought I knew him. Dammit, I *do* know him. I'm *sure* he checked that guard's breathing before he left him. Alex, I *know* him."

"Tell it to the coroner. Tell it to Rice, for that matter." Alex fought to keep irritation from his voice. This wasn't what he wanted to talk about, or what he wanted to say. Maybe he should just leave . . .

But Gwen reached across and touched Acacia's shoulder, and her budding anger melted.

"All right. It was all his fault."

There was a hollowness in the air that Alex wanted to fill with something. Words . . . touches . . .

But he sat there next to her, almost touching but not

quite, until Ollie tugged at Gwen's hand. "Come on, hon," he said, "I think we should go count some sheep. These two need to talk. Acacia—breakfast tomorrow?"

"You know it. Goodnight, Gwen."

"Good Game, Griffin." Gwen hugged Acacia goodnight.

Acacia watched the two of them leave. "You should have seen the reunion."

"Ollie and Gwen?"

"Yes. It was weird. Ollie seemed scared to touch her at first. She had to grab and kiss him before he could move."

They both laughed, and both knew it was only postponing the inevitable. When the chuckle died they said nothing, then Griffin's hand stole over to find hers. She squeezed it weakly.

"Leaving tomorrow, Cas?"

She smoothed her hair back with her free hand. "That's what the ticket says."

"Then I guess that's it. Nice knowing you. I mean, really."

She clenched her teeth and bored into the rug with her eyes. "I wish I could say the same thing."

Alex felt her hand cool, and withdrew before she could break contact. "It's down to that then?"

"Don't misunderstand me. You're fascinating, Griffin. And sexy as hell. And a little frightening. Did you seriously come in here to put the make on me after sending my boyfriend up for ten years?"

That was that. The air clouded with frost. Oh, for a word, a clever line. *It's just the neutral scent talking, babe, don't flatter yourself . . .*

"I was invited," he said, and stood up.

"Griffin," she called up to him, her eyes impossibly wide. "There was an accomplice, wasn't there? An inside man? *Suppose Tony was set up.* What if they did get away with whatever it was that they wanted? Suppose Tony was just a patsy, and while you prosecute him, the big people are all getting away?"

Alex's expression didn't change. "The fantasy is over, Acacia. Tony played the wrong game in the wrong place, and he's going to have to pay for it." *Damn, you just can't say anything without being* Mr. *Griffin, can you?* Then the only words that mattered bobbed up in his mind like letters in a bowl of alphabet soup. "I'm just sorry we had to meet like this," he said.

She was silent, but the air was just a shade warmer, and he knew she had believed. And then, all that could be said having been said, he left.

Griffin felt his weight settle into his mattress, a two-hundred-pound deadweight of human being.

The temperature in his bedroom was seventy degrees and he didn't bother pulling the sheets up over his body.

He watched the sleep pattern dancing in the air in front of his eyes, soothing pastel freeforms that pulsed and bobbed at eighteen beats per minute.

Here, the distant gurgle of his living room aquarium and his low steady breathing were the only sounds. Here, away from the babble outside, he could listen to his body, feel the bruises and hurts, the places where he felt good, the clean spot in his mind that would fill in with work.

Here he was free to let his control go, and sleep.

And he couldn't sleep. Not at all.

His job was done. There was nothing he could do, should *want* to do, about Acacia. Tomorrow he would wrap up his report with Harmony, be de-briefed, and that would pretty well end his personal involvement.

Rest. For days he had thought of nothing that would

make him happier. And now, with the sleep-pattern snaking in front of his eyes, the warm air circulating around his naked body, nothing seemed further away.

Murder in Dream Park. God, what a nightmare. Could it have been an accident, despite what Novotney said? Doctors weren't omniscient . . . Could Tony be a consummate liar, despite everything Griffin thought he had seen in him? The Griffin wasn't omniscient either . . . Or had he been set up?

Suppose, just suppose, Rice was the inside man? What a grim joke that would be. Rice was in a good position to commit the burglary. Suppose Rice handed the notes and neutral scent to Tony, then allowed Tony to tie him up . . . both following instructions . . . wrap him up like a Christmas present so that a third accomplice, unsuspected by either, could shut Rice's mouth by pinching his nose shut . . .

Griffin shook his head. It was the kind of thought you could only have about a man you disliked. It irked him to admit that he had never warmed to Rice. But then, Rice had never given Griffin much chance to warm to him. Distant. Polite, but cold. Capable of that total indifference even toward the man to whom he owed his job.

Alex squinted in the darkness, following a disturbing train of thought. If Rice was the true thief, still, why should he be killed? If he knew too much . . . but why should he have been told any more than Tony? No, that wasn't it.

Because Rice was in the wrong place at the wrong time, then. What did he see? What did he know . . .?

Griffy, you're definitely detective material.

Griffin listened to his breathing: thunder in his chest, the blood roaring in his ears; and knew that he had to call Millicent. He propped himself upright and said, "Switchboard."

The screen formed, a pale violet rectangle of light. A voice asked, "Yes, Mr. Griffin?"

Stifling a yawn, he said, "Summers, Millicent Summers. Priority call."

Twenty seconds later Millie rippled to life in front of him, her eyes puffy and half-crossed with bleariness. "Chief? What's up?"

Gotcha! he thought; but it didn't seem to matter. "I need your help, Hon. You did the research—"

Even as he spoke she was coming alert, her eyes focussing, mouth hardening. *By God,* he thought to himself, *maybe I never will learn her secret.*

Chapter Thirty-One

DEPARTURES

At ten past ten that Wednesday morning, Skip O'Brien looked like the surviving Gamers had looked stumbling out of the Goose. Smiling, successful, but very tired. He blinked at Griffin and Harmony and, seeing no returning smiles, lost his own. "Am I late?"

Alex felt awake and alert after ten hours of sleep. "We haven't been here long. Coffee, Skip? You look like you need it." He was already holding the pot.

"Good. Black, thanks. I didn't get to bed till two this morning. Worth it, though." Skip slid his briefcase onto the desk and took the cup Griffin handed him. Griffin refilled Harmony's empty cup, then his own.

Harmony gulped, made a face. "Good. Well, I'm glad to be wrapping this mess up, finally. Skip? Your report, please?"

Griffin watched Skip remove three sheets from his briefcase and sort through them. Skip adjusted his glasses and skimmed down the chosen sheet.

"We recovered almost half of the neutral scent. Considering the level of impact felt by the Gaming party, I believe we can safely conclude that we've got it all. The formula has been recovered, and we have stress-analyzed testimony indicting no copies were made. Although we don't have tapes to study, the report filed by security chief Griffin would seem to indicate that the drug performed at a level beyond our most optimistic expectations." He smiled shallowly. "I think we've got a winner, gentlemen." He settled the papers back in his lap.

Harmony tapped a thick finger on his desk pad. "Very good. Alex?"

"It's not quite so neat on my end, Mr. Harmony."

The bald man's face remained immobile. "Explain, please."

"I'm just not sure that we know the truth yet. There are some questions about Rice that need to be answered."

"Wasn't it murder?"

"The coroner says so. McWhirter says he left Rice alive and healthy, and the voice-stress test says he isn't lying. But McWhirter's no doctor. . . Incidentally, we picked up his accomplice at five this morning when he tried to recover the notes and the neutral scent." Alex grinned suddenly. "Wet as a cat in the rain, he was, and not happy. McWhirter was supposed to leave the stuff behind the fake waterfall. He's given us that much, anyway. We don't know who the man in Sacramento was . . . yet. We will. My question is: was Rice involved? His apartment was rifled only two days before, he was taking an unscheduled break . . ."

"Exactly what are you saying?" Skip's eyes were narrowed.

"It's pretty thin, but thieves have been known to fall out among themselves."

Harmony's finger tapped more quietly. "I'm still not sure I follow."

Griffin sighed. Here it came, and it wasn't going to be pretty. But he could be wrong; he could still hope he was wrong.

Alex said, "Rice claimed that nothing was missing from his apartment. We think he lied. A statue was missing. The statue was known to be hollow. Two days later, Rice is dead and the neutral scent turns up missing. Skip, when exactly was the last time that the contents of that cabinet had been checked?"

"I . . . see what . . . you mean." Skip thought a moment. "I'd have to check."

"All right. Now, think with me. Suppose the neutral scent was already gone? Suppose Rice stole it, and the whole thing went down to divert suspicion?"

"Then . . ." Harmony's frown deepened. "You think that the statue held the vial and someone stole it back? Gave it back to us? That doesn't make sense."

"A lot of this doesn't make sense, Mr. Harmony. Maybe Rice got greedy and didn't sell the drug to his friends. Maybe McWhirter is a more calculating man than any of us realize. All I know is that something's wrong and I'm having Bobbick check Rice's place again. What we need may be there."

O'Brien squinted. "Haven't you already searched Rice's place?"

"Not thoroughly. Just photographed."

"Well, *somebody* searched it."

"True. And maybe they didn't get what they were looking for. There are a lot of ways to hide things in a CMC apartment, that an outsider might miss."

"A place large enough to hide a statue?"

"No, no, only enough to hide what someone thought was in it. Rice was a sculptor, you know. It wouldn't have been hard for him to rig a fake brick for his fireplace. A holo projection of a book could cover a hole in his shelf . . . I don't really know." Alex glanced at the cuff of a fresh shirt. "Bobbick must be almost there by now. If there's anything there, we'll find it."

Skip snapped his briefcase shut. "Whew. This sounds pretty bad. I'd better go and check the dates on that cabinet. If you'll excuse me—"

Alex thought a wordless curse.

Harmony patted the air with his hand. "That can wait, Skip. I need to know about the formula we recovered. How familiar with it are you? Enough to be sure it's the real thing?"

"I—it's hard to say. I, uh, I could check with Sacramento, but if the leak's there, the real formula could be switched already. And if it isn't, we can't compare them over an open line." He sat down, reluctantly, then popped up again. "Listen. I may have some notes on this in my lab. If I match them up . . . ?"

Harmony looked at Griffin, then back again. He hadn't liked this when Griffin broached the subject earlier, when it was still hypothetical. Now he hated it, and it showed in his face. "Why don't you just get them on the phone. Have your office check. We'll have a courier bring it over if necessary."

"I—we can't, uh . . . There's been too much trouble already. It's too valuable."

"You're too valuable to us here, Skip," Griffin said gently. He turned to Harmony. "There's only one person in Sacramento whose name turned up in Albert Rice's telephone book. Lady named Prentice, Sonja Prentice."

Harmony nodded grimly.

The blood was draining from O'Brien's cheeks. His eyes flicked from Harmony to Griffin to Harmony . . . "What the hell is this about?" He could barely speak, the breath whistling weakly in his throat.

"It's about getting to the truth, Skip."

O'Brien's mouth worked wordlessly. "You can't—"

"Yes, we can." Griffin said. "We know about Sonja and we know about you and Rice."

"Jesus . . ." O'Brien whispered. Then his eyes blazed and his lips set in a taut pale line. "I'm not saying a goddamned thing until I talk to my lawyer."

Harmony spoke now, and his voice, cultured and precise, was an ugly thing to hear. "I'm not sure you appreciate our position, O'Brien. Alex and I talked this over before you arrived. We *can't* have you prosecuted. Unfortunately."

Skip's eyes narrowed. "What do you mean?"

"What do you think would happen if it was known that Cowles Industries' chief psychiatrist, the man who has headed up our child research division for six years, is a cold-blooded murderer?"

"You did it, Skip." Griffin said hollowly. "You were in a position to alter Rice's computer records. You could 'discover' the forgery later, after Rice was dead. You were working in R & D the night he was killed." He leaned close to Skip, whose eyes were closed now, his breathing heavy. "We just need to know the truth, Skip, all of it. Either we get it from you, or the police come in and drag it out for us; and the papers get everything."

Again, O'Brien's mouth worked without sound, then a long, arid sigh. "It was the girl. Prentice. My god, it was so long ago . . ."

He lit a cigarette with a shaking hand. Griffin watched the smoke haze around Skip in a cloud until Harmony whisked it into the ceiling. "Rice was my student at Sulpher University. Bright. Promising. We became friends. My wife found it so damn easy to get into the swing of being a University wife. The entertaining, the parties . . . Albert could talk sense, and he . . . he listened to me. Looked up to me."

He gestured aimlessly with the cigarette, the smoke making spirals in the air. "We had a thing. It didn't last for that long, but it was pretty intense. More of a crush, maybe. When I tried to back off, he got crazy. Just nuts. Swore to tell the University. Said I was abandoning him, that I didn't give a damn about him. I tried to show him that I did."

Griffin waited for him to continue, then started to prod gently, but Skip continued by himself. "Sonja was a girl who had taken a class from me the semester before. She was lonely, I knew that, and I thought that maybe . . . maybe there was enough common ground to form a bond between them."

"Had you had a 'thing' with her too?" Alex's voice was dangerously quiet. O'Brien nodded miserably. Good old Skip. Giving his all for the youth of America.

"For a while, it worked. Maybe only to spite me, to prove he wasn't the emotional cripple he accused me of making him, Albert and Sonja starting relating. It was

during this time that she modeled for his statue. Sometimes . . . sometimes the three of us would . . . play
together." He closed his eyes and swallowed. "By damn,"
he whispered, "as an officer of this municipality, Alex, you
had better know that none of this is admissible in court."

"I know." Griffin said, flatly. "Finish it. What was supposed to be in the statue?"

"Albert was . . . into drugs. That was why he made the
hollow statue. He had made some freebase cocaine in the
lab. One night we all got incredibly high smoking it. Sonja
got too high, too damn high. I don't know why Albert kept
feeding it to her, but he seemed to enjoy watching her
literally lose her mind."

"And she lost more than that."

He nodded. "We were all zonked out, and finally I
noticed that Sonja was having trouble breathing. I was
stoned, and scared, and I tried to apply some kind of
resuscitation. She just stopped breathing, that's all. I
couldn't believe it. I was too scared to call the ambulance.
Christ. My job, my wife . . ."

"So she died."

Skip couldn't face them. "She died. Honestly—please
believe me—I did try to call the police, then. But Albert
pleaded with me. Begged me not to. Said that we could get
her back into the dormitory without getting caught. I was
still high. I didn't know what to do."

Harmony was pitiless. "So you let him talk you into it."

"Yes. Albert went out to dispose of the smoking kit, and
the drugs in his apartment. Then, at three in the morning,
we carried Sonja into her dormitory, got her into her room,
and left her undressed in bed. I remember reading the
papers, hearing them talk about 'the suicide . . .' " He
buried his face in his hands. "I stopped seeing Rice, and

that was the end of it, until two years ago. He called me at home, the bastard! He said he knew I worked at Cowles Industries and he needed a job. He didn't make any threats, but it was there, hanging. I should have gotten rid of him somehow . . . I got him the job."

"Then the demands started, right? A better job . . . Manipulate his psych profile . . . Just a little twist of the arm, a little blackmail that grows—" Griffin left it open.

But O'Brien was shaking his head. "It wasn't like that, really. It was *do a favor for a friend*. Then it was *make sure you stay my friend*. He kept pushing and I kept trying to draw the line. Finally he told me that he still had the smoking kit, and that all those sets of fingerprints were on it. His. Mine. Hers. If I didn't do as he said, the police would get it. He told me I had more to lose than he did. He was right.

"So I broke into his apartment and ripped it apart looking for the kit. I broke the statue open but there wasn't anything in it. The next day he told me I had twenty-five hours to falsify his records, or he would go to the police. I did it. The night that the R & D center was broken into, I went to meet him, to tell him that now he had as much to lose as I did, and that all bets were off."

Skip seemed to have forgotten them. His eyes were dreamy, peaceful; he wasn't seeing anything in Harmony's office. "I found him in the break room, trussed up like a turkey. I already knew it wouldn't work. It couldn't. He'd keep pushing me as long as there was a reasonable doubt as to my weakness. I wanted my job, my freedom . . . my marriage. He could ruin me. And there he sat, looking at me over that big wide bandage across his mouth, waiting for me to turn him loose. He was sniffling, trying to suck in enough air."

Skip's voice was shot through with horrified fascination, fear and heady power. "He was sniffling. Like calling attention to his nose. Alex, it was like finding an Easter basket the day after Easter's over. When I held his nose shut he went crazy. I had to kneel on his chest to keep him steady. It took two minutes before I could get a good grip, and another three before he finally stopped struggling . . ."

He looked at his fingernails, chose one after careful deliberation, and began to chew on it. "I never found the smoking kit. Maybe your man Bobbick will have better luck."

Alex said, "I doubt it. Rice must have dumped it, just like he told you the first time."

The office was deadly quiet for a while. Smoke wafted silently into the ceiling fan. Three still and silent men watched each other with calculating eyes.

Harmony said it first. "Well, what do I do? We know you did it, but probably can't prove it. Even if we could, we couldn't afford to turn you in. Too many innocent people would suffer. Cowles Industries would suffer." He drummed those thick fingers on his desk. "Griffin? You've called the shots on this thing so far. Any ideas?"

"Yes." Alex kept his voice cold, and refused to allow himself to look at Skip. "First, Skip resigns from Cowles Industries, effective immediately. Second, he agrees never to work with children *ever, anywhere* again. If he does—" Now he looked at Skip. From the way his former friend pulled back, shrinking into his chair, Alex knew that O'Brien was seeing a Griffin he had never seen before. "Then we have a talk with his employers. *And* his wife. Do you understand?" Skip nodded.

Griffin closed his eyes lightly. "And then there's the matter of Tony McWhirter. He may be a thief, but he's no killer, and I don't want him treated like one."

"Alex, we can't tell the District Attorney—" Harmony began.

"No, we can't. But we can offer Tony legal assistance. I can testify that a reasonable doubt exists as to his capacity for coldblooded murder. That, together with the voice-stress analyzer, if he takes it, may well counterbalance the coroner's report."

"All right . . ."

"And one more thing. Even with that, a couple of years are going to be added on his sentence for . . . oh, negligent homicide at the least. When he gets out of jail, I'm going to offer him a job. With me. He beat my security system, and I can use him. Well, what do you say?"

The man with the linebacker shoulders nodded. "That seems fair." He turned to the man with the briefcase, the man with the flesh stretched tight across his cheekbones, who seemed to be trying to hide in the plushness of his chair. "All right, O'Brien," Harmony said, his voice for once unmelodic, ugly. "I'd like you to dictate your letter of resignation, and then go clean out your desk. I want you out of the park by 1400, and out of CMC by next week."

Griffin stood.

"Aren't you staying, Alex?"

"No, I don't have any stomach for this."

He had reached the door when he heard Skip whining, "But . . . what do I tell . . . Melissa?"

And before he could stop his tongue, he heard himself say, "'Just follow your instincts, Skip. Tell her anything but the truth."

Then the door sighed shut behind him.

Alex watched the towers and domes of Dream Park shift in his office, shadow-puppets that swirled and loomed at his command.

There were people in the streets. He couldn't see their faces or hear their sounds, but he knew they were happy. Their balloons and cotton candy and plaid cotton shirts said so. The children that skipped to a faroff jaunty melody said so.

There was sunshine out there, and color and magic and music. But tomorrow, or next week, the people would leave, go back to their worlds carrying a little bit of the Dream with them to lighten their lives. And when those lives grew dreary again, they could think of vacations, and holidays, and travel . . . and Dream Park.

He had to laugh at himself. How often had he accused the Gamers of blurring the line between fantasy and reality? The truth was that their fantasy was his reality, and their reality his fantasy.

Tony would go to his grave thinking he had killed a man, and there was nothing to be done about it.

For that matter, it was true enough. Tony McWhirter had gambled the lives of anyone who crossed his path that night. He might have found a witness waiting when he emerged from G. A. 18; and then what? He might have crushed Rice's windpipe; Rice might well have died of a stopped nose; McWhirter could have died in that fight, leaving Rice to carry the guilt of the manslayer. Instead, he had left Rice as a gift to anyone with the whim to hold his nose shut.

Tony must have known the odds when he set forth to rob Dream Park. People *die* during burglaries.

But if Tony McWhirter was getting justice, then what was Skip O'Brien getting?

Alex's fingers dug into the controls on his desk, and the shadows shifted, now the abandoned Gaming area, now the streets of Section One, now the hotel transport strips . . .

It wasn't fair. It just wasn't. For Skip O'Brien to escape was obscene.

"See you later, Chief—"

Right. And maybe if Griffin had consciously noted that Rice had no words for O'Brien, his former teacher, the man who got him his job at Dream Park . . . if he had noticed that Rice had been talking to him for O'Brien's benefit, taunting . . . *They must have skipped over anything important.*

But that was expecting too much of himself, and that wasn't fair, either.

A holo window opened up in the air above his desk, and Millie's face materialized.

"You have a visitor, Griff." Millie was unusually subdued, eyes worried. She and Bobbick had been treating him with kid gloves ever since he'd laid out his suspicions about O'Brien. Friend. Buddy. Killer.

"Can't it wait, Millie?" His voice was more petulant than he cared to admit. *Leave me alone. Let me hurt . . .*

"I don't think so, Alex."

He sighed and faded the holo map to black. "Send 'em in."

When she stood in the doorway, outlined in the darkness, her brown hair flowing behind her like a scarf, he swallowed, not knowing if this was something he wanted. He thumbed up the light.

"Hello, Alex."

"Hello, Cas. What brings you here?"

"Do I need a reason?"

"No. No, but you've got one."

She nodded, smiling. "I just wanted to tell you that you were voted fifty bonus points for Best Novice Player."

He leaned back in his seat and folded his hands behind his head. She walked a few steps closer. "May I sit down?"

"Please." She folded herself into a chair, and wiped her hands on her slacks.

"I thought you might want to know the final score."

He was silent, just watching her.

"As a party, we won almost 2100 points. Personally, I walked away with a hundred and sixty." She paused. "You earned a hundred and seventy-four, counting your bonus. Congratulations. You're no longer a novice player."

Somehow her smile grew so warm and alive that it crossed the distance between them, and they shared it. "Thank you. I really appreciate that. I've been feeling very much the novice, lately."

"There's something else, Alex. I care about Tony . . . Maybe I love him. I'm not sure. But he used me to get into the Game—"

"Hey, no. They probably propositioned him after he was already registered. They'd have wanted a novice."

Her brows contracted. "Oh." She shrugged, her strong smooth shoulders lifting under her blouse. "Never mind. What he did—I can't let what happened stop me from letting you know how much I like you."

"Not now, Cas—"

But she already understood. "No, not now. But you're not rid of me, and I'll be back." Her dark eyes twinkled at him. "Sooner than you want, probably."

"I doubt that," he heard himself say, surprised and glad that he had been able to get it out past numbed lips.

"My train leaves in twenty minutes," she said, rising. He stood, and the gulf between them grew great, impossibly great again. He held out his hand.

She looked at it for a second, then took it. Gently he pulled her closer, feeling only the slightest tug of resistance, and kissed her. It was a light, brief kiss, but it was less an ending than a promise, and he was happy.

She turned, pausing only at the door. "I'll be back, Alex," she said.

He fumbled in his mind for something appropriate to say.

"Good Game," he said, finally, the beginning of a grin framing the words.

"Good Game," she echoed, and closed the door behind her.

He sat there in his office, grinning like an idiot. Presently he tapped the Com line. "Millie?"

His dark genie materialized. "Yes, Griff?"

"My desk is irritatingly clear. Dammit, isn't there some work to do?"

"You bet, Chief."

"Then wire it in here." He stretched his head side to side, listening to his neck pop. *Good Game.* Damn straight, it had been.

"On its way," she said. His desk printer began to hum. "Oh, and one more thing."

"What's that?"

"I've never met a Slayer of the Unclean before. Can I have your autograph?"

"We heroes are a busy lot," he said blandly. "I'll try to work you in Tuesday." He watched the sheets of fanfold paper sprout out of his desk. When it reached a pile an inch high, it stopped.

Millie whistled. "That's a lot of business backed up there. Good luck. Personally, I'd rather be fighting monsters."

Wouldn't we all? he said silently. *Wouldn't we all.*

He tore off the sheets and went to work.

Afterword

The authors had a wonderful time researching Dream Park. As we hope you will agree, Melanesian myth patterns are as bizarre, convoluted and imaginative as any in the world.

All of the various monsters and most of the magics are taken from the literature available concerning New Guinea and its sibling isles. *Road Belong Cargo* by Peter Lawrence was the single most informative work; Albert and Sylvia Frerich's *Anutu Conquers in New Guinea;* Benjamin T. Butcher's *My Friends The New Guinea Headhunters;* Roy Wagner's *Habu;* and Ian Hogben's *The Island of Menstruating Men* (honest!) are also worth reading.

The Cargo Cult is the Melanesians' attempt to explain the disparity between their own lifestyle and the superior technology of the "Europeans" who changed their lives.

The Melanesian approach was and is pragmatic. They adapted Christian deities to their own naturalistic pantheon, to form such entities as God-Manup, Jesus-Kilibob, and God-Dodo. They hoped that the right combination of

431

ceremonies and imitation of Europeans would "open the road of the cargo", bringing them the wealth that God intended for all his children equally. When one approach to the *rot bilong kako* failed—and they have all failed, to date—the Melanesians always tried something else. Even twenty years ago there had been at least five systems of Cargo Cult belief; and where it stands now is anybody's guess. Because it is intended to divert goods now reaching "Europeans" alone, the Cargo Cult is by nature a secret society, and illegal.

The worship of European artifacts created some truly bizarre situations. One tribe did indeed try to hatch an "airplane's egg" in a fire, with results better imagined than witnessed. Europeans ignorant of the Cargo Cult have found themselves involved in strange schemes intended to divert mail or to build airfields.

There seems no sure way to convince a Melanesian native that his world-picture is wrong. If present spells are not effective, he tinkers some more with the system—as if a European were working on a car that has been seen to run. Consider the case of Yali—

Born in (approximately) 1912, Yali was undoubtedly the secret leader of the Cargo Cults in the late 1940s and mid-1950s. He enlisted in the Army during World War II, and was trained in Australia. He toured European-style factories. He returned to New Guinea claiming to have seen God and His Cargo workshops. A highly intelligent, charismatic war hero, he amassed great power through his system of "Boss Boys" who controlled political and religious activity in dozens of villages. His legend includes a tale of Yali's death and rebirth in the jungle.

Depending on who's talking, he was either a saint or one of the greatest con men who ever lived. Peter Lawrence

(Road Belong Cargo) sees Yali as himself a victim of the Melanesian world-picture. He saw those factories as an elaborate ritual intended to divert goods created and sent by God.

Cargo Cult, or the worship of material goods, is only one facet of Melanesian mythology. The winds, the tides and rains all were influenced by an incredible array of gods, goddesses, spirits and nether-beings.

The Foré do indeed exist, and are the only group of people on earth known to be carriers of Kuru, the laughing sickness. They are feared as magicians and cannibals of terrific ferocity.

Giant snakes, lizards, birds and other "natural" creatures abound, and required no modification to bend them to our story needs.

Magical creatures needed a bit more modification.

The *Nibek* is a village monster or "big thing". It is generally described as having a head like a snake's, a body like a huge stone, and legs like a centipede's. It has a tiny mouth that expands "in the manner of a python swallowing a rat."

The dread *Bidi-taurabo-haza*, the "man ripe making animal" is precisely as presented, a tropical Gorgon of immense lethality.

The *Haiavaha* was a demigod who guarded the secret of fire. According to legend, a dog stole the secret and brought it to mankind. We added the "reverse fire" as well as the Just-So type "Why dogs can't talk" anecdote.

Zombies of one kind or another are common to many cultures. The Melanesians are no exception.

The Spruce Goose is, of course, an actual plane. It flew only once, off Long Beach, California, with Howard Hughes aboard. The fantastic troop-transport was constructed almost totally of wood, and was never put into production.

The concepts of Gaming used in *Dream Park* are drawn from many sources: computer-gaming, Dungeons and Dragons, the Society for Creative Anachronism, and the fiendish imaginations of fans throughout the Southern California area.

To the many friends who contributed eyes, ears and voice to the creation of this book, a hearty thanks. Without your knowledge and enthusiasm, writing *Dream Park* would have been far less than the exhilarating experience it was.